SKIN SHIFTERS

By T. J. MacGregor

His fingers went to the alien's neck. Nothing.

Was is breathing? He pressed his ear to the alien's back. Nothing.

Did it have organs? A heart? Blood? He didn't have any idea how he might determine whether it was unconscious or dead, so he touched the shoulder to turn it over. He did so carefully, afraid he might break one of its bones. Then it was on its back and everything inside of him went utterly still. It seemed his heart no longer beat, that he no longer breathed, that he'd flat- lined but was still conscious. If his body had been working the way it was supposed to, he would have leaped to his feet and scrambled up the side of the cliff. The only thing he could do was stare, then he remembered to breathe, and the scientist in him snapped to attention.

The alien's eyes, closed now, looked slightly larger than human eyes, but weren't the huge almond-shaped horrors depicted on Greys. Its face was almost human except it had only a single nostril. Its long legs had dual knee joints, which was why they had looked so strange while it was sprawled face downward. Only one foot and hand were webbed. At its throat was an extra flap of skin, which also appeared on its right side. Amphibian? The only visible body hair was on its head, that odd blue tuft. Gender: unknown. No breasts, smooth skin between the legs, no genitals.

For Rob & Megan with much love always
& for Nancy Pickard and Hilary Hemingwayy

Prologue

Tango Key
February 6, 2017

L uke Pierce drove like a madman through the Tango Key hills, his heart hammering, his hands gripping the steering wheel so hard his knuckles turned white. The back road twisted and curved through ceiba trees so massive and lush that the branches weaved together overhead, blocking the view of his destination. The lighthouse. Old Post Road was the faster route, but not during the morning rush hour at the height of the tourist season.

"C'mon, c'mon," he muttered and floored the accelerator. The speedometer needle swung toward 100 and he entered a sharp turn, tires screeching.

His cell rang, the call went straight to Bluetooth, and Josh McMullen's name popped up on the navigation screen. "Luke, shit, you nearly here? We've got to move the body before the lighthouse opens at ten. I got a tarp we can wrap it in."

It was 9:09 right now. "I'm a minute away. Had to dig my rappelling equipment out of the garage, lost some time. Any change in the ET?"

"It's dead, Luke. It hasn't moved since I first spotted it. I'm at the edge of the cliff now, staring at the damn thing down there, sprawled on that jut of rock. I took some pics, like you suggested. It's... it's *grotesque*. I don't know how you're going to be able to haul it up."

"How far down the cliff is it?"

"Midway. Too far for me to reach."

"Okay, nearly there."

"Just pull into the vacant lot next to the lighthouse. That's where I am."

The car screeched out of the turn, the overhang of trees ended, and there it was, the lighthouse perched on a cliff, the tallest and oldest structure on the island, rising against the clear blue February sky, an icon of an earlier time. Excitement and a terrible urgency surged through him. He'd been waiting for something like this his entire life. And how fitting that an alien body had been found this close to the lighthouse.

For the dozen years he'd been investigating sightings, the lighthouse and the northwestern part of the island had been a focal point. But all the questions he had—how, where, when, and WTF—would have to wait. Right now, the most important thing was retrieving the body, then hiding it some place safe until he could notify his boss, Ted Fisher, and they could figure out what to do with it. No way would he allow this to go the way of Roswell, with the government and the military moving in and whisking the body away, then denying anything had happened.

Pierce swung into the vacant lot, past half a dozen palm trees, and saw McMullen crouched at the open gate of the metal fence that ran along the edge of the cliff. Pierce honked and McMullen bolted up and gestured for Pierce to drive in closer. He brought the car right up to the fence, parked parallel to it, leaped out. McMullen, wearing his brown custodian uniform, hurried over, looking deeply shaken. "We gotta hurry, Luke. It's nine-thirteen now."

"Need to get my gear." His voice sounded calm, but his hands shook when he opened the hatch and grabbed the canvas bag that held his equipment. Yeah, he was rattled. "Those trees give us some protection from being seen by anyone driving past on Old Post. Any idea where we can hide it?"

"Yeah." McMullen moved alongside him to the gate. "Old freezer in the shed out back. We can keep it there till Wednesday, when the lighthouse is closed, then move it somewhere else. But fuck, Luke, this is… my God…"

Pierce dropped his gear to the right of the gate, on top of the tarp McMullen had mentioned, and peered over the side. His breath exploded out of him and he nearly passed out. He rocked quickly back on his heels, eyes squeezed shut, hands gripping his thighs, shock shuddering through him. *It's real, don't blow this. Get down there, retrieve it, hide it.*

He pushed his shock into a back room in his head, slammed and locked the door, then peered over the side again. He forced himself to notice the details. The body, which looked to be all bones, was about thirty feet below him, sprawled facedown on a jut of rock just like McMullen had said. It had a sprig of blue hair sprouting from the top of its head, super long legs. There was something odd about the backs of the knees, but he was too far away to be able to tell what it was.

Its right foot was webbed, he could see that clearly, and its hands were thrust out in front of it. The left hand was webbed and it, like the right, featured four fingers and two thumbs. The skin was pale, like that of someone who had spent years underground. Pierce didn't think this being was a Grey, the most commonly reported alien, the one whose terrifying face had graced the cover of Whitley Strieber's book, *Communion*, years ago. Beyond that, he knew nothing.

"Can you get down there?" McMullen asked anxiously.

"Yeah. It shouldn't be a problem." *Except it's an alien.* And he would have to touch it. Suppose it was still alive? "You're sure it hasn't moved? Or breathed?"

"Not that I've seen."

Pierce unzipped his bag, pulled on his chest harness, a rappel belt, rigged the anchors, ropes. He kicked off his sandals, put on his climbing shoes, slipped on his helmet, gloves. He decided to take a second harness with him to put on the body so that he and McMullen could pull it up. But a lot could go wrong with that plan. A rope might get caught on rock, the body might swing, and slip out. And that would be it. Proof of alien life would plummet a hundred feet to the rocky beach below and that bony body would break apart. Just the same, he brought it along as a backup.

"Keep your phone handy, Josh, in case you can't hear me shouting. We may try to pull it up separately. I'll have to, uh, see what the situation is."

The situation. He had never been in this situation. Never imagined it. Omega didn't have a protocol for it in their handbook. But their primary directive was to get the body some place where it wouldn't be found by those people who would take it away and deny its existence.

"Hurry, Luke. We've got forty minutes till the lighthouse opens."

Pierce glanced out at the gulf and was relieved that he didn't see any boats in the immediate vicinity. No telling what some fisherman might think if he saw someone rappelling down the face of the cliff. "Here goes."

He started down, eyes pinned on the being below him. The closer he got, the more freaked out and alarmed he felt. Where the hell had it come from? Given that one hand and one foot were webbed, it seemed reasonable to assume it had come out of the Gulf of Mexico. But how did it end up on this jut of rock seventy feet above the beach? Had there been a sighting this morning that he'd missed? Had the damn thing been dropped out of a craft?

Stay focused.

Despite the cool weather, he was sweating.

Questions stumbled around inside him, screaming for answers.

Right now, he and McMullen were the only people in the world who knew about this alien body. Once they hid it in the shed freezer, he would notify Fisher and his wife, Carmen. That would bring the count to four. And beyond that, he thought, he would have to get in touch with Sofia Lopez and somehow convince her to come back to work for Omega. She'd spent eight years working side by side with him and was the only psychic he knew or trusted who might be able to read an alien. But she hadn't spoken to him since she'd ended their relationship a year ago and resigned from Omega.

His feet touched the jut of rock, his heart pounded in his ears, the inside of his mouth flashed dry. *Fuck, it's two feet from me.* "Easy, easy," he murmured, and moved closer.

He came along its right side, crouched, stared. No sign of clothing. But maybe the skin was the clothing, a body suit or something. Or maybe he'd watched too much *Star Trek*. He brought out his phone and snapped a dozen photos. Proof, these pictures were proof that he wasn't hallucinating, that he was crouched next to an alien body. He removed his gloves, reached out to touch its back, but everything inside him recoiled and he jerked his hand back.

You can't move it without touching it.

Slowly, he would do it slowly. Fingertips first.

The alien's skin felt cool, like the air. And smooth, almost silken, like a baby's skin. Pierce trailed his fingertips up the back, to the tuft of blue hair. It felt strange to the touch, some strands like wire, others soft and pliant, others sort of oily.

"Hey, Luke, you okay?" McMullen hollered.

"Yeah. I'm..." *Freaking the fuck out.* "Just trying to figure out how to get it up there."

Pulse? Did it have a pulse?

His fingers went to the alien's neck. Nothing.

Was is breathing? He pressed his ear to the alien's back. Nothing.

Did it have organs? A heart? Blood? He didn't have any idea how he might determine whether it was unconscious or dead, so he touched the shoulder to turn it over. He did so carefully, afraid he might break one of its bones. Then it was on its back and everything inside of him went utterly still. It seemed his heart no longer beat, that he no longer breathed, that he'd flat-lined but was still conscious. If his body had been working the way it was supposed to, he would have leaped to his feet and scrambled up the side of the cliff. The only thing he could do was stare, then he remembered to breathe, and the scientist in him snapped to attention.

The alien's eyes, closed now, looked slightly larger than human eyes, but weren't the huge almond-shaped horrors depicted on Greys. Its face was almost human except it had only a single nostril. Its long legs had dual knee joints, which was why they had looked so strange while it was sprawled face downward. Only one foot and hand were webbed. At its throat was an extra flap of skin, which also appeared on its right side. Amphibian? The only visible body hair was on its head, that odd blue tuft. Gender: unknown. No breasts, smooth skin between the legs, no genitals.

Horror, then awe washed through him. He snapped two photos, zipped his phone into the back pocket of his jeans, then brought out the extra harness and tried to fit it on the alien's body. But he couldn't adjust it to fit. The being was too skinny.

"Luke!" McMullen shouted. "Twenty minutes and counting till the lighthouse opens and this place is flooded with tourists."

Shit. Twenty minutes. Forget the harness. The best he could do with the time he had was to rig a rope around the alien's waist, hope it didn't slice the body in half, and connect it tightly to his harness. The body felt light enough so that he probably could drape it around his shoulders. As long as he didn't screw up in his ascent and make any jarring moves, he could get to the top with the alien and himself intact.

Maybe.

"Luke, you okay?" McMullen yelled.

"Yeah, nearly ready to come up," he called back.

He slipped his arms under the body's back and slowly lifted it and draped it around his shoulders. It weighed—what? Sixty or seventy pounds? He could do this. He had to do it. But he couldn't climb with just one hand, so he couldn't hold on to its hand while he climbed. If the body fell back, away from him, or hit the rock, it might break apart.

If, if, if. Just climb, he thought. *Climb.*

He made the first ten feet without any problem. But the body shifted on his shoulders and he had to pause to adjust it. That sixty or seventy pounds started feeling excessive during the next ten feet and by now, perspiration poured off him and oozed into his eyes. He paused to wipe his arm across his forehead and eyes, then started up the final ten feet. He could see McMullen leaning over the edge of the cliff, hands extended for help if Pierce needed it.

When he got to within a foot of the top, he realized the body had shifted too far to the right and he had to stop again to reposition it. McMullen shouted, "Grab my hand, Luke! I can help you up the rest of the way!"

"Don't want to let go of the rope."

He strained to make it another half foot, then McMullen took hold of the rope and pulled him up and over the lip of the cliff with surprising strength for a guy in his seventies. Pierce collapsed against the ground, gasping for breath, and McMullen moved the alien body off his shoulders and onto the tarp he'd spread out against the grass.

Pierce lay there for a few moments, catching his breath, then ripped off the helmet, gloves, and unhooked himself from his gear. He left everything on the ground and hurried over to the tarp, where McMullen was removing the rope from the body. The old man looked up at him, shook his head. "I... damn... I never thought... what the fuck, Luke. Once we get it into the freezer, we've got to wait until the day after tomorrow to move it."

"Unless we move it tonight."

"Move it where?"

"I don't know."

Stretched out against the tarp, the body looked to be at least seven feet long, maybe longer. No telling what those double-jointed knees or dual knees or whatever they were could do. Jump great distances? Extreme heights? They rolled the body up inside the tarp, Pierce picked up one end, McMullen picked up the other, and they moved quickly toward the gate in the fence that surrounded the lighthouse. "Quickest way to the shed is across the back lawn," McMullen said. "You reckon it's alive in some way we don't understand?"

"No idea. Right now, this can't go any farther than the two of us."

"Damn straight. We'd have the feds all over us."

"Or worse. Josh, was there a sighting earlier today that I didn't hear about?"

McMullen glanced back at him, surprised. "I thought you'd heard."

"I was on my way back from Key West when you called. I haven't heard anything."

"Around eight-thirty, I was cleaning up the telescopes out on the porch and I saw this...ball of fire, that's what I thought it was, plunging out of the clouds. Then I realized it was sunlight hitting what might've been a jet in big trouble, spiraling downward. It slammed into the gulf several miles offshore. I ran back inside to grab my phone and called 911. But the number was busy, so I'm guessing other people saw it hit the water."

That meant cops and paramedics were going to be combing the gulf in boats and walking the beaches on the western side of Tango, searching for survivors. "What time did you first see the body?"

"A few minutes before I called you."

"Who else has access to the shed?"

"No one. I've got the only key. I'm the lighthouse museum custodian. Technically, the mayor is my boss and has access to it, but he doesn't give a shit about the museum."

They reached the shed, McMullen slipped a key into the padlock, and they walked into a surprisingly cavernous room. Air-conditioned, no windows, jammed with boxes and shelves filled with museum stuff—old maps, books, telescopes, ship logbooks. McMullen flipped on the lights, Pierce shut the door, and they moved the body over to the long freezer against the wall, set it down.

It required a combination to open, McMullen keyed it in, and raised the lid. Not much food in here, but it was deep and they could arrange the several dozens bags of ice around the body and cover it with the tarp. "This will do, Josh. It's long enough if we bend its knees."

"Let's do it. We've got eleven minutes."

Tick-tock.

Once the body was encased in bags of ice, knees bent, and covered by a tarp, Pierce shut the lid, McMullen keyed in the code, and on their way out, Pierce killed the lights. A car had pulled up to the front gate. "Who's that?"

"One of the clerks. She sells tickets. The guide should be showing up shortly."

"I'd better move my gear back into the car."

"And then?"

"I have to make some calls. Let's meet here early Wednesday morning."

"Six? It'll still be dark then. We can move the body into the freezer in the employee kitchen in the lighthouse. It's long and deep enough."

"Six it is." Pierce slung his arm around the old man's shoulders. "I'm going to see if I can get Ted Fisher to give the governor a call. He's a big donor. They're friends. Shut the lighthouse down for renovations or something."

"Good idea. Yeah, that'll work."

"Now you're part of Omega, Josh. I can't thank you enough for everything."

"You kidding, Luke? This is the most awesome thing that's ever happened to me. I'm thrilled to be a part of this."

He hoped that McMullen still felt that way if and when this whole thing slammed into a high strangeness that none of them had ever encountered.

Part One

TANGO KEY

"If aliens visit us, the outcome would be much as when Columbus landed in America, which didn't turn out well for the Native Americans."

- Stephen Hawking

Chapter 1

February 8, 2017

The closer Sofia Lopez got to Tango Key, the queasier she felt. Twice, she had started to turn back. But now only a few miles remained on the twelve-mile bridge that connected Key West and Tango. She again felt the simplest thing would be to make a U-turn as soon as she reached the island, then text Pierce and tell him she had changed her mind.

But if she did, that decision would also impact her son, Mike, now trying to rearrange his schedule for the semester so that he could join her. Mike would tell her she was nuts, that it would be a bad move and she couldn't afford to turn down the job Pierce had offered her.

And he'd be right. With certain foreclosure on her Key West home in a matter of months, she couldn't turn down Pierce's offer of $250,000 for a week of her time. It wasn't as if she had other options, like her parents. They had pretty much disowned her when she'd gone to work for Omega years ago. As strict Catholics, they believed that by investigating sightings, UFOs, and all the rest of it, she was colluding with demons, which qualified her for hell. Now in their eighties, her parents still lived in the Little Havana neighborhood where they'd been since they fled Cuba.

The last time she'd spoken to her mother several months ago, her parting words were, *I pray for you daily.* Her father, now in advanced stages of Alzheimer's, hadn't said anything. He'd cried.

Sofia shook off her depressing musing about her parents

and thought back to her vision two days ago. She had seen two men carrying something wrapped in a blue, paint-splattered tarp. She hadn't been able to see their faces, but had heard them whispering.

You reckon it's alive? the older man had said.

No idea, the younger man had replied. *Right now, this can't go any farther than the two of us.*

Damn straight. We'd have the feds all over us.

Or worse.

There had been more to the vision than that, an old floor, a musty smell, the men's fears, their urgency. Mike had helped her sort it out, just as he'd done since he was a kid. The two of them had sat at the kitchen table over a breakfast she'd whipped up, and he'd fired questions that prodded her to re-enter the vision in her head and flesh out details. They had talked about whether the vision was clairvoyant—something happening now—or precognitive, something that might happen in the future, but hadn't come to any conclusion.

Several hours later, when they'd been repainting the back bedroom, which she planned to list on airbnb to bring in extra income, Pierce had texted her. *How much would you charge for a week of your time?* Pierce, whom she hadn't heard from in a year. Pierce, who didn't bother with any prelude like, *Hey, how're you doing?* Or: *I know this is outta left field…* Nope. Not Pierce. He jumped right in. She'd felt like telling him to fuck off and nearly deleted the text.

Now that she knew she'd been seeing a future event—i.e. Pierce and her reason for being on Tango Key—she wondered why the vision had totally failed to show what Pierce had called the *mother lode*. If it was an artifact, then it ought to be tangible, something she could feel, touch, investigate. If it was ephemeral—a theory, speculation, another *what if*—then forget it. Omega would be paying her a shit ton of money for nothing.

Bottom line: her unease was caused by Pierce's involvement.

The island now loomed before her, a picturesque green emerald floating in the endless blue of the Gulf of Mexico on a beautiful February morning. The breathtaking hills began just outside of the bustling marina to the south and reached their highest point, a hundred feet above sea level, at the north end of the island. Hills, she marveled. Cliffs. In the Florida Keys. Tango, a geographical anomaly.

In between the island's low and high points lay neighborhoods, equestrian farms, groves of mangos, citrus, papaya, three schools, a hospital, hotels, businesses, a small airport, and a wilderness preserve that covered much of the northern part of the island. In many ways, the self-contained world of Tango Key with a history as rich and quirky as its topography, was like her relationship with Pierce. Odd, uneven, strange, unpredictable. It seemed oddly fitting that they would see each other here for the first time in a year.

She thought back to her first visit to Tango seven years ago, when she and Pierce investigated a UFO sighting with multiple and credible witnesses all over the island. Mike, just fourteen and on his spring break, was with her. He'd accompanied them around the whole island as they interviewed witnesses, studied witness videos, sorted through photos. Steve, her ex, had considered her work delusional and had objected to Mike being there. But he really didn't have any say in it. He'd left them seven years earlier and was on a honeymoon in Europe with his new wife.

Omega's investigation of the Tango Key Lights had triggered her son's interest in her work, her passion, and marked the beginning of the attraction between her and Pierce. She knew other sightings had occurred on Tango over the years, but the Tango Key Lights incident remained the most convincing. In the expanding annals of UFO sightings in the twenty-first century, this case stood out because there had been so many credible witnesses—police, pilots, engineers, scientists, individuals trained to distinguish farce from fact.

Since she'd moved to Key West a year ago, she had been to Tango for the farmer's market, art fairs, book fairs, concerts, day trips that invariably included a visit to One World Books, her favorite independent bookstore in the universe. But these trips always had been overshadowed by a nostalgia for her first visit here with Pierce.

Once she escaped the crowded bridge of commuters and tourists, Sofia followed the GPS instructions to Gulf Avenue. It led her through downtown Tango, past businesses, restaurants, cafes, the marina and the seaport where cruise ships were anchored offshore. She hung a right finally onto Old Post Road. It twisted and climbed along the rocky western coast and at times was so steep she had to downshift her VW into second gear.

She came out of a particularly sharp turn and there it was, the Tango Key lighthouse, rising a hundred and fifty feet at the edge of a cliff, majestic against the perfectly blue sky. Now a museum and an historic landmark, the structure was built by the Spanish in 1568, just three years after the founding of St. Augustine, the oldest city in the country. A large red sign, posted on the front gate, read CLOSED UNTIL FURTHER NOTICE.

Sofia swung into a culvert at the side of the road, stopped and snapped several photos of the lighthouse with her cell phone. She texted them to Mike.

Arrived.

Fits your vision, Mom. And it has plenty of history. Pirates, plundering, murder.... Is Luke meeting you there?

That's the plan.

Why's it closed?

Don't know yet. Will keep you posted and see you and Cooper later!

The plan was that Mike and Cooper the dog would meet her at the lighthouse after he'd gotten his college stuff sorted out. With Pierce, she had insisted that Mike be part of this investigation, that he act as her monitor. Pierce had been offended at that.

I thought I was your monitor.

You were my lying lover who wasn't honest about your relationship with your ex-wife.

She pulled back onto the road, drove another three hundred yards, and turned into the lighthouse driveway. She felt alternately euphoric and depressed about seeing Pierce again and this seesaw in her emotions frustrated her. She only wanted to feel indifference toward him. Or anger. Even that would be preferable. She parked to the left of the CLOSED sign, yanked up the emergency brake, and texted Pierce. *Am here.*

Be there shortly.

Since Pierce was probably on island time, *shortly* could mean anywhere from five minutes to an hour. Sofia slung her bag over her shoulder and got out. The gate was electronically controlled and the iron fence that surrounded the lighthouse looked too formidable to scale even if she'd wanted to try it.

So she walked along the northern side of the fence, through a field filled with weeds, that ended at a guardrail at the edge of the cliff. A sign here provided a short history of the lighthouse and noted that at one time, a stable had occupied the field where she stood. It had been burned down in the late 1600s by fundamentalist settlers who believed the stable was run by a coven of witches.

Mike, a history major at the University of Miami, hadn't told her about the witch part of the lighthouse history. Maybe he didn't know about it. Or care. His interest had been the UFO sightings that had occurred around the lighthouse over the years.

"Hey, Sofia!"

She glanced around. Pierce bounded through the field in jeans and a windbreaker, a slender, agile man in his mid-forties who looked like a bearded businessman on vacation. A good cover for a UFO investigator and researcher. She insisted to herself that she didn't feel anything at the sight of him, but her body betrayed her. Her pulse had quickened, she could actually feel the fevered sensations his hands had aroused in her in their three years together, and heard the soft whispers of his voice in the darkest pockets of the night.

She waved and they met in the middle of the field. But instead of hugging hello or even shaking hands, they just looked at each other, their past now a mountain between them. His dark, curly hair shone in the morning light, his seductive mouth smiled.

"Damn, it's good to see you, Sofi."

"You too, Luke. It's been awhile."

"Twelve months and three days since you quit us."

"But who's counting, right?"

He gave a quick laugh. "I've missed you."

"Ha. You've missed the information I provide."

"That's cynical."

"But also true."

He reached for her hand and she didn't pull back, didn't stop him. His fingers touched hers there in the cool sunlight, in the middle of this deserted field. The touch softened her, just as he must have known it would, and the barrier between them suddenly didn't seem quite as insurmountable.

She noticed he no longer wore a wedding ring. "You got divorced?"

"The day you quit, I took the damn ring off, filed for divorce, and she left."

Interesting, Sofia thought, and wished he'd done it when it would have counted. She reclaimed her hand. "When did you move to Tango?"

"Two weeks after you resigned. They don't care where I live. Besides, the Fishers are living here now."

Ted Fisher and his wife, Carmen, a Cuban-American, officially opened Omega fourteen years ago and one of the first people they had hired was Pierce, now considered an expert in this strange, rarefied field. Fisher had been investigating UFOs for years before that, but not in an official capacity, and Omega had given him that platform. Pierce had been teaching science at the University of Miami and had written several academic papers about what might occur when aliens and humans actually met in the real world. One of those had been picked up by a science magazine and because of it, Fisher had hired him.

"Is their son living here, too? Is he still your boss?"

Pierce made a face. "On paper. But he's never around. He's living in Miami with his family and runs the main office. Ted has made it clear I'm my own boss."

"Is he still an asshole?"

"Yeah," Pierce laughed. "Pretty much. Ted is the one who suggested I get in touch with you, see if you'd reconsider for this job. He insisted on the twelve-month contract as part of the deal." He paused. "So remind me of the invaluable information you provided Omega over the years that makes me miss you."

By then, they were walking toward the lighthouse. "Remember that supposed artifact you brought back from Guatemala? My reading was that it was fake. Or how about the crystal skull Ted found in New Mexico? I told you guys it was a convincing fake. Then there was…"

"Okay, you made your point."

"Hey, you asked."

They fell silent. When Pierce had recruited her, she and Mike had been living in the same place they had lived before her husband had walked out. She'd been teaching ESOL—English to speakers of other languages—through Dade County. On weekends, her time had been divided between Mike's activities and her psychic work with a Miami UFO network. They had paid her, though not well, but she would have done the work for free. Her interest in the field had begun with a daylight sighting she and her *abuelita*—her grandmother—Rosa had when she was a kid.

She'd met Pierce during a UFO conference in Hollywood, Florida, where she'd been one of the featured speakers alongside some of the luminaries in the field. She'd given a talk about how psychics might contribute to the research and had ended up doing her psychic carnie act on a lush back patio—fifteen minute readings for twenty-five bucks a shot. A tall guy wearing a blue t-shirt with three aliens on it—Greys with the huge almond-shaped black eyes—had sat down at her table.

I want to know how you and I can work together. I was impressed with your talk.

In that t-shirt he looked like a nut from one of the fringe groups that often attended UFO conferences. *And who are you, exactly?*

Luke Pierce. I'm the lead investigator for Omega. He dropped a hundred dollar bill on the table. *And I'd love to get a reading.*

As soon as she heard *Omega,* excitement coursed through her. *So you're testing me. Fair enough. I'll need something you wear often, preferably metal.*

My cell? I practically live on it.

Sure.

She closed her fingers over the cell, adjusted her breathing, but for the longest time, nothing happened. Then she saw him as a young boy sitting in a yard, staring in wonderment at an object in the sky. Cigar-shaped. Brilliantly lit. Hovering. It looked identical to what she and her *abuelita* had seen that day in Little Havana so many years earlier. She described the image. *Ever since that sighting, this work has been your greatest passion.*

She didn't realize her eyes were shut until they opened and she saw the shocked expression on his face. *I've never shared that incident with anyone except my parents, who applauded my imagination. When can you come to work for Omega as a psychic consultant?*

Today?

He laughed and a handshake sealed the deal. She started working for Omega two days later, earning more than she'd ever made in her life. As a single mom, she had welcomed that spike in income.

"So you've found—what, Luke?" The loaded question.

"Something here on Tango."

"Connected to the multiple witness sightings two days ago?"

He nodded.

"I didn't connect anything in my vision to those sightings. What were you and the older man carrying in that blue tarp?" she asked. "No, forget it. Let's follow the same protocol we always did. Don't tell me anything. I want to get a feel for things when we're inside the gates."

"Sure. However you want to work this is fine with me." He glanced at her. "What'd you pick up when our hands touched?"

He asked with the eagerness of a little kid. "Nothing. I've never been able to read you very well. If I had, I would've known things with your ex weren't exactly how you described them." Okay, it was a low blow, but also happened to be true.

"The whole marriage was fucked up from day one, Sofia. We never had a thing in common and the only reason I stuck around was because of our daughter. Then she's the one who told me to just file for divorce because she couldn't stand the bickering. Now she's in college."

Sofia held up her hands. "Look, I'm sorry. I shouldn't have said that. Let's keep things simple right now, okay?"

"Fair enough."

"What college did she end up at?"

"University of Florida. Veterinary school."

He punched in a code on the gate keypad and the old twin iron gates opened slowly, creaking like a sound effect in a horror movie. Her unease rushed back. Her temples throbbed. She nearly spun around and fled and perhaps Pierce sensed it. He touched her arm and they made their way up the winding sidewalk. "Is the lighthouse closed for repairs or something?" she asked.

"Or something."

In other words, it was closed for the same reason they were here. "So now they close historic monuments for a government outsourced outfit that investigates UFO sightings?"

"When the right people ask. And we're not really government outsourced, you know. We help them out when we're asked."

"Ted Fisher asked the mayor?"

Pierce made a face. "Mayor Willford is no friend of Omega. He thinks we're outliers. Ted asked the governor. They've known each other for years."

It felt odd to be alone with him here on this deserted piece of property, out in the cool February air, like they were the last two people on the planet. She knew he felt it too. Their mutual attraction felt visceral, like an electric current that danced and hummed and connected them just as strongly as it had the last time she'd seen him, in the parking lot behind Omega headquarters in Miami. She had been hurrying out to her car, carrying a large plastic container with her laptop and office supplies inside of it. He'd come running out of the building, shouting her name, and she'd stopped only when she reached her car.

You resigned, Sofia? Why? Why would you do that?

It's the only way I can end our relationship.

But why?

Because you haven't been honest about your marriage.

She shook off the memory.

"When is Mike arriving?" he asked.

"Knowing Mike, later this afternoon. He's bringing Cooper with him."

"Look, I know you and Mike and Cooper can drive home to Key West every night, but there's an apartment above my garage you can use while you're here."

The idea of staying might have thrilled her if the invitation hadn't felt like another attempt at controlling her. "Thanks for the offer, Luke. We'll play it by ear."

He unlocked the lighthouse door and they walked in. Stone floors, display cases, a gift shop, four telescopes set up on the balcony that overlooked the gulf. The stunning view of water and sky made her feel as if she were on a ship in the open sea. Colorful, tropical art and tasteful, framed antique maps decorated the walls. She felt like she had walked back into an earlier time, when this place had a lighthouse keeper who scoured the gulf for enemy vessels. The air was cool and quiet and yes, it smelled musty, just as it had in her vision.

"This way," he said.

Pierce led her into a hall on the left and down a flight of stairs to an area with empty employee desks, computers, bookcases, filing cabinets. Sunlight spilled through a large window that faced the gulf, highlighting family photos and name plates on the desks. He unlocked a door on the right, flicked on all the lights. An employee kitchen. Fridge, stove, sink, dishes, a table, and a long, padlocked floor freezer against the wall.

When Pierce went over to the freezer, her earlier queasiness roared back. The muscles in her legs tightened. Why would he store an artifact from a crash site in a freezer?

Sofia hung back, watching as Pierce unlocked and removed the padlock, raised the freezer's lid. She didn't move. Dread churned across the pit of her stomach. She knew that if she approached the freezer and peered inside, she would be committing to an irrevocable path. There would be no going back. Whatever the freezer held would captivate her completely.

But she'd known that when she'd answered his texts.

"You going to take a look inside?" he asked.

"I did once and my whole life got turned upside down."

Pierce frowned, the vivid blue of his eyes dimmed. He didn't understand the reference. "Which case was that?"

"You, Luke. How the hell can you be so dense?"

"Oh." He looked embarrassed, then touched his hand to the edge of freezer. "Trust me, Sofia. This is way stranger than I am."

She hesitated, then moved forward, and looked down. Everything inside of her went motionless—her heart, breath, lungs, the rushing of blood through her veins. She gasped, her knees turned soft, she grabbed onto the edge of the freezer to keep herself upright. "Holy fuck, Luke."

She felt lightheaded, started hyper-ventilating and knew she was on the verge of passing out. She slammed the lid shut, spun around, bent forward at the waist so blood flowed into her head. She dropped to the floor and forced herself to breathe slowly and evenly until she was no longer lightheaded. Her mind raced, questions without answers stampeded around inside her. *Leave now and leave fast.* She pressed her hands against the floor to push herself to her feet, but her muscles refused to work.

Pierce dropped to a crouch beside her. "You okay?"

"I... need some info."

"You said you didn't want me to tell you anything, that I should follow the old protocol."

Sofia looked at him, Pierce with that square, stubborn, bearded jaw, dark, windblown hair now threaded with gray, those intense blue eyes, that sensuous mouth and those hands that once had excited her beyond anything she'd ever known. "Forget the old protocol. This is..." She pressed her hand to the freezer. "Without precedent. Old rules out the window. Why isn't this place swarming with feds? The military?"

"Because only four people know about it—five now, counting you. And when Mike gets here, it'll be six. And your dog will make seven."

"Where was it squished together?"

"On a jut of rock halfway up that cliff out there."

"By who?"

"The lighthouse/museum custodian, old dude I got to know because I use the museum's library so often. He called me when he found it. I rappelled down the cliff and retrieved it. We hid it in an air-conditioned, locked storage shed at the back of the property until today, when the lighthouse is closed."

She could see him doing this, rappelling down the side of the cliff like he'd been doing it his entire life. Give him a goal, a target, and he would find a way to reach it. She, on the other hand, knew her limits. "I don't think I can do this, Luke."

"Of course you can."

"You guys needs to hire someone else. I know a couple of really great psychics who would be ideal for this."

She got up, surprised that her legs could now move, that her breathing and heartbeat were normal, that whatever had afflicted her minutes ago had vanished so completely it was as if none of those sensations ever existed. She grabbed her shoes, her purse, and headed for the door.

Pierce hurried after her, clasped her arm gently. "Please, Sofia. Please reconsider."

She turned, faced him, and instantly regretted it. The expression on his face was that of the man she'd once loved— and, if she were honest with herself, still loved.

"Look," he said, "I know it hasn't been easy for you financially since you left Omega, that you're in deep shit financially and..."

She wrenched her arm away. "You ran a *check* on me? Seriously?"

"I wish I could say it was Ted's idea, but it was mine. I... I needed to know what it would take to get you here."

"Christ, Luke, that's really unfair. I would have come just because you'd asked. This work is also my passion, you know."

"Yeah, and when you were on the Tango bridge, you might've had some major second thoughts and turned around. I figured you would need a kick in the ass incentive and I had to know what that was."

How well he understood her, she thought.

"Look, I can pay you more to see this through to the end.

It would mean a two-year contract, but would enable you to pay off your house, your debt, and leave plenty left over to do whatever you wanted with the rest of your life."

"You're trying to buy me off, Luke."

Exasperated, he burst out, "I'm trying to make this job tenable for you. I can't just bring in some other psychic who..."

"What you've offered is fine. Better than fine." She threw her hands up in front of her, a gesture with an unequivocal meaning: *back off.* "But I have some conditions."

"What?"

"I don't know if I can read that...body in the freezer, okay? I've been so off on reading my own life, sensing my own future, that I got myself into a financial mess. So, my first condition: I'll do my best, but no guarantees."

"Okay. What else?"

"Nothing happens between the two of us. I just... can't have that emotional entanglement."

"I don't like that one at all. But I get it. I didn't give you too many reasons in the past to trust me. What else?"

"You're missing the point, Luke. What went wrong between us is that you *lied to me.* Don't lie to me. About anything."

"Okay. You have my word."

"And Mike has full access to whatever we know."

"I already agreed to that when we spoke earlier. Is that it?"

"I think so."

"The money, by the way, has already been wired to your account." Pierce extended his hand. "Is a handshake good enough for now?"

Sofia nodded and they shook.

She felt a quick, sharp sensation in that touch, that electrical current, and thought it boded well for what lay ahead. *I can do this*, she thought, and she and Pierce walked back into the employee kitchen.

2

Now that they had agreed on terms and conditions, doubt crept through her. Had she just sold out? Compromised herself beyond redemption? Was she taking advantage of Pierce and Fisher, the two men who had been enormously helpful to her when she worked with Omega? If they'd been feds who intended to hide or get rid of that alien body then yes, she would be selling out by accepting anything from them. But she knew that was the last thing that Pierce and the Fishers would do.

In the kitchen, Sofia slipped off her shoes, dropped her handbag on the table, and joined Pierce at the front of the freezer. She raised the lid and stared at the frozen entity in a transparent body bag. A thin, long being.

It lay on the floor of the freezer, surrounded by bags of ice, frozen loaves of bread, meats, fish. It didn't look anything like the usual images of aliens. It wasn't a Grey. Its face reminded her of a grasshopper's, insectile, and its thinness was like the body of a dragonfly. No wings, but those weird twin thumbs really disturbed her. What could you do with four fucking thumbs? And the flipper foot and webbed hand and the gill at the throat all suggested this alien had been amphibious.

Conflicting emotions swept through her—horror, intrigue, nausea, excitement, revulsion. When she'd worked for Omega, she'd seen numerous sketches and drawings of aliens. But this... seeing an ET in the flesh... was altogether different. Sofia stared at its dual-jointed knees and recalled drawings of ETs made by children at the Ariel primary school in Ruwa, Zimbabwe during a mass sighting in 1992. More than sixty children claimed to have seen a disc-shaped object land behind the school during the morning break time. Two strange beings were reported, one of which approached the children. Several of the sketches the children at Ariel had done included a being with dual jointed legs, like this entity. She started feeling lightheaded again, looked away. "Omega finally has proof, Luke."

"Yeah. And if we release it, we'll end up like John Mack."

Mack, a professor of psychiatry at Harvard and a writer and researcher in the alien abduction phenomenon, had died under suspicious circumstances in 2004, when he'd been hit by a car while crossing a street in London. Speculation was that a covert government agency had killed him to shut him up. But long before she and Pierce any of them were knocked off, she thought, the U.S. military or agents from some other government faction would sweep in just as it had at Roswell and other sites over the decades and the evidence would vanish. "So what's your plan?"

"I stored dozens of photos on the Dark Net and sent them to Ted Fisher. I haven't heard back from him, he's traveling. But he's supposed to be back tonight or tomorrow. He'll probably want the body moved elsewhere."

Fisher shared their belief that extraterrestrial life existed, but that the evidence had been covered up by various governments with disinformation campaigns, ridicule, propaganda. The idea behind the cover-ups, she thought, was that the public wouldn't be able to handle the truth. This excuse was clearly absurd because thanks to countless Hollywood depictions of aliens and their invasions, the majority of the public already believed.

The bottom line was that the covert agencies keeping the truth under wraps did so because they hoped to weaponize whatever technology they might be able to glean. They also knew a discovery like this would shift everything in a heartbeat— science, politics, religion, psychology, cultures. In short, they believed it would result in global collapse and bedlam. The deeper truth, though, was how such knowledge would impact every individual personally.

She brought out her cell, snapped photos, and would send them to Mike later, from her own dark corner of the Internet. "When you brought it up from the cliff, was it alive?"

"It wasn't conscious. I had no idea what to look for in terms of life or death. Does it have a heart that beats? Blood? Organs? I don't know. There's no X-ray machine here. No MRI, no CAT scan. When we moved it out of the storage shed, the body wasn't decomposed, it had been in an old freezer. Tell me what you can, Sofi."

"Can we lift it out? Set it on the floor?"

"Sure. It isn't very heavy."

He reached into the freezer, picked up the ET gently, reverently, and set it on the floor between them. It might not weigh much, but she guessed its long legs put its height at seven or more feet. She didn't want to touch it, didn't want to know its story, didn't want to walk through this door. But her *didn't want* was overpowered by her *I gotta know.*

Sofia sat back on her heels and peeled the body bag down to the being's feet—and the webbed toes on its right foot. Her heart pounded as she brought her palms to the sides of the ET's face, the skin as soft as rose petals. She might not be the first human being to touch an alien, but she suspected she was the first psychic to ever do so.

She waited—and nothing happened. No physical sensations, no impressions or images, no clicking sounds in her ears. The alien body could have been just a weird-looking movie prop. "I'm not picking up anything, Luke."

"Because it's dead?"

"That shouldn't make a difference. I've read bodies in the past."

"Take a breather or something."

"I just started. I don't need a breather."

She started to slip her hands to the ET's blue hair and discovered she couldn't move them at all. Her hands and arms didn't work—not a muscle, not a single joint. Some force or power kept her hands against the being's face like a magnet holding iron. "What the hell," she said, then panic poured through her and behind it, rushed images of the craft plunging out of the sky, swirling into a death spiral. Suddenly, Sofia was *there*, inside the ETs craft, experiencing what the ET did as it struck the water.

A fire breaks out in the craft. Panicked and terrified of burning to death, Mira slams her body repeatedly against the hatch until it finally opens. The webbing between her fingers and toes snaps into place, her third eyelids roll across her eyes, the flaps of skin at her throat and side flutter open.

She shoots into the salt water and the pressure of the gravity nearly crushes her. Her body struggles to adjust, strength pours into her arms and legs, the flaps at her throat and side open and close, allowing her to breathe underwater. She's as much a creature of the sea as she is a creature of the earth. But it's not enough, she feels as if an unendurable weight pushes her down, down, intent on drowning her.

Above her, the craft keeps burning.

Her feet sink into the soft, cold sand that eddies and shifts and threatens to bury her. In a last, desperate burst of strength she propels herself upward, swimming frantically. Her dual knee joints enable her to leap like one of the strangest insects on this planet, a grasshopper. She catapults out of the sea and lands clumsily on a jut of rock on the face of a cliff. She crawls frantically forward, as far as the rock will allow, then collapses, too weak to become fully air-breathing again. As she gasps for air, she watches her craft sinking. Her scream for help bursts out of her...

Then the force released Sofia's hands and she fell back, legs flopping out in front of her, back and head hitting the floor. Air rushed from her lungs. She lay there, stunned and wheezing, her vision blurred.

Something had happened to one of her hands, Sofia felt it, like gum stuck between her fingers. She knew she should look, check it out, but didn't have the strength. It was as if the muscles in her arm had atrophied and her will had been squashed.

C'mon, do this. Lift your goddamn arm.

And finally, she did. Her arm felt as heavy as wet cement. But when she saw her hand, the webbing between her fingers, a scream clawed its way up her throat. It never reached the air. She passed out.

The Fist of Destiny

I *understand now. She has The Sight and when she touched me, she was able to see the crash of my craft, the fire that broke out, my escape. She believes I suffocated to death on that cliff and that is to my advantage. Only so much I can do in this dormant state until my body heals, but I may have changed her enough to establish a rudimentary basis for communication and control. Her webbed foot is our connection.*

Sofia, Sofia. I like her name, how it sounds in my language, like a series of notes that create a music so seductive that even dolphins and whales will hear it and obey. She will make a perfect host for me.

Once I take on her appearance and she takes on mine, her skills will become mine. I will gain her Sight. The people she loves will love me. Her son, ex-lover, parents, the people around her will be fooled. I don't know about the dog. My tribe's experiences with these creatures is limited. In our world, there is not enough land remaining for dogs or any other land creatures this planet has. If the dog becomes a problem, I'll eliminate it.

I suddenly hear the call of Acia, my equal in the tribe, who is in charge in Cuba. Her voice sweeps through the telepathic web that connects all of us. Mira, you must stay where you are, change the woman with The Sight, then come here as human. We need one like her.

You don't tell me what to do, Acia. I know what to do. How many has the tribe transformed in Cuba?

Not as many as we would like. For some, the metamorphosis is slow.

Your job is to take as many humans as possible. When I am healed, I will do what circumstances and opportunity permit.

But we need a human on our side with The Sight, we...

Enough. *I disconnect from the web. I do not have the strength to argue with her. Perhaps being in charge of the tribe in Cuba has convinced her she rules us all. I open a private channel in the web to Lotus, my advisor and friend.* What is wrong with Acia?

She is failing at what she is supposed to be doing. Fear cripples her. She hides all day in the caves, watching the ones we are transforming as they become more and more like us, watching our kind take on human appearances. She despises how humans look, she tortures some of them. Please get here as quickly as you can, Mira.

I must heal first.

How badly are you injured?

Badly. Am dormant now. It takes most of my strength just to hold Sofia's webbing until it begins to grow capillaries and veins and become a permanent part of her. Do not let Acia torture the ones who are changing. We need them. We need as many as we can successfully take.

Some of the humans are going mad. Those who now have gills claw at themselves. Others try to escape the caves. I will do what I can. Heal quickly. Acia suspects I am speaking to you on a private channel, so I will detach now.

Wait! If Acia goes completely out of control, have Jez eliminate her.

Jez, one of our warriors.

Okay. It is not at that point yet, but I will speak to him, have him follow her.

We need this world, Lotus.

I know. Until soon.

Our world is a parody of this world's science fiction movies. It's mostly water, inundated centuries ago when its axis tilted and lakes and rivers and streams poured into oceans and seas and turned salt to brine, killing off marine life. Our air is toxic, our food sources are limited to crops grown on islands that don't exist in our own time, to cloned marine life farmed in other times.

We have evolved from chaos, three billion of us left from nine times that, have developed skills that enable us to survive, but we lack The Sight. We cannot see our own future. We no longer reproduce and it is our hope that we will be able to reproduce with the humans we transform. Hybrids.

I transmit a message through the web to the entire tribe. Information moves through it faster than the speed of light. Maintain resolve. Take as many as possible. Do not torture. That island is already ours.

The web trembles and shudders. My message has been heard. I detach from the web.

I'm not sure what happened to my craft, why the navigational system failed. But I'm so close to Cuba that when I am fully healed, I will be able to get there even if Sofia is only partially changed. She will facilitate that journey. The crushing weight of this planet's gravity has killed many of us, but now that her transformation has begun with the webbed feet, it will be easier for my body to adjust.

So perhaps the fist of destiny determined my crash here. Acia is correct about one thing. The tribe needs someone like Sofia, someone with The Sight. Her skill will enable me to lead my tribe to the conquest of Cuba and from there, the world.

Chapter 2

Pierce stared at her. One moment she had rocked away from the ET, fallen onto her back, and lay there, breathing hard. Then she had lifted her hand—and passed out.

"Fuckfuckfuck... Sofia." Pierce touched her shoulders. "C'mon, snap out of it."

He leaned over her, made sure she was still breathing, slipped his hands under her head. He lifted it and set it on his thigh and smoothed her dark hair off her forehead. He longed to press his mouth to her beautiful skin, to trace the shape of her mouth with his thumbs. But he was afraid that if he did she might suddenly stop breathing.

"Hey, if you... die on me, I'll... I'll..."

What? Just what the hell would he do? Scream at her? She would laugh at him from the afterlife.

Her eyes flitted back and forth beneath her lids, as though she were dreaming. Her breath remained soft, even. Pierce moved her head from his thigh, set it carefully on the floor, got up. He stepped over the alien to the freezer. Lid up. He broke open a six pack of frozen water, pulled out a bottle, moved back to Sofia's side and rolled it across her face, her forehead—and the webbed fingers of her left hand.

No wonder she'd passed out.

He glanced down at her feet. The toes on her right foot were webbed. Just like the alien's right foot.

Webbed. "Fuck." Pierce rocked back on his heels, unable to wrench his eyes away.

He slipped his fingers under her hand and raised it. The webbing was grotesque yet eerily beautiful, thick but translucent, and extended from the upper joints in her fingers and down the length of them. Terror crawled through him. *What happened here?*

He touched the webbing. The skin felt tough, resilient, but lacked any network of capillaries or veins.

Document everything. It helped to take photos, made him feel useful and less freaked out. In his eight years of working with her, knowing her, loving her, he had witnessed a lot of strange things. But never anything like this, where she took on a physical manifestation of whatever she had tuned into. Remorse filled him. He should have just let her leave. Shouldn't have contacted her at all.

He pressed the bottle of water to her forehead. She twitched. Pierce spun off the bottle's cap and ran over to the microwave, hit defrost, melting the ice enough so she could sip it. He hurried back to her side. Blood had drained from her beautiful face, her right foot twitched, as if the webbing was painful. He couldn't understand how this had happened. None of it was possible.

Then again, mainstream science insisted that man was alone in the universe and that the alien on the floor couldn't possibly exist. He lifted Sofia's head, touched the bottle to her lips. "Drink a little, Sofia, c'mon."

When she didn't, he dabbed cold water on her lips, poured some on her face. She didn't move. His alarm deepened. He considered taking her to the ER, but how would he explain the webbing? *It happened when she tuned in on an alien.*

"Shit, shit."

Pierce examined her webbed right foot, the sole, the top of it. He ran his fingers over the webbing here, too, and thought it felt thicker. He took photos, lifted her foot and propped it on his thigh. He shone his cell's flashlight at its underside. Translucent. And again, the light didn't reveal any capillaries or veins.

He tried once more to get her to sip from the bottle.

Nothing.

Pierce pressed his knuckles against his eyes and flipped through a mental list of contact who he might call. The Fishers, sure. But they weren't in town. If they had been, Carmen would have raced over here with her *santero*, who would have performed some weird ritual, decreed that Sofia was possessed by a malignant spirit that had to be eradicated. Fisher would have arrived with the staff physician at his side. If Pierce called his daughter, she'd tell him she was in the midst of a veterinary crisis and couldn't talk. The only people he could call were Sofia, who was *out*, or Mike, who would arrive with a chip on his shoulder and whisk his mother out of here.

"Luke?"

McMullen's voice echoed through the stone walls of the lighthouse. Thank God, now he wouldn't be alone with this. "Down here, Josh," he called back.

He appeared at the top of the stairs, saw Sofia laying on the stone floor, and trotted down. "Holy shit." He raked his fingers back through his thick gray hair, crouched beside her. "Is she okay? Should we get her to a hospital?"

"Give her a few minutes. Maybe she's processing what she picked up."

"What happened, anyway?"

"I don't know. She had her hands against this thing's face, said she wasn't picking up anything, and then her body...it was weird...her body just seemed to freeze for two or three minutes. Then she made a strangled sound and she fell back and lifted her arm, saw this..." Pierce touched the webbing on her hand. "And she passed the fuck out."

"Shit, man, I woulda done the same." McMullen paused, stared at her. "She's really beautiful, Luke."

Like he needed to be reminded.

"Except for the webbing on her hand and foot. How do you explain that?"

"I... can't."

McMullen gestured at the ET. "And what happens when that thing thaws out?"

"I don't know." This weirdness had left him feeling disassociated from science, from facts, from whatever he thought he knew about anything. He'd felt like this ever since he'd rappelled down the cliff and retrieved the body.

"Has she passed out before when she reads stuff?"

"No. And that webbing, Josh. It appears on the same hand and foot as that of the alien."

He touched Sofia's hand. "Yeah, even looks like the same color, the same texture. But, uh, how come the alien's right foot now looks as human as Sofia's?"

Pierce hadn't noticed that until McMullen pointed it out, and wondered how he'd missed it. Selective perception was something that happened frequently in his investigations. But not when it involved Sofia. "I... don't know." He whispered the words, cleared his throat. "Like a transfiguration. She took on its foot, the ET took on hers."

"Excuse me, Luke. But from what my very Catholic daughter tells me, a transfiguration involves a complete change in appearance to something more beautiful and spiritual. Like Christ into radiant light. That fucking exchange of feet is not more beautiful or spiritual."

He shook his head. His parents had been atheists or agnostics or something. His mother had read tarot cards from time to time and for years, his idea of Christ was that of the image depicted of *The Hanged Man*, key 12 of the Major Arcana. The poor dude hanging upside down on a cross. "Take religion out of it, Josh, and transfiguration literally means a complete change of form or appearance. Tadpoles are transfigured into frogs. Caterpillars are transfigured into butterflies."

"Is that what's happening here?" McMullen looked as horrified as Pierce felt just then.

"I don't know what the fuck's happening."

He touched the flap of skin at the alien's throat. A gill? Had something like that appeared on Sofia? He glanced over but didn't see anything like this at her throat. With his thumb and index finger, he opened one of the alien's eyes, something neither he nor McMullen had done before. "Josh, what do you see?"

The old man shone his cell's flashlight there. "It looks like... a... a translucent piece of skin is covering the eyeball."

"A third eyelid?" Pierce said.

"There's a name for that."

"Nictitating membrane."

"Yeah, that's it. Does Sofia now have them?"

Pierce hadn't looked, didn't want to look. But his body had other ideas. He knelt next to her, opened her right eye, her left, saw third lids. This level of strangeness was so high he had no idea what to do next.

And now he saw the webbing on her hand was gone. Withdrawn into her fingers? He moved his hand to her fingers, her eye shut. He spread her fingers apart, ran his thumb down one finger and up another. No nicks, no protrusions, just soft, smooth skin.

"Well?" McMullen asked.

"She... has the third lids. And the webbing between her fingers is gone."

Pierce jerked his hand away, scooted across the floor and sat back against the wall, gripping his knee caps. His thoughts scrambled around, terrified rats in a cage. What the hell had he unleashed here?

"I'm moving it back into the freezer, Luke." McMullen pulled the body bag back over the alien, then slid his muscular arms under it, picked it up, and set it down carefully in the freezer. He shut the lid, leaned against it. "Hey, man. Deep breaths, okay? I don't need you going comatose like her."

Deep breaths. Right. Like deep breaths would solve anything. Pierce forced himself to breathe slowly and evenly, and after a few moments, felt *almost* normal. But he knew *almost* could burst apart at any second.

"You think we might grow webbing?" McMullen asked.

The possibility had occurred to Pierce. But it seemed unlikely. Neither of them could read the ET psychically and he was fairly certain the psychic facet had helped establish a connection between Sofia and the alien. "Not unless we're psychic."

"Mayor called me earlier, Luke. He wanted to know when the renovations would be done to the lighthouse, said it's costing the county money, having the place closed."

Ted Fisher had spoken to the governor, not the mayor, and asked that the lighthouse be closed for several days. Pierce didn't know what explanation he'd provided. But the mayor, he knew, could make a stink about the closing of the museum and cause them problems. "We could move the body to a freezer in my garage."

"After his call," McMullen said, "I decided that moving it soon would be smart. Is your freezer long enough?"

"I think so."

"So the sooner we move it, Luke, maybe the safer we are." His bushy white brows shot up, forming peaks over his eyes. "The mayor was making noises about stopping by to see what was going on."

"Great." Pierce looked down at Sofia. "As soon as she comes to we'll move the alien body."

"I'll bring my van around to the back. That's the best place to park. But first I should destroy the security feed for the last several days."

"Who has access to it?

"Relax. It's just for me, unless there's something big, then I'm 'sposed to send it out to the mayor, chief of police, and so on. In my twelve years here, that's happened only twice." He paused. "Okay, just curious, why'd she leave Omega?"

"She got fed up with me." Pierce rolled the bottle of cold water over her face and neck again. "I'll bring the ET's body upstairs and set it in front of the rear exit, so you don't have to come back down here."

How easily those words came out. *The ETs body.* Sweet Christ, he'd been dreaming of something like this ever since he'd seen that UFO when he was a kid, the night after his sixth birthday. He'd been outside in the backyard with Lynx, his Border Collie, the sky so cloudy that it hid the moon and stars. Occasionally in the distance, lightning unzipped the darkness, promising rain. He and Lynx had been sitting together on the grass when something bright, almost luminous, had shot out of the clouds.

It seemed to be only a couple hundred feet above them, so close he could see that it was shaped like a gigantic cigar. But in retrospect, he figured it had been at five or six thousand feet, had hovered for several breathless moments, casting a soft blue light that spilled into the yard. Lynx had whimpered and moved closer to Pierce, and he'd thrown his arm over the dog's back, afraid he might try to chase the light. Then the object shot away so impossibly fast that he'd known right then it couldn't be a plane.

He'd run inside and awakened his parents, but they'd had a party that evening, had both been drinking, and told him he'd imagined it. *Go back to bed, Luke.* Next morning over breakfast, his mother had asked him about it, so he told her. She sort of smiled and shook her head. *Honey, there's no such thing as UFOs.*

His father had laughed. *Honestly, the stuff you cook up, Luke.*

But he knew what he'd seen and never allowed their opinions to sway his belief. And now he wasn't about to let the mayor or anyone else ferret the ET's body away and pretend it didn't exist.

"If she hasn't come to, Josh, I'll bring her upstairs, too, and we can put her in your van."

"And since her car's parked out there, we'll have to move it."

After McMullen left, Pierce spread out a blue tarp, the same one they'd used initially to carry the alien into the storage unit and then into the lighthouse. He lifted it out of the freezer again, set it carefully on the tarp. He considered peeling the body bag away from its head and checking both eyes for that third lid. But he felt a greater urgency to get the body out of here. It would be just like the mayor to suddenly show up. He knew the security code, had a key, could just walk in unannounced. And he would immediately see that not a single renovation was happening.

Pierce glanced once more at Sofia. Still out. The webbing between her fingers hadn't reappeared. Incredulity welled up inside of him and behind it whispered a near panic.

Don't think about it. Just move, get the thing outta here.

Pierce murmured, "Be right back, Sofia." He carried the body upstairs to the lobby, down a side hall to the rear exit, set it down on the floor in front of the door. He then immediately had second thoughts about just leaving it here for McMullen to retrieve, and texted him.

Am @rear door. U done?

On my way.

I'll wait here with the body.

The alien with its webbed hand and foot. Nictitating membranes. A flap of skin at its throat and on its side that looked like gills. A single nostril. Extremely long legs and dual-jointed knees. A weird sprig of blue hair. "Fuck me," he whispered. In all these years of investigating sightings and abductions, of gathering evidence, he'd never imagined himself in this situation.

As soon as McMullen appeared, Pierce opened the rear door and peered out. Old Post Road had more traffic now, but McMullen's van was behind the lighthouse, not visible from the road. Pierce opened its rear hatch and motioned for the old man to hurry and load the body in the back. McMullen stepped outside, cradling the wrapped entity in his arms the way he might one of his grandchildren. He set it between a pair of ladders, with cleaning supplies and a tool kit and shut the hatch.

"Luke, you think this alien is radioactive or carries disease or something?"

Pierce had considered that possibility after he and McMullen had carried it into the lighthouse, touched it, and placed it in the body bag. "Well, if it does, it's too late for us."

The old man slipped on his sunglasses, rubbed his hands against his jeans. "Shit, maybe I'd better stay away from my grandkids right now. I'll wait for you and follow you to your place."

Pierce nodded and hastened back inside. If Sofia hadn't regained consciousness, he would have to call Fisher's physician and explain the situation to him. If he was on the island, maybe he'd examine her. Good plan, but not one that he wanted to act on. He could text the Fishers, but they hadn't responded to texts, emails, or calls since he'd texted Fisher two days ago, the same day McMullen found the alien.

He hurried downstairs and when he was back in the lighthouse employee area, Sofia was sitting up against the freezer in the kitchen, staring in horror at her webbed toes. "What the fuck *happened* to me? Am I hallucinating? Do you *see* this?" She grabbed her webbed foot, lifted it off the floor. "It's *real*, it feels *real*, I can see it…" She let go of her foot and it plopped to the floor, the webbing twitching. "Fuck!" she shrieked, and ground her fists into her eyes. "I knew I shouldn't have read that thing. I knew it." Her arms dropped and he pulled her to her feet.

"Do you otherwise feel okay?"

"*Okay?* How the hell can I feel okay, Luke, about hobbling along with a webbed foot?"

She looked scared shitless, he thought. "I know, I know. I meant, are you in physical pain?"

"No. Just… my foot feels weird. Uncomfortable." She held up her left hand. "The webbing between my fingers disappeared."

"It happened pretty soon after you passed out."

"Then why the hell hasn't *that* vanished, too?" She pointed at her foot.

"I don't know. I don't understand any of this."

She hobbled over to the freezer, threw open the lid. "Where is she?"

"Her? The alien is female?"

"Definitely. And you moved her?"

"Upstairs. Josh McMullen, the custodian, thinks Mayor Willford is on his way over here. He put the body in his car to take to my place. I've got a huge floor freezer in my garage where we can put the body."

"Do you think the webbing can be surgically removed, Luke?"

"Probably. But do you want to go there?"

"I just want it *gone*," she whispered. "*She* did this to me. That alien shit turned my foot and she exuded a force that wouldn't let me move my hands off her face, she…"

"Wait. She's *alive*?"

Sofia looked bewildered. "I thought she had suffocated on the cliff because her gills didn't close fast enough. But if she died, where did that force come from? Jesus, I need to get outta here, into the air."

"Yeah, good idea if you follow Josh to my place. We need to keep reminding ourselves that what we think is true and real has changed dramatically." Even to himself, he sounded manic. "We don't know the parameters and rules yet."

"We don't know *squat*," she spat, and wagged her hand in the air. "Why was my hand webbed? Where'd that extra skin go? I know it was there, I saw it. You saw it. And... and my toes..." Her voice choked with fear.

"Will your shoe fit over it?"

Sofia scooped up her shoes and sat down on a step. She tried to pull on her right shoe, but couldn't. "Great. I'm one of Cinderella's wicked stepsisters." She threw the shoes across the kitchen. "Fuck it, I'll go barefoot."

Pierce picked up her shoes, pocketed the freezer lock, and she grabbed her purse. He took a quick look around to make sure he hadn't left behind anything important, and followed her up the stairs. He didn't tell her the alien body now had her foot. "What happened? Do you remember?"

"Yeah. All of it." She turned on her phone's recorder and told him to do the same. "It's best to do this now, while the memory is still fresh."

As they climbed the stairs to the lighthouse lobby, she told him what she'd seen and felt from the moment the craft had crashed to when the ET leaped from the water to the side of the cliff. "So it was definitely amphibious. I think when she was submerged, cartilage must have closed off the inside of her nostril so she didn't drown. And she had nictitating membranes."

"So do you."

"Not now I don't. Listen, I don't even want to think about what any of this might mean." She tucked her hair behind her ears, pointed at her webbed foot. "Or why I would take on physical manifestations of this alien's body. But it happened and I... I need to... to..." She raised her eyes, tears leaking from them. "... to figure out why."

Pierce felt like gathering her into his arms, holding her tightly, reassuring her that he was here for her. But he didn't. Considering their past, she had no reason to believe in him. During their three years together, he had never been truthful about his marriage, Whether he was divorced, separated, or living with his wife and daughter. Why should she trust him now?

Sofia paused in the middle of the hall, her recorder still on. "Another thing I remember. When she was suffocating on the cliff, she watched her craft sinking and screamed for help."

"She could *speak?*"

"No, not that kind of scream, Luke. It felt telepathic, but maybe a high-pitched sound. I'm not sure. I feel she sent out a call to the rest of her kind."

Her *kind?* Where? How could they get to her sunken craft? If there had been a fire onboard, was anything left of it? And if so, how would they haul it up? "Did it come from a larger fleet?"

"I don't know."

As they reached the back exit, Pierce heard the heavy front door of the lighthouse slam open. "Hey, Luke, you here?"

"The mayor," he whispered. "Follow Josh to my place. I'll deal with him."

She nodded and quickly hobbled out the rear door.

2.

Rattled by the mayor's sudden appearance, Pierce took a moment to compose himself and come up with an excuse about why he was here. As far as Ben Willford was concerned, Pierce was a weirdo who worked for a company that investigated and researched fringe stuff. He knew that Pierce was often at the lighthouse, going through the museum's vast collection of old books on the second floor. He also knew Pierce and McMullen were friends.

When he walked out into the lobby, Willford was studying one of the old maps on the wall of old maps. Big guy, broad shoulders, gym rat, early fifties. Married, two kids, five grandkids, southern to the core. "Hey, Ben. What's going on?"

"Luke." Willford turned. "Saw your car and another parked outside. The lighthouse is closed but not to you, huh?"

Oh Ben, if you only knew... "I told Josh I'd give him a hand cleaning up so the museum can reopen tomorrow."

Willford tipped his shades back onto the top of his head, his eyes darting about. "Well, that's good news. County can use the revenue. Height of the tourist season and all. Josh said some renovations were going on? Don't see much of anything torn up here."

Of course not, Ben. We had an alien here. Pierce just wanted to get away from Willford as quickly as possible. "The plumbers have been here and left. Some problems on the lower floors. I figured while I was here, I'd spend a little time in my favorite library."

"Did Josh already leave?"

"Probably. He was loading up his gear."

"Uh-huh." He turned back to the wall of maps and pointed at one of Tango dated 2010. "You know what that there map shows, Luke? Those red dots?"

"Sure. Where people all over the island saw the lights seven years ago. The Tango Key Lights, one of the best cases in Omega's files."

"Why one of the best?"

"Because of the credible witnesses, their testimonies, the photos, videos."

"And you were here then."

"And now I live here." His phone vibrated, a text from Sofia. *On the road, following Josh.* "Your point, Ben?"

"So, just curious," Willford said. "I was off island for several days and when I got back, I heard two things—one is multiple reports of a sighting near the lighthouse, in broad daylight, on February 6. Then I hear the governor issues a close up order for the lighthouse. Seems he got a call from your boss, old man Fisher. Look, when one of the richest men in the state, who also happens to be a friend and a donor, calls the gov and requests a favor, well, sure, no problem. We'll close the museum for a couple of days. Now here you are, Luke."

"And that's a surprise, Ben? My job is to investigate sightings."

"I've got a nose for bullshit, son." He tapped his plump finger against Pierce's chest. "And right 'bout now, my nose is workin' overtime, if you catch my drift."

Pierce felt like shoving his arm away, but he took a step back and Willford's arm swung to his side. "Actually, I'm missing your drift. I'm not breaking any laws, Ben. What're you getting at?"

Willford whipped out his phone, brought up something on the screen. "Listen real close to this recording. She's one of the ones who called in about the sighting. I spoke to her in person. Talked to several of the witnesses."

He started the recording:

Willford: It's Tuesday, February 7, 2017. State your name, address, profession, ma'am.

Woman: Annette Proodian. I'm a flight attendant for American Airlines. When I'm not flying, I live at 516 Doubloon Drive just outside Pirate's Cove.

Willford: And what did you see, Ms. Proodian?

Proodian: On Monday, February 6, 2017, around eight-thirty or so a.m., I'm on Flight 156 coming in from Miami, about fifteen hundred feet and descending. I was walking up the aisle, picking up glasses and reminding passengers to fasten their seat belts. One of them, a man, suddenly started shouting and pointing at something outside the window.

Willford: Which side of the plane?

Proodian: Well, we were headed south into Tango, so he was on the east side. I leaned over to take a look and I have to tell you, it was one of those oh my God moments. I saw—everyone on that side of the plane saw it—a craft spiraling out of the clouds. And headed for us.

Willford: An aircraft?

Proodian: Nope. A UFO craft, oblong, large enough to kill us if it plowed into us, but not huge. Morning sun was hitting it, lighting it up. We all saw it clearly and recognized what it was. Captain Piper, too, because the plane suddenly banked steeply away from it.

Willford: So what happened to the craft?

Proodian: After we banked, I couldn't see.

Willford: Did the pilot file a report?

Proodian: Probably not. Most pilots are afraid that if they do, they'll be blacklisted or something. But they don't give a crap what flight attendants say. When I got home awhile later, I drove over to the lighthouse. I was pretty sure the craft had come down offshore from there. I went inside and used one of the telescopes, but didn't see a thing. That's when I called your office, Mayor. And the police station. Turns out the cops had been inundated by calls.

Willford: Thank you for your time, Ms. Proodian. If you remember anything else or hear from any of those passengers, please let me know.

The recording ended and Willford now stood there, gloating. "Well?"

Pierce felt like wiping that smirk off the mayor's face. "Are you kidding, Ben? I'd like to talk to this woman. Omega has a hotline, we got some calls on February sixth and seventh, but nothing like that."

"So it's just a wild coincidence that you're here at the lighthouse, helping ole Josh with some repairs."

"Not at all. The day the calls came in, a colleague and I went scuba diving four hundred yards offshore, hoping to find this alleged craft. We were out there five hours but never spotted anything. Yesterday, I helped Josh out here and spent awhile using one of the telescopes, hoping to spot, you know, maybe some aliens swimming the breast stroke to shore."

"Very funny, Luke."

"Yeah? I'm delighted you're amused because I find this entire conversation tedious. What really puzzles me is why any of this would even interest you, Ben. I thought you considered this stuff to be total bullshit."

"This is *my* island."

"You *bought* Tango Key? With what, an inheritance?"

Willford now looked pissed off. "My island by virtue of the fact that I received sixty-five to nearly eighty percent of the vote for mayor in my first and second terms. My third term is going to be higher than that. "

And that vote would be in a few weeks, Pierce thought.

"Been mayor for eight years. I know this island attracts all types. And it's my business to know what's going on even with weirdos like you and Omega. If Tango Key is being invaded by little green men from Mars, then I need to know about it."

Little green men from Mars. Pierce laughed and shook his head. Where had that phrase originated, anyway? The invasion consisted of one dead amphibious female ET with pale skin, a sprig of blue hair, a single nostril, gills, double knee joints, four thumbs, nictitating membranes in both eyes, and a hand and a foot that were webbed. Well, the foot was originally webbed, but now looked like Sofia's very human foot, toenail polish and all. "Ben, I can assure you no little green men from Mars or any other planet are invading Tango Key."

"Well, in a few days we'll really know. Called a friend in the Coast Guard. He and his team will scuba dive in the area, deep dives, and then we'll know one way of another."

"Great. Good luck with it. And if you find any alien treasures, invite me to the showing. I need to get to work, Ben. You've got the key. Lock up when you leave."

Pierce was out the door before Willford could think of anything to say.

The mayor troubled him. Willford had been born and bred on Tango, so that made him part of an exclusive group that called themselves Tango Fritters, good ole home boys with roots here going way back to the first overzealous American settlers from Salem. Pierce had no idea whether Willford descended from those witch-burning freaks, but it wouldn't surprise him. He was an authoritarian who allowed his police boys to deal with suspects any way they wanted to.

Stop you for a dead tail light and if you're a minority, check you for drugs. Check.

You're a woman who claims to have been raped, but because you're a woman, you enticed the guy. Check.

If Willford won the election in a few weeks, it would put him in for another four years. Up against him was a man Pierce liked who was so liberal he probably would welcome aliens into the electoral process.

But the mayor's sudden appearance kept eating away at Pierce, and his creepy spider sense sprang into action. He stopped a mile south of the lighthouse, in a culvert of trees. He walked to the back of his Prius, ran his hand under the rear bumper, into the wheel wells, up and down and sideways, and finally found it.

The tracking device was small, about the size of a quarter, stuck way up in the well of his front right tire. He peeled it off with his thumbnail, studied it, smiled. *Asshole.* Pierce set it on the passenger seat and drove toward his house. En route, he stopped at a Cuban market and slapped it under the rear fender of a truck parked at the side of the market.

Track that, dickhead.

Out of the Freezer

Even from the back of the old man's van, I finally can smell the richness of the sea, of the lakes that exist all over this island, of the food sources they hold. My hunger hasn't reached epic proportions yet, but it won't be long. The driver might make an excellent meal, but he is old and I may need him later. I cannot reveal myself that way until I am fully healed.

Besides, human flesh isn't my preference. Give me frogs, turtles, seaweed, octopi, fish, clams, oysters, the fresher the better. Fruits, coconuts, and leafy greens are also excellent. Through the web that connects my tribe, I have learned they found a source of food in Cuba that does not exist in our world. They do not have a name for it yet and eat it sparingly because it is rich in the nutrients our bodies crave. It makes them feel so sated that some of them become lethargic, stupid, clumsy. Several in my tribe have grown so careless after eating it they make mistakes that get them killed. I do not understand how this happens, but it should be something that Acia can control.

The web shimmers and Acia's voice reaches me. Lotus and I and several others are going to attempt to rescue you. We need you here.

It is too soon. I am not healed.

We can heal you.

Even these injuries are beyond our tribe's capacity to heal, Acia. The healing must come from within me and the human I am slowly changing.

But we have a plan, Mira. We can get to you, take this human you are changing…

No!

I jerk my attention away from the web, my anxiety weakening me even more. Why does Acia fight me on this? Does she hope it will exhaust me to the point where I cannot heal? Where I perish? Is that her intention? Her plan? Has the journey from our world changed her so profoundly?

If I perish, then she will assume control of the entire tribe. Alarmed, I try to contact Lotus through our private channel. Minutes pass. She does not respond. My alarm deepens and in desperation, I contact Jez, the warrior who commands the warriors.

I am here, Mira. Lotus has left the caves and gone into hiding. She fears for her life. Acia is turning the tribe here against you.

And you, Jez? Where do you stand?

Where I have always stood, with you and Lotus. Acia will not dare threaten me. She knows I command more than 500 warriors. But we may have a greater threat than Acia and her supporters. Humans have a compound near here and are taking some of us captive. To study us. Lotus and I have discussed attacking this compound and freeing our kin. But we feel such an attack would be premature. We want you here first.

If I were inside my craft, I would be healed in minutes. Its environment is calibrated to match that of my home. But just being out of the cold helps. The cold slows everything down, leaves me feeling thick, weighted, stupid. It's why Cuba is ideal for us.

When I am healed enough to travel, I will contact you. Until then, please keep Lotus safe, in a secure place. Unless Acia and her supporters become aggressive toward you, do not make any move against her. I will deal with her when I arrive.

Stay safe, Mira. I will be in touch on this same channel.

I disconnect from the web, struggle against waves of pain brought on by the bouncing of the vehicle. I find comfort in the knowledge that Jez and his warriors are still with me, that they will keep Lotus safe. I am healing, slowly, and Sofia's webbed foot alleviates some of the discomfort of this world's gravity.

Her webbed foot also transmits her distress but not her plans, her fear but not her speculations. The capillaries and veins, the intricate network of muscles and cartilage, skin and bones, must be more firmly rooted in her body before I will be able to spy on her, eavesdrop on her conversations with other humans. Once that happens, I won't need to be physically near her.

I seek to tap the web once more, to ask Jez something else, but can no longer remember what I want to ask. And I lack the strength to open a channel to the web.

Chapter 3

Sofia followed McMullen's van along back roads that cut through the middle of the island. Her right foot felt awkward, too large and floppy against the accelerator, the brake. The webbing was astonishingly sensitive, too. She felt the grooves in the gas pedal, the reverberations of the VWs speed. Now and then, the webbing pulsed, as if with a heartbeat, and it deepened her fear that it might become a permanent part of her.

She entertained the thought, again, of having it surgically removed. But suppose it was already too late for that? Suppose the webbing was developing a network of capillaries and veins that now ran through the tendons and muscles in her foot?

The more she thought about it, the more freaked out and terrified she felt. The physicians she knew made up a short list. One client was a dermatologist, another a general practitioner. Occasionally they did exchanges with her—an office visit for a reading. But they weren't podiatrists and she sure as hell didn't want to explain to them or any doctor why her foot was now webbed.

The dead alien did it to me.

That alone would land her in a psychiatric unit.

But was it actually dead? If so, how had it exuded a force that had kept her hands glued to the sides of its head? Dead, but not in the way she understood death. Was that it?

She stared at the back of McMullen's van and shrieked, *"Why'd you do this to me?"*

Screaming made her feel moderately better, but didn't solve a damn thing. Her webbed foot, like almost every facet of the UFO field, was inexplicable. But now it had become too damn personal.

She now understood emotionally, viscerally, how some people who had experienced encounters or whose kids had been abducted, could descend into a place so dark and hopeless that suicide or madness were their only way out of the horror. Three years ago when she and Pierce had investigated a tragic encounter in Sarasota, her grasp of such horror had been only intellectual.

The encounter itself had been fairly simple, straightforward. Several students at New College, which backed up to the Sarasota Bay on Florida's west coast, claimed they had witnessed an encounter one evening near the campus sail club. Justin Dylan and his girlfriend, Barb, were refurbishing a sailboat when a thick fog rolled in from the water and a short luminous entity lumbered into their open work area on the beach. Justin reportedly had stood there entranced, but Barb had freaked out and taken off, screaming and shrieking her way back toward the dorm.

When she returned awhile later with half a dozen friends and two professors, Justin was gone. Three days later, his body washed up on the beach, covered with mysterious burn marks, cuts. abrasions. By then, Justin's father, George Dylan, had arrived and when he told her and Pierce that he worked for "The Agency," they'd assumed that meant the CIA and decided to cooperate with him in whatever way they could. Pierce, of course, had an ulterior motive—to enlist George Dylan's help in getting whatever classified information the CIA had on alien life.

Thinking back on it now, she sensed a connection between that encounter and her own situation. One weird event after another, one puzzle after another, and no satisfying answers. Justin's cell phone, she recalled, had been found on the beach by a student who had turned it over to Dylan and he had given her and Pierce copies of the three photos of the being his son had seen.

The photos hadn't looked anything like the alien in the back of McMullen's van. If anything, it had resembled some religious painting of an angel or a divine being—all light, nothing but light. They had worked on those photos for months, she remembered, trying to strip away the light so they could see what it actually looked like. But when they finally got rid of the light, nothing was there.

Nothing.

Dylan's work partner, Lia Graham, had shown up as well, to help on the investigation, and she was present with Sofia and Pierce at Justin's autopsy. The coroner had found an implant behind Justin's right ear and when he'd attempted to extract it, the implant had wormed its way through bone, directly into the kid's brain. They'd all seen it happen, it was on X-rays. The coroner had hurled his scalpel across the room and backed away from the table, his bloody, gloved hands in the air. *I don't know what the fuck is going on, but I'm done here.*

She and Pierce had stood there in shock, but Dylan had snapped, *Follow the damn thing.*

I'll have to cut and drill through your son's skull to follow it, Mr. Dylan.

Do it.

Sofia had watched until she nearly puked. But she'd seen the implant as it had exited through Justin's left ear and had fallen, motionless, onto the autopsy table, where it turned dark and flat. She and Pierce had gotten photos of it and Dylan had scooped it onto a piece of paper and pocketed it.

The coroner's official cause of death was anaphylactic shock.

The Sarasota incident had resulted in the death of a young man, video images that revealed nothing, and a physical object, the implant. But the thing in the back of McMullen's van... *Real.* She had touched it. Read it. And it had turned her foot into a webbed monstrosity. "Fuck!"

This time, screaming didn't make her feel better. But remembering helped. It helped to recall that Dylan had his son's body cremated and that after the memorial service, she and Pierce didn't run into him again until they investigated a case in 2015. After that, nothing. Now and then, rumors surfaced through the grapevine—that Dylan had suffered a breakdown and was in a psychiatric facility somewhere in South Florida. Sofia didn't know if any of it was true. But she suspected it was.

In his shoes, if it had been her son's body that had washed up on that beach, she would have lost her mind.

She texted Mike to meet her at Pierce's place and gave him the address McMullen had provided. *I think we should stay in Luke's garage apartment. Can u toss some of my clothes & shampoo & stuff into a pack? Grab my computer and iPad. Bring food for Coop.*

Is it the mother lode? Mike texted back.

U decide.

Steve, her dead ex-husband, would have dismissed all of this as delusional. The best thing that had come from their tumultuous six years together was Mike. Their son was the only thing they had in common, she thought, except for their mutual fascination with *The X-Files*. Steve had wanted to believe but wasn't able to move beyond his scientific indoctrination.

If Steve were alive now, he would take one look at her webbed foot and remind her of her obsession with frogs when she was a kid. *You're becoming the amphibian that so intrigued you.* Well, not exactly. A webbed foot didn't make her a frog. It made her a goddamn freak.

2.

Pierce's home, tucked back on a dead end dirt road in the Tango hills, was shrouded in pines and old banyan trees. It fit what Sofia had imagined. Given the nature of his work, Pierce tended toward seclusion and the house probably had heightened security—video cams, bells and whistles and alarms that shrieked at the first hint of intrusion.

She followed McMullen's dusty van up a winding driveway, through a braided overhang of branches. A tall wooden fence surrounded the place and McMullen stopped at the front gate. She didn't see any security keypad or video camera and was surprised when McMullen got out and simply flipped up the gate's latch and drove on through.

They continued up the driveway, through the trees, past a pond, beds of colorful flowers, bougainvillea vines on trellises, lush ferns, bushes. Not much grass, she noted, but plenty of stones and mulch in a small front yard that was easy to care for. The brick house came into view, a one-story with large bay windows at the front and a second story above the garage that she guessed was the apartment he'd offered to her and Mike. It looked like the sort of place, she thought, that should be a home to a family, pets, people who were happy with their lives. The fact that Pierce lived here alone saddened her.

McMullen backed up to the garage, she pulled alongside him, and they both got out. She waddled awkwardly over to him, he raised the garage door. She knew that if any of this had happened to her before she'd started working for Omega a decade ago, she'd now be a screaming banshee. But in this line of work, you learned to compartmentalize certain horrors, though this was the most personal yet. Panic clawed away inside her.

"I thought he'd have more security." Her voice surprised her, too calm, too normal.

"He does. He controls everything from an app. I texted him a few minutes ago and he unlocked the front gate, garage, even the door into the house. I'm going to back the van in."

"Hey, did anything weird happen to you on the way over?"

McMullen's bushy white brows knitted together. "Like, uh, with the ET?"

"Yeah."

"Not that I noticed. But it's dead, right?"

"I'm honestly not sure now, Josh."

"I was hoping you wouldn't say that, Sofia. You think it's infected with anything?"

"Could be."

"Not a comforting thought."

He hopped back into the van and she ducked inside the garage and immediately spotted the large floor freezer where Pierce intended to hide the body. It looked new, more than seven feet long, probably four feet wide. It took up most of the wall to her left. To her right she saw a rack that held two bikes, storage shelves where boxes, suitcases, and backpacks were neatly lined up. Directly in front of her stood storage cabinets, a small workbench, tools tidily arranged on hooks. The place was so clean and organized it put her garage to shame.

Pierce, neat freak.

Sofia flicked on all the wall switches. Overhead lights flared, two floor lamps came on. She set her bag on the workbench and as soon as McMullen pulled in, she punched a button that lowered the garage door. The moment it clattered shut, sealing them inside with their secret, some of the pressure she'd been feeling eased up. Her eyes no longer throbbed, she now felt *invisible.*

She moved awkwardly over to the freezer, absurdly grateful and relieved that the webbing between her fingers was gone. Why didn't the webbing on her foot vanish, too? Would she have to wear socks the rest of her life or two different sized shoes?

Stop it. Not yet. Not ever.

Sofia raised the lid on the freezer and began rearranging the items inside so there would be an unobstructed space for the entity. The ET. The alien. *Call it what it is.* Pierce's freezer held more stuff than the freezer at the lighthouse had. She guessed he'd been stocking up for some monster hurricane like Danielle, that had hit Tango in 2005, knocked out power for months, and hurled the island back to the Dark Ages. Or he was stocking up for his version of Armageddon—*the aliens land and take over the planet.*

Was that what was happening?

She moved the bags of ice and bottled water to one end of the freezer, took out some of the meats and breads to put in the freezer in the house, and set the rest of it on the workbench. "I've cleared some space, Josh."

"Great." He turned away from the van with the ET in his arms, still wrapped in the tarp. "It feels heavier."

"She."

"Yeah?" His eyes widened. "You're really sure about that?""You and Luke seem to have this automatic assumption that the ET is male. This one isn't, okay? It's female. Wherever she comes from, women seem to be truly equal." Or maybe in charge.

McMullen, carrying the ET toward the freezer, laughed.

"Daily, my wife and daughters remind me that women really rule the world, Sofia." He set the ET in the space she had cleared. "Shit, listen to us. We're talking like this is… is normal. Business as usual."

"Right now, we have to pretend it is. Otherwise…"

"… we lose it." His voice, soft and scared.

"Yeah."

They looked at each other. He finally said, "Maybe we should cover her with something else. I mean, if we're not sure she's dead, she might get cold in here, right?"

Sofia felt like hugging him. A man who spoke like this about an alien being that had fallen into his life was the kind of person she wanted to know. "You're a sweetheart, Josh." She bussed him on the cheek. "Yeah, maybe we should cover her with something else. Or not leave her in here at all. What do you think?"

"But if she defrosts and she's dead, she'll decompose."

"Will she? Maybe her species doesn't decompose after death. We just don't know enough."

"Can you, uh, ask her?"

Thanks to the earlier events, Sofia didn't want to read the ET again. Ever. No telling what attributes she might take on—a single nostril, extra thumbs, gills, the webbing on her fingers, another webbed foot. "Let's wait till Luke and my son get here."

"Yeah. Good idea." His head bobbed in agreement. "I'll find another tarp to put over her."

McMullen went over to the storage cabinets and Sofia reached inside the freezer and drew back the edges of the tarp so she could see the ET, encased in that body bag. She looked different, denser, more complete, something. McMullen had said she felt heavier. Was that what she was seeing? Physical bulk?

"Josh, did you guys weigh her?"

"Yes, ma'am. Right after we found her. She came in at around seventy pounds."

"We should weigh her again."

"I think there's an old scale in one of these cabinets. I'll bring it over."

Sofia unzipped the body bag and folded it down the ET's body and past her webbed foot. Except her foot was no longer webbed. It looked like Sofia's foot, right down to the color of the polish. Shock tore through her, she nearly grabbed that foot, *her* foot, but was suddenly terrified that if she did, it might disintegrate or fall off and she would be stuck with this goddamn flipper forever.

"Jesus...you stole my fucking foot, you monster!" she shouted, backing away from the body.

McMullen hurried over with the scale, set it down. "I thought you already knew."

"I... " She shook her head, unable to speak.

"We're going to figure this out, Sofia."

"Yeah? How?"

"A step at a time. Look at it this way. You've got her flipper. It may prove useful somehow."

"Right now, it... it only scares me, Josh." And enraged her.

She moved toward the body, grabbed it by the sides of the head, lifted it toward her and hissed, "Listen closely, you piece of shit. You can't have my body, we clear?"

Then she jerked her hands away, the alien head fell back against the ice, and McMullen tossed a second tarp over the body. "I'll lift it out," he said. "And get it on the scale.

As he was doing that, she stared at her webbed foot, her hatred for this alien as great as her curiosity. "Josh, when you found the body, how'd you feel?"

The old man laughed, a sharp, almost choked sound. "Terrified. At first, I wasn't sure what I was seeing. But when I knew something really extraordinary and... and strange and tragic had happened, I ran. When I stopped running, I called Luke."

The bathroom scale, old and rusted, was too small for the ET's long body, so they had to slide a bag of ice under her legs and head so they could get an accurate weight. "It looks like she's up to eighty-nine pounds, Josh."

"How the hell is that even possible? That would mean she has gained twelve pounds in just the two days since I found her."

"You and Luke might not have gotten an accurate weight the first time."

"We weighed her on one of those scales you find in a doctor's office."

"They're sturdier, but not much wider than this one."

"Doesn't the body get lighter after death?"

"Human bodies do."

"Yeah, okay. I keep forgetting all the rules are new."

Sofia brought out her phone, recorded the time, date, and the ET's weight now—and two days ago. She snapped two photos of her—full body, and then just that human foot. *My foot.* Then McMullen put her back into the freezer, against the blue tarp, and zipped up the body bag, and covered her with the second tarp.

"She's too exposed in here," Sofia said.

"Let's cover her with all that frozen food you put on the workbench," McMullen said. "That way, if someone opens the freezer, the tarp won't be the first thing they see."

"Good idea."

Sofia went over to the workbench, plucked a plastic container off a lower shelf, scooped all the frozen food into it. She hurried back to the freezer and she and McMullen moved the frozen loaves of bread, chicken, turkey, fish, and chopped up fruits into the freezer and distributed everything evenly over her body. She could do this easily enough because it didn't entail touching the body. Here and there, the ET was still visible, so they broke open a bag of ice and McMullen emptied it up and down the length of the alien's body.

There. The ET was completely invisible—unless someone dug through the cubes of ice. "Okay, this is as good as it gets for hiding an ET, Josh." She snickered, a small, frenzied sound, almost insectile, like that of a swarm of mosquitos. Or bees. She slammed the lid and they both backed away from it. "Is that door unlocked?" She nodded toward a door to the right of the freezer.

"Yeah."

McMullen hurried toward the door and Sofia moved awkwardly over to the workbench to retrieve her handbag. But before either of them reached their destinations, the lid of the freezer snapped upward, slammed against the wall behind it, and ice cubes exploded outward in every direction, pelting the ceilings, walls, workbench, van, and her and McMullen. They dived for the floor.

Frozen stuff rained down on them. Sofia scrambled to the other side of the van. "Inside!" she shouted. "Get inside the van!"

Moments later, McMullen appeared at the rear of the van, jerked open the passenger door, and they threw themselves inside. A frozen chicken slammed into the windshield, fissures spread through the glass, and any second now, Sofia knew the windshield would explode.

"What the fuck," McMullen breathed.

She scrambled into the back seat with him and the two of them huddled on the floor. He texted frantically and she turned on the video on her phone and moved it back and forth above her as more frozen shit struck the van.

The windshield exploded, glass flew wildly around inside the van, and McMullen scrambled into the driver's seat, turned on the engine. The windows went down, the swirling glass flew out, the garage door went up and he slammed the van into reverse. Tires shrieked against the pavement as the van careened back down the driveway.

Sofia raised up only once, her phone in front of her, video engaged. So much stuff was airborne inside the garage that it resembled a scene from a movie—*The Fury, Matilda, Carrie*—the laws of physics turned upside down and inside out, telekinesis gone wild.

McMullen slammed on the brakes when they were a safe distance from the garage and they both jumped out of the van and stood there, stupefied. The rampage continued for another few minutes, then everything swirling around in the garage suddenly dropped to the floor. The van's engine died, the air went still, she didn't move. Her knees had turned to Jell-O and she sank to the ground, staring, unable to speak.

Something warm dripped into her eyes and when she ran her hand across her face, it came away streaked with blood.

Cuts, she thought. From the flying glass. Blood also speckled her arms and she ran her hand over her right arm and felt the bits of embedded glass.

"Josh?" She pressed her hands to her thighs, pushed up and hurried to the other side of the van, her webbed foot slapping against the concrete.

McMullen, sprawled facedown. His arms, flung out to either side of him. Head turned to the left. Sofia dropped to her knees beside him, frantically felt for a pulse in his neck. Quick. Erratic.

She turned him over, slid her arms under his head, raising it. "C'mon, Josh. One good breath. C'mon, c'mon…. Please, wake the hell up…"

His face was cut up from the flying glass. A large gash over his left eye bled freely. She set his head on the ground and tore off the long sleeve shirt she'd been wearing over her t-shirt. She pressed it against his eye and held it there, fear slamming around inside her.

After a few minutes, when the flow of blood seemed to be abating, she grasped his forearms and pulled him across asphalt, mulch, through a bed of flowers and finally to the front porch. She brought her fingers to his neck again, checking his pulse. Not quite as erratic. Hoping that Pierce's app had unlocked the front door as well, she tried the knob, the door swung open.

Sofia dragged McMullen into the living room, kicked the front door shut, sank to the floor next to the old man. Her phone rang. Pierce. Before he could say anything, she blurted, "Something happened. Get here fast."

She dropped her phone on the floor and lurched into the kitchen, wet a dish towel, raced back into the living room. She cleaned up McMullen's face, picked bits of glass out of his cheeks. His breathing seemed more normal now, but maybe she imagined it.

"Josh?" She leaned over him.

His phone rang and she dug it out of his jacket pocket. Ben Willford's name in the caller ID. The mayor. The call went to voicemail. The transcription read: CALL ASAP.

Her phone, on the floor to her left, also rang. Pierce again. Sofia knuckled her eyes, hysteria climbed up her throat. She shot to her feet, grabbed him again by the forearms, dragged McMullen across the shiny wooden floors, up a hall to the first bedroom she reached.

She pulled his torso onto the bed, it slipped off, she tried again. After the third try, she yanked the mattress to the floor and was able to get McMullen onto it. She removed his shoes and socks, covered him with a sheet. He appeared to be sleeping comfortably now, but beneath his lids, his eyes moved in that restless, constant rhythm of REM sleep. He was dreaming and she felt like puking.

Sofia fell back to the floor, clasped her legs against her chest, her forehead dropped to her knees. She rocked. Sobbed. She got disgusted with herself and pushed back across the floor, away from mattress, from McMullen.

Sunlight streamed through the window, across the bed, the mattress, his body. *Calm down.* Sure. Of course. Calm the fuck down. Like that would solve anything.

She snapped to her feet and ran out of the house, her webbed foot making a weird sucking sound against the floor. She burst through a rear door to the backyard. Stopped. A man scooped up papayas that had fallen off the trees and dropped them into a large fabric bag that hung from his shoulder.

"Hey, you!" she shouted.

He looked up.

Sofia reeled in shock. Steve, her ex-husband, dead for seven years, raised his hand. *"Hola, Sofia. Como andas?"*

She stood barefoot in a patch of ivy that reached to her ankles, staring at him. *Como andas?* literally meant, *How're you walking?* He used to say this to her after they'd argued and he wanted to reconnect, to pretend they had no differences, to cozy up, make love.

"Con los dos pies," she replied. With both feet.

He threw his head back, laughing.

And those feet, *her* feet, moved toward him quickly, moved even as she thought it was all smoke and mirrors. When only a yard separated them and he hadn't vanished, she said, "How can you be here?"

He stared at her webbed foot. "That thing in the freezer. It makes some impossible things possible."

"But you're dead," she blurted.

"Well, yes and no." He brought a small, ripe papaya out of his fabric bag, set it on the ground in front of him, slipped a switchblade from the pocket of his windbreaker, and sliced the fruit open. The interior was sunrise gold, with dark seeds clustered straight down the middle. He drew the knife through the seeds, flicking them to the ground, then scooped out a piece of the fruit, stabbed it, held it out to her. "See how this tastes."

She stared at the bit of papaya, raised her eyes to his face. Right then, with the sunlight angling through the trees and spilling across his handsome face, he looked so much like their son she nearly wept.

"C'mon, try it," Steve said.

She plucked the chunk of papaya off the tip of the knife, popped it in her mouth. It tasted real—succulent, sweet, divine. "How... long will this last? Where we can talk like you're... actually alive?"

He shrugged. "Beats me. This has never happened to me before."

"How do you know that alien in there..." She stabbed her thumb over her shoulder. "... is making this possible?"

"It's what I sense to be true."

For the first time since she'd met Steve two decades ago, he was speaking her language. *What I sense...* But he'd had to die before it could happen. "What else do you sense about this being, Steve?"

"That if it's dead, it isn't dead in the same way that I am."

"I don't understand."

"I don't either. But what I do know is that one of the reasons this is possible is because I need to apologize to you for making our marriage so difficult."

His words stunned her, but before she could say anything, she heard McMullen calling her name.

She glanced around, delighted to see him up and moving and looking normal. "Josh!" She waved her arms, as though they were separated by a great distance and were hidden from each other by trees and vegetation. As she got up, she looked back—and it was all gone. Steve. The papaya. The switchblade. But on the dry leaves close to where he'd been sitting lay a clump of glistening papaya seeds. She touched them to make sure the seeds were real. Solid. Still moist. She scooped up the leaf, went over to McMullen.

She wasn't nuts. These seeds proved it. They constituted tangible scientific evidence of... *what?* That a papaya had been cut open recently, its moist seeds discarded. It didn't prove shit, except to her because she knew she hadn't cut the damn thing open.

"What happened?" McMullen asked.

"The garage. Do you remember what happened in the garage?"

He frowned, his gaze went fuzzy, then he snapped his fingers. "The alien had a tantrum, Sofia. She didn't like being covered in all that ice."

Something snapped inside of her. It felt like a metal ball hitting her squarely between the eyes and blowing her skull open. She realized the ET emitted some sort of telekinetic field that not only resulted in frozen goods flying and zooming around the garage, but also might have ripped a hole large enough in the veil between the living and the dead for Steve to slip through. Contact with the dead had been reported in some of the encounter cases she and Pierce had investigated. And she had, from time to time, seen the spirits of the dead. But not like this, as though the spirit were alive. Solid.

"Josh, was I alone in that yard? Did you see anyone else?"

"At first, I thought that Luke had gotten here. But the man I saw wasn't Luke."

"Describe him."

"Tall, slender, dark, curly hair, a handsome Latino around forty or so."

"It was my dead ex-husband." She held out the piece of palm frond with the damp papaya seeds on it. "He sliced open a papaya and cut me a piece. Here're the seeds he scooped out."

McMullen looked at the seeds, touched them, and raised his eyes, haunted now by the implications of everything that had happened. "Is the garage door still open?"

"Shit." In the turmoil and chaos. she'd forgotten completely about the door. "Yes."

She and McMullen tore back through the house. He threw open the door from the utility room to the garage and they lumbered into a scene so perfect and tidy that they both stopped, gawking. Sofia felt as if a fist were being ground into her solar plexus. Her breath burst out of her.

The garage door was still open, McMullen's van parked out in the driveway where he'd stopped, the front doors gaping open like mouths, the front windshield gone. "What the hell," McMullen said, his voice tight, scared. "Did you clean up the mess?"

"No."

... if it's dead, it isn't dead in the same way that I am.

Sofia's feet came uprooted from the concrete floor, she moved to the freezer, flung open the lid.

All the frozen goods that had been flying around in the garage were arranged neatly inside. Sofia frantically shifted bags of ice and dug down through everything else, hoping to uncover the body.

But the ET was gone.

Escape

No! No more ice, no more cold, no more! I muster the little strength I have and hurl all of it away from me. I cannot heal buried in ice and frozen foods. I cannot heal as a captive in this long, cold box.

Frozen foods and ice swirl and spin through the air and Sofia and the old man dive for cover. I leap out of the freezer, my knees creaking and burning with pain, and escape through a side door, into a grassy area that leads to the dock. To water. Three leaps bring me to the dock, the warmth of the sun against the old wooden boards seeps through my human foot—Sofia's foot—suffusing my body, but that warmth doesn't extinguish the agonizing pain of my abrupt and frantic movements.

Another leap takes me into the water, my gills open, and I swim madly, fast and deeply. The beauty of it, of the water, the lush smells, fills my senses but the pain persists. Food, I need food. I grab a handful of seaweed, stuff it in my mouth. It tastes too salty and I nearly spit it out. I can exist in salt water, but not at full capacity and I'm going to need fresh water before I can fully recover.

The web blows open and my tribe feels and sees what is happening to me. Jez shouts, Eat anything.

A school of silvery fish swim past in front of me and I inhale them, chew. Salty, it's all too salty, and I spit out most of it. The piece I swallow makes me gag. I swim more deeply and touch the muddy bottom of the canal.

Dig into it, Mira, into the mud, I am with you, Lotus is with you, the warriors are with you. We lend you our strength and resolve.

I dig into it, down deep into moss, into holes where crabs and clams burrow, and quickly draw the mud around me, over me, so it forms a bank that covers me. My webbed hand slides down into the mud, searching for crustaceans, I find two. My teeth tear into their shells and down into their meaty bodies. They aren't nearly as salty as the fish and the seaweed, and they awaken the depth of my hunger. My full body burrows into the mud, and for a long time I become a creature of the mud. I find more crabs, a handful of them, gobble them down.

If you can get near the coast of Cuba, we will meet you, guard you, support you, whatever must be done, Mira.

Cuba? I will be fortunate to escape mud that now clogs my gills. I must surface into the clear water in order to breathe. Ahead of me, something large splashes into the canal, stirring up mud and muck so I cannot immediately see what it is. Human? Fish? A shark pursuing fish? Then something strikes me from behind, slams into my legs and feet with such a tremendous force that I am knocked sideways.

I fling my arms back, turning, and face an alligator as long as I am tall. Its tail whips back and forth, propelling it toward me, its huge jaws open, teeth bared. Panic pours through me.

Speak to it, Jez shouts.

Stop! *I hurl my arms toward the gator, flinging a wave of energy toward it that is pathetically weak, incomplete. My power has been depleted by the chaos I created in the garage when I escaped and this creature is so primal, it's unresponsive, oblivious, and keeps racing toward me, intent on eating me alive.*

My only option is to leap to land. But I am so weak that the leap falls short. I hit the side of the bank, my feet slip on the wet moss, and I fall back into the water and land on top of the gator. It roars, thrashing its tail, forcing me to sink my dagger teeth into the back of its neck.

I feel the full strength and force of the web behind me, Lotus and Jez and his warriors rising up in my defense, scrambling the gator's brain, confusing it. The creature's skin is so thick that my teeth must keep lengthening, sinking in deeper, deeper even as the gator thrashes, trying to throw me off. I cling to it, blood pours out of its neck, its tail whips back and forth, its body jerks erratically.

Its tail slams into my legs, forcing me to loosen my grip on the back of its neck or risk breaking off my teeth. I press my feet against its back and struggle to leap to shore, but my legs are too weak and I land clumsily on my torso, my legs still dangling in the canal.

I jerk my legs up toward my chest and manage to take several pathetic hops toward the trees. The gator launches its entire body toward me, but is so badly injured it dies before reaching me. I feel its death, the rushing of its being into the afterworld as it leaves that primal body. My gills are slow to close, I can barely breathe, and collapse just inside the perimeter of trees. The fertile scent of the woods, of the dead leaves beneath me, follows me into a healing darkness.

And there in that darkness that is nowhere and everywhere, I find Lotus, Jez, his battalion of warriors, all of them safely hidden for now.

More are joining them. My tribe in Cuba is now divided.

I pull a dark curtain over myself, and follow the softness of Lotus's voice, whispering, I am here, my friend. I am here.

Chapter 4

George Dylan located the pilot's place on Amelia Street in old town Key West. Two-story house, small front yard dominated by a pair of magnificent banyans that shrouded the house in perpetual shade. A white picket fence like something out of *Tom Sawyer* surrounded the property. Potted plants festooned the wide front porch, which also featured a colorful hammock and a couple of rocking chairs.

Now: a parking space.

Lack of land, of course, was the major challenge for every island in the Florida keys, but particularly for Key West and Tango Key during the snowbird season, when the islands' populations tripled. He drove up and down a couple of narrow, cobbled streets, where cars were jammed bumper to bumper, and houses and duplexes were built practically on top of each other. He found a spot just two blocks away and slipped his mini-Cooper into a tight space between a Fiat and a Ford truck. He felt a familiar surge of excitement, that fire in his belly.

Finding a parking place this quickly was a good sign. He was big on signs like this.

He grabbed the small case that held his iPad and got out of the car. He didn't bother locking it. What was the point? A determined thief wouldn't be deterred by sunlight and locked doors. Besides, the car didn't hold anything of value.

Dylan walked rapidly up the block, his Fitbit tracking every step. He'd already surpassed his ten thousand steps today because he'd gone for a three-mile run this morning before leaving Key Largo. This brisk walk would bring him to just under twenty-thousand steps, or nearly ten miles. Not bad for a guy pushing fifty.

One of his agency buddies had given him a Fitbit when he was in the nuthouse. *This will help you shift your focus, Dylan. Start running and you'll be outta here in no time.*

And his buddy had been right. Less than a year after his son had washed up on the beach in Sarasota and Dylan had lost his mind, he'd been declared cured of the depression that had nearly obliterated him—as long as he took his meds. By then, it was the end of 2015 and he was on his third Fitbit and flushed his meds away. Using the proceeds from the sale of his home in Florida—his ex had gotten the house in Virginia—he'd bought a small place in Key Largo. Since he'd been on medical leave and pulling in a salary, he invested a good chunk of his savings into the stock market and had doubled his net worth.

One thing he had to say about being in a nuthouse was that it sharpened your instincts. He bought and sold stocks based on nothing more than that fire in his belly. If the fire burned, he bought. If the fire wasn't happening, he sold. And right now, the stock called Captain John Piper burned so hot and furiously, he felt sure he would find a lead.

Before he reached the gate, he activated the recording feature on the phone in his shirt pocket. He had a second phone in the pocket of his lightweight jacket, but left it alone. Just in case. Dylan always had backups. The Agency had taught him that.

When he reached the house, he paused at the gate, and checked to make sure that belly fire was still burning. It was. He flicked up the latch on the gate and walked up the tree-shrouded sidewalk, to that beautiful front porch with all the glorious potted plants. Someone, he thought, had a powerful green thumb.

He saw hyacinth, lavender, miniature citrus and mango trees, impatiens, roses, orchids. Along the front of the house were more plants, bursts of color, a schizophrenic explosion of nature. Two pairs of sandals sat side by side at the front railing. He rang the bell.

An attractive brunette in her early forties opened the door, a yapping Corgi at her heels. "May I help you?"

"Hi, is Captain Piper home?" he asked.

She stepped outside onto the porch. The now growling Corgi slipped out before she shut the door behind her. "You a reporter?"

"Nope." Dylan held up his ID, courtesy of his former partner, Lia Graham. The photo was a bit dated, but showed a handsome man, a lean six foot two, with blue eyes and dark curly hair threaded with gray. A man whose face now held traces of deep bitterness and sadness. But the only thing the woman noticed was *The Agency*.

"The agency as in the *CIA?*" she exclaimed.

He didn't confirm or deny it.

"But why?" she asked.

"Same as the reporters. Flight 156."

She looked exasperated. "Okay, he was the pilot for American Flight 156 from Miami to Tango Key. And his full name is John Piper. And contrary to what the crew and passengers are saying, it was a routine flight. Thirty-three, maybe thirty- four minutes. We don't want any more publicity. Our phone and doorbell have been ringing nonstop since this happened."

"I'm not interested in publicity, either, Mrs. Piper. I'd just like to speak with your husband."

"He's my brother."

Behind her, the door opened and a tall, lanky man with thick gray hair stood there in running shorts, bare feet, a t-shirt. His face looked ravaged by lack of sleep or stress or both. "I don't have anything to say beyond what my sister just told you," Piper said.

"Look, I know what your flight path was, Captain Piper. I have the FAA report on my iPad. I have the control tower audio, I have..."

"In other words, you came prepared. I like that. But why is the CIA interested in this?"

"They aren't. But I am. For personal reasons."

Piper considered this, seemed to weigh it against something internal, then nodded. "Fair enough." He came out onto the porch, walked over to the larger pair of sandals, slipped them on. "Let's walk and talk."

"Let's not," his sister snapped.

The Corgi barked louder and Piper dismissed the dog and his sister with a flick of his hand. He and Dylan headed down the porch steps, up the sidewalk, and out the gate. Dylan liked that progression of prepositions: *down, up, out.* In the nuthouse, the inmates had used a lot of prepositions. When Justin's body had turned up on that Sarasota beach three years ago, he'd heard mostly adjectives. *Inexplicable. Eerie. Strange. Horrifying.* What he wanted to hear were nouns and verbs that would fill in the details. The *craft slammed...* The craft *missed* us... A *being shot out...*

"Just in case your ID is fake and you're actually a journalist," Piper said, "I'd like to hold your phone while we walk and talk."

"My phone? Sure." Dylan slipped his backup iPhone from his jacket pocket and passed it to Piper. "Your paranoia is revealing."

"Revealing?" Piper snorted. "You talk like a shrink."

"I've known my share of them. Tell me about your flight."

The air was cool, a slight breeze kicked in off the Atlantic, shadows and sunlight eddied across the sidewalk. Piper moved at a brisk pace that Dylan matched. He noted that Piper also wore a Fitbit.

"So here's the truth, George. May I call you George?"

For some reason, Dylan got a kick out of the question. "John, you can call me asshole if you want."

"Great." Piper grinned. "Okay, Asshole. Flight 156 from Miami to Tango usually takes between thirty and forty minutes in good weather. The plane's maximum speed is nearly six hundred and thirty miles an hour. I was doing about three hundred and sixty and was holding at fifteen hundred feet, aiming for a landing on runway eleven. I suddenly spotted..." He paused. "... well, *something*, at about twelve thousand feet hurtling toward us. And I mean *hurtling.* This sucker was plunging earthward at a thousand or fifteen hundred miles an hour, and coming at us from an angle so the passengers on the east side of the plane saw it clearly. I immediately banked steeply to the right. It missed us by less than a quarter of a mile."

"What did it look like?"

"Oblong, shaped sort of like a cigar."

"How large?"

"A whole lot larger than a cigar."

"How long?"

He thought about it, glanced behind them, stopped. "Stay right here." He walked deliberately along the sidewalk to a black truck parked at the curb and turned toward Dylan again. "About this long. Fifty, maybe sixty feet. Maybe as long as eighty." He trotted back to Dylan.

"Do you think it was a satellite, John? Or a meteorite?"

Piper's laugh this time was derisive, mocking. "C'mon, is that a serious question? I've been flying for more than twenty-five years and I've never seen anything like this. It was a UFO. That specifically means an *unidentified flying object*."

"Did it have windows?"

"It was moving too fast to see that kind of detail."

"Was it on fire?"

"At first, I thought it was. But that may have been the reflection of the sunlight. What was obvious was that the craft was in distress, rather like when a plane stalls out. If you can't pull out of the stall, the plane goes into a tailspin, just like this craft was doing."

"Did you see it crash?"

"Yes."

"Did it break apart?"

"It slammed into the gulf, but I didn't see it break apart. It must have, but I didn't see it. We were past it by then. A couple of the passengers reported seeing smoke or flames at one point."

"How could a craft moving at a thousand miles or more an hour not break apart immediately upon impact?"

"*Now* you're asking the right questions, George. There should've been pieces of that craft washing up on Tango's western beaches. But I walked miles of beach Monday afternoon, from just north of downtown Tango to Pirate's Cove at the other end of the island. I didn't find anything that resembled a piece of a craft."

"If this craft was, uh, alien, then how would you even know what to look for?"

"Another good question."

Dylan didn't realize they'd walked so far. He motioned at a Cuban café on the corner across the street. "How about a shot of caffeine?"

"Sounds great."

"I'm beginning to think I need a shot of something stronger."

"I know exactly what you mean."

"So reporters have been bugging you?"

"Non-stop. And the Tango mayor and the chief of police and people from MUFON and local UFO groups."

"Anyone from Omega?"

"Got a couple of calls from them, but I let them go to voicemail."

"Any feds?"

"Just you. Unless you count the airline official who called and told me not to talk to reporters and threatened to ground me if I did."

"So you haven't spoken to anyone about what happened?"

"I gave a statement to the mayor and I spoke to a reporter from the *Tango Gazette* because I don't like an asshole from the airline bureaucracy telling me to keep quiet about something that presented a threat to the plane I was flying. Something *happened* and at least half the passengers on board that flight saw it. The flight attendant gave a statement to the mayor and the press and I wasn't going to contradict her story, particularly since it closely paralleled what with I saw."

Dylan decided he liked Piper. "And what did the airline do?"

"Grounded me. With pay. An investigation is pending."

"Or a massive cover-up. How far off the coast do you think it went down?"

"Two to three miles."

Precise. Certain. The best witnesses, Dylan thought, were often pilots.

They crossed the cobblestone road and got in a short line at the sidewalk window. Latino music drifted through the air, everyone around them chattered away in Spanish. Dylan realized he was famished and ordered a chicken and cheese empanada and an espresso. Piper ordered the same, but in fluent Spanish, and Dylan paid.

They walked over to a small park next door, empty of people, and sat on a bench in the shade. The park was filled with crows and doves that pecked at bread crumbs that had been tossed around.

"So what's your answer to my second good question, John?" asked Dylan.

Piper nibbled at his empanada, sipped at the coffee. "After I'd walked the beach, it occurred to me that the craft might be made of some kind of organic material that soaked up water, like a sponge, on impact. If that's the case, then it makes sense that it didn't break apart immediately. If the craft was inhabited, then the entity inside would have had to escape quickly or drown. Unless it's amphibious. If the reports about flames and smoke are true, then it would have had to get out of the craft quickly enough so it wouldn't die."

"Your speculations are fascinating."

"You didn't see what I saw, asshole."

I saw worse. I saw a coroner's drill rip apart my son's skull in pursuit of an implant that was alive, conscious, until it hit the autopsy table. Dylan pulled a chain out of his shirt. Justin's implant hung from that chain, shaped like a comma, dark and dead now. "Three years ago on a beach in Sarasota, my son was abducted. His body washed up several days later, covered in mysterious burns, cuts. This thing?" He touched the implant. "During the autopsy, the coroner found it behind my son's right ear. When he tried to remove it, it wormed its way through his brain and exited through his left ear and dropped to the autopsy table, dark and motionless, like it is now. Sarasota abduction, 2014. Google it, dude."

Piper stopped, touched the implant, looked at Dylan. "I read about it. I've read about a lot of this shit in the last several days. Your son's abduction is a well-cited case and experts consider it to be genuine. But I never read anything about an implant."

Experts. Who were these so-called experts? Bloggers? MUFON? Omega? Dylan was an expert on his son's disappearance and everything that had followed. He had documented every second of that encounter, was still in touch with Barbara, Justin's girlfriend at the time. He regularly emailed with the group that had accompanied her to the beach that night. Both professors still worked at the college. The students had moved on with their lives, but all of them recalled the events of that night.

"You never read about it because only the coroner and I and three other people witnessed it. I want to know why my son was tortured and killed. I want the details."

They resumed walking. "I don't know if what I'm about to tell you will help."

"It all helps."

"Or it just confuses everything. I also walked back to Tango on Monday, alert this time for any type of unusual organic material on the beach."

"Challenging. Beaches are filled with organic material."

"True. But not like this." He reached into a pocket of his running shorts and brought out a folded Baggie that he held up to the light. "What's it look like to you?"

"A shell." A piece of broken shell about half the size of his palm. "And it looks like it has been scorched around the edges. Or maybe it's dirt?"

"Burn marks, not dirt." Piper tilted his head at a trellis of bougainvillea vines bursting with bright red blooms. "Let's step behind there so we're not as visible from the sidewalk."

They ducked between the trellis and a tall hedge. Piper opened the Baggie and shook the shell into his hand. "Watch what happens as the heat from my skin interacts with the shell. You might want to record this on your phone, George."

Dylan recognized this as a clever ploy from Piper. A test of his character? "You've got my phone."

"Oh, right."

Piper passed him the phone and Dylan turned on the video feature and held it out in front of the object. In less than sixty seconds, the shell or whatever it was became pliant, like soft rubber, and morphed into a perfect circle. It turned translucent and swam with color, a vast spectrum from shimmering blue to mango yellow to popsicle orange to a hue like dust.

That color turned kaleidoscopic and, like a special effect in a movie, burst open and revealed what Dylan thought might be the interior of a craft. Some sort of craft. Not that he'd ever seen a cockpit anything like this. No buttons or switches, just small circles and squares of swirling colors similar to what initially had appeared when the shell had turned translucent.

One of the squares turned transparent. Dylan gasped as sky and earth and water rushed toward him. Then a fire broke out in the cockpit, and a hand—four fingers and two thumbs—passed quickly over one of the bluish green circles and everything went dark.

"Holy shit," Dylan breathed, and grabbed onto the trellis to keep from falling over. "It..."

"Yeah. The craft was inhabited."

Dylan's knees buckled, he sank to the ground. Three years and he finally had found *something*. This being's hand looked nearly identical to the one in a video Lawrence Aldridge had shown him and Lia Graham during an investigation two years ago. He fumbled with his phone, turned off the video, and wondered if it would disappear. If his phone might disintegrate. Or blow up.

Piper slipped the object back into the Baggie, sealed it, and lowered himself to the ground. He set the Baggie between them. The object looked like a large, flat, broken piece of a shell once more. "Holy shit," Dylan said again.

Piper nodded. "I know. Believe me. I know. I've hardly slept the last several nights. My sense is that the craft is a hologram. Each piece contains the whole. If one of us found another piece of it somewhere, we would see the same or similar scenes. What we saw there, when everything rushes toward you, was happening as it plunged toward the gulf. But the craft itself..." He touched the Baggie. "... that piece of what looks like shell... I think that's the organic part, that it absorbed the water when the craft hit. That's why it didn't break apart on impact."

"And it got scorched when a fire broke out in the cockpit."

"Yeah, that's my guess."

"And the craft broke apart later, underwater?"

"Apparently. This piece was still damp when I found it. Once

I set it in the sun, it was completely dry within an hour. I chipped off a piece of it and gave it to a buddy over at the college who's a chemist."

"What's he say?"

"He ran tests on it all day yesterday. So far, he doesn't know what the hell it is. He only knows it isn't a shell. It's not like anything he has ever seen before. When he was working on it, he saw images, too. He speculates that the control systems may be part biological and organic and part physical, that the craft is a hybrid system composed of something grown within a material framework."

"What the fuck does that even *mean*? That it's... *alive*?"

"I think so, at least in part, but maybe not as we currently understand life."

"Did he see the image of that being?"

"Yes. But he saw more of it than we did. He saw a webbed hand and foot."

"So that's where you got the amphibious bit."

Piper nodded.

"Does it show the same scene each time you hold it?"

He shook his head. "This is the third time I've held it. The first time was on the beach, right after I'd found it. It showed the craft as it was starting to sink. And it had sound. I could...could hear the alien's panicked breaths."

"So it didn't die at the moment of impact."

"I don't think so."

"What did the object show the second time?"

"That was yesterday morning. At breakfast. I had my sister sit with me while I held it." Piper raked his fingers back through his hair. "It was... an image of the alien's world. At least, that's what I think it was. Mostly water. Land was... scarce, really scarce."

"Like *Water World?*"

"I guess that's the closest analogy. But there *was* land. It just wasn't abundant. We could see beings swimming, George. Amphibious beings. Tall, graceful beings that could be the evolved and adapted version of us hundreds of years in the future when no one denies climate change anymore because it's already happened."

The heat of the fire in Dylan's belly suddenly felt like it was scorching him from the inside out. He nearly puked. "Do you think this being *escaped*? That it's somewhere on Tango Key?"

"It could be. But if it is, it's not walking around in its natural form, that's for sure."

"I've wondered about that. About the ET form. The alien's shape. " He navigated to his most secure and hidden place on the Internet, brought up the three photos, handed the phone to Piper. "Take a look at what my son saw."

Piper stared at the pictures, enlarged them, studied them, and finally looked up at Dylan. "What the fuck. Four thumbs. Webbed hands and feet. One nostril. Gills. Christ."

"I figure that as soon as Justin saw this grotesque thing, he reached reflexively for his phone and snapped that... that.... bulb of luminous light. That's what this generation does, John. It's all about the phone, the apps, the instant communication. He definitely put it on his Facebook page, because that's where I first saw it. And not long after his body washed up on shore, someone in the government had that post taken down. But by then it had been shared all over social media and that's one of the reasons the encounter is still talked about three years later."

"These other images..."

"Yeah. You're only the only person besides my ex-wife and former partner who has seen them. They were part of a short video. Omega was investigating my son's death and encounter and they have three copies of that first photo. Not much there, except something that looks like an infinite pool of light and energy. A psychotic's vision of an angel, a divinity. Omega was helpful initially, but I felt like they might be the sort of group that would try to usurp the control of *my* investigation. So I never gave them the video you just saw."

"Fuck." Piper didn't look away from the images on the phone.

Dylan felt enormously grateful that someone else seemed to grasp what was really happening here. For three years, he had kept these secrets held tightly within himself. Sharing them now, with this man whom the fire in his belly had promised would yield something valuable, felt like vindication, validation. He remembered telling one of his early shrinks about the being—and afterward, his meds had been increased, he couldn't do much more than drool and sleep.

"Those other images," Dylan rushed on. "That's what the ET actually looks like, an abomination of an insect. A BIG insect. Those long grasshopper-like legs, that preying mantis sort of face. But then that image becomes...almost human, doesn't it?"

"A single nostril? Gills? That's not human, George. Not by a long shot."

"Compared to the insectile thing it is."

"Yeah, but it's still a big stretch."

"So is your theory about the shell."

"Sure. Except we saw that it isn't a shell."

"What're you going to do with it?"

"Keep experimenting with it."

"May I have a piece?" Dylan asked.

"What're *you* going to do with it?"

"Try to find out what happened to my son."

"Why do you think a piece of this would help you do that?"

"You ever get a fire in your belly, John?"

Piper held his gaze, smiled. "Every time I'm in the pilot's seat." He opened the Baggie, shook the object into his hand, and quickly set it on grass, presumably so the heat of his skin wouldn't activate it. He slipped a penknife from his pocket. "How large a piece, George?"

"Whatever you think is appropriate. We don't want to destroy it."

"Not likely. After I gave my buddy the chemist a piece, the damn thing re-grew. It healed itself. The parts are definitely greater than the whole." He sliced it down the middle, neat as an apple, then sliced the Baggie up one side and down another and folded Dylan's piece of the object inside half of the Baggie. "It'll be interesting to see if both halves grow back."

"What's your interest in all this, John?"

Piper looked at Dylan like he was nuts and burst out laughing. "I've been flying since I was sixteen. After college, I was in the Air Force for four years. Before I started flying with American, I flew for Delta, United, puddle jumpers, private jets. I've flown throughout the Mideast, Southeast Asia, South America. I've got more than forty thousand hours of flight time. Until the morning of February sixth, I'd never seen anything that even suggested we aren't alone in the universe. Flight 156 was a game changer for me."

His eyes held Dylan's for long, strange moments, then he handed him the treasure, half of the mysterious object wrapped in part of the Baggie. "Take care of that. And let me know if it helps you find out what happened to your son."

"Let's exchange numbers." The fire in his belly burned fast and furiously, confirming the connection with Piper. "I'm staying at the Cove B and B. I suspect I'm going to be there awhile."

"Do you scuba dive?" Piper asked.

"Yes."

"How about if tomorrow at low tide we go scuba diving around where the craft went down? We can rent gear at the dive shop in the Cove. I've got a boat that will get us out there."

The suggestion exhilarated Dylan. Finally, an ally. "Count me in." He ticked off his phone number, Piper texted him, and Dylan entered the number into his contacts.

As they walked back toward Piper's block, he gestured at the implant dangling from the chain around Dylan's neck. "Since that thing crawled out of your son's ear, has it ever moved? Shown any sign that it isn't as dead as a battery?"

"No. Nothing."

"Maybe it will now."

Dylan shuddered and slipped the chain back inside his shirt.

Chapter 5

Lia Graham had an agenda and as soon as she exited the plane in Miami, she was eager to set it in motion.

But her agendas often seemed to be complicated by things beyond her control, details the ETs manipulated in some way. Her boss, Jerry Fleming, understood this intellectually, but not viscerally. She suspected that would change soon. He was alone down there on the compound in western Cuba that the U.S. government had leased last year from the Cuban government.

It might seem like a small point to an outsider—intellectual versus visceral—but for her, it was the whole point. The bigger picture. None of what was happening could be understood just intellectually. It wasn't like you could connect a bunch of dots and the entire blueprint of this alien phenomenon would make sense. It wasn't rational. Or reasonable.

She drove her rental car out of the Miami airport and, following the GPS instructions, headed south on I-95 toward an assisted living facility in Homestead. It had taken some research to find out where Larry Aldridge and his wife lived now, but the assisted living facet of all this didn't surprise her. When she'd seen Aldridge two years ago, during the investigation into the disappearance and the subsequent metamorphosis of his daughter, his Parkinson's had progressed to the point where he couldn't walk without a cane or a walker. She wouldn't be surprised to find him housebound in a wheelchair now.

Aldridge, now in his late seventies, was once the shining star of the University of Miami's neurology department and had succumbed to what eventually afflicted every human being: old age and a body that slowly failed.

She was forty-five. A widow with some ex-lovers. No kids. She was in charge of a bunch of these captured ET skin shifters. They were now in an aquarium on a Cuban compound, ugly fucks that might include her husband, Neil King, abducted from a beach in Costa Rica in 2011.

Don't go there.

But it was the only place she could go, the dark, terrible place she often went in her memories. They'd been investigating an alleged encounter on the west coast of Costa Rica. Neil hadn't been a field agent, but Jerry Fleming had urged him to accompany her and George Dylan because it involved a Costa Rican scientist and climate change expert, Neil's expertise.

The three of them had spent two days in San Jose, then traveled to the beach town where the scientist's encounter had occurred. They'd interviewed multiple witnesses, had compiled videos that clearly showed three triangular-shaped UFOs hovering over a long stretch of beach, and the scorched circle in a nearby wooded area where one of the UFOs had landed. It had been here where the scientist had come upon the craft. Because he believed he was missing time, he'd undergone a regression shortly after his encounter and had provided her, Neil, and Dylan with that recording.

Even now, six years later, she recalled the emotional and harrowing account of his abduction, where he was shown scenes of massive climate changes—rising oceans, devastated coastal cities, landscapes changed almost instantly. It was never clear to the scientist or to them whether the scenes were of the alien world or Earth.

The day Dylan left to drive the scientist back to San Jose, she and Neil were sitting on the beach that evening when a thick fog had rolled in, lit up from the inside as if with bright flashlights or lanterns. Because her field experience was greater than his, she'd known immediately what was happening, and leaped up, shouting, *Run, Neil, get out of here!* But Neil had just stood there, spellbound. And seconds later, he'd been dragged off into the ocean, just as Justin Dylan would be three years later. The difference was that Neil's body never washed up on a beach.

A year after he'd disappeared, she and Dylan had been in

San Francisco to interview a possible abductee and she'd seen Neil's human counterpart on a street in Haight-Ashbury. The man had looked like Neil, walked like Neil, dressed like Neil. A twin. That's what these aliens did. But when she'd run up to him, overjoyed to see him, his vapid eyes told a different story. He hadn't recognized her. He smiled politely, looked her over quickly from head to toe, decided he liked what he saw, and said, "Wow. You're a knockout. Let's go get a drink."

Lia had raced off in the opposite direction. From this horrifying experience, she had determined that a skin shifter who had been changed into a human didn't necessarily retain the memories of the metamorphosed human. Some probably did, but not Neil. That night, Dylan had been her refuge, the only time they'd slept together until she'd rescued him from the nuthouse and he'd lived with her.

Stop. Fleming had sent her to the U.S. because of the sighting on Tango Key on February 6. Focus. It was all about that focus.

The assisted living facility, The Moors, backed up to a salt marsh and looked like most of these places did, a pleasant prison for the remainder of your life. Trees, walkways, solariums, patios, and locked wards. Christ, it depressed her to even walk inside the facility.

At the front desk, she told the young woman she was here to visit Larry and Arleen Aldridge.

"Are they expecting you?"

"No." *I'm a surprise.*

"Are you on the visitors' list, ma'am?"

Lia shook her head, set her ID on the counter.

"The CIA?" the woman exclaimed, eyes wide with alarm.

"That's it."

"Just a minute." She got on the phone with someone—her supervisor, the head office, maybe the Aldridges, who knew? A few minutes later, she swiveled around in her chair. "Apartment one twelve. Past the stairs, first hallway on your left."

"Thanks very much."

Lia passed a spacious room where men and women in wheelchairs or with walkers were watching TV, playing cards, reading. Apartment 112 was at the very end of the hallway and the door was already open, a trim and stately Arleen Aldridge standing there.

"Lia," she exclaimed. "The woman at the desk said CIA, so I was expecting some dude in a suit and tie."

Lia laughed. "Just me. So good to see you, Arleen."

They hugged hello. Arleen felt thin, frail, as if she were melting away. Inside the apartment, the living room opened onto a deck surrounded by a lush garden that ensured privacy and plenty of morning sunlight. A gray cat was curled up on a wicker table, watching something in the garden, and Lia heard cascading water from somewhere nearby.

They sat out on the deck, where the cat settled in Arleen's lap. "Larry's going to regret missing you. He's on Tango Key. What brings you to Homestead?"

"I just wanted to check in on you and Larry. Find out how you're doing, if there have been any developments."

"You're in a better position than I am to know about developments." She stroked the cat with her manicured nails. "The Agency is still investigating these monsters, right?"

Lia nodded. "Have you had any dreams about your daughter and son? A sense they might be around?"

"Around as what? Ghosts? I feel strongly that Cat and Duncan are both still alive." She leaned forward slightly. "Let me be frank, Lia. When you lose both of your children in the way Larry and I did, your life is never the same. My life fell apart two years ago—first when Duncan vanished in Puerto Plata, then when he was spotted by a field biologist in the Yaque River down there. Then it fell apart a final time when Cat... was changed."

Lia didn't know what to say—that she understood? The loss of her husband had devastated her, but she didn't understand how anyone could survive the loss of two children.

"Some days, it's all I can do to get out of bed. And... sometimes when I close my eyes at night, the only thing I see is that horrifying video ...of Cat after your agency brought her back from the Dominican Republic, and took her to Homestead Air Force Base and she...she had started changing and ... then fled from that swimming pool on the base. I see her like she was in that video… seven feet tall, a sprig of cinnamon colored hair on her head, her double jointed knees, her… four thumbs…" She began to cry and Lia went over to her, slipped her arms around her, and held her while she sobbed.

"There's still hope, Arleen. That's why I came here."

She drew back from Lia, her mascara now smeared under her eyes. "Hope? I've forgotten what that word means."

Lia pulled her chair over closer to Arleen's. "Look, one of the reasons The Agency funded the search for Duncan in the DR was because we've had experiences with these aliens before. In 2011, my husband, Neil—who worked for The Agency at the time—was abducted. From what we've learned, these abductions have been going on since at least the late nineties, when the agency was formed."

Arleen sniffed and wiped the back of her hand across her eyes. "Larry has done a lot of research on this. That's why he's on Tango. Because of the recent sighting. You know about that, right?"

Lia nodded.

"He has proof that these abductions have been going on since the early sixties. Similar MOs."

"They've probably been ongoing even before then. But in this era with social media and You Tube and the rest of it, we're able to keep closer tabs on these events and that's where our hope lies. I've been in Cuba for the last thirteen months. After Cat's husband was taken and we rescued her, that pod of ETs was spotted on satellite, headed for Cuba. We couldn't do anything about it until President Obama opened diplomatic relations with Cuba. Then their government reached out to us for help because so many of their people were being abducted by these monsters, which now number in the thousands."

"*What? Thousands?* In Cuba? Is there… an invasion underway? Is that what you're saying, Lia?"

"I don't know about an *invasion*. It's not *Independence Day*, but it's coordinated. And what better place for an invasion than an island like Cuba? Isolated, a dictatorship… We've captured a hundred of these ETs and are keeping them in huge tanks on a compound our government leased from Cuba. The problem is

that we don't know which ones are humans who were changed."
She spoke softly, aware of how nuts she sounded. "But once we
figure that out, my hope is that Cat and Duncan are among
them. I remember what Cat looks like, but since we never met
Duncan, could you text or email me a photo of him?"

"Sure. Of course." She sniffled, slipped out her phone. "Are
you going to Tango? To talk to Larry?"

She felt she should, but she honestly didn't want to go to the
keys. The temptation to stop in Key Largo and see Dylan would
be too great. When he'd moved out of her place a year ago to
live on his own, he'd made it clear his only goal in life was to
find the alien fuck who had abducted his son, tortured him, and
killed him. She hadn't heard from him since and hadn't tried to
get in touch with him.

"I can't go to Tango on this trip. But I'd love to talk to him."

"I'll text you his cell number."

"Why'd he think it was so important to investigate this
sighting on Tango?"

"He chases every sighting."

Maybe, but Aldridge had impressed her as a detail man. As
a former neurosurgeon, he had to be. "I'll give him a call. How
come you haven't joined him on these investigations?"

"I did several times. But then my sister's husband died and
she got sick, so I've been helping her out." She texted Duncan's
photo and her husband's cell number. "Are you going to tell him
about this, uh, compound in Cuba?"

"I shouldn't even have told you, Arleen. " *But I wanted to
give you hope.* "At some point, we may need Larry's help but
right now the operation is classified."

"I understand. But if you could...keep me in the loop, Lia, I
would really appreciate it."

"I definitely will."

Arleen walked with her to the door and they hugged
good-bye.

As Lia walked out toward her car, she tried Larry Aldridge's
number. It went straight to voicemail. She started to leave a
message, but decided she would text him later. Right now, she
had a date with Publix and the hardware store for supplies and

provisions they needed on the compound.

The closest Publix lay south of The Manor and she thought how easy it would be to keep driving for another 39 or 40 miles to Key Largo. She knew where Dylan lived. She'd helped him move. For all she knew, one of the ETs on the compound or in the underground rivers in Viñales had killed Justin. Dylan deserved to know about the compound.

But she wasn't ready to see him again. She still remembered the last time they'd made love. It had been in that bungalow he'd bought in Key Largo, and she remembered every detail, every nuance, every emotion she'd felt. And she remembered how crushed she'd felt the next morning when he'd told her he no longer had room in his life for her, that his search for his son's killer was the only thing he cared about.

That wound still festered and until it had healed, she was better off not seeing him.

Chapter 6

As Pierce came out of the last bend in his driveway, he saw McMullen's van with the front doors ajar, the garage door wide open, the back windshield cracked, the front windshield shattered. Crouched in the yard near the bay windows were Sofia and McMullen, studying something.

Alarms screeched in Pierce's head.

He pulled up behind the van, the damage to it more visible now, and slammed on the brakes, leaped out. "What's going on?"

Sofia glanced around, her face pale, haunted. "The ET is gone."

"Gone? Gone where? She was dead."

McMullen shook his head. "Apparently not."

Sofia brought out her phone, sat on the ground, her right leg stretched out in front of her, the webbed foot grotesque in the light. A flipper. It twitched, turned toward the sun, basking like a reptile. She clicked to a video. "This is what happened after we put her in the freezer and covered her with ice and frozen food so she wouldn't be visible."

Pierce clicked on the video and for the next 93 seconds, reeled from the implications, the impossibility, of what he was seeing. Stuff flew around in his garage in some mind fuck whirling carnival, hammering the van, the walls, Sofia and McMullen.

"I backed the van outta the garage," McMullen said, and at some point got hit with something. It knocked me out. Sofia pulled me into the house..."

"I couldn't wake him up," she said quickly. "I was so freaked I walked into your backyard to calm down and there... collecting papaya... was my ex."

"But he's dead," Pierce blurted. "Steve's been dead for years."

"And we thought the ET was dead, too," McMullen reminded him.

Beats passed. Pierce struggled to absorb the words. Dead but not dead.

"Steve told me the ET had made some impossible things possible," Sofia said.

Pierce felt so disoriented by all this he lowered himself to the ground next to McMullen. He needed facts, a timeline. "Did you see her talking to Steve, Josh?"

"I saw her talking to a man. At first, I thought it was you. He just faded away."

"We realized we'd left the garage door open and ran back through the house," Sofia added. " But when we reached the garage, it looked just as tidy and neat as it had when we got here. And the ET was gone."

Pierce pressed his fists against his eyes. *Shit. Dead but not dead. What's it mean?* And where would something that looked like this creature actually hide? "Where have you looked?"

"Nowhere. This just happened. But... wait." Sofia clicked on her phone's recorder. "Luke Pierce's front yard on Tango Key, February eighth. Luke, what time do you have now? My phone says it's 2:15."

Pierce understood she was trying to establish a timeline of events that would give them a baseline from which to work, to figure things out. He glanced at his watch. "Same."

"Me, too," McMullen said. "And you and I loaded the ET into my van at 9:36, Luke. I remember checking the time because I was worried that the mayor might come by the lighthouse."

"And I went back into the kitchen and found Sofia conscious," said Pierce. "We got upstairs to the back door and then the mayor arrived."

"It took eleven minutes," McMullen said. "I kept glancing at my watch. I was uneasy with that ET in the back of my van. I was anxious to get the hell outta there."

"So call it 9:47 when the mayor arrived," Pierce said, and took a look at his text messages. "Two minutes later, Sofia, at

9:49, you texted me that you and Josh were headed to my place."

She double checked on her phone, nodded. "The trip from the lighthouse to your place, Luke, took about five minutes because we were on back roads. Let's say 9:54 or 9:55. How long did you spend with the mayor?"

He wasn't sure. It had felt like hours, but at the most had been perhaps twenty or thirty minutes. "I probably left at 10:25 or 10:30."

"And got here at... 10:35? 10:40?" she asked.

"Uh, no. I found an electronic bug in the wheel of my car." Pierce told them about slapping the bug under the bumper of a car parked at the market.

McMullen snickered. "Good for you. Asshole Willford."

"So let's say I got here at close to eleven," Pierce said.

Sofia paled. "I took that video about ten minutes after Josh and I arrived. What's the time on it, Luke?"

He looked and experienced one of those all too familiar moments that he was losing his mind. In this business, that feeling was a professional hazard. "Uh, 11:11."

"Oh my God," Sofia whispered.

"But... but..." McMullen stuttered, his face now as pale as his gray hair. "Now it's 2:15. That's not possible."

Impossible, yet it had happened. That made it possible. "It means the three of us...with me in a different location...lost a lot of time," Pierce said, and looked at Sofia. "It's classic Budd Hopkins."

"What's *that* mean?" McMullen looked alarmed now. "Who's Budd Hopkins?"

"A researcher." Sofia explained that in 1988, Hopkins published a book called *Missing Time*, about seven people who experienced alien abductions but all traces of the trauma were erased from their memories—until they were hypnotized.

"Fuck," McMullen breathed. "We were *abducted*? By an alien we thought was dead but isn't dead? What the hell, this whole thing is nuts."

Pierce, still seated in the shade of the tree with the others, gripped his knees, struggling to assimilate everything. He quickly checked his arms and legs for any injuries that would suggest abduction. He noticed that Sofia already was doing the same thing.

"I should be checking myself?" McMullen asked. "For what?"

"Bruises, nicks, cuts," Sofia said. "Scars you don't remember having. I'm clean, Luke."

"Me, too."

McMullen twisted his arms this way and that, rolled his jeans to his knees and examined his legs, tore off his shoes and socks and ran his hands over his feet. "Hell, I'm older than you two. Got a lotta scars. But I don't see… anything new. So that's good, right?"

"Yeah, definitely," Sofia replied. "But if we weren't abducted, then what happened?"

About the only thing Pierce knew for sure at that point was that when Sofia and McMullen had left the lighthouse, the timeline had diverged. If he supposedly had arrived at his home close to or at eleven a.m. and the video had been taken eleven minutes later, then what the hell had happened between then and 2:15 p.m. when they'd all checked the time? He didn't remember anything except driving and feeling eager to get home, to dive into the details of what this ET was.

"I don't know." Pierce's left brain screamed, *Pay attention.* "What do you two remember of the drive to my place?"

"Paranoia because I was following a car that was transporting an ET, because my foot is webbed, because I was scared of getting stopped," Sofia said. "That's about it. What about you, Josh?"

The old man's frown pushed his bushy gray brows together. "I just remember one thing that seemed sort of weird at the time. I was fiddling with the dial on my radio, trying to pick up NPR, when there was this really loud burst of static. And then… I thought I heard stuff moving around in the back of the van."

"*Stuff?*" Pierce said. "Like the cleaning supplies? Tools?"

"I don't know."

"Did either of you stop at any point?" Pierce asked.

"No." McMullen shook his head. "I don't remember stopping."

Sofia held up her hands, patting the air. "Not so fast. I have a vague recollection of stopping for some reason."

"How can that be?" McMullen asked. "I was checking on you in the rear view mirror, making sure you were behind me. I didn't want us to get separated. You didn't stop. I would've seen it, and you would've called me, right?"

Not good, Pierce thought. Missing time, messed-up time, different memories of the same event: these elements were all part of the MO of encounters. "Check your phones."

He watched them scrolling through their call logs and when Sofia looked up, Pierce saw the truth in her haunted eyes. "At... 9:51, I called Josh. He didn't pick up."

In other words, she'd called McMullen two minutes after Pierce had received her text message that they were on their way to his place.

"She's right." McMullen checked his phone logs. "9:51. I didn't answer. I don't have any memory of the call."

Pierce asked if he could look at their phones. He set them side by side on the ground, snapped photos of their call logs so he had proof of this discrepancy, and noted that they had spoken at 10:58, about two minutes before they supposedly arrived at his house. "Do you remember speaking to each other shortly before you got here to my place?"

"No," they replied simultaneously.

His head ached with questions. But he knew none of them would be answered now. He would take these discrepancies to Fisher, whose field experience far surpassed his own. "Okay, going forward, we need to keep close tabs on the time. I've got 2:23."

McMullen and Sofia glanced at their watches, nodded.

Pierce pointed at the ground. "What're you looking for here?"

"I think it's a footprint," McMullen replied. "We know this ET can *jump*, right? And the soil is damp enough from sprinklers and a brief shower last night. One foot landed *here*."

Pierce saw a human footprint.

He shot to his feet and moved fast through the yard, eyes fixed to the ground, looking for another print, somewhere, anywhere. If what Sofia had seen psychically was true, then the

ET had leaped from the floor of the Gulf of Mexico to the face of the cliff at the lighthouse. The ET hadn't died on that cliff, at least not in any sense that he, as a human, understood death, but she'd been injured severely enough so that she had gone into a kind of dormant state.

A theory. He desperately needed a theory and right now, this one felt good enough to pursue. How far had she jumped from the floor of the Gulf to the cliff? A mile? Two? More? He trotted forward now, scouring the grass, the fallen leaves, the damp dirt, for signs of another footprint.

He found a print at the side of his house, beneath one of the tremendous banyan trees. It was deep, suggesting she'd landed hard. He dropped his head back, peering up into the tree, through the branches. He didn't see anything except green leaves. Would she have vaulted into one of the high trees? To the roof? Or would she head for water?

He threw open the gate to his backyard and ran down to the canal that paralleled the back edge of his property. High tide. The water washed over the top of his deck. Pierce stretched out on his belly in front of the canal and stared at the water. Nothing unusual. If the ET was in the canal, then she was hugging the sandy floor, perhaps digging her way into mud so that she wouldn't be seen at low tide.

Or maybe she wasn't anywhere nearby.

2.

By the time Sofia's son, Mike, and their dog, Cooper, arrived shortly before six p.m., with Chinese food for everyone, Pierce still didn't have a plan. He didn't even have a *concept* of what a plan might look like. He didn't have any answers, either. It would be dark soon and just the idea of darkness scared him.

"I don't think we should do anything, make any move," Mike said, setting a bowl of food for Cooper on the floor. The dog hurried over to it.

Mike had watched the videos, seen the evidence, the timeline, they'd told him all of it. But Mike could still sit here at the kitchen table in the apartment above Pierce's garage, and tell them not to worry, they would find their alien, their answers. He was 21 years old and full of shit, Pierce thought, and said as much.

Mike, to his credit, just laughed. "Suppose this ET is just trying to fuck with your head, Luke?"

Yeah, there was that.

"Or everyone's head?" Mike went on. "The three of you are missing time. It means the ET can control our perceptions. Or can manipulate time itself. Or both. Hopkins implied as much. So did Whitley Strieber. So did Betty and Barney Hill. So do most abductees. None of this is new. The alien as a dark trickster. But until now no one at this table has experienced anything like this. Agreed?"

Mike's words suddenly struck Pierce as the voice of reason, and it soothed him. Calmed him. Yes, they were in the grips of some sort of terrible high strangeness. But as long as they could communicate with one another, could document the time and what they felt and experienced, they had a chance of understanding it. "Agreed that it's a new experience for all of us. But we thought... the ET was dead."

"Maybe it was," Mike said. "But it sure as hell isn't now."

"A dormant state," Sofia said. "That's my guess. Dormant, it can heal?"

McMullen looked so stricken that Pierce didn't want him returning alone to his empty condo. "Josh, why don't you stay here tonight? Take the extra bedroom. We'll get up early tomorrow and take my boat out to the crash site."

"I'm sposed to go into work at noon."

"Call in sick," Sofia suggested. "I bet you have a load of sick days."

"And annual leave days," McMullen said.

"Good." Mike slapped his hands against the table. "It's settled then. Three humans and one dog are crashing at your place, Luke."

"Time?" Sofia said. "Anyone? Everyone?"

It was 8:17 p.m.

3.

Dark outside. Daylight savings wouldn't start until next month, March 12, but since the winter solstice, the minutes of sunlight had become longer, the time of sunset later. Pierce was no fan of darkness and would be ecstatic in a place where the sun shone twelve hours or more a day. This fear of darkness had begun when he and Sofia had started working together on these investigations, and she had become the only light in the darkness of his marriage back then. She was still his light, and now, surprisingly, so was her son.

Mike offered to drive McMullen to his place to grab clean clothes and whatever else he needed and when they left, it was just him, Sofia and the dog in the apartment over the garage.

It felt odd to be alone with her in the place he'd bought after she'd left Omega and ended their relationship. She stood at the kitchen sink, rinsing dishes, loading them in the dishwasher, and he relished the sight of her, all that flowing dark hair that his fingers had so enjoying slipping through, the blades of her hips, her long legs. He even loved the webbed toes on her right foot.

"I'm going to need some other shoes," she said.

"We can buy some tomorrow on the way to the Fishers' place. In the meantime, I might be able to enlarge the one shoe so you can get your foot in it."

"Yeah?" She turned, wiping her hands on a dish towel. "How?"

"By mutilating it."

She laughed. "Give it a shot, Luke."

Sofia scooped the shoe off the floor, handed it to him, and sat at the table as he went to work on it with a large pair of scissors. He snipped off the toes, made slits on either side, then cut off the toes on the other shoe so they would match. "Voila. See how it fits."

She slipped her foot into it, stood, walked around, and nodded. "Not bad. It'll do for now. Thanks." Then: "How'd we get into this mess? Find an alien, lose an alien. And she leaves her calling card." Sofia pointed at her webbed foot, toes peeking out the open end. "And the fucking ET has my foot. I mean, how? How's any of this possible? Have you told any of this to Ted?"

"Only that we'd found an ET."

"She has to be somewhere on the island, Luke."

"I hope so."

"It's the closest spot to her craft."

"Why did that webbing happen?" he asked.

"I don't know. I've been thinking a lot about that. I wonder if it might facilitate communication between her and me."

"Does it feel like it's part of you?"

She sat again, slipped off the shoes, lifted her webbed foot to the edge of the chair. "It feels... foreign, like a big splinter, but without the discomfort."

"May I touch it?"

"Sure."

She extended her leg and rested her foot on his knee. Pierce ran his hands over the webbing. It felt different than it had earlier. Warmer, as though her blood now flowed through it, and the texture was softer, more like her skin.

He raised her foot so the overhead light shone on it and, sure enough, he could see thin capillaries, a network of them, absent earlier. It creeped him out. What he felt must have shown in his expression because Sofia said, "Yeah. Capillaries. I think it's becoming a... permanent part of my foot."

"You seem pretty calm about it."

"*Calm?*" Her brows shot up, she emitted a sharp, clipped laugh. "Hardly. But what the hell am I going to do about it? Rant and carry on? Freak out? Kill myself?" She drew her foot away, dropped it to the floor. Cooper came over and sniffed at it, growled softly, then licked at it. "I now have a very personal motive for finding this alien. She did this to me, so she can undo it."

Excited, Pierce leaned forward. "Sofi, maybe that's exactly why she did it, to create a connection between you. Maybe it really does facilitate communication. Can we capitalize on it? Use it to our advantage somehow?"

"Well, Christ, if that's true, she could've figured out something other than mutilating me."

Pierce suddenly recalled the Aldridge case from 2015. He and Sofia had investigated it but not in depth because Dylan and Lia Graham had been directly involved. Usually, when a government agency was in charge of an investigation, Omega was permitted only limited access. Someone had sent Pierce a file with a number of emails exchanged between Dr. Lawrence Aldridge, a retired neurologist from the University of Miami, whom he and Sofia had met, and his daughter, Cat, a biologist.

She was in the Dominican Republic searching for her brother, who had been abducted and supposedly transformed. If he remembered correctly, there had also been emails between Aldridge and Lia Graham, who had investigated Justin Dylan's disappearance the year before and had been present at that shocking autopsy. Pierce never knew who had sent him the file, but had suspected either Aldridge or Dylan.

"You remember the Aldridge case, Sofia?"

Her eyes lit up. "Damn straight. I read those email exchanges a zillion times. My God. If there's a connection between what's happening to me and what happened to Cat Aldridge... "

"Be right back."

Pierce was sure he'd stashed a hard copy of those email exchanges in a wall safe in the apartment's back bedroom. He hurried down the hall, dialed in the safe's combination, shuffled through the folders inside until he found it, a skinny unlabeled folder. He opened it, read: *From the 2015-2016 e-mail files of Lawrence Aldridge, PhD, M.D.*

He hurried back into the kitchen, dropped the folder on the table, flipped through the pages. "Listen to this. It's from Cat Aldridge to her dad. She and her husband are camping in the wilderness of the interior of the Dominican Republic, following a pod of amphibious ETs that she believes her brother, Duncan, is a part of."

"Yeah." Her eyes lit up. "I remember that part."

"Okay, so Cat is hot and sticky and goes down to the river to fill a bucket with water." He paused, then read what she'd written her dad. "'Suddenly, the water three feet away from me exploded upward and there he was, Duncan, totally unrecognizable except for his eyes. I know it was him, Dad. He's tall, at least seven feet, has the dual- jointed knees, just one nostril, a gill at his throat, four fingers and two thumbs on either hand, a gill on his left side. His beautiful black hair has been reduced to a weird reddish brown sprout."

"That description, except for the color of the hair, could be the ET I read, Luke."

"Exactly. And I should've realized it when I first laid eyes on that thing."

"Hey, don't blame yourself. I didn't make that connection, either. Probably because we didn't investigate it in any depth."

Or maybe they hadn't remembered because the alien had fucked with their memories, he thought.

Sofia turned the folder around, flipped through the pages until she found what she was looking for. "This is from Lia Graham to undisclosed recipients. I figure that means the rest of The Agency people. 'Satellite images show pod moving from the coast of the Dominican Republic toward Cuba. This could be a big problem for us unless, hey, they stop at Gitmo for refreshments.'" Sofia glanced up. "Suppose that's where the ET was headed when she crashed, Luke? To Cuba? It makes sense. Tango Key is less than ninety miles from Havana."

"Maybe. But just because they were headed to Cuba two years ago doesn't mean they're still there. It's possible they move around throughout the Caribbean and the Atlantic." Pierce sat down, rubbing his hands over his face, his excitement growing. "There's a description in there somewhere of what Cat Aldridge looked like when she escaped from Homestead."

"Yeah, I remember that, too." Sofia flipped through more pages. "Here it is. An email from Jerome Fleming, the director of The Agency, to Aldridge's attorney, who had threatened to go public. 'I don't know what happened there. I don't know what Larry's daughter became. But I'll tell you this. During the ensuing chaos at Homestead, she was sighted racing toward the nearest canal. One witness described her as at least seven feet tall, with a weird topping of cinnamon-colored hair, and not running but leaping from one point to another until she splashed into a canal and swam away.'"

"And who was this agent Lia Graham was married to, Neil King, who was either killed or transformed? Do we know anything about him?"

"We weren't involved in that case. But that certainly gives Graham a personal stake in all this."

"But when we met her in Sarasota during the investigation of Justin Dylan's disappearance, she never let on what her personal stake was in this. And somewhere in these emails, Graham tells Aldridge these ETs have been up to no good since at least 2001. He sends her his research that says they've been doing this shit since the sixties. That means that when she and Dylan investigated the disappearance of Dylan's son, they already knew about these alien fucks, Luke."

"They also seem to believe the ETs are in Cuba because since August 2016—at least according to these emails—our government has had a compound on land they've leased from the Cuban government and they were planning to trap these things and study them," Pierce added. He straightened the papers, slapped the folder shut. "I'm going to leave this out so Mike and Josh can read it. We have to figure out what our next step is."

"Do you have any way of getting in touch with Dylan? Or Aldridge?"

"Old email addresses. I'll try those first."

She nodded, her face drawn with lines of fatigue, pushed up from the table, picked up one of the packs Mike had brought. "I need to go shower and get some sleep. I'm whipped."

In the old days when she'd said something like this, he would have replied, *Want some company?*

Now he simply sat there, silent, and watched her walk out of the kitchen.

At the Mercy of

*I*am not sure how I made it back to this dock, how I crawled out of the water, but now I am lying here, the gill in my side torn, the gill at my throat struggling to close. I couldn't stay in the woods in my weakened state, night predators were already circling. I could hear them—hordes of fire ants, carrion beetles preparing to lay their eggs in my dying flesh, demestids that love to feast on the dead and dying. And in the trees, the hawks and buzzards gathered, my stink drawing them out of their night nests to investigate.

The web shimmers and I feel Lotus's presence. Mira, Jez told me he was in contact with you. Do not worry about me. I am well protected in an area away from the caves. If you are going to arrive in Havana, I will meet you, travel with you to Viñales. The human I am changing is not fighting her transformation. But it is a slow, often tedious process and I wonder if it is because Acia keeps these partially changed humans as prisoners in the caves. Taunting them. Torturing them.

I demanded that she stop and sent out a message to the tribe about it, *I tell her.*

She has poisoned them against you. I feel you are weak, still badly injured. Remain vigilant. One of Jez's warriors infiltrated Acia's followers and learned she is sending a Blue, loyal to her, to eliminate you.

The news does not surprise me, but alarms me. I am in no condition to battle another Blue. All Blues have the same powers, but those powers are more developed in some. The Blue's name?

It will come as no surprise—Ravina.

My oldest adversary. Before we decided to leave our world, Ravina fought me for control of the tribe. She lost and went dormant for months in order to heal. Acia revived her, brought her to this world. Is she transformed?

I am not sure. Rumor is that she is partially changed. She has great control over others' perceptions, however. Jez believes this control grew more powerful because of the injuries you inflicted on her—a permanent limp that she disguises with beauty and presence.

I wish I could say I will be ready for Ravina, but right now I am not strong enough for any kind of conflict, Lotus. Thank you for the warning. I will focus more intently on healing.

The web shimmers and trembles again. Acia, trying to contact me. I tell Lotus and we disconnect. When I tap into Acia's channel, a shrill screeching noise tears through the web, her call to battle. I do not disconnect or respond. Instead, I hurl open all channels in the web so that the rest of the tribe hears her, understands her intent, and can declare their loyalty to her or to me.

The web fills with discordant music—songs, screeches, hums, wails, cries, clicking, moans, and then it all melts together and explodes with images of our violent, ancestral past. Wars. Plundering. Hunger. Deprivation. The waters rising, rising, until nearly every bit of land is inundated, until billions are dead. Then, as if to reminds us of our own evolution, the images illustrate how we became amphibious, infertile, desperate, how we learned to move through and beyond time to cultivate food in places outside of time. These images assault me, wear me down, and exhaustion overpowers me. I seek solace in a darkness thick with the past.

Rest, *Lotus whispers.*

This invasion was not supposed to be difficult. It has been ongoing for years, with a few successes here and there, particularly in tropical climates. But this planet has more than seven billion inhabitants and perhaps the invasion would have occurred faster if we had targeted poorer countries or areas torn apart by war and religious strife. But those areas can also present a greater risk to us. Many are deserts where water is such a precious commodity that our presence would be known too quickly. And few of us want to trade places with humans who have little or nothing.

Some of my tribe landed in the northern countries and eventually died of the cold. Canada, the Scandinavian countries, Russia, China, parts of Asia: their winters are too brutal. Yet, China in the spring and summer is a possibility we should explore. Its population is large enough to accommodate all of us. But only after we have taken over Cuba and some of the other Caribbean islands.

I press my hand over the torn gill at my side. It allows me to breathe a little more easily. What I need is fresh water. Or more of Sofia- her human hands, her remaining human foot, her human throat that lacks a gill, both of her nostrils, her luxurious hair. I need all of her. But most of all, I need her Sight so that I can peer into my own future, into the future of my tribe. But as long as I am not at full strength, it's all I can do to maintain the webbing on her right foot, so that my right foot is human. I might be able to transform her left hand again, the nubs from which the webbing grows still covers the inside of her fingers.But not right now.

For now, I shut my eyes, turn my head toward the water and search for the healing darkness. I drift to sleep, but suddenly the frantic barking of the dog wakes me. I roll into the deeper shadows where trees shade the dock and struggle to reach out to the creature, to silence it with my thoughts. But it doesn't understand my thoughts, doesn't understand anything except my scent.

The only way I can erase my scent is to move time back a bit. But I'm too weak to do that. Too weak to hurl energy at the dog that would stop it. Too weak to even roll toward the water and drop into the canal.

A human male whistles for the dog. Pierce. He has hunted for evidence of my kind for most of his life. We found him years ago, a young boy in a backyard with his dog, watching the night sky. He was marked then. We became his destiny.

"Coop," he calls. "Wait up."

I struggle to speak, to create the sounds that will shatter the darkness and stop him in has tracks. The most I manage is a wheeze, the noise that precedes death. I try to create an atmosphere that will enable him to see his dead parents, to communicate with them, a distraction that will remove his attention from the dog's steady trek toward me. But I can't even do that. And now I'm thinking in contractions, like they do, and I hate that.

A breeze rustles through the trees, causing the fronds to click and clack. The smell of salt water thickens in the air, as if to remind me that if I can't muster the strength to reach the water, I'll die here on this old, weathered dock.

The dog sees me, snarls, moves around me slowly but not too closely. I can smell Pierce's fear now, a thick, unpleasant odor. He approaches slowly, shines his phone's light at me.

"Holy fuck." He grabs Cooper's collar, pulls him back. The dog keeps snarling but stays close to Pierce. "Jesus. She's dying." His fingers move rapidly on his phone.

The doors of the house slam open and Mike and Sofia rush down the stairs, through the yard. Cooper breaks away from Pierce and moves toward me, circling me, barking softly, barks that seem to say, Get up, move.

Sofia and Mike lumber out onto the deck. I am at their mercy and they know it. Instead of letting me die, which I would do if our situations were reversed, Mike slides his arms under my head, Sofia grabs my feet, and they carry me to the edge of the dock.

Pierce shouts, "No, you can't do that! She'll swim away, escape!"

"She's going to die," Sofia screams.

And Mike, frantic, adds, "We can't let that happen."

They drop me into the canal.

I can breathe again, I can swim in spite of my injuries, and even as I move rapidly away from the dock, from them, I hear Pierce yelling, "Do you have any idea what you just did?"

Sofia: "We saved her life. Fuck off, Luke."

"My God," Mike spits out. "You were just standing there, watching her die. She needed to be in water and didn't have the strength to get there herself. What the hell were you thinking, Luke?"

"What was I thinking?" Pierce yells. "Look at your mother's feet, Mike. Both of them are webbed now. Even while you two were helping that alien fuck, she was taking your mother's feet. Did she take your hands, too, Sofia?"

Then their voices are lost to me. But what isn't lost is that I owe them. I don't want to owe them anything. I hate them. They're my enemies, I'm supposed to control them, control her, and I didn't. I couldn't. She and Mike acted out of an emotion that is foreign to me and my tribe—compassion. Altruism. It enrages me that I need Sofia's body to gain her Sight, but that it can't happen until I repay my debt to her and her son.

Chapter 7

Sofia's eyes snapped open, heart hammering against her ribs. A dream? A vision? She bolted upright, the images looming brightly in her head, and fumbled with the lamp switch. A quick glance around the room told her she was alone. Even Cooper was sleeping elsewhere.

The wind outside had picked up and even though the windows were shut, they creaked and rattled. It was warm in the room and she was tempted to get up and open one of the windows for fresh air. But she was afraid the images would get away from her. She reached under her pillow for the pad of paper and pen she'd put there before she'd gone to bed and scribbled down what she'd seen. Letters, words, but not in any language she could read, followed by a sequence of numbers.

As soon as she started jotting down the words and numbers, the dream dried up. Sofia shut her eyes, tried to move back inside the dream, but ran into a wall. She could see the wall in her head, impossibly high, thick, impenetrable. She imagined running her hands over it, and asked that it yield, open, that it surrender to her need to know what lay behind it.

Nothing happened.

She opened her eyes and stared at what she'd written—*gratias tibi ago.* That last word sounded like English, *gratias* was close enough to Spanish for *thanks,* but she didn't have any idea what *tibi* might mean. Was it Latin? She Googled it on her phone. Sure enough, the translation from Latin meant *I give thanks to you.*

For the second set of letters—*ecce ego ad te*—the closest

thing Sofia found was: *Ecce ego ad te mei canis Raelyn* or *Behold I come against thee, shall a dog Raelyn*. That sounded too biblical to be relevant, but maybe the alien's world was based on biblical tenets. At this point, she didn't discount anything. When she Googled the third phrase—*Quomodo auxilium i*—she didn't find much of anything. She needed to show this to someone who actually knew Latin.

Was this just the stuff of her dreaming mind or did the ET speak Latin? And if she did, how had she invaded Sofia's dreams? Stupid question. The alien had swapped her flippers for Sofia's feet, had facilitated her dead husband's appearance, and she had witnessed the ET's telekinetic power. If the alien could do those things, then entering people's dreams was the proverbial walk in the park. But the most obvious vehicle for the alien entering her dreams was her webbed feet.

The webbing hadn't withdrawn while she'd slept. She felt it there, connecting her toes. But she suddenly remembered that when she had grabbed the alien's feet to hurl it into the canal, its feet had looked human, like her own had looked yesterday morning before she'd read the ET. The toenails were painted the same shade as hers—a coral pink.

Sofia pulled her legs up toward her chest and ran her hands over the webbing—*my flippers*—and experienced an almost crushing despair. *Hey, Mom , guess what happened to me?* Her mother would tell her the demons finally had entered her, that she should get herself to church immediately, go to confession, tell the priest everything. Like that would return things to normal.

If her grandmother, Rosa, were still alive, she would advise Sofia to explore the webbing, talk to it, engage in conversation with it, ask what it wanted. She would tell her to view it as an ally not enemy. She would look at it as evidence that Sofia had entered a profound mystery, that she, like the alchemists of Medieval times, would have to draw on all the skills and resources at her disposal to travel through the labyrinth of illusions and deceptions to find the truth.

The problem with all of Rosa's the mumbo jumbo was that Sofia had been through countless alchemical journeys. Her childhood as a young girl who had seen spirits and experienced visions was one version of that journey. Her Catholic parents had believed she was possessed and had hired a priest to exorcise her. In that journey, Rosa had been her mentor, her beacon, her salvation.

Her marriage to a man who was a complete skeptic about the paranormal had been another journey. In that one, her son had rescued and redeemed her. The fourth journey had been her relationship with Pierce and the years she had worked for Omega, doing what she loved. In that journey, she had rescued and redeemed herself by resigning and terminating her relationship with Pierce, but had ended up facing financial ruin.

Now here she was, in the midst of a new journey that was stranger and riskier than all the rest combined. There would be no Catholic exorcism this time, no new son or daughter, no new lover or job or career. Rosa would call this journey that of the warrior.

Thanks to Pierce and Omega, she could now pay off her debts, her house, and still have money left over to help Mike through college and grad school, if that was his choice, and to live for a long time doing whatever she wanted to do. Except her feet were webbed. Except that she now had irrefutable evidence that alien life existed. Those two details couldn't be translated into some lofty metaphysical quest. They had changed everything. And so had Pierce's reappearance in her life.

A divorced Pierce. For the first time since he'd seen that UFO as a kid, he had his proof. The alien. When he'd thought it was dead, he'd touched it, moved it, protected it, puzzled over it. Once you found proof of what you sensed to be true, your life couldn't be the same as before, she thought. So why had he just let it lay there on the dock, dying?

She decided it hadn't been a lack of compassion, but the paralysis of fear.

Sofia shut her eyes and tightened her hands around her webbed feet. Her breathing deepened, she slipped easily into her zone.

What do you want from me?
Silence.

Why did the webbing between my fingers disappear?
Silence.

How can I help you? With this question, she felt a shift within herself.

I need to find my people.

The answer came to her as an image—ETs that looked like the amphibious being, swimming through deep ocean.

You don't need me to do that.You don't need to keep my feet webbed to do that.

The webbing is a conduit between us. It enables us to talk, share ideas, find common ground. This image looked almost cartoonish—an old dial phone and a smiley face.

I'm happy to do that, but my feet don't need to be webbed for that to happen.

I need your Sight. To use it, I must be physically connected to you and the webbing is my connection.

The image for this: her webbed feet connected to the ET's hideous body by a thin, luminous thread. So Sofia replied with an image—that of a surgeon cutting the webbing off her feet. The ET's alarm radiated through her.

Remove the webbing and I'll be happy to use my Sight to help you in any way I can.

Her feet suddenly throbbed, pulsed, and ached as if in response to her remark. Sofia slung her legs over the side of the bed, not entirely sure that what she'd just experienced was real.

She set the pad on the nightstand, checked the time on her phone—5:33—and took a screen shot of it. Sofia emailed it to herself with a note that it was the time she'd awakened this morning. Now if she experienced another time anomaly, she would have her baseline for the day. She got out of bed, stared at her webbed feet. If the converstion she'd just had with the alien actually had happened, then the ET wasn't willing to withdraw the webbing.

Fuck it.

She hurried into the bathroom and showered, brushed her teeth, dressed. Jeans, t-shirt, denim jacket. Her right shoe, the one Pierce had customized for the webbing, fit okay. But she couldn't get her left foot into the left shoe.

Forget shoes.

She regretted that the webbing prevented her from jogging. In Key West, she used to run three miles in the evenings, usually with Cooper, until the weather got too hot. Now she could hardly walk normally.

Sofia slipped her phone into the back pocket of her jeans, zipped the pocket shut, and padded quietly through the apartment to the back door. Cooper joined her, tail wagging, and when she pushed open the screen door, he darted outside and down the stairs.

He waited for her at the bottom of the stairs—her ally and protector—and walked with her through the starlight to the edge of the dock. The tide was moving out and off to her right, fish splashed. She didn't sense anything unusual. Neither did Cooper. When she crouched, he sat, ears twitching, tail flicking back and forth, snout lifted into the air.

Sofia rocked forward onto her knees, pressed her hands to her thighs. Given her webbed feet, she felt reluctant about trying this again, but since she was going to read just the ET's residual energy, if she could, she doubted there would be any physical repercussions this time. She adjusted her breathing, slowing her breaths, deepening them until she was in the zone. Then she brought her hands to the dock where the ET had lain.

Yeah, it was a long shot. No telling how many people had walked on this dock since it was built. But in the last eight hours, only the four of them, Cooper, and the alien had been on the dock. She kept patting the old wood, searching for some trace of the being. Minutes passed, her hands kept moving. Then she hit a hot spot, a place where she sensed Pierce's anxiety and paraslysis out here last night as he'd realized the ET was dying.

She moved her hands to the left. Suddenly, that force, that power she'd experienced yesterday in the lighthouse, seized her hands. It alarmed her, but she didn't struggle to free herself. Cooper whimpered and licked her arm. "It's okay, boy." *I hope.*

No images rushed through her. But she felt a pervasive awareness of the ET's residual energy. She felt it viscerally, a kind of slow heat that started in her solar plexus and spread out through her organs, blood, skin. She experienced an odd discomfort in her fingers, still splayed against the dock, then a sharp pain in the bones and joints that made her gasp. Webbing sprouted like weeds between her fingers on both hands, her horror caused her to wrench back, but her palms stuck to the dock as if they were super-glued to the wood.

Panicked, she struggled to jerk her hands off the dock, but the force held fast. The muscles in her arms screamed, she kept struggling to wrench her palms free, but they remained stuck.

She screamed.

A chair on the dock abrupty lifted into the air and swirled ten or twelve feet above her. The hose connected to a nearby faucet uncoiled like a snake, leaped upwards, and ripped the faucet out of the ground. The wooden railing along the side of the dock snapped in half and the pieces joined the maelstrom whirling through the air. A thick fog rolled in, covering her and the dock.

Cooper now barked frantically, wildly, and raced around her in circles, snarling and snapping at the fog. A plank of wood in the dock tore loose and catapulted into the stuff whipping around overhead. Sofia shrieked unintelligibly, the whirlwind grew fiercer, the fog thickened, dust and dirt blew into her eyes. Another plank of wood ripped away from the dock and vanished in the foggy whirlwind. The dock shook so violently that Cooper ran away. Her hair blew across her eyes, so she couldn't see him, but heard his wild barks nearby. She also heard shouting—Mike, McMullen, Pierce.

"The dock's collapsing!" she yelled.

The front pilings snapped, she slid forward, and the plank that held her captive tore loose and hurled upward. Sofia, now airborne and somersaulting like some acrobat, was still stuck to the plank, the pressure on her hands and arms, her feet and legs, nearly unendurable. She screamed, the force suddenly released her, and she dropped like a stone and slammed into the water so hard her breath rushed from her lungs. As she sank, she had the presence of mind to twist her body around, and started swimming. *Fast.*

The webbing on her hands and feet enabled her to move

through the water with the ease of a giant fish. She surfaced once, gulped at the air. But the swirling tempest hugged the ground and the surface of the water, so she sank and swam faster and harder and hoped she didn't suddenly grow gills.

Sofia didn't have any idea how long or far she swam or how many times she surfaced for air. But at some point she realized she had nictitating eyelids that allowed her to see clearly underwater. She swam madly toward the surface, exploded out of the water, into full, bright sunlight, and felt the eyelids recede. Treading water, she realized the tornadic whirlwind and the fog were gone and she didn't have any idea where the hell she was.

She looked around anxiously, trying to orient herself. There: Key West in the distance. And high above her arched the bridge between Key West and Tango. She was miles south of Pierce's place.

Her drenched clothes weighted her down, her shoes were gone, her cell phone—still zipped in the back pocket of her jeans—was ruined, and her fingers and toes were still webbed. Despair filled her.

She might be able to make it to the canal behind her house in Key West, but then what? Lay low until the webbing vanished? Suppose it never did? What then? Her son, dog, and car were on Tango. She needed to go back there to collect the pieces of her life and to tell Pierce to forget it, she was out, she would refund his goddamn money. The alien was hostile and no telling what might happen next time—gills, double jointed knees, a single nostril, a tuft of blue hair.

A piercing whistle cut through the air and she twisted around, the salt water splashing into her eyes. One of the Tango Key ferries was nearing the island and passengers stood at the railing, gesturing and waving their arms. At her? The ferry suddenly slowed and turned toward her. Crew members started lowering lifeboats into the water.

They thought she'd fallen overboard.

"Shit."

She took a deep breath, dived. Her third eyelids slipped into place. She saw so clearly now she could estimate the distance to the bedrock on which Tango Key rested. Two to three miles. But unless she found the canal where Pierce's house was located, she would end up swimming along the shore for miles or, worse, would be forced to get out and walk.

Sofia swam faster, surfaced for air, saw two lifeboats headed toward the bridge, and dived again.

How'd this happen?

She should have left yesterday, when the webbing between her toes hadn't vanished. She shouldn't have tried to read anything about the alien. *You shoulda walked fast.* Too late now.

When Sofia surfaced again, she couldn't see the lifeboats. She had moved too far south, but still heard the ferry's whistle, louder and more insistent. Even though she was distant from the bridge, it was so high up she could see crowds of people along the railing. And if there were crowds, it meant that traffic had come to a full stop. It meant social media would be buzzing about a passenger who had fallen overboard from one of the many boats and was spotted moving toward Tango. It meant trouble.

She finally reached the southeastern tip of Tango and crawled onto a spit of deserted beach and just lay there, too exhausted to move. The warm sand felt good against her cheek, the salty scent of the air smelled familiar and clean and reassured her she hadn't grown gills, that she still had two nostrils. Just to be sure, though, she touched her face, checking. Two nostrils. Lots of hair. Same skin, mouth, chin. No gill at her throat. After awhile, she raised her head and stared at her hands, fingers splayed against the sand.

Different story here.

On her right hand, the webbing was partially gone and looked even more bizarre than it had when it was fully webbed. The flaps of skin hung off the insides of her fingers like leaves of wilting lettuce except they were thicker than lettuce, and looked like the aberrations they were. She rolled onto her back and lifted her hands skyward, so the light shone through the webbing. Eerie, disturbing, and in its way, also beautiful.

But not so beautiful that she wanted it to become permanent.

She sat up, looked at her feet, and a choked sob fell into the air, a soft, pathetic sound that only disgusted her. She peeled away her wet denim jacket, spread it out on the sand, and dug her ruined iPhone from her back pocket. She set it on top of her jacket. Her entire life was inscribed somewhere on that phone. Texts, emails, ebooks, photos, videos, contacts, memories that dated way back.

Sofia wrapped her arms around her legs and rested her forehead against her knees. *Gratias tibi ago.* Thanks be to you. Yeah, right. A trickster joke. "You piece of shit." she spat. *"Eres un maricon."*

That sure helped, swearing at an alien who was undoubtedly long gone by now. But gone where? The goddamn alien had turned her into a freak, so it could also turn her back into a full human. "Hey, ET!" she shouted. "How about making things right again?"

Her voice echoed in the warm air.

She finally picked up her phone, blew on it, wiped her fingers across the screen. "Please work," she pleaded. "Please, please... "

Sofia pressed the home button. Nothing happened. The screen remained black.

Start walking.

As she hauled herself to her feet, her dead ex took shape in front of her, Steve cross-legged on the sand, his expression bewildered. As before, he looked as solid and real as any living person. His dark hair even looked shiny in the sunlight. "Just so you know, Sofia. As long as I can appear like this and you can see me and we can talk, then the ET is still around."

"Not in the immediate vicinity."

He pointed at her feet. "I think that webbing connects you to her in some way."

"Thanks for the tip, Steve. But I'm frankly more concerned about how to get *rid* of the webbing."

"Not my department."

"Then what're you doing here?"

"I'm not sure. But part of it, for me, is our son. He's one of your greatest resources. Hug him for me, *chica*. Tell him I didn't mean to be a shit to him, to leave him. I didn't know what I was doing back then."

"Yeah, you were thinking with your dick."

"You're right. I was. She was pretty and seductive and turned out to be a complete bore. My only out was to die. So I did." He stood, held out his hand. "Lemme see your phone. Maybe I can do something about it." She set the dead phone in his hands, he sandwiched it between his palms. "Do you realize that the iPhone didn't exist when I died?"

"Then how do you even know what that is?"

He shrugged. "People use them in the afterlife."

"For what?"

"Texting, emailing, taking photos, whatever suits you."

The idea of the dead using iPhones struck her as comical and she laughed. "Can you have sex in the afterlife, too?"

"Sure. Whatever you can imagine is possible." He kept rubbing his hands over the phone. "You know, you really should give Luke a chance. He's still crazy about you."

How odd to hear this from her dead ex-husband. "You didn't like him when you were alive."

"I didn't have a right to any opinion about him."

"That's true."

"But I like him now. I like his perseverance, his dedication, and I like how much he loves you."

"You may just be one of the ET's trick manifestations."

"I thought about that. Then I decided that if I can think of myself as an alien manifestation, then I'm probably not."

Good point, Sofia thought. "I don't know if I trust Luke."

Steve rolled his eyes. *"Mira, chica.* You need to lighten up, okay? None of us is perfect. The circumstances back then were different."

"Yeah, he wasn't honest about his relationship with his ex."

"Just sayin'."

"The alien's hostile, Steve."

"And scared. And injured."

"She attacked me back on that dock. She created this...this whirlwind and shit flew into the air and... and... this... " She held up her hands, kicked up her feet. "She turned me into a fucking freak."

"If it was an attack, she would've done worse. You would look exactly like her."

"I think that's her ultimate intent."

"Maybe."

"I was trying to help her, to… "

"No, you weren't. You were trying to do what Luke hired you to do. Read the alien, glean as much info as possible…and for what? So Omega can justify its existence? Next time, if there *is* a next time, just ask her what *you* can do to help, Sofia."

"I already asked her that. And besides, Mike and I saved her life last night."

"And she may save yours in return. Starting here." He handed her the phone, the screen fully lit, five bars of power, all her icons lined up, 22 text messages waiting for her, 49 emails.

"My God," she whispered, and glanced up.

Steve was gone.

2.

Pierce, Mike, and McMullen stood at the edge of the yard, at what remained of the dock, attempting to explain to Lt. Ray Hayes of the Tango Key PD what had happened here. But it was like talking to a wall, Pierce thought.

The neighbors up and down the road had called the police when they'd heard Sofia shrieking and had seen her huddled on the deck with the tornadic maelstrom roiling around her. Now Sofia was gone and the cops wanted to know where she was.

"I don't know where she is," Pierce said for the umpteenth time. "We came running out here and couldn't even get near the dock, that's how violent this… this freak weather thing was."

"*Weather* thing?" Hayes shook his head. "Sorry, but I checked with Tango weather and there wasn't any *freak weather thing* at any point this morning, Mr. Pierce."

"I don't know what to tell you, Lieutenant. We know what we saw. We've got it on video."

Hayes looked at Mike and McMullen. "You guys concur?"

"There's nothing else it could've been," Mike said.

"Damn straight." McMullen nodded enthusiastically. "You

know me, Ray. I've lived here for twenty-two years. I've never seen anything like this."

"Email it to me."

"Done," McMullen said.

"And this woman, Sofia Lopez... " Hayes spoke to Mike. "She's your mother?"

"Yes, sir." His voice was choked with emotion. "And... I would appreciate it if we could get on with looking for her."

"And where will you start looking for a woman who, as some of the neighbors describe, was *carried* off like Dorothy in the *Wizard of Oz*?"

Pierce felt like grinding his fist into the man's smirk.

"I don't know. But her dog might." He whistled for Cooper and the two of them headed toward the front of the house where the cars were parked.

"If you'll excuse us, Lieutenant Hayes," Pierce said. "We need to get out there and search."

Hayes looked confused. "Do you, uh, need police help?"

McMullen snorted. "Ray, all you've done so far is delay the search."

"Feel free to look around, Lieutenant," Pierce said. "But we need to get moving."

With that, Pierce and McMullen turned away from the cop and hurried after Mike and the dog. When his phone dinged, he looked down at his text messages and saw one that had been sent to both him and Mike.

Am @ southeast tip of Tango, tiny deserted beach with historic sign that says, Here in 1570 Spanish forces fought marauding Caribbean pirates.

Pierce didn't know this spot, but he suspected that Mike, the history major, did. He broke into a run, McMullen trotting after him, and they piled into the back seat of Mike's old truck. Cooper barked at them, as if telling them to hurry up.

"You know where this place is, Mike?" Pierce asked.

"Bet your ass. But the sign is wrong. It was pirates who fought off the Spanish. The pirates had a settlement at the south end of the island and the Spaniards had the north end but wanted the entire island. " He tore up the driveway, swerved out onto the road, then shot south along back roads. "But the Spanish lost and the pirates moved inland and got as far as the low hills before they were ambushed and slaughtered."

"Christ, Mike, how do you know all that?" McMullen asked.

"The University of Miami library has a bunch of historical documents written by the Spanish about the early days of that struggle with the pirates. And it was 1571, not 1570. Josh, is that cop going to be trouble?"

McMullen laughed, but it wasn't a happy sound. "You shittin' me? You can bet he'll go straight to the mayor with this and when the neighbors add their witness reports, he's going to come sniffing around your place, Luke."

"Sniff away," Pierce said. "It's not like we're hiding anything now."

They came out on Old Post Road and followed it past the entrance to the bridge, jammed with commuter traffic in both directions. Pierce glanced at his phone. The time read: 9:11. Bad omen, he thought, and asked Mike and McMullen what time they had rushed outside.

"Just past six, I think it was," Mike said.

"I remember the sun rising," McMullen added.

Pierce quickly Googled sunrise for Tango Key today. "Uh, the sun rose today at 7:04."

"No way," Mike said. "That means we were standing out there for *more than hour,* watching everything?"

Messed-up time once again, Pierce thought. "Time now, guys?"

"9:12," they replied simultaneously.

"So something is seriously wrong," Mike remarked.

"*Everything* is seriously wrong," Pierce said.

Mike pulled into a deserted cul-de-sac and they leaped out and ran to the edge of a hilltop. Pierce saw Sofia standing on the beach below, water lapping at her ankles. She looked slight and forlorn in her drenched clothes, a jacket tied at her waist. When they shouted, she turned and waved her arms and moved awkwardly toward them, like a kid just learning to walk.

Cooper tore past them and reached Sofia first. She threw her arms around him and plopped back in the sand. Pierce scrambled down the hill, knocking loose stones, clumps of dirt and grass and it wasn't until he reached the beach that he understood why she moved so clumsily. Both feet webbed. Her left hand was also webbed and her right hand was partially webbed.

He pulled her up, her arms came around him, she sobbed softly. "I quit, Luke. I can't do this. It's going to turn me into some hideous amphibious creature. It's... "

"It's okay, Sofi. He held her tightly, loving the feel of her body, her wet clothes, overwhelmed with gratitude that she wasn't dead. "It's okay."

She jerked back. *"No, it's not okay."* She shouted the words, hurled her arms out at her sides. "I'm becoming like her, like the ET. She did this to me when I was reading the dock and she froze my hands against the wood and started... started tearing things apart and... and suddenly I was airborne on that fucking plank and then I slammed into the canal and I... swam like hell and came out under the bridge, halfway to Key West."

C'mon, Mom." Mike slipped his arm around her shoulders. "Let's get you up the hill and into my truck."

Cooper trotted alongside them, Pierce and McMullen followed. The old man looked worried. "Right now she's a missing person, Luke. If we go back to your place, Lt. Hayes may still be there and unless she's got her hands in pockets and her feet inside shoes, it's too risky to talk to cops. They'll take her to ER or a psyche unit or something. Mayor Willford is already suspicious. This will just complicate things."

Like he didn't know all this. Like he hadn't been doing this work for more than a dozen years. Like the woman he loved hadn't turned into a partially amphibious being. *Jesus. Shut up, Josh, shut the fuck up and let me think.* "I know. I know. We're going to Ted Fisher's place in the preserve. She'll be safe there until we can, uh, figure out what to do."

Once they were all in Mike's truck, with Sofia and Pierce in the back seat and Cooper between them, Pierce gave Mike Fisher's address. "The GPS won't show his place, but follow the directions as far as they take you, then I'll direct you in."

"How come he doesn't show up on GPS?" Mike asked.

"You'll see when we get there."

Mike nodded. "Sounds very mysterious, dude. Okay, there's a small cooler in the well behind you. The bottled water in there should still be cold."

Pierce reached into the well, flipped open the cooler's lid, and brought out four bottles of water. He twisted off the cap of the first and handed it to Sofia. She held it awkwardly in her partially webbed hand and gulped at it. He passed out the rest of the bottles and poured some of his into the dog bowl and held it for Cooper.

He desperately wanted to ask Sofia for specifics, for details of what had happened out on the deck before they had burst out of the house. But her face was turned away from him and he knew her well enough to understand she didn't want to talk. Not yet. Maybe never. He started to text Fisher, but suddenly remembered that when he'd first heard Sofia screeching, he had rushed to the porch door but it wouldn't open.

McMullen had hurried up behind him, shouting, *It's her, it's Sofia, we need to get out there, man!*

The goddamn door won't open.

Fuck it, McMullen had snapped. *It's a stupid screen door.* And he punched his fist through the screen and jerked up on the outside handle.

Pierce leaned forward. "Josh, do you remember... "

"Yeah, just now, all of it," the old man said. "The ET was trying to block us from getting to Sofia. I slammed my fist through the screen."

"The back door in the apartment wouldn't open, either," Mike said.

"Oh, for Chrissake's," Sofia burst out. "When she didn't succeed in keeping you guys away from me, she created that tornado of shit and started ripping wood out of the dock until the sucker collapsed. Listen, Luke. I quit. I can't do this job, I'll refund your money. I don't want to do it. If I keep working at this, I'll turn into what she is. I'll..."

"Yeah, you already said that." *No way you can quit, you can't do this, can't strand me now when we're so close... But close to what?*

He'd seen the alien, touched it, moved it in and out of a freezer. He had seen it laying on the dock last night. He had video, photos, *proof*. Ever since he'd seen that UFO in the backyard of his childhood home, he had speculated and dreamed about seeing an alien. He had hungered to know, without any doubt, that man wasn't alone in the universe. Now he knew. He had his answer. What more was there?

Everything else. The rest of the story. Every piece of knowledge gave birth to new questions and his list of questions read like an elementary school guide to interrogatives: *Who? What? Where? When? How?*

Sofia might not have all those answers, but she was a conduit to them. If she was made to feel like a prisoner, a hostage to what Omega had paid her for this job, she would bolt and go off the grid and he would never see her again. He didn't give a shit about the money or his job. He just couldn't risk losing her again.

"Keep the money," he said. "And get out of here. Go home, pack your bags, and get out of the country. Go to Costa Rica. You'd be safe there, you're fluent."

"To Costa Rica?" She laughed. "A tourist with webbed hands and feet? Sure, Luke. I wouldn't even get into an airport. I'm not going anywhere. I intend to find this ET so she can undo what she did to me."

"I thought you just told me you quit."

"I take it back. Short of surgery, the ET is the only way I'm going to get rid of the webbing. And I may have to kill her to do that." With that, she turned toward the window again, everything about her screaming with resolve.

Pierce texted Fisher. *All hell broke loose. On our way to your place.*

Social media lit up with mermaid sighting under Tango bridge. Is that what we're dealing with?

WTF? A *mermaid* sighting? He clicked through the Tango Key website, Facebook, Twitter, Snap Chat, Instagram, MSNBC, CNN, and it was everywhere, blurry videos, witness testimonies, man overboard stories from passengers on a Tango ferry. In one video, Sofia was clearly visible—not her face, but her head and shoulders above the water, and then she had dived.

He texted his reply to Fisher. *Yeah, you got it. A mermaid. Daryl Hannah.*

Deep breaths, Luke. When John Mack and I were investigating the Zimbabwe sighting, we reached the point where you are now. You want to believe, you can't believe, you know you believe...all that dichotomy fucks with your head.

Pierce didn't even think about it. He texted, *I'm Mulder. I believe.*

Great. And that's where we'll start.

Chapter 8

Dylan followed his GPS toward the neighborhood social media had pinpointed as the site of the raging, tornadic storm. He knew those storms, had seen them before. The night his son had been abducted from that Sarasota beach, a violent whirlwind and thick, dense fog had been captured on video by some random guy on the beach. He still had that video on his phone.

But the storms dated farther back than that.

When Justin was young, seven or eight years old, they had gone camping in the Ocala National Forest. His wife hadn't wanted to go, she hated sleeping bags and those kinds of physical discomforts. So it had been just dad, son, and the family dog, a big black lab named *Hombre*. They'd found a perfect campsite and everything had unfolded smoothly, joyfully, until dusk.

I'm afraid of the dark, Daddy.

They'd been sitting at the campfire and Justin's voice, so small and terrified and *naked* in this admission, had puzzled and alarmed Dylan. His first thought was that his son had been abused, but instead of asking that straight out, he'd said something stupid like, *Aw, c'mon, Jus. There're no bogeymen.*

Yeah, there are, Daddy. And they're out there. Waiting for us to go to sleep.

Hombre will keep us safe.

That night, a violent storm had swept through the park and in the morning, both of them had inexplicable cuts and bruises on their bodies, the area around the campsite looked like a tornado had ripped through it, and they found Hombre dead in the debris.

Dylan was fairly certain it was the first time he had been abducted, but just one of many times his son had been taken. These incidents had persisted over the years, not with any regularity or predictability, but frequently enough so that he finally requested a transfer to Virginia.

For their six years in Virginia, until Justin had left for college, they'd lived relatively peaceful lives. No abductions. He didn't have any idea why the move had made the difference, but it had been a particularly happy time in their lives. Then three years ago, he and his wife had gotten that call from the college. *Something has happened to your son.* And he'd known immediately what it meant—but hadn't suspected that Justin's body would wash up on that Sarasota beach days later.

He wasn't sure anymore about the sequence of events after that and the autopsy. His marriage had fallen apart, he remembered that much. But the rest of his memories were chopped up, disconnected from each other, the result of whatever they'd done to him in the nuthouse. Anti-psychotic drugs, electroshock, something worse, who knew? But here he was, an ex-agent with current credentials that would enable him to find out whatever he needed to know.

The gate to Luke Pierce's home stood open, several cop cars were parked in the driveway, the house had been cordoned off with yellow tape. A van parked haphazardly close to the garage had a cracked back windshield, a shattered front windshield, a flat tire, flat, the thing so battered it looked like it had barely survived a war zone. He got out, ducked under the tape, and walked up to the closest cop.

"Morning." He held up his ID. "I'd like to speak to whoever is in charge."

The cop looked at his ID, at him. "A spook? Whole scene's pretty messed up. You want to talk to Lt. Hayes. Or Mayor Willford. He's around here somewhere."

"Thanks."

Dylan hurried alongside the house and emerged in the sloping backyard. A dock that used to jut out into the canal lay in ruins, branches had been torn off trees, chairs were overturned, a faucet had been ripped out of the ground. Neighbors mulled around as the cops interviewed them. Ordinary people, he thought, locals who had witnessed something unusual or extraordinarily weird. Or something that was a flat-out mind fuck.

He walked among them, listening, vigilant until a skinny cop noticed him and marched over. "You a neighbor, sir? A witness?"

"Nope. Name's Dylan, George Dylan." He brought out his I.D. and the cop looked surprised. "CIA? Why?"

Dylan didn't clarify. "Your name?"

"Lt. Ray Hayes."

"So tell me what happened here, Ray."

The lieutenant rubbed his hand through his neatly trimmed dark beard. "Wish I knew. According to witnesses... " He gestured at the men and women talking to a big guy with broad shoulders and muscular arms, dressed in jeans, a t-shirt, running shoes. "... a woman, Sofia Lopez, was carried away in some sort of freak weather phenomenon, except Tango weather wasn't reporting any freak weather thing here or anywhere else in the keys."

"What kind of weather?"

Hayes twirled his index finger in the air. "Tornadic activity."

"A tornado tore up that dock?"

"Yes, sir."

"But didn't touch the trees on the other side of the canal or tear up any yards nearby."

"You got it."

Yeah, he got it, all right. "People actually saw Ms. Lopez being carried away'?"

"That's right."

"Is she still missing?"

"Yes."

Was she even alive? Sofia Lopez had been working with Luke Pierce when they had investigated Justin's disappearance. She and Pierce also had been around when he and Lia Graham had investigated the strange Cat Aldridge case in 2015. That was right before he'd been committed and if he remembered correctly, he hadn't been included in the finer details of that investigation. He did recall talking to Sofia and Dr. Lawrence Aldridge, Cat's father. He had given them copies of his email exchanges with his daughter when she and her husband were in the Dominica Republic, searching for her brother, Duncan. He supposedly had been morphed into an amphibious being like the one Piper had shown him. Sofia and Pierce also had been at the autopsy, had seen the implant scurry through his son's skull when the coroner had tried to remove it. She and Pierce had witnessed the horror Dylan and the coroner had seen.

"And the owner of the house?"

"Luke Pierce."

He'd figured as much. "Is he here?"

"He left with her son and Josh McMullen to look for her."

"Why'd you let them leave?"

"Unless they killed her and got rid of the body—a damn unlikely scenario—they didn't break any laws, Mr. Dylan. Right now, my job is just to take testimony. A missing person report on Ms. Lopez can't be filed until she's been missing for at least twenty-four hours. They have every right to look for her."

"Look where?"

"Beats the crap outta me."

"You another witness?" The big dude joined them.

"This is Mayor Ben Willford," Hayes said. "Mayor, this here is George Dylan, with the CIA."

Willford looked amused. "No shit. You got creds to verify that?"

This man already annoyed him. He held up his ID and the mayor's eyes widened. "So why's the CIA interested in anything that happened here, Mr. Dylan?"

"Our interest is in the recent sightings here on the island and what Omega may know about them. Both Luke Pierce and Sofia Lopez work for Omega."

Something new came into the mayor's eyes, Dylan thought, something dark, strange. Curiosity? Eagerness? Or something more sinister, like a bone to grind with Omega or with Pierce or Sofia? "So the CIA's chasing UFOs now?"

Dylan forced himself to chuckle. "C'mon, Mayor Willford. Not officially, but that's nothing new."

Hayes jammed his hands into the pockets of his jacket and rocked forward and back on his heels. "So you spook guys actually think those sightings were of an honest-to-Christ UFO?"

"Let me put it this way, Ray. UFO means unidentified flying object. So far, satellite photos haven't been able to identify what that object was. That makes it a UFO. The fact that it crashed several miles off the island's west coast makes it particularly interesting."

"And means it's likely no one is going to find it," Willford said. "Couple miles out, the Gulf floor drops off more than a mile."

"Anyone have video of this tornado?"

Willford nodded. "We have several. Give me your number. I'll text them."

Dylan reeled off the number for his burner phone and when the videos came through, a chill gnawed up his spine. *Same whirlwind. Identical.* He forwarded the videos to John Piper. "Thanks, Mayor."

"You look sorta spooked, Mr. Dylan. You seen something like this before?"

"Yeah, I have. You mind if I have a look around?"

"Go right ahead. We'll be here for awhile yet. If we can be of any help, give a holler."

"Thanks." Before Dylan turned away, he caught the look that passed between Willford and Hayes, common among law enforcement personnel. *Keep an eye on him.*

Dylan wasn't at all sure what a *look around* might reveal other than the level of destruction to the dock. He snapped photos of the scene—the collapsed pilings, the planks torn out of the dock and littering the yard, the deck's aluminum sink in pieces, a fishing pole snapped in two. The hose that presumably had been attached to the faucet had been shredded to the consistency of coleslaw.

When he'd seen the video of the tornadic whirlwind that had occurred the night of Justin's disappearance, he finally had understood what had eluded him for years, the source of that spinning maelstrom. It was telekinetic. In the nuthouse they'd called it psychoshit because the guy who claimed he could move objects with his mind, a vet suffering from PTSD, had been totally nuts. Yet, one night, he'd shown them what he could do.

Dylan recalled how the vet had thrown the bolt on the living room door of the nuthouse and stuff immediately had leaped and somersaulted into the air, almost as if the ability, the power, had been itching to escape. The table had spun across the room and blocked the door, lights had shattered, flowers in plastic vases lifted up and drifted like butterflies around the room. Dylan and five other patients had witnessed the spectacle.

When pounding had erupted at the door, everything that had been airborne dropped to the floor, the table slid back across the room to its former position, and the only light bulb that hadn't shattered flared again. It had impressed Dylan. But the energy the vet had triggered was nothing compared to what the ET had created the night that Justin was abducted.

The nuthouse experts—shrinks and neurologists and nurses—had questioned him and the other witnesses relentlessly. But they'd refused to accept Dylan's contention that the vet was telekinetic. They believed it had been sleight of hand, something pulled out of a magician's bag of tricks.

He walked up to the house and paused outside the open garage. Close up, the old van in the driveway looked worse. He opened the rear hatch and was struck by a familiar odor. His son's body had smelled like this the day he'd washed up on the beach—not of rotting flesh saturated with salt water, not of death, but of something so terribly sweet that if it were a taste, it would make your mouth pucker. He didn't know what it meant.

Dylan checked the rest of the car—the shattered windshield, shards of glass on the floor and seats, dirt and dust and debris. Had the damage to the van been done by the tornadic wind? This seemed unlikely since nothing else in the immediately vicinity looked damaged. He turned on his phone's video and walked into the tidy garage, capturing the white Prius, the workbench with tools organized neatly on hooks, the two bikes on a wall rack, a rope hanging down from an attic door. He moved the camera slowly through the garage, looking for anything unusual, anything that stood out.

The size of the floor freezer bugged him. He walked over to it, raised the lid, took a video of the interior. The contents were precisely arranged, organized, tidy. Frowning, he stopped the video. Why was water running from the back of the freezer out into the garage? He moved around to the far side of the freezer, peered behind it, and spotted two previously frozen and now melting whole chickens and a melting steak.

Weird. How had those items gotten back there in an otherwise fastidiously organized garage and freezer? He moved the freezer out far enough from the wall so he could videotape the items clearly, then used the handle of a broom to push them out into the open.

He crouched and examined them. The steak, broken into four pieces. The chickens were also broken—legs snapped off, breast bones shattered, pieces now floating in an inch of water. You could slam a hammer against a frozen chicken or steak and not break it the way these items were broken. Given the condition of the garage compared to that in the backyard, the tornadic whirlwind hadn't been in here. So what had happened?

He opened the freezer lid again, touched the items inside. Frozen solid. But as he dug around, he found other broken items—a frozen pizza in a dozen fragments, two shattered Cornish hens, plastic bottles of frozen water that had split in two, plastic containers of orange juice and lemonade that had broken apart and then refrozen just like the water.

The sound of an arriving car distracted him and he glanced out toward the driveway. A Mercedes SUV stopped at the crime tape and a tall, gray-haired man got out, leaning on a cane. He looked vaguely familiar to Dylan but it wasn't until the man faced the cop who approached him that the familiarity clicked into recognition.

"Holy shit." He moved the broken frozen goods back into the freezer, shut the lid, and hastened out of the garage.

"I'm sorry, sir," the cop was saying. "But without the proper credentials, I can't..."

"He's with me," Dylan told the cop. "Dr. Aldridge, thank you so much for coming."

Aldridge's eyes bulged like that of a man choking. "I got

here as soon as I could, Agent Dylan."

They walked past the cop, Aldridge moving slowly, his cane tapping along in front of him. When they were far enough away from the cop so they couldn't be overhead, Aldridge said, "My God, George, what in the world are you doing here?"

"The same thing you are, I imagine."

"I'd heard you had a breakdown shortly after the debacle at Homestead, when my daughter escaped."

"I did. I'm no longer with the agency, but Lia Graham made sure I have the ID that says otherwise. I heard that you became a consultant to Omega."

Aldridge shrugged. "I did for awhile. I loved working with Sofia and Luke, but Ted Fisher was too dogmatic. He started ordering me around and I told him to fuck off. He didn't lose two kids to these monsters."

"What tipped you off to come here?"

"It's going to sound nuts."

"Nothing sounds nuts to me anymore."

"In a dream, my daughter tipped me off. She told me to look for freak storms."

Interesting, Dylan thought. "So she and your son have never been found."

"Nope. They supposedly have been sighted, though, around the Bahamas and Tango Key. I don't know if it's accurate. At any rate, this is what I do now, follow sightings and freak storms."

"Me, too, Larry."

Aldridge held his gaze for a moment, his haunted eyes searching Dylan's face. "These aliens fucks have defined our lives." He paused. "Have you heard from Lia Graham recently?"

"Not for a year. Why?"

"She called me yesterday, but didn't leave a message."

"Maybe she heard about the sighting." How odd, though, that she would call Aldridge and not him. He felt he should text or call her or something, but didn't want things between them to start all over again. It wasn't fair to her.

They entered the garage and Aldridge looked around slowly. "What happened here?"

"Damned if I know. " Dylan explained what he did know,

then raised the lid of the freezer and showed Aldridge the frozen items that had broken apart, pointed at the chickens and steak. "This garage is so fastidious that I'm puzzled why a couple of chickens and a steak were behind the freezer."

Aldridge examined everything with the careful precision of a physician. "Fascinating."

"It takes an enormous force to break frozen foods in that way."

"Let's conduct a little experiment, George. Is there a hammer anywhere in this garage?"

Dylan nodded and went over to the meticulous workbench, grabbed a hammer, returned to the freezer. Aldridge dug deep into the frozen goods and came out with a slab of what looked like frozen venison, another whole chicken, and a package of four turkey patties.

"I don't know why a single guy has a freezer filled with so much food, but it sure looks to me like he's stocking up for a bad hurricane season," Aldridge remarked.

"Or for the apocalypse."

Aldridge set everything on the floor of the garage, poked his fingers at each item. "Frozen solid, right?"

Dylan poked his fingers into them, verifying. "For sure."

"Okay, here goes." Aldridge set his cane against the freezer, then raised his surprisingly muscular arms and slammed the hammer down against the turkey paddies. They broke apart. Next: the whole chicken. The package that held the chicken—cardboard and cellophane wrap—popped open, but the chicken remained intact. "Shit," Aldridge said.

"Yeah."

"Okay, the venison." He struck the slab ferociously half a dozen times and the venison didn't break or chip, but the head of the hammer flew off and clattered against the garage floor. He dropped the handle. "Christ, George, I think you're onto something. And you said you found those two chickens and a steak behind the freezer?"

"Yeah." Dylan nodded and showed him the video, then picked up the stuff from the floor, dropped it all back into the freezer, shut the lid.

"And the van. What damaged that van?"

"No telling," said a man behind them. "And you are who, exactly?"

Dylan and Aldridge looked around. Mayor Ben Willford stood there, staring suspiciously at Aldridge. "I called him," Dylan said, and introduced them.

"A medical doc?" Willford asked.

"Right."

"You practice on Tango?"

"Did for awhile, after I retired from teaching at the University of Miami medical school."

"Really." Willford looked impressed. "What type of medicine did you teach?"

"Psychiatry."

The right answer for Willford, Dylan thought.

"Considering the level of weirdness that occurred here..." Willford gestured at the van, stabbed his thumb over his shoulder. "... and out back, we could use a shrink's expertise."

"A tornadic wind?" Aldridge asked.

"That's what the videos show, what the neighbors report. I'm no expert on this anomalous stuff. But Tango Key has had its share of strange things over the years—sightings, reports of alien abductions, ghosts, all sorts of woo-woo shit. At the very least, I'm a skeptical researcher. Granted, I'm less skeptical these days, but my sense is that you guys aren't skeptics or amateurs."

"We've been doing this a long time," Aldridge replied.

"With the CIA?" Willford asked.

"And other federal agencies," Dylan replied. "Dr. Aldridge keeps things grounded and in perspective. Question, Mayor. Did that tornadic wind come in here?"

"Doubtful. Why?"

Dylan explained what he'd found, showed him the video, and Aldridge added, "So we conducted our own little experiment, trying to figure out what would be powerful enough to break frozen chickens and a frozen steak."

Willford's eyed them both. "Why?"

"Isn't it obvious?" Dylan said. "Something strange happened here, Mayor Willford. A UFO supposedly crashed off Tango's western shore on the sixth, both Pierce and Sofia Lopez work for Omega, an outfit that..."

"Yeah, I know what they do. So tell me, gentlemen. Are we being visited by little green guys from Mars?"

Aldridge looked amused. "They're not green."

"You have proof?" Willford asked.

"What constitutes proof for you?" Aldridge asked. "Videos? Photos? Those things can be photo shopped."

Willford laughed, an odd chopped up sound like a hiccup or a burp. "Oh, I don't know. How about an alien body? And the two of you, my first name's not mayor. It's Ben."

And because Dylan felt the good ole boy mayor might facilitate things for them and because Aldridge hadn't seen it yet, he slipped the Baggie out of his jacket pocket that held the bit of shell that pilot John Piper had given him yesterday. The mysterious thing he'd experimented with for half the night. He held the Baggie up to the light. "What's this look like, Ben?"

"A shell."

"Dr. Aldridge?"

"A piece of a broken shell, burned around the edges."

"Uh-huh. That's what I thought, too. Now watch."

Dylan opened the Baggie, removed the shell, set it in the palm of his left hand. As the heat of his skin penetrated it, the shell expanded, turned colors, and repeated every step that he'd seen yesterday when Piper has shown this to him. When the image of the cockpit and the being's hand and dual thumbs appeared, Ben Willford wrenched back, gasping as if he'd been struck in the chest.

Aldridge stood there in shock, blood draining from his face. "My God."

"I believe this entity is what was in that UFO that crashed off Tango's western shore."

"And it's *alive*?" Willford burst out. "It survived the crash?"

"I think so."

"And the piece of shell that is... is showing this?" Aldridge asked. "Where did you get it?"

"Found it on the beach. I think it's part of the craft, that the craft is organic, holographic... " Dylan launched into the truncated version of the explanation Piper had given him, but didn't mention the pilot's name.

Willford struggled to absorb the information, undoubtedly all new to him. But Dylan suspected that for Aldridge, it was a confirmation of what he'd uncovered since the loss of his son and his daughter. Dylan returned the shell to the Baggie, slipped it back into his pocket. Willford leaned against the freezer, lit a smoke, tried to compose himself and failed.

"You two want to hear my theory?" Willford asked.

"About?" Aldridge asked.

"About what's going on here. I think Luke Pierce found the alien at the lighthouse, brought it back here, maybe thought it was dead, put it into his freezer only to find out it wasn't dead. And that it had some sort of, I don't know, weird power that defies gravity. That would explain the chaos in the freezer, the tornado in the yard that destroyed the dock, and what happened to the Lopez woman."

"Why do you think that?" Dylan asked.

"Because a day after the sighting, the governor closed the lighthouse for repairs. The governor is close buds with Ted Fisher, who owns Omega and is Luke Pierce's employer."

"And Sofia Lopez was Omega's employee for eight years," Dylan added. "She left about a year ago, but is apparently back again."

"What's her expertise?"

"She's a clairvoyant," Aldridge said.

"Aw, c'mon, a psychic? As *I come into your vibration* shit? Like that?"

"Uh, no," Dylan replied. "As in, the real deal."

"Doc, as a shrink, are there *real deals* among psychics?"

"Yes."

"And how do you guys know about her?"

Here goes, Dylan thought. "Because three years ago she was part of the Omega team that investigated my son's disappearance." He provided an abbreviated version of the story, enough so that Willford would believe him, but not every sordid detail. And nothing about Sophia's impressions of what had happened to his son.

"Jesus," Willford murmured. "And what about you, Doc?"

Aldridge looked stricken. "I lost two children."

With that revelation, Willford stopped asking questions.

"Look, we've shared some classified info here with you, Ben. Please keep it to yourself," Dylan said.

"Yeah, no problem. But where do you two go from here?"

"Find the Lopez woman. Find Luke Pierce. Go to Ted Fisher. Uncover what they suspect, what they know. Do they have the body? Is it dead or alive?"

"Fisher. He's got twenty-five acres in the wilderness preserve that's like a fortress," Willford said. "Private security. Impenetrable."

"That's where he lives?"

"That's the location of the Omega headquarters. I don't have any idea where he actually lives. No one does."

Aldridge looked surprised. "How's that even possible? Tango's not that big."

"When you're worth nearly a billion bucks, Doc, anything is possible. Anything at all," Willford remarked. "Word is that Omega has completed a spaceship that's going to colonize an asteroid. Or Mars. Or some damn place. They've got ex-NASA engineers working for them, men and women who are among the brightest on this planet."

Dylan filed all this information in that mental folder labeled, JUSTIN. In the three years since his son's death, this was the closest he'd gotten to the truth. The closest he'd gotten to one of the aliens responsible for the tragedy that had defined his adult life. He sensed it was also the closest Aldridge had gotten, too.

The fire in his belly burned fiercely.

"Mind if I take a look out back, Ben?" Aldridge asked.

"No, no, of course not. I'll walk back with you."

"Me, too," Dylan said.

Not much had changed out back. Neighbors still being interviewed, videos exchanged, but Aldridge apparently wasn't interested in talking to people. He made his way to the edge of the ruined dock, leaning more heavily on his cane now, and surveyed the destruction. He snapped photos. Spoke into his phone. One of the cops called Willford over and Dylan joined Aldridge at the edge of the yard.

"Incredible, isn't it, Larry."

He looked at Dylan, his glasses magnifying the blue of his haunted eyes. "It was telekinetic. Do you know the full story on my daughter?"

"Only what I learned when Graham and I first looked into the case. I had my breakdown midway through the investigation. You sent me some of the email exchanges. I know that Cat went to the Dominica Republic with her husband to look for her brother, who had been turned into one of the amphibious things."

Aldridge nodded. "That's only the tip of it. Your agency knew about it and Director Jerry Fleming came to me offering whatever help he could, like with funding. He and I go back a ways. His son was one of my students some years before."

New details. Dylan listened closely.

"My daughter and her husband already had planned a trip to the interior of the DR, where Duncan was last sighted. Long story short, she had an encounter with her brother, her husband was captured by this...this pod of unspeakable monsters, and she fled. A transport from Gitmo picked her up and took her to Homestead. Lia Graham was my contact throughout this horror.

"During the night at Homestead, Cat started to change and was transferred to a swimming pool on the base. I wanted to transfer her to the Miami Seaquarium, the chopper had arrived to do that, but at this point my attorney and I were escorted from the base. Here's what followed."

He brought up a video of a huge swimming pool surrounded by total chaos, with chairs and towels and lockers swirling above the pool, windows exploding, and a tall, strange-looking being loping toward the exit.

"That's Cat." He pointed at his transformed daughter. "She was last seen leaping into a canal behind the base. That chaos in the swimming area? Telekinetic. The tornadic wind that allegedly ripped up Pierce's dock? It was also described by witnesses at Homestead. It's the same MO, George."

"I know."

"Now tell me how you got that piece of shell that isn't a shell."

"From John Piper, the pilot of Flight 156, who I'm going to meet up with when I leave here. Want to join me?"

"Definitely."

With that settled, they walked over to Willford. Dylan said, "We need to get moving, Ben. But let's stay in touch."

"Dude, I'm in your back pocket."

He didn't want the mayor quite that close. But a handshake sealed their new partnership and Dylan and Aldridge started toward the front of the house where their cars were. "Here's a quantum physics question for you, George. If the parts of the craft are greater than the whole, will it show you where the remains of the craft are?"

"Maybe. But John has a pretty clear idea of where the craft went down, so the plan is to take his boat out to the area and dive for a look."

"I don't dive, but I'll man the boat. Okay with you?"

They were standing by Aldridge's Mercedes then and Dylan took his hand and held it tightly between both of his own. "Larry, I'm so grateful you showed up." He started choking up, tears burned the backs of his eyes. "Losing my son... was... "

"I know," Aldridge said gently.

"But losing two children like you did, I can't... even imagine what kind of hell you've gone through the last two years."

Emotion collapsed Aldridge's face and he hugged Dylan. "We're going to win. One way or another, we're going to get our kids back."

Aldridge might, Dylan thought, since his kids were still alive. But Justin was dead.

The neurologist stepped back, his eyes bright with tears. "I'll meet you at the marina."

"Slip twenty-two."

Dylan followed Old Post Road along the western side of the island, glancing periodically in the rear view mirror to make sure Aldridge was still behind him. He called Piper en route. They had touched base earlier this morning after Dylan had heard about the freak storm. Piper had told him to call when he finished, that he didn't intend to go diving until it was low tide. That was now.

Piper answered on the second ring. "Hey, George. I'm about to head out. Where're you?"

"Almost to the marina. We're going to have a third person with us." He quickly explained.

"Goddamn, George. You may be my lucky charm. Should I rent gear for him?"

"No need. He doesn't dive. He'll man the boat."

"The tide's perfect. Hurry up."

Several minutes later, Dylan swung into the marina parking lot, and Aldridge pulled in alongside him.

2.

At one time, the Tango Marina had accommodated boats and seaplanes in the same area. But when the marina was expanded and deepened and cruise ships began regular stops here, the seaplane tie-down part of the marina had been moved to Pirate's Cove and the small vessel section had been moved behind the scuba and bait shops. Not exactly the easiest cove to get out of during the tourist season, he thought, but it made Piper's blue and white boat easy to spot.

Dylan grabbed his pack out of the trunk and waited for Aldridge to catch up. A small pack was slung over his shoulder. "Where're you staying, Larry?"

"Nowhere yet. I was in Key West with a friend when I had that dream. I'm loose and ready for anything. My stuff's in the trunk. You?"

"B and B on the island. I've got an extra bed. You're welcome to stay with me."

They strode through the warm sunlight, out toward the dock where the boat, Mile High, was tied up. It had two outboard engines, a canopy, and a small cabin.

Piper welcomed them aboard, gestured at the scuba gear. "Two tanks of air apiece. That should be plenty for what we're going to do. And Larry, with the canopy, you'll have plenty of shade, there's cold water and food in the cooler, and the Internet signal is good out on the open water."

"Great. Thanks for letting me tag along."

Piper got a kick out of that. "Hey, from the little George told me, you know a hell of a lot more about all this than we do. I'm glad you're joining us."

"Mayor Willford said that a few miles offshore, the Gulf floor drops to a mile or more," Dylan remarked. "Is that true?"

"Yup." Piper nodded. "It's a trench that runs for ten, eleven miles. But just beyond it, the floor rises again. And that's where the craft came down. I rechecked the coordinates I'd noted the day of the sighting. Go change and I'll get us out into the open gulf."

Dylan went below deck with his pack and in the tiny head, changed into swimming trunks and a tank top. One of the first things he'd done when he'd been released from the nuthouse was to renew his diving certificate. Scuba diving was something he and his son had done often together. When he was underwater, he often felt that Justin was there with him, pointing our coral reefs, interesting fish, caverns, the diving buddy who had his back.

Piper took them more than three miles offshore, stopped the engine, dropped anchor, and put up a dive flag. As they geared up, Aldridge helped with their tanks, and Piper asked him if Dylan had shown him the shell.

"To me and the mayor."

"Bet that blew Willford's mind."

"Mine, too," Aldridge said.

"I told him I found it on the beach, John," said Dylan. "Your name wasn't mentioned."

"Thanks, but Willford isn't a threat to me. You got your shell with you, George?"

"Yeah, zipped into a pocket in my swim suit."

"Good spot for it. I've got mine, too, and an underwater GoPro that will capture everything we see."

"You think these shells will help?"

"Definitely. I've been experimenting a lot with mine. What'd you find out about that weird weather anomaly?"

"That it wasn't weather," Dylan replied, and explained. "It felt right to engage Willford, get him on our side. I told him only what he needed to know. He speculates that Luke Pierce found the ET's body, took it back to his place. If that's true, then the ET he found wasn't dead, but was badly injured and revived and created such complete havoc that a psychic who works for Omega was taken. There were witnesses, the video I emailed you."

Piper nodded, dipped his mask into the water to clear it, fitted it on top of his head. "Right now, I believe almost anything. Let's go find our own proof, George. You good, Larry?"

Aldridge flashed a thumbs up, poked his glasses farther back up on the bridge of his nose, helped himself to a bottle of cold water from the cooler, and sat down. Piper fitted the mask over his face and tumbled backward off the boat.

Dylan followed him.

3.

The water was achingly clear and Dylan sank with complete abandon, loving the environment in which he found himself. Small, colorful fish swam past his mask, close enough for him to touch. Ten yards to his right, he spotted a manta ray, moving gracefully along with the current, away from him and Piper.

Piper gestured at a coral reef thirty feet or so deeper than where they were. The GoPro was attached to his forehead, with a bright light that pointed downward. Dylan started swimming in that direction. His breathing was good, the air in his tank was at full capacity. He unzipped the pocket in his swim trunks and brought out the Baggie that held the shell. He noticed that Piper had done the same. Nothing about the shell looked unusual and he was afraid that if he removed it from the Baggie, it would float away from him. The Baggie, of course, might do the same, so he stuffed it back in his pocket, zipped it shut.

When they were at about seventy feet, Dylan's ears started popping, the part he hated about diving. Then he was at the coral reef, marveling at the shape and texture and pallid color. The reef was dying and there was nothing he, an ordinary citizen, could do about it. Somehow, the survival of coral reefs—something so basic to the survival of the planet—had gotten entangled in politics and now reefs all around the world were dying.

He swam closer to the reef and suddenly saw his son in full dive gear on the far side of it, wiggling his gloved fingers. *Over here, Dad. Take a look. What d'ya think?*

Justin looked whole, alive, *real*, that most of all. "Justin," he shouted.

It sounded like baby talk, the inside of his mask clouded up. Was he hallucinating?

Then Justin was at his side, touching his arm—a physical touch, he could feel it through his suit—and stabbed his hand below them, indicating something partially buried in the sand. Dylan didn't give a damn about finding pieces of the craft. He just wanted to stay close to his dead son's side. He clasped Justin's arm, their eyes met. *Love you,* his son's eyes signaled, and he hugged Dylan awkwardly, tightly, an embrace so real that Dylan's heart nearly burst with joy. Bubbles floated up around them, between them, an indication that his son was breathing, *alive,* that Dylan wasn't hallucinating or imagining this.

He moved back, still clutching his son's forearm. *How? How's this happening?*

Justin pointed down at the rocks and sand below them, then broke away from Dylan and swam fast toward the Gulf floor, leaving a trail of bubbles behind him. Dylan swam rapidly after him, through all those bubbles, evidence of life.

When he reached the rocks and sand, Justin was nowhere in sight. Dylan looked around desperately and saw Piper swimming toward him, gesturing wildly. Dylan's flippers touched the sand. Like powder, it drifted upward, revealing the curved edge of an object. With his gloved hands, Dylan reached down and struggled to pull the object out of the sand. He couldn't do it. He clawed at the sand, dug around it, clearing it away from the object, and when Piper reached him, they managed to pull it free.

It looked like a much larger version of the bit of shell in his pocket, perhaps fifteen feet wide, twenty feet from top to bottom, but lightweight. And it appeared to be glowing. Piper looked at him, eyes wide with shock, and held out the Baggie with his piece of shell in it. The thing glowed and so did the shell in Dylan's Baggie.

Dylan stabbed his thumb upward, Piper nodded. They shoved their respective Baggies back into their pockets and, clutching either side of the object, swam toward the surface. They were at ninety-two feet when they started, so they surfaced slowly, pausing every five or six feet. He knew that for every 33 feet in ocean water, the pressure due to nitrogen went up another 11.6 pounds per square inch. As the pressure due to nitrogen increased, more nitrogen dissolved into their tissues. The longer they remained at depth, the more nitrogen dissolved, and the more likely it was that they would develop the bends. The problem was that Dylan didn't know how long they'd been down here.

He tapped Piper's arm, then his watch.

Piper shook his head. He didn't know, either.

Slow, we need to take this really slow, Dylan thought.

Awhile later, his gauge said they were still deep—72 feet. And his air gauge told him he would run out of air before they reached the top. He motioned at Piper, tapped his air gauge. Piper glanced at his gauge, flashed a thumbs up. They would share his air if it came to that. Even so, panic built up inside Dylan and he forced himself to breathe slowly, evenly. They moved up another five feet, paused, then another ten feet and paused again.

Piper turned off the GoPro, let it hang around his neck. Dylan wished he hadn't done that. The bright light had helped him see details that were now lost in shadow. As if to compensate, the glow of the object strengthened, brightened, a luminous blue tinged with violet.

The light from the piece of the craft was now so bright he couldn't look at it directly. The Baggie in his pocket abruptly burst through the zipper in his suit, the Baggie shredded, and that bit of shell zipped toward the larger object they held and glommed onto it. The same thing happened to the piece that Piper had. Suddenly, as if these two missing pieces energized the larger piece, the craft started moving upward of its own volition, up and up at a pace so rapid that Dylan feared both he and Piper would end up with the bends. But neither of them was willing to release it, not now, not when they were so close to whatever secrets it held.

They burst through the surface, Dylan gulping at the air, and the object dragged them thirty yards across the water as though they were skiers. Then it lifted about twenty feet from the surface of the water, the two of them clutching it, their masks askew, regulators dangling around their necks, their flippers gone, their tanks a terrible weight.

When the object was over Piper's boat and Dylan saw Aldridge gesturing frantically for him to drop onto the canvas awning, he did so. Dylan slammed into the awning, it ripped but not completely, and he was able to shed his tank before he rolled off the awning and onto the deck. He landed so hard on his feet that his knees gave way.

Aldridge was instantly at his side, helping him up. "My God, I can't fucking believe what I just saw," he burst out. "You okay, George?"

"I... think so."

Seconds later, Piper slammed to the deck on his side. Groaning, he pushed up. "What the hell just happened?"

Before Dylan could find his voice, the object dropped, light as a feather, onto the back deck.

4.

Dylan stared at it. From where he stood, he could see the left side of it, the perfect curve of its edge. It no longer glowed, but a pulsating noise emanated from it, like the amplified sound of a beating heart.

He stood shakily, peeled off his wet suit, tore off the mask, dropped the regulator, and made his way toward it. Slowly. Heart hammering. Aldridge, just ahead of him, limped without his cane. Dylan gripped the side of the boat to keep himself steady, kept blinking hard to clear his vision, and tried not to think about his interaction with his dead son down there at ninety-plus feet. Tried not to think about how real that embrace had been. Tried and failed.

When he reached Aldridge at the back of the boat, he dropped to his knees, and sprawled across the object, whispering, "Please bring him back. Please." His cheek pressed against the wet warmth that covered the surface of this strange, alien object, a broken craft. "Please let me be with him again."

The pulsating sound stopped.

Aldridge touched his back. "George, take it easy. Breathe through it."

Breathe, yes, breathe.

Dylan lifted his head, ran his hands over the markings on the surface of the object, then crossed his arms and rested his forehead against them. He had never felt so alone.

After what seemed a long time, he heard Piper and Aldridge talking. About the cut on Piper's forehead. About what Aldridge has seen. Then Aldridge said, "John, boats are headed toward us."

Dylan wanted to move, but couldn't.

"Larry, can you get into the cabin?" Piper's voice sounded urgent, scared. "There're tarps in there. We need to cover the craft. I'll get us underway."

Dylan finally sat up, glanced at the two men. "I saw my dead son. He was scuba diving with us. He hugged me. He was alive."

Piper, now on his feet, held a towel to his temple that was soaked through with blood. "I saw my old man, dead for twenty years. He was scuba diving, too." He paused, looked down at the remains of the craft. "I don't know what the hell this is, but we need to get it somewhere safe."

Dylan knew it wouldn't fit in the trunk of his car and said as much.

"It might fit in the back of my SUV if the seats are down," Aldridge said.

"Or in the back of my truck," Piper said. "And we can stow it in a storage unit I rent in Pirate's Cove."

"It's alive," said Dylan.

"Not in the way we define life," Aldridge said. "But yes, there's life here. Consciousness."

Piper patted the object twice, pressed his hands against his thighs, and the bloody towel fell away from his temple. Blood remained, a lot of it smeared across Piper's temple, into his hair, but Dylan didn't see a wound—no gash, no cut, just the drying blood. "Your head, John."

"Yeah, when I hit the deck. It felt like it took away a chunk of my temple."

"No." Aldridge touched Piper's forehead. "Nothing's there. Just dry blood."

"*What?*" Piper's fingers flew to his temple. He hurried to one of the cabin portholes, where he would see his reflection in the glass. "What the hell." He leaned over the side of the boat, splashing water onto his face, washing away the blood, and returned to the window. He touched his temple. "The gash was deep. And it's healed. There's just a hairline scar." Alarmed and bewildered, Piper sprang into action. "Get into the cabin, find those tarps, cover this thing. We're outta here."

Chapter 9

Mike's old truck moved deeper and deeper into the wilderness preserve at the north end of Tango Key, bouncing over dirt roads, gravel roads, footpaths that weren't meant to be roads at all. Trees rose up on either side of them, graceful pines so tall that Sofia couldn't see the tops of them. Spears of sunlight lit up the space between them, birds sang, the air smelled almost sweet.

In the years Sofia had worked for Omega, she'd been to the main office a number of times. She had seen the space craft Ted Fisher was having built for a manned mission to Mars, had met the ex-NASA engineers who were making Fisher's vision a reality. But she'd never been to his private home. In those days, she hadn't even known he and his wife owned a home on Tango Key.

But she wouldn't exactly call the spot that Mike approached a home. It looked like a Hobbit's place, a mountain of rich, dark Tango soil covered with colorful flowers and blooming shrubs with a strange door in the center of it. Surrounding the place were pastures where horses grazed, chickens roamed, cats darted through the sunlight. She spotted a lake where ducks and swans drifted in the heat of midday and could hear an orchestra of frogs. A vast wooded area lay beyond the pastures. Dogs barked somewhere nearby and Cooper immediately sat up, ears twitching, stepped across her to the open windows and barked in response.

"And people say dogs can't communicate," McMullen remarked.

"People who say that have never owned a dog," Pierce said.

An odd remark coming from Pierce, she thought. In the past, he might have made some sarcastic comment like, *Oh, it's just noises they make.* Now that they lived with so many impossible things, maybe his previous worldwide had been turned inside out.

"Stop here, Mike," Pierce said.

Mike pulled up to the Hobbit home and they all got out. When Sofia's webbed feet touched the ground, she once again felt like the outlier. No one else in the group walked as she did, looked at she did, or even thought as she did. She felt less human than she had before the series of events that had begun on Pierce's deck.

She also felt certain the ET was hostile.

The webbing on her right hand had withdrawn completely, giving her hope that the webbing on her left hand and on her feet would do the same. But so far, it hadn't happened.

"You doing okay, mom?" Mike fell into step alongside her.

"Better, hon. Thanks. At some point, I need to get my pack from Luke's place."

"Your stuff is in the back. I grabbed everyone's pack before we left, took everything visible."

She touched his arm, they stopped. "I talked to your dad, Mike. He said he was sorry for the way he treated you but he was thinking with his dick at the time."

"The ET enables you to talk to the *dead*? Jesus, Mom."

It wasn't the response she'd expected from him. "That's your dad's theory."

"Where did you see him? When?"

Sofia told him about the two events, painfully aware of just how strange it sounded even to her. "My phone was ruined from water, Mike, and he picked it up and held it between his hands for awhile and then it worked."

"Wow." Mike looked down at the path, kicked at some stones. "Look, Mom. Just so you know. I forgave him a long time ago. He did the best he could. And I came out pretty good, right?"

She slung an arm over his shoulder. "You're the best."

They stopped behind Pierce as he rapped his knuckles against the arched, wooden Hobbit door, a rustic green wooden door that had been sanded and refurbished to look old and weathered. When the door opened, Carmen Fisher threw out her arms. *"Bienvenidos, todos!"* She motioned them inside and hugged Sofia hello.

"Sofia. Que magnifico que estas aqui!"

"Soy un monstruo." I'm a monster. Sofia stepped back, holding up her hands, pointing at her feet.

"Ay, Dios mio, eres una sirena!" Oh my God, you're a mermaid.

Sirena sounded more romantic and mythic than mermaid. Or monster. "No gills yet."

Carmen patted her shoulder. "We're going to figure this out." She went over to Mike. "You've grown since I last saw you, Miguel. *Bienvenido a mi casa."*

In perfect Spanish, Mike told her how wonderful it was to see her again and gave her a hug. The Fishers were always big huggers.

Pierce introduced her to McMullen, who looked nearly overwhelmed. "Luke tells me you're worried about your job at the lighthouse, Mr. McMullen. But please know you'll have a job regardless. You've helped us immeasurably."

"Thank you, ma'am. I appreciate it."

"Let's get you all comfortable and fed. Ted should be along once he finishes whatever he's doing."

Carmen looked just as Sofia remembered her, salt and pepper hair gathered at the back of her head with an ornate wooden comb, a colorful silk skirt tied at her slender waist, a violet silk shirt tucked into it. She was barefoot and wore a necklace that held a beautiful piece of moldavite, known as the "ET " stone.

They followed her into a spacious living room where sliding glass doors were open to the February air. It overlooked a wide veranda that offered a stunning view of the preserve and, beyond it, the glistening Gulf of Mexico. A banquet of food was set out on a large glass coffee table with pitchers of lemonade, iced tea, hot coffee, plates, glasses, mugs. "Help yourselves. Sofia, if you want to get out of those damp clothes, your room is the first door on the left, down the hall."

"Thanks, Carmen."

She waddled over to her pack, which someone had set against the wall, and felt Carmen's eyes burning holes through her webbed feet. Imagine, she thought, how a stranger would react to her.

Sofia slung the pack over her shoulder and made her way toward the hall, her feet making sucking sounds against the terrazzo floor. The hall was long and wide, the walls decorated with family photos of Ted and Carmen and their son at various ages through the years. But there were also photos of Pierce, like a second son to them, and of the engineers who were building the Fisher craft and their families, of the massive buildings that contained pieces of that craft. She saw photos of Ted and Carmen with John Mack, Whitley Strieber, Budd Hopkins, Betty and Barney Hill, some of the fearless explorers in this field.

All the photos screamed, *This is who we are.*

Sofia ducked into the first bedroom on the left and realized it was Carmen's Cuban sanctuary. Cuban art covered one wall, most of them paintings of the *orishas*—saints—in Santeria. Decorating another wall was a gallery of photographs of Havana that spoke to Carmen's sense of history. Against the wall under the windows stood an altar with burning candles, bowls of magical shells, other bowls that held offerings of fruit and candies and honey to the *orishas*. A painting of the Virgin Mary graced the altar—half of her face white, the other half black.

Sofia dropped her pack beside the bed and sat down heavily against it. Her exhaustion was so deep and extreme it was an effort to untie the damp jacket at her waist, to strip off her shirt and jeans, to make her way toward the bathroom.

When the hot water pounded down against her head and shoulders, she pressed her hands against the walls and stared at them. Along the inside of the fingers on her right hand were barely visible bumps that she could feel, the places where the webbing had emerged. The webbing on the fingers of her left hand now felt as soft as her normal skin.

She didn't understand how this had happened.

Over the years, she had read a vast spectrum of individuals with different types of issues—health, emotional, spiritual, past life, jobs, lovers, spouses, kids—but never had she taken on symptoms of whatever ailed them. For her, their issues had served as conduits to the deeper parts of whoever they were. But this was something so entirely different that she had no name for it, no place where she could file it to scrutinize later. It was *on* her body, *of* her body, a grotesque switch that made her feel, ugly, freakish, like a carnie act, some weird scientific experiment that had gone horribly wrong.

Worse than the obvious physical ramifications was the internal stuff- the change in her emotions, her perceptions, her senses. When she'd been underwater, with the nictitating eyelids in place, her vision had been shockingly clear. Her sense of smell was so sharp now that she understood what Cooper experienced when he caught a squirrel scent on the ground, in a tree. Her hearing was so acute she could detect Cooper panting just outside the bathroom door, and even caught snippets of what the others were talking about in the living room.

"… trauma… "

"… tornado… "

"… mayor, cops, witnesses, video, social media… "

She could hear McMullen complimenting Carmen on the delicious food, hear Pierce and Mike commiserating about the events in his backyard, on his dock. She heard Ted Fisher's booming voice when he entered the living room, greeting everyone. She could hear more than she needed to hear and understood that the alien heard all of it through her. She had been transformed sufficiently in a physical sense so that she had become the alien's spy.

If the ET intended to change her completely, as had happened to Cat Aldridge, did that mean there would be some human that looked like her twin but was actually a transformed alien? Did it mean Cat Aldridge had a human twin somewhere who was a transformed alien? How did that work exactly? Did each retain its own memories of life before the transformation? Its own consciousness? She thought that the aliens who now looked human probably did. And they probably retained their paranormal powers, which gave them such a distinct edge over humanity. Otherwise, what would be the point of all this?

It wasn't enough to just *look* human, she thought. They had to know how to *act* human, how to *speak* the language of whatever country they were in, how to *interact* with other humans.

Did the same apply to humans changed into aliens? Would Cat Aldridge recognize her father? Her mother? Her friends and colleagues? Had memories of her life as a human dimmed in the last two years? When she had broken out of Homestead Air Force Base as an amphibious being, she'd left telekinetic chaos behind her. That meant she had been able to draw on the alien's power. Was that true across the board for all the humans who had been changed? Sofia doubted it. Perhaps now, two years later, Cat Aldridge was just an ordinary monster who, if she retained any memories about her human life, might be totally crazy.

If the ET succeeded in a switch that changed her completely, would she remember Mike? Pierce? Cooper? Her grandmother? Would she still be psychic? Would she be able to create conditions conducive for humans to communicate and see their dead loved ones?

This line of thought exhausted her. She pressed her forehead against the tile and stood under the deliciously hot shower for a long time. Could the alien feel the water drumming her back? Could it taste the water when she opened her mouth and it slid down the back of her throat? Could it smell the steam? How far had its senses invaded her own? She was no longer completely human.

She screamed, beat her fists against the wall, begged the alien to switch her back. Nothing happened. When she was thoroughly disgusted with her tirade, she washed her hair and shaved her pits and legs, and thought, *I'm not entirely alien, either, you piece of shit. Even if you succeed at turning me completely, I'll remember everything. And I'll fight you to the death.*

When she opened her eyes, she saw a tree frog in a corner of the shower, watching her with its topaz eyes, its little sucker feet clinging to the tile. She remembered how she and her *abuelita* Rosa used to drive out into the Everglades National Park and walk around looking for pools of tadpoles they would scoop up and transfer to the lake behind Rosa's house.

Then she and Rosa monitored their progress from tadpoles to frogs, recording the various stages of their existence. In the evenings, they sat on her grandmother's back patio, listening to the orchestra of croaks that filled the air, and she would imagine herself as a frog, able to exist on land and in water, her long, beautiful tongue darting here and there to nab insects.

They are symbols of profound transformation, Sofia, her grandmother told her. *When a frog lands on your window, your doorstep, in your home, then you know that big changes are headed into your life. The condition of the frog tells you whether the change is negative or positive. And urges you to act.*

The frog suddenly hopped to the floor, near the drain. Sofia quickly turned off the shower so the creature didn't get scorched by the hot water. She watched it half-swim, half hop to the back of the shower, then it moved up the wall to the panes of the jalousie window. Sofia realized that it eventually would die in here for lack of food. She rolled the window open, punched out the screen, and the frog hopped through it to the outdoors.

How were these amphibious aliens changing the ecological balance in nature for creatures like frogs? For the first time, she fully understood that what was happening to her wasn't just about her. It was that the entire planet—all wildlife, from the smallest insects to the largest mammals—would be drastically changed by the presence of these amphibious ETs. Oceans, continents, weather patterns, food sources, lakes and ponds, jungles and deserts, none of it would escape the terrible imbalance these ETs would create.

The realization stunned her.

She rolled the window shut, whipped a cranberry-colored towel off the rack, rubbed it through her wet hair, wrapped it around her body, and stepped out of the shower. Her feet hugged the thick cranberry-colored bath mat. Infused with a greater awareness of the ramifications of the alien presence, Sofia felt that her group might be all that stood between the aliens and a global ecological catastrophe. And that terrified her. They weren't an army, they didn't have weapons. They were four people—six if she included the Fishers—and a dog.

She moved in front of the sink and the steamy mirror, swiped her palm across the glass to clear it. As she brushed her wet hair, something took shape in the mirror, the reflection of a form behind her, indistinct at first, hazy, like a figure in a dream. Then it became clearer.

The alien.

It—she—looked like Sofia, except much taller.

Sofia spun around. The ET didn't disappear. She stood there, back to the door, watching Sofia. She was at least seven feet tall, had almost human eyes now, a pair of nostrils, a nearly normal mouth, humanlike skin, and in place of that weird tuft of blue hair was Sofia's own hair, damp and thick, tumbling almost to her shoulders.

Fuck.

An illusion? A perceptual manipulation? *Does it matter?*

The alien tucked her hair behind her nearly human ears, held up her human hands with ten fingers splayed—no extra thumbs, no webbing- and glanced down at her human feet with ten toes and no webbing. She looked at Sofia again.

This is how I will look, Sofia.

"Jesus." The words hissed between her lips and suddenly her rage exploded from her. "*You bitch, you can't have my body, you can't switch your hideous body for mine! You lied!*"

The alien stepped closer.

Sofia, paralyzed in front of the sink, couldn't move her arms, couldn't even blink. The alien drew Sofia's hands between both of her human hands, a touch that felt strange, bizarre.

Were tears glistening under the alien's eyes? Or was it a trick?

Sofia struggled to scream, but couldn't, except in her head. *What do you want?*

The answer came as an image—of the ET's craft, whole and undamaged and ready for flight.

Panic coiled in the pit of Sofia's stomach. *You want to go home? Home to your water world, your own kind? Then why are you taking on human attributes? Why are you starting to look like my twin and I'm looking more like you?*

A second image came to her- of this ET now completely changed into a second Sofia, walking through a street somewhere, sipping an espresso. From Starbucks?

It horrified her. "Fuck you! Never!" She tried to shout the words, but they fell into the air as a pathetic whisper.

She finally wrenched free of the spot in front of the sink and mirror and stumbled past the alien, nearly tripping on her webbed feet, and threw open the door. Steam drifted out into the bedroom and when her head snapped around for another look, the alien was gone. But her hands, my God, her hands were completely normal again, all traces of the webbing gone.

Sofia slammed the bathroom door and backed away from it, breath exploding from her lungs, webbed feet slapping the floor, and stumbled out onto the small balcony. She fell forward at the waist, her human hands pressed to her thighs, and struggled to understand what had happened. The healing of her hands, the ETs tears that had indicated compassion, not hostility.

But it was a trick. No compassionate being would do to someone what the alien had done to her. The message was *control*, as in *I control you, Sofia Lopez. You are mine.*

2.

Dylan and Aldridge followed Piper's truck to the outskirts of Pirate's Cove, where the storage facility was located. Flanked by a field with grazing horses on one side and a community of two-story townhouses on the other, the place was deserted at this hour of the day, an enormous relief to Dylan. On the drive over here from the marina, with the huge piece of the craft covered by tarps in the rear of Piper's truck, anxiety nearly had eaten him alive.

Piper pulled up to his unit, hopped out, unlocked the aluminum door, raised it. It clattered noisily and the sound echoed across all the asphalt. Dylan and Aldridge parked parallel to the pasture fence and got out to help. "Can you direct me in?" Piper asked. "It's crowded in there. We're going to have to move stuff around."

Dylan trotted into the storage unit. The truck's headlights illuminated the crowded interior—boat parts, plane parts, a workbench loaded with tools, odds and ends of furniture, cartons stacked like blocks from floor to ceiling. He and Aldridge moved stuff to either side, clearing a path for the truck, and Dylan flicked on the light switch just inside the door. Overhead lights and several floor lamps winked on.

Piper pulled in slowly and Dylan lowered the door of the unit, sealing them inside. The three of them hurried to the back of the truck. "Unless we move a lot of this shit, there's not going to be any room for the craft," Aldridge said.

Piper pointed at the stairs that led to the second story of the unit. "The craft should fit in the loft. Let's lay out some tarps up there first." He grabbed a pair of tarps off the workbench and they started up the stairs.

Dylan noticed that Aldridge had a difficult time negotiating the climb. "Larry, we can spread out the tarps. And John and I can carry the craft up here."

"I'll help you with the tarps and pass on getting the craft up here. Damn Parkinson's has made stairs a challenge."

"You did great on the boat today," Piper said. "Especially in light of all the strangeness."

"A boat, even at sea, is a flat surface. It's stairs that give me fits."

The loft area on the second floor was larger than it had looked from below. Dylan estimated the area was twenty feet by twenty-five or thirty. "Part of it may extend over the railing, but I think it's large enough." They spread the tarps out end to end.

"I've got more tarps that we can use once we've brought it up here."

They returned to the main floor of the unit, Piper lowered the truck's gate, and Dylan peeled back the tarps that covered the craft. It looked like ordinary metal now, its shape less defined, the edges not quite as curved as before. The color seemed darker, as if the power that had propelled it out of the water with the two of them hanging on to it had gone dormant or dissipated altogether.

"Even from up here, it looks dead." Aldridge stood at the loft railing, looking down. "But maybe it's just the light."

Piper stared at it. "Like we talked about earlier, I don't think it was ever alive in the way we understand life."

Their comments hung in the cool silence, riddles without answers. Dylan yearned to touch it, to reconnect with his dead son, to see Justin striding over to them to help move the craft. But when he finally brought his hands to the dark, cool surface, nothing weird happened. He felt the grooves and nicks in the metal that were the inscriptions or symbols he'd seen when they were out on the boat.

He slid his hands along the underside, lifted it slightly. "I think it's heavier than it was, John."

Piper nodded; his hands were also touching, lifting. "We won't be able to carry it by moving side by side up the stairs."

Dylan climbed into the truck, grasped the back curve of the craft, and Piper took hold of the front it. The overhead lights glinted against the dark metal as the craft tilted downward toward Piper. Its shape seemed erratic—no cigar or football now. It rested briefly against the floor, Dylan jumped down from the truck and they moved it away from the vehicle toward the stairs.

He had no idea how much it weighed, but it was definitely forty or fifty pounds heavier than it had been on the truck. Was that significant? Did it mean something? And if so, what? If the craft was conscious or alive in some sense, did the increased weight mean it was succumbing to gravity? Adjusting to it? Had that even been an issue?

Before they reached the stairs, the craft became lighter, started humming, and a soft, pulsating blue light spread from its curved edge across the rest of it. Then it lifted into the air. Dylan and Piper, too shocked to move, watched as it neared the ceiling of the storage unit and hovered there.

"What the fuck," Aldridge burst out, and backpedaled out of the way, toward the mouth of the stairs.

The craft finally began to sink slowly downward, almost as though it had been waiting for Aldridge to move.

Dylan and Piper raced up the stairs and paused next to

Aldridge, who grasped the railing with one hand and leaned heavily on his cane with the other. The truncated craft settled against the tarps they had spread out, the pulsating light faded. The three of them approached the craft slowly, warily.

"It looks too… flat to be able to accommodate anyone inside of it," Aldridge said.

"Maybe it's like the shell," Pierce speculated. "And expands with heat."

"It wasn't flat as it was plunging toward the Gulf," Piper said. "I'm a hundred percent certain of that much."

A faint mist emanated from it, odorless and barely visible. Dylan felt it against his face and arms as a cool dampness. "You feel it?" he whispered.

Piper grunted, Aldridge nodded. They moved to the far side of the craft, their backs to the wall. "From there." Piper pointed at one of the inscriptions on the surface of the metal. "I think that's where it's coming from."

The mist thickened and spread, eddying like a rapidly moving current to every corner of the loft. Dylan had the presence of mind to bring out his phone, to videotape what was happening. Three figures appeared in the mist at the top of the stairs. One of them moved toward Piper.

"Dad," he gasped.

The second figure, also male, stepped toward Aldridge. "Duncan?" he burst out. "My God, is it you?"

The third figure was Dylan's dead son. Justin walked over to him as though there was nothing unusual about his presence here. "The mist creates an atmosphere more conducive to our communication, Dad."

Dylan's eyes brimmed with tears. He touched his son's face, ran his fingers through Justin's hair. "You feel so damn real. Just like before, when we were diving."

"Right now, I *am* real. So are John Piper's dad and Larry's son. I think we're, like, three of the alien's emissaries or something. You did the right thing by retrieving what you could find of the craft, by allowing it to reunite with those pieces of the hull you and John had. Now it can keep itself hidden here. I think it needs more of the shell-like pieces. The more complete the craft is, the greater its strength. And you should find the two people who investigated my disappearance."

"Luke Pierce and Sofia Lopez?"

"Yes."

"Why?"

"Because they hold pieces of the truth you don't have yet and vice-versa. You'll find them through Ted Fisher and Omega."

Dylan glanced at the craft, the mist still pouring from its surface, then drank in the sight of his son. "If I walk away from all this, what happens?"

Justin looked bewildered. "Walk away? Why would you do that?"

"That's not an answer."

His dead son frowned. "I don't know what would happen. I guess that nothing would change for any of us, for the craft, for the alien. We all would remain stuck where we are."

"And if I do what you're saying? What then?"

"The ET gets to where it was headed in the first place, finds its kin, and goes home."

"Great. And what do *we* get out of it?"

"I don't think it's a *you get* or *it gets*, Dad."

"For me it is." He slung an arm around his son's shoulders and shouted, "Hey, mist, craft, alien, whatever the hell I'm talking to. Here's the deal. If you need help, great, I'll help. But in return, I want my son alive. I want the last three years not to have happened. It's the Many Worlds theory, okay? You hearing me? The incident on that Sarasota beach *never happens*. He isn't abducted or tortured or whatever the fuck you did to him, and he DOES NOT die."

His voice echoed in the storage unit, he felt Justin flinch. Then the mist suddenly vanished, sucked back into the craft. Justin was gone, Piper's father was gone, Aldridge's son was gone. The craft went dark, lusterless. Piper lay on his side, sobbing like a child. Aldridge looked like he was about to keel over. Dylan swayed like a drunk, grabbed onto the railing to steady himself, his stomach lurched. He somehow made it down the stairs and outside before he doubled over and puked.

His legs gave way, he fell to his knees. The warm afternoon

sun beat over him, sweat poured off of him. When he finally raised his head, he spotted a piece of a shell on the ground in front of him. It looked like what Piper had given him yesterday. Impossible. Their pieces of shell had glommed onto the craft when they'd been scuba diving. But because his life was now populated by impossible things, he picked it up, held it in the palm of his hand, rocked back onto his heels.

After a moment, it expanded and a single image appeared on the screen: the Sarasota beach where Justin had had his encounter, where he'd been abducted, where his body had washed up several days later. In this image, though, Dylan was with Justin and Barb, his girlfriend, on the beach, helping them refurbish a sailboat. As the shadows of late afternoon lengthened against the sand, Dylan heard himself say, *Hey, let's grab a bite to eat in town and come back in the morning to finish this.* They gathered up their things and left.

But this didn't confirm anything. It didn't tell him that Justin hadn't been abducted, that he hadn't died. Dylan waited anxiously for a scene that would confirm these details. "C'mon," he muttered, certain he'd gone around the bend. "I need the rest of it, the *certainty*."

And gradually, a new image took shape and he videotaped it with his phone in one had, the shell in another. He and Justin were on the same Sarasota beach, now strewn with debris of what had once been the sail club, helping in the clean up. Sofia Lopez and Luke Pierce were there, moving through the crowd, talking to people. But Dylan and Justin were just two among many.

"Are you bullshitting me?" he snapped.

Was this the alternate timeline or was it just another illusion?

The shell went dark, reshaped itself, and dropped against his palm, as flat and uninteresting as a postage stamp. His fingers closed over it, he squeezed his eyes shut, and struggled with what he had seen just now and what he knew had happened three years ago and in the months since *on this timeline.* If these scenes were possible, it meant that Justin would live, that Dylan might still be married to his ex, that he wouldn't end up in a nuthouse, that he probably would still be working for

The Agency, that he might not have made a small fortune in the stock market. It meant his life would be vastly different.

He embraced that possibility.

When he opened his eyes, Piper and Aldridge stood in front of him, their faces ravaged. Piper spoke first. "It seems... that nothing is what it appears to be, George."

"That's the only goddamn truth that matters." Dylan slipped the bit of shell back into his shirt pocket, and stood. He looked over at Aldridge, now leaning against Pierce's car. "What did your son say, Larry?"

"That... he's with Cat. His sister. My daughter."

"Where?"

"Cuba."

"Cuba?" Piper looked excited. "My dad said I would return to Cuba and embark on the most extraordinary journey of my life."

"Return? You've been there already?" Aldridge asked.

"Sure. American started flying there last year."

"Where are there caves?" Aldridge asked. "My son said something about caves, an underground river that runs through them."

"Viñales, an area west of Havana, several hours by car. But there are hundreds of caves, miles after miles of them."

"Justin didn't say anything about Cuba," Dylan told them. "But he did tell me to find Pierce and Lopez because they have answers that I don't."

"The Omega people, right?" Piper asked.

"Yes."

"I liked the two of them," Aldridge said. "But forget Ted Fisher. I'm not dealing with him."

"Look." Piper leaned in close to Dylan and Aldridge, his eyes sort of wild, his voice a frightened whisper. "I don't have a clue what the fuck's going on here. But I think the three of us are going to Cuba." With that, he walked back into the storage unit, got into his truck, backed it out.

Dylan shut the storage unit door and Piper drove off, calling, "Keep me posted!"

He and Aldridge walked toward their cars. Dylan noticed

he wasn't leaning as heavily on his cane.

"You think there's a chance, George, that I can find my kids?"

"I sure hope so. But what then, Larry?"

"I don't know. I heard what you shouted back in the loft. You want these monstrous fucks to erase the last three years. To make it so your son never died. I want the same thing. I want my kids back, as humans. My horror show happened a year after your son's death. If we have a chance of creating a different timeline by going to Cuba, I'm all for it." He paused. "We're assuming, though, that they can change time."

"We know they mess with it. We know they have telekinetic abilities. We know they can transform humans physically, that they essentially switch an alien body for that of a human. I think it's entirely possible that they can change time. But if we go to Cuba, we're going to need weapons."

"Weapons? We'd be arrested in the TSA line. Why do we need weapons?"

"Because if they won't consent to an agreement on my terms, I'll kill them."

Aldridge looked horrified. "I don't think that's the answer, George."

"For me, it is. Think about it. If this species has a hive mentality, like the Greys supposedly do, then the death of one or dozens of them will reverberate throughout the hive and… "

"And what? Bring them around to our way of thinking? C'mon, at the first sight of a weapon, all that telekinetic power would be unleashed against you."

It was a risk he was willing to take. "I say we go back to the B&B where I'm staying, get a bite to eat, track down Pierce and Lopez, and keep Piper in the loop."

"And then?" Aldridge asked.

"I don't know."

Chapter 10

Ted Fisher was a thorough man, a detail guy who understood the importance of gathering information when it was still fresh, vivid. Pierce wasn't surprised when he invited them up to the library on the second floor so that he could record their testimony of everything they'd experienced since McMullen had found the ET on the side of the cliff.

Once they were all seated comfortably on couches and chairs arranged around a large oak coffee table that matched the wooden floors and bookcases, Cooper plopped down on a throw rug in the middle of the room. He worked away at a marrow bone Carmen had given him. A good sign, Pierce thought. When Cooper was calm, it meant things were on an even keel.

Fisher said, "Let's start with you, Josh."

The old man rubbed his palms against his jeans. "Good enough."

Fisher reminded Pierce of an eccentric academic just then, his thick white hair windblown, his blue eyes wild with passion for his work, his tall, lean body decked out in jeans and a faded blue cotton shirt. He kicked off his sandals, signaled Carmen to begin the videotaping and recording.

"It's now 2:38 p.m. and we're in the Fisher library on Tango Key," Fisher said. "We're going to hear from Josh McMullen first. He's the custodian at the Tango Key lighthouse and found the ET. Josh, tell us what you experienced on the morning of February 6."

Pierce kept glancing at Sofia, sitting in a wedge of sunlight that illumined her profile. He noticed that the webbing on both of her hands had disappeared and wondered when it had happened and why she hadn't said anything about it. But why should she? Of them all, her situation was the strangest and most frightening.

"I got to work around eight that morning. It was Monday, one of our busiest days in the snowbird season. I did my usual walk around the outside of the lighthouse. The exterior security lights are on all night because in the past we've had some homeless people sleeping on the grounds. So I did my rounds, then unlocked the front door and went inside. Usually on Mondays before we open at ten, I straighten things up, clean, toss out the trash, do general housekeeping.

"Around eight-forty, I was out on the deck, cleaning the lenses of the telescopes mounted out there. Not sure how long it was before I saw something plunging out of the clouds. At first, I thought it was a plane going down in flames. But it was dropping so fast I didn't really get a good look at it. Then it slammed into the water and started sinking."

"You never told me you saw the craft," Pierce said.

McMullen shrugged. "After I found the ET, the craft seemed beside the point."

"So go on, Josh," Carmen urged him.

"I scanned the water with one of the telescopes, but didn't see anything. No smoke, no flames, no debris, nothing. Your mind plays tricks on you at times like that and I wondered if maybe it was a meteorite or space debris that the sun had hit at just the right angle. I left the porch and ran alongside the lighthouse to the gate that opens into the adjacent field. I was digging around in my pocket for my phone just in case what I'd seen really was a plane that had gone down, and realized I'd left it on the deck railing. Just as I was about to race back to the deck to get it, something exploded out of the water and hit the side of the cliff."

These details were new for Pierce and he regretted not being more thorough back at the beginning of all this on February 6. "At which point did you call me, Josh?"

"I ran to the edge of the cliff and saw... the ET clinging to the side, struggling to crawl onto a flat surface. I could hear it gasping for air, making this horrible gurgling sound. I flattened out on my stomach and tried to reach it. I guess I had some half-assed idea that I could pull it to safety. But it was about midway up the cliff and no way I could climb down to reach it. That's when I ran back to the deck, grabbed my phone and called Luke."

"Time?" Fisher asked.

"A few minutes after nine."

Pierce scrolled through his call log. "Josh called me the first time at three minutes after nine and then again nine minutes after. By then, I was a minute or two away from the lighthouse."

"Did you bring your rappelling equipment with you to the lighthouse or did you have to return home to get it?" Mike asked.

"I brought it with me. It was tricky rappelling down the face of that cliff, so I took my time. As soon as I reached the ET, I thought it was dead. It wasn't moving or struggling to breathe."

"What did it look like at that point?" Sofia asked.

"Eyes shut, throat gill open, side gill closed, legs splayed at strange angles, arms thrust out overhead, fingers and thumbs limp. I was freaked. I knew we had half an hour to move it before the lighthouse opened."

Fisher frowned. "You should've taken photos, Luke."

"I took two while I was on that jut of rock."

"I don't recall getting anything from you."

"I forgot. There was a lot going on."

"How'd you haul it back up the cliff?" Carmen asked.

"I somehow managed to get the body around the back of my neck so I could rappel with both hands. As I got close to the top, Josh was able to grab hold of the body and haul it the rest of the way. We wrapped it in a tarp and carried it into the storage shed at the back of the property until we could figure out what to do with it. We put it in the old rusted freezer."

McMullen said, "We padlocked it. Two days later, on Wednesday the eighth when the lighthouse is closed, we got there around seven a.m., moved it to the floor freezer in the employee kitchen. A much larger freezer."

"My vision happened on February eighth, hours before all this," Sofia said.

"Tell us what you saw, Sofia," Fisher said.

She recounted it in detail, with Mike adding comments about the questions he'd asked her. "Around eight a.m., she got a text from Luke."

Pierce nodded. "I texted Sofia right after Josh and I had unrolled the tarp and put it in the freezer."

"I got to Tango the next day," Sofia said. "On the ninth. Yesterday."

"Why did you move the body from the shed to the lighthouse, Luke?" Carmen asked.

"We could keep a closer eye on it. And the freezer in the employee kitchen is larger and newer."

"Was there any sign of decomposition when you two moved it from the shed?"

"None." Pierce replied.

"You're sure about the ET's gender, Sofia?" asked Carmen.

"Yes."

"We've seen the video of your reading," Fisher said. "Were you aware of the moment when the webbing grew between your fingers? Your toes?"

Sofia looked uncomfortable. "I wasn't aware of it until I raised my arm and saw the webbing between the fingers on my left hand and on my right foot. The other foot happened early this morning, when I was trying to pick up information from Luke's dock. During that fiasco, both of my hands became webbed."

Carmen frowned. "But when you arrived a few hours ago, *mi amor*, your hands weren't clear, as they are now."

"The webbing comes and goes of its own volition."

As soon as she said this, Pierce recognized it as a half-truth and knew she was hiding something. What? When she didn't elaborate, Fisher continued with his questions and they took the story up to the moment when they had arrived at his and Carmen's home.

"So what does all of this tell us that we didn't know before?" Fisher paced, raked his fingers back through his hair, and looked at each of them.

The question sounded stupidly rhetorical to Pierce, as though Fisher were a professor posing a theoretical question to his students. It irritated him. "What we've got is a hostile ET loose on Tango that has telekinetic ability. It wrecked my dock, whisked Sofia away, and is turning her into something that looks like it does."

"It actually tells us quite a bit more than that, Luke. For the last several days, Carmen and I have been in Cuba. We're going to show you a video of what we discovered there."

Cuba? It was news to Pierce. But it explained why Fisher had answered just one of his texts, emails, or calls—the one in which he'd suggested that Pierce hire Sofia for whatever sum she requested. The postscript to that text was that Fisher would ask the governor to keep the lighthouse closed for "renovations."

Fisher fiddled with a remote that turned on the large computer monitor mounted on the wall and Carmen brought her laptop online. Within moments, the video started. Fisher stood on the bank of a river wearing shorts, a t-shirt, hiking shoes, and a pale straw hat identical to the one worn by the short *campesino* next to him. The Cuban man gestured at the water and spoke rapidly in Spanish. Pierce spoke the language well enough to get by, but he wasn't fluent like nearly everyone else in the room. Fortunately, in the video, Fisher translated.

"Carmen and I are here in the area of Viñales, in western Cuba, with Pedro Mateo, who works on a nearby tobacco plantation. He tells me at least three unusual creatures— probably many more—live in the river and the locals have been bringing them papaya, guava, plantains, corn, rice, and yucca. They used to be very shy, but now they come right up to the shore when people come around with food. He wants to know if we would like to see them." Off camera, Carmen said, *"Claro que si. Como se llaman estas creaturas?"* What are these creatures called?

"Sirenas," Pedro replied, and gestured at someone off camera.

An older woman hurried into view, carrying a straw basket jammed with fruit and vegetables. She set it down close to the water, and Pedro stuck two fingers into his mouth and whistled shrilly. He and the woman stepped back, Pedro motioned for the Fishers to do the same. The image wobbled, steadied, and suddenly, a hand with four fingers and two thumbs reached out of the water and grabbed a large, ripe papaya.

"My God," Pierce exclaimed.

Sofia gasped. "How long have those ETs been there, Ted?"

"We're not sure. We first heard about them a few years ago through a UFO group in Havana. They may be part of the group that Dr. Aldridge told us about. They could be the group that included his son and daughter. We just don't know yet. But we couldn't go there to see for ourselves until commercial flights to Cuba started for Americans."

Carmen resumed the video. The alien's hand tossed the papaya to the other side of the river. A second hand shot out of the water, caught it, then the ET's head popped through the surface. It looked identical to the alien he and McMullen had brought to the lighthouse, except its clump of hair was yellow instead of blue. "Pause it," he said, and went over to the monitor. Sofia also had gotten up and stood at the monitor.

"It has two gills at its throat," she said, her hand moving to her own throat. "And yellow hair. Does that make it a different species?"

Fisher shrugged. "The color of the hair could be the equivalent of skin color in humans. But we don't know."

"The alien we found has blue hair," Pierce said.

"Are there any frames where one of them stands?" Mike asked.

"Yes," Carmen replied, and the video picked up where it had left off.

The second being tossed the papaya upriver and a third hand darted out of the water. Then this being stood, water slipping away from its body like a translucent silk veil, and Pierce saw it was shorter, lacked the double jointed knees, and seemed to have more of a shape—a suggestion of breasts, a flare to the hips. It also had two nostrils, a face that looked almost human, and hair that was vastly different—a dark mass that flowed to the being's shoulders.

"We initially thought this third being might be a different species," Fisher said.

"Now we know otherwise," Carmen said.

"Why?" Pierce asked.

"You'll see."

Her response annoyed Pierce, but he understood that the Fishers were presenting the information chronologically. The ET slipped back into the water and Pedro talked excitedly as he and Fisher moved quickly along the riverbank. In the video, Carmen's voice could be heard off camera, translating what the *campesino* said.

"Pedro says he believes the mermaids have a home in one of the nearby caves where there's an underground river. I asked why this one looks so different from the others and the question seems to upset him."

The older woman who had left the basket of fruits and veggies near the water now rushed to Pedro's side, babbling way, waving her arms wildly. *"Cálmate, mama,"* he said repeatedly.

When she didn't calm down, Pedro clasped her arm and they walked quickly away from the others, their argument inaudible.

Carmen paused the video. "The older woman is Pedro's mother. They were arguing about the third ET, but at this point we weren't sure why she was so upset."

"Did you keep following them upriver?" Sofia asked.

Fisher nodded. "Yes, for maybe another quarter of a mile. Then they submerged and didn't surface again." On the monitor, photos appeared of a narrow street lined by small, colorful concrete buildings. "Pedro and his family live in that coral-colored house in the middle of the block. We took them back there, paid Pedro, and he and his mother hurried inside without saying another word to us. We hung around for hours in the back of truck until Pedro and his mother left the house. Then Carmen went up to the front door and knocked."

"A young woman answered the door," Carmen said. "Pedro's granddaughter, Lucia. We'd met her before. She was really nervous but drew me into the house, said she knew why I was there, and led me into a back bedroom. The room was hot and dark. She allowed me to take video. These images are... disturbing. They're of her older sister, who's in her mid-twenties."

The video showed the woman laying on a narrow bed, covered by just a sheet. Her face looked alien—a single nostril, a tuft of red hair, a gill at her throat that moved frantically, her breathing labored. Carmen drew back the sheet, revealing the woman's webbed hands and feet, the gill at her side.

Lucia took a photograph off the wall over the bed and held it up to the camera. In broken English, she said, "This... my sister before."

The photo of Lucia's sister resembled the third ET in the video, the one with the long dark hair. Pierce realized that the young woman's grotesque switch was what was happening to Sofia. Horror crawled through him. Sofia looked like she was ready to bolt from the library, the house, the island.

"Before what?" Carmen asked her.

"Antes que ella encontró el extraterrestrial."

Before she found the extraterrestrial? *WTF?* "Where did she find an ET?" Pierce asked.

"Near the river," Carmen replied. "It was dying. She brought it back to her home."

On the video, Carmen's urgent voice told Lucia her sister was suffocating, that she needed to get her into water—a bathtub, a lake, the river. Alarmed, Lucia lifted her sister and carried her into the bathroom, Carmen hurrying after her, their frantic chatter too rapid for Pierce to understand. The image bounced around as Carmen turned on the bathtub faucet and plugged the drain with a flat piece of old rubber. Lucia set her sister carefully in the tub and as the water rose, it covered her face and she moved her webbed hands and feet as if trying to swim.

What disturbed Pierce most about these images was their similarity to reports from the Cat Aldridge case in 2015 that he and Sofia had talked about last night. "Could you pause the video, Carmen?" he asked, and she did. "Carmen, there are eerie parallels between this video and the reports we received about the Cat Aldridge case."

She nodded. "Yeah, there are."

"I don't know about that," Fisher said. "Mostly, we read email exchanges and had Larry Aldridge's side of the story."

Carmen frowned. "Uh, Ted, Dr. Aldridge provided video of his daughter in a swimming pool at Homestead Air Force Base when she was almost completely transformed into an alien and it clearly shows the telekinetic nightmare she wreaked as she fled. We have images of what she looked like as she raced across a parking lot and leaped into a canal."

Sofía had remained silent during most of this exchange, but suddenly spoke up. "Excuse me, Ted, but I have a copy of that video. There's a distinct MO to all this." She worked her shoes off her misshapen feet and lifted her legs so that everyone in the room could see her webbed feet. "And for Cat Aldridge, it started with her feet, just like it did for me. And the telekinetic activity is just another facet of it."

Fisher looked embarrassed, Pierce thought, a difficult response to evoke in him. "Well, yes, there are parallels, certainly, but two cases don't equal an MO, Sofia."

"What about the tornadic wind that ripped apart my dock?" Pierce said.

"When we finally got to my mom after that cyclone on the dock that whisked her away," Mike said, "her hands *and* feet were webbed. Sorry, sir, but there's a huge connection here."

Fisher patted the air, a gesture that reminded Pierce of what a matador might do in the seconds before he pierced a bull's neck with a sword. "Granted, there are similarities."

"And the Justin Dylan case," Sofia said. "The fog, the tornadic wind... "

"Justin was dragged away and killed," Fisher said. "He wasn't changed. It's just that I'm not willing yet to call any of this an MO. Can you resume the video, Carmen?"

"Hold on, Carmen." Sofia glared at Fisher. "I realize you and Larry Aldridge didn't get along, Ted. But you can't allow that bad chemistry to influence the facts. And the facts speak for themselves. This is their methodology."

Pierce had worked with Fisher long enough to read his body language, and it was saying he was pissed at Sofia for contradicting him. His cheeks flushed. His nostrils flared. "My disagreements with Dr. Aldridge have nothing to do with my own assessment of all this, Sofia."

"Ted, there's a tornadic wind. Fog. Telekinetic activity. And then someone is taken or changed in some way," she argued. "That's an M.O."

He ignored her outburst and signaled Carmen to start the video again. Pierce stared at the screen, where Lucia now was crouched beside the tub, sobbing, begging her sister to *breathe*, dear God, *breathe*. Suddenly, Pedro and his mother burst into the bathroom, screaming and shouting, "Get out, *vete*, you have no right... "

On the video, Carmen leaped up, the image went haywire, then black.

"I ran back outside and leaped into the truck and we got out of there," Carmen said. "Ted and I believe that some sort of transference occurred between Lucia's sister and that unusual being we saw in the river."

"It's not a *transference*," Sofia snapped. "It's fucking *theft*. They switch their bodies for ours." She turned away from the wall monitor, her face now drained of color. "Earlier, after I showered and was standing at the mirror brushing my hair, the ET's reflection... appeared. I spun around and she was still there. She had... my hair. She had two nostrils... she looked almost like my twin, okay? I think it was a trick, that she was fucking with my perceptions just to show me she eventually would look like me. And vice-versa."

Total silence.

Then McMullen coughed and Carmen turned off the computer and the screen went blank.

"But then a really weird thing happened," Sofia went on. "The ET took my hands between hers. It looked as if tears glistened on her cheeks. Two images came into my head. The first was of her craft, whole and ready to fly. In the second image, she looked like me and was walking somewhere, sipping a goddamn latte. Her intention is to keep switching out parts of my physical body until she looks so much like me that no one can tell she *isn't* me. Somewhere on the planet, there're a Cat and Duncan Aldridge walking around who look human but are actually ETs. And meanwhile, the real Cat and Duncan are amphibious creatures swimming around in a river or harbor somewhere. There's no better way to take over a planet than to exchange your appearance with that of the inhabitants. Think about *that* MO."

No one spoke. Pierce felt physically ill.

"And when I finally ran out of the bathroom," Sofia rushed on, "I realized she'd healed my webbed hand and the nubs on my other hand where the webbing had sprouted. At first, I thought she felt sorry for me and remorse for what her species is doing to us. Now I believe she was demonstrating her *control* over me."

"This is too weird," MuMullen whispered.

Pierce went numb. Mike and Carmen looked stricken to the core. But Fisher snapped, "Why didn't you say something about this when we were all downstairs? Right after it had happened?"

Sofia looked at Fisher with such fury that Pierce flinched. He'd been the target of that fury only once. "Are *you* the one being turned into a goddamn merman, Ted? Are you the one being torn apart and made to feel like an outlier because of what's happening to you? To your body? Are your senses changing and sharpening because you're not entirely human anymore? *No.* So get the fuck off my back. I don't know about the rest of you, but I'm going to Cuba. That's where my answers are. That's where we stop these fucks. And that's where I kill the alien who did this to me and regain my human body."

She got up and moved rapidly and clumsily down the library stairs, Cooper shadowing her, Mike and McMullen following her. Pierce stayed where he was, silent, staring after them, then pressed his hands to his thighs and got up. "She's right."

Fisher shot to his feet, pacing like a madman, his fingers sliding back through his wild hair. He looked to be on the verge of stroke. "You need to stop this, Luke."

"*Stop it? Why?*"

"Because the story's going to get out and we can't have that kind of thing circulating when Omega doesn't have full control of the narrative."

Huh? The *narrative?* Fisher was talking like some political spin doctor. "Control over it? My God, Ted. Listen to yourself. There are at least three of these ETs in Cuba and one of them is doing to a young woman what this ET is trying to do to Sofia. The ET here was trying to get to those ETs in Cuba, Sofia is right about that. And the answers are *there*, not here."

"If she goes to Cuba, I'll have that money we paid her rescinded."

"You can't. It's cleared. It's in her account."

"Ha. Just watch me. And if you go to Cuba with her, you're fired."

Pierce couldn't wrap his head around that one. He'd worked for Omega for a dozen years. Ted and Carmen had become his adopted parents, the family he no longer had. "Wow."

"Don't be an asshole, Ted," snapped Carmen. "This isn't just about you and your reputation and some goddamn mission to Mars. This isn't about you and funding for Omega. They've stumbled across something that holds important implications for all of us. And for the planet." She set the remote on the coffee table. "Now that we know the same thing is happening to Sofia, it's obvious that Cuba holds answers. I'm with them."

Pierce hurried downstairs. Behind him, the Fishers kept arguing, their angry voices rattling away in Spanish, English, a mix of the two. He joined the others outside on the wide back porch, where the late afternoon sun slanted across the table and chairs, the burnished wood, and blazed against the trees beyond the deck. Cooper stood at the railing, panting, aware that something had happened, and stuck close to Sofia.

"We can't stay here," Pierce said. "And we can't return to my place. The cops may be watching the house."

"We can go to my apartment," McMullen said. "It's small but we'll fit."

"Or my house," Sofia added.

"Josh's place is two miles from here, Mom," said Mike. "Home is fourteen miles. I'm opting for Josh's."

"I'm going with you," Carmen said, coming up behind them. "If you'll have me."

Sofia turned, went over to Carmen and slipped her arms around her.

It was done, Pierce thought. Fisher's team had defected.

2.

Sofia's fingers felt a little stiff and they tingled as if, at any second, the webbing might reappear. She could use the computer keyboard easily enough, though, and booked a flight for all of them from Tango to Key West to Havana. She had twenty-four hours to hold the reservation before paying for it and needed to check with the others. They were no longer solo players, but a team with at least three players who were fluent in Spanish—herself, Mike, and Carmen—and that would make a huge difference. Since Carmen had been to the river where these beings lived, she would know the best way to get to Viñales.

The flight would leave the day after tomorrow, took about half an hour, and then they could make arrangements to travel to Viñales to find these river mermaids. These river aliens. As long as she wore socks over her webbed feet and mutilated a pair of shoes so her feet would fit in them, she figured she could get through TSA.

She planned on taking Cooper. When she had been working for Omega before, she'd had him certified as a rescue dog so that he could accompany them overseas and never had any problem. Cuba might be different, but she hoped that once she showed his rescue certificate and vaccination papers, the airline would allow it. Since he was so large—110 pounds—she would have to reserve a seat for him.

She was in McMullen's small office, where a futon would be her bed for the night. It was already made up with soft pillows and a quilt where Cooper had made himself at home. His topaz eyes followed her as she moved around the room and she sensed he was afraid of being left behind. Sofia went over to him, ran her hands over his back. "Not to worry, Coop. You're going with us."

His tail beat rhythmically against the futon.

A quick rap at the door, then Pierce's voice: "Hey, there's been a development. Can I come in?"

"It's unlocked," she called back.

Pierce rushed into the room, clutching his phone in one hand, and two small bottles of Perrier in the other. He was barefoot, wore nylon shorts and a t-shirt, his usual sleep attire. She remembered peeling those shorts off his body one afternoon when they were in Chile, investigating a mass sighting in Santiago. *Don't go there*, she thought.

He handed her a bottle of Perrier. "Thanks," she said. "So what's going on?"

Pierce sat on the futon next to Cooper. "You aren't going to believe this. Two hours ago, I got a text from George Dylan. I didn't see it because my phone was off. He's on Tango."

"*The* Dylan?"

"Yup." He touched his phone. "I just forwarded it to you."

Good, she thought. He hadn't forgotten that for her to pick up anything psychically from an electronic communication, she had to see it on the screen of her phone, iPad, or computer where she could touch the letters.

Her phone dinged and she read the full text message:

Hi, Luke. George Dylan here. Am on Tango doing the same thing you & Sofia are. Am working with John Piper, pilot of Flight 156, and Larry Aldridge. We've recovered a large piece of the craft that crashed 3 miles off Tango's west coast. It has unusual properties—telekinesis, for instance, & is able to create a climate conducive for spirit contact. I saw & spoke to Justin. John saw & spoke with his dad. And Larry conversed with his son, Duncan. That's just the beginning of the high strangeness. We'd like to talk to you and Sofia. We were told you're going to Cuba.

Seeing and talking to the dead. Telekinetic shit. Cuba. Those three things alone told her that Dylan and Piper had been experiencing the genuine effects of this phenomenon. She didn't need to touch the letters on her screen. But had either of them grown webbed hands or feet? Gills? If so, they weren't telling. But how did they know about Cuba?

"I'd like to see photos of what they recovered," she said.

"I already texted Dylan and asked for that. Haven't heard back yet."

"Let's meet with them, Luke. Tonight."

"Where?"

"There's a café down the street."

"How about the Relax Grille? We can sit outside, take Cooper."

Sofia didn't want it to seem like a date, didn't want Pierce to get the wrong idea, didn't want to lead him on. Then again, she with the webbed feet couldn't be particularly attractive to any man, even Pierce, who had loved her at one time. "Ask him. I'd like to buy our tickets to Cuba tomorrow, so the more we know tonight, the better off we are."

While Pierce texted Dylan, she went into the bathroom and changed into jeans, a long-sleeved shirt, a jacket. Nothing had changed with her feet. Nothing had changed with her senses, either. She heard Pierce tapping away on his phone, heard Carmen in another part of the apartment, on her phone, arguing with her husband, heard McMullen talking with his wife. She heard too much that was none of her business, and yet all of it was the alien's business.

Why?

As she pulled on one of her shoes, she sensed the alien nearby—not physically, but telepathically, energetically. Its presence manifested itself as a taste—an unnatural sweetness along the surface of her tongue—and then as a scent of salt and lavender, a weird mix.

An image took shape in Sofia's head that looked like a *National Geographic* photo, an aerial shot of Cuba surrounded by the sparkling blue waters of the Caribbean. She took this image to mean that the ET was headed there.

Sofia refused to acknowledge the communication and kept her mind blank. Moments passes. The scent of lavender and salt faded, she no longer tasted that unnatural sweetness. The ET had left.

Good riddance, fucker.

Her right shoe didn't fit. Pierce had customized the left shoe for the webbing, but with both of her feet changed, the right one refused to squeeze into the shoe. She was now Cinderella. A woman in a fairy tale who awaited the prince to save her.

Forget that.

She rifled through the drawers in the bathroom cabinet, hoping to find a pair of scissors. The best she could do was an electric razor, which cut through the back of her shoe just fine but probably wouldn't work ever again on McMullen's face. Her foot slipped into it, but not comfortably.

Back in the main room, Pierce looked excited. "We're a go," he said, then pointed at her shoes. "You got the other one to fit?"

"Only with surgical intervention."

Pierce laughed and suddenly she was laughing too and he wrapped his arms around her, holding her tightly. It felt so good to be held the way only he could hold her, with one hand at the small of her back and the other hand against her neck or hair, that her arms responded. The part of her that was still human wanted very much to kiss him, to feel his hands and mouth. The non-human part of her understood the pleasure of those sensations intellectually, but not emotionally, viscerally, sexually. And this was one of the reasons the alien was becoming more human, why it was adapting Sofia's physical traits bit by bit.

When Pierce kissed her, the past flooded back in all its perplexing passions and contradictions. She wanted to lead him over to the futon to make love. She wanted to banish him from this room. She wanted him, didn't want him, wanted, didn't want... Sofia pulled away from him.

"Let's go see what they have to say."

Pierce held out his hand and she grasped it and he grinned. "Hey, I know you love me, Sofia."

"Ditto, Luke."

She snapped the leash on Cooper's collar and they left McMullen's place. When they were outside, Pierce said, "So if it's true that we love each other, why aren't we doing the, you know, fuck your brains out thing?"

"Because I have webbed feet and that would be too weird for you."

Pierce still clutched her hand, his thumb moving over the tiny grooves between her fingers where the webbing had appeared—and vanished. The air was cool enough so they both wore jackets and the slight breeze carried the salty scent of the

Atlantic and the Gulf.

"Look, all joking aside, I don't give a shit if you have gills and webbed everything, Sofia. I just want you to know that."

Pierce in his naked honesty held such appeal that she stopped and brought his hand to her curly hair. "When she appeared to me, she had my hair, Luke." She moved his hand to her chin. "She's taking my face. When she's done changing herself she could be standing right here with you and you wouldn't know the difference between her and me."

"I'll always know the difference."

"How?"

His thumb tapped out the response in a secret code they had developed over the years. *Your eyes. The way Cooper reacts to you.*

Of the two, she banked on the last one.

Her fingers still remembered this code. *We should talk like this when we can. Otherwise, she can hear us through me.*

He blurted, "How do you know that?"

"I just do." She tapped, *My webbing.*

Pierce released her hand, slipped an arm around her shoulders and leaned in close, his breath warming her ear, and whispered, "Is she going to Cuba with us?"

Sofia shrugged. "I think she's already headed there."

As they neared Relaxed Grill, Cooper paused to sniff at some bushes and she and Pierce stopped. He turned to her, cupped her face in his hands, brought his mouth to hers. If there was an art to kissing, Pierce had mastered it. Her resistance to him and to the previous intimacy of their relationship, melted away, and it felt strange and yet familiar to her, a kind of homecoming.

"Webbed feet and all, huh?" Her laugh sounded self-conscious.

"Hey, maybe I find webbed feet erotic."

She poked him in the chest. "And maybe you just want to get laid." Cooper started moving forward again and she trotted after him.

Pierce caught up to her. "Question. Personal."

"Just one."

"Has there been anyone else since you left Omega?"

"I'm the one who should be asking *you* that question, Luke. You were the infidel."

"Christ, spare me Fitzgerald."

"He beats out Hemingway any day of the week. At least he didn't hunt big game. You're avoiding the question."

"No one for me," he said.

"Me, either."

"Clean slate, Sofi?"

"I can't promise anything. But I'm willing to try."

He did a little jig there on the sidewalk that made her laugh and then Cooper—lured by the delicious odors of grilling chicken and fish—tore away from her and bounded toward the restaurant, his leash slapping the sidewalk, the grass. She and Pierce ran after him.

Connections

*M*y debt to her is repaid. She may not see it that way, healed
hands in return for her and Mike saving my life, but it's
how I see it. When I skewed her perceptions so that she saw me
as I will look at the end of my metamorphosis and took her hands
between my own, the connection between us was solidified. She
understood that I control her, that she is mine, that I own her.
And I can now hold this illusion long enough to fool most of the
people most of the time.

I'm on a ferry headed to Cuba and the other passengers see me
as a tall, attractive woman in sandals, jeans, a t-shirt, who stands
alone at the railing, staring out at the moonlit water. I don't yet
have Sofia's Sight, but that will come in time. At the moment, my
strength is consumed by holding this illusion.

My tribe already controls certain places and humans in Cuba
and the fist of destiny will make sure that Sofia is directed to these
areas. Some of the humans whose loved ones we have taken do
our bidding in the hopes that we will return those they love. We
use that hope and their fear to our advantage.

Standing here, the smell of the sea nearly intoxicates me. I
pluck the web, searching for my allies and find Lotus. I am on my
way to Havana.

So am I. How are you traveling, Mira?

By ferry. Human in appearance. You, Lotus?

By land, as who I am. But in these many months in Cuba, I
have learned how to control the camouflage, so that when I am
in a populated area, I appear to be human.

And Acia? And Ravina?

Acia has taken over the caves and our supporters have gone into hiding until you arrive. Our sources say that Ravina made it to your location.

Excellent. She cannot locate me through the web. I will be in touch.

There is information you should know, Mira.

The web trembles again with information that has been withheld from me. I learn that the humans have captured nearly a hundred in my tribe and keep them captive in large tanks, as if they are pet fish. Some of them have died. This news enrages me to the point where my control over the illusion starts slipping.

I quickly go downstairs to the restroom and hurry into a stall, struggling to maintain the illusion. If I can't hold onto it, I will have to dive overboard and swim the rest of the way to Cuba. How far? How many miles is it now? Fifty? Sixty? I won't survive a swim that far, not in salt water, not in the aftermath of my injuries. My plan all along was to fall overboard once we were within a few miles of the harbor. I can survive a few miles, but not fifty or sixty.

Suddenly, I feel something on my foot and look down. A frog, it's a frog, and I scoop it up and pop it in my mouth and bite down. The exquisite taste of it fills me with such pleasure that I'm able to control the illusion again. I'm still chewing when I step out of the stall. A young woman and her daughter are at the sinks. The child watches me in the mirror.

"Mommy, that lady is really tall."

"Yes, she is. Wash your hands, honey."

I dislike human children. I feel a nearly overwhelming urge to grab the girl, sink my teeth into the back of her neck as I did to the alligator, and kill her mother as well. I stifle the urge, it would cause trouble I don't need right now. Besides, the girl is an innocent, too young to understand anything.

In the mirror, I see that a piece of the frog's leg clings to my lower lip. I swipe my arm across my mouth and turn to leave the room.

Suddenly, the mother speaks. "Hello, Mira."

"Ravina." *By human standards, she is stunning. Tall. Raven-haired. High cheekbones. But behind this camouflage, I see her as she truly is, shoulders hunched, her left leg permanently deformed.* "How sneaky of you."

The child, the small girl, looks at the woman she thought was her mother, then at me, and backs away slowly, eyes wide, bewildered, terrified. "Mo-mmy, what's going on? What... "

"Shut up!" *Ravina snaps.*

The girl keeps moving back, back, until she is up against the trash can, both hands pressed to her mouth, tears filling her eyes.

"You have scared your human child, Ravina."

"Such an ugly little thing."

She moves toward me, her camouflage melting away from her, and the girl shrieks and races wildly to the door, but Ravina flings her arm outward, hurling a wave of energy that slams the child into the ceiling, crushing her skull. She drops to the floor, bleeding profusely, twitching, her eyes frozen open, gazing into the maw of death. Before Ravina can attack me, my camouflage vanishes and time races backward ten, twenty, thirty seconds until Ravina, the girl, and I are as we were before, the terrified child backing away from us.

Ravina now looks confused, as if she has forgotten that I can manipulate time in this way. Before she remembers, I launch a powerful wave that lifts her off the floor and throws her through the bathroom window, out onto the deck.

The girl just stands there, paralyzed with fear. I grab her hand and leap toward the restroom door, ripping it off its hinges. The girl screams and struggles and when we reach the stairs, I pull her against me. She pounds her puny fists against my chest, but I force her to look at me. "Run!" *I tell her.* "Find human adults who will help you!" *Then I no longer have a human voice, only the voice of my species, shrieks and clicks and jarring notes. I release her and race up the stairs, into the bedlam that has erupted as panicked passengers race madly for the lifeboats, screaming at* the sight of Ravina in her true form, leaping from one end of the ferry to the other.

She grabs people, tossing them overboard, twisting their necks, waves of energy pulsating from her and punching holes in the hull of the ferry, causing waves twenty and thirty feet high to crash over the deck. I leap at her, slam into her from behind, her knees buckle, and she goes down. Just as I sink my teeth into the back of her neck, the ferry lurches in the tumultuous water and I lose my grip on her. She leaps over the side and vanishes into the dark, the violent waves.

Then the panicked crowd turns on me and I try to move myself back ten, fifteen seconds, but I can't do it. Something is wrong. This has never happened before. It's something all Blues can do at will, with practice, as long as it's done within sixty seconds of the event to be changed. By the time I had crashed and was injured, it was already too late. But now... it hasn't been sixty seconds yet, has it? I race toward the front of the ferry, leap onto the highest point, the roof of the pilot cabin, and catapult myself out into the darkness, into the warm, salty, and stormy Caribbean water.

I sink and swim frantically away from the sinking ferry, the chaos, the horror, the public exposure that will surely follow.

Chapter 11

Dylan, Aldridge, and Piper sat at a table on the deck that faced the Atlantic. They had just ordered drinks when a large Golden Retriever raced across the deck and stopped at their table, tail wagging, and sat down, eyeing the three of them.

"Uh, your dog, George?" asked Piper.

"Not that I know of, but I'll adopt him." Dylan extended his hand toward the dog. "You're one handsome dude, you know that?"

The dog barked and licked his hand. Piper laughed. "Egotistical. He knows he's gorgeous." He tore off a piece of bread from a fresh, warm loaf, dipped it in olive oil, held it out. The dog gobbled it down and licked his hand, too. Piper glanced at his nametag. "Name's Cooper. No phone number. Probably lost and joined one of the wild dog packs on the island."

"He doesn't seem too wild to me," Aldridge remarked. "I don't see his pack anywhere."

Dylan glanced around, expecting to see other dogs hanging out in the shadows, waiting for whatever goodies Cooper might bring back to them. Instead, the dog's humans hurried toward them—Luke Pierce, Sofia Lopez.

Pierce looked like Dylan remembered him- lean, tall, bearded, imbued with nervous energy. Sofia looked unchanged, too—a knockout beauty with a certain untamable wildness about her. "There's Cooper's pack." Dylan nodded toward them.

Piper gawked. "Damn. She belongs on the cover of *Sports Illustrated* or something."

"She's breathtaking," Aldridge said. "And if you've got

secrets, John, don't let her touch you."

"*Omega's psychic*? Wow. I expected some overweight woo-woo type."

Woo-woo: the same phrase the mayor had used, Dylan thought, and figured the worldview that had given birth to it was the same one that referred to aliens as little green men from Mars. He and Aldridge pushed back from the table and got up. Dylan noticed he didn't use his cane, still hooked over the back of his chair, and he seemed to walk fine without it. No shuffling gait, no missteps. Was it significant? Since Justin's death, he questioned everything. Cooper glanced back, barked, and trotted over to Pierce and Sofia.

"If the dog's yours, Sofia, I'll adopt him any day of the week," Dylan said.

Aldridge nodded. "Me, too. It's wonderful to see you again, Sofia, Luke."

He and Dylan shook hands with Pierce and Sofia threw an arm around each of them, an awkward group hug. "Wow, the two of you!"

Dylan hoped the hug was too brief for her to pick up anything. But so what if she did? She had witnessed the most terrible moments of his life three years ago in that coroner's office, when they had watched the implant scurrying through his dead son's brain and exiting his left ear. At this point, he had nothing to hide from her, no horrifying secrets—except that he intended to kill the ET if it didn't create an alternate timeline that restored his son's life.

She broke the group hug. "Anything new on your kids, Larry?"

He rocked his hand from side to side. "Maybe."

"How did you both end up here? Now?"

Aldridge stabbed a thumb toward Dylan. "I guess you could say George and I have similar missions. I've been following reported sightings for the last two years. George has been doing it for the last three."

"Except for a hiatus in the nuthouse," Dylan added. "The sighting on the sixth brought us here and we both ended up at Luke's house this morning. His neighbors have video and witness testimony. Were you, uh, really whisked away by that tornadic anomaly?"

Her smile faded, she gave a slight nod. "Introduce us to Mr. Piper and we'll all catch up."

"The guy who didn't return my calls," Pierce remarked.

"I'll break the ice," Sofia said. "Introduce me, Larry." She and Aldridge walked over to Piper, her dog trotting alongside her.

Dylan, now alone with Pierce, didn't know where to begin. So he went directly to the proof. "Photos and video, Luke." He held out his phone, Pierce took it and reciprocated with his phone and the proof it held.

The sight of the alien on the floor of the employee kitchen in the lighthouse nearly did Dylan in. If he'd had a bad heart, high blood pressure, a blocked artery somewhere in his brain, he would have died right then. Instead, his tongue tied into knots and as he kept scrolling through the pictures, his anger escalated. This ET—or one just like it—had abducted his son. This monstrosity with a single nostril, a truncated Mohawk of blue hair, a gill at its throat... An ET capable of creating a chaotic weather phenomenon that had destroyed a dock, could flatten a town, a city, that had obliterated his son's life.

"Where is it?" Dylan asked.

"Sofia thinks it's headed to Cuba. Where's the craft?"

"The part we recovered is hidden in a storage unit." And if he got the chance, Dylan thought, it would become his bargaining tool for his son's life. "So when the ET escaped, did any of you see it again?"

"Sofia did. I'll let her tell you what happened."

Then Pierce blurted the rest of it, as though he desperately needed to tell someone, Dylan thought. The ET's escape from his freezer, the missing time, the messed up time, the skewed perceptions. Dylan immediately felt ashamed of himself for distrusting people generally, but these UFO people specifically. None of them had ever done anything but try to help him. He told Pierce more about the craft.

"So the craft is as powerful as the alien?" Pierce asked.

"Hell, maybe it's *part* of the ET, Luke. Conscious, alive in some way we don't understand. That's John's theory, anyway."

"Where's this leave us? And how'd you come up with Cuba?"

"I didn't. I think Larry did and then John confirmed it. It's part of what they learned when the dead spoke to us in the storage unit." *When the dead spoke to us...* The words came out so easily, Dylan thought, but when he heard them aloud, it made him sound like he should still be in the nuthouse.

"So it seems we have a whole new way of talking about this," Pierce said. "A new lexicon."

"Yeah, but if anyone not familiar with all this heard us talking, they'd think we were crazy."

"Is Cuba important?" Dylan asked.

"We think so." Pierce tilted his head toward the table. "Let's talk. The five of us."

Dylan introduced Pierce and Piper, the waitress came over with a basket of chips and dips and they ordered drinks. Then the five of them sat there, silent, staring at their phones. Dylan, like the rest of them, didn't know where to begin, didn't have any idea what Sofia and Pierce knew or didn't know, so he blurted, "John, Larry, and I will tell you two what we know and what we suspect. Then you guys can do the same and... "

"That's a waste of time," Sofia said. "We've exchanged the big pictures of what we know. Except this." She worked off her shoes, raised her legs and rested her feet against the edge of Dylan's chair.

Webbed feet, just as Dylan had seen in Pierce's videos and photos. But seeing them in real time, perched at the edge of his chair, nearly made him puke. *Is this what they did to Justin?*

"It's changing me," she said. "There are at least three other beings in western Cuba and one of them is turning a young woman into an amphibious creature and taking on her human attributes in the process, just like this ET is trying to do to me. Just like the ET did to Larry's daughter and son."

Dylan couldn't wrench his gaze away from her feet. "May I take a photo?"

She nodded, he snapped his picture, and she dropped her feet to the floor and slipped on her shoes again.

Piper leaned forward. "Is it still on the island?"

Sofia shook her head. "I don't think so." She described the image she'd seen earlier. "But I think she can eavesdrop through the webbing."

Dylan recovered enough from his initial shock to ask, "Are you experiencing any psychological changes? Sensory changes? Anything internal?"

Sofia stabbed a thumb over her left shoulder. "That group of four on the other side of the deck? They're talking about how wasted they were at the last concert they went to. The female bartender is sucking on a peppermint I can taste." She gestured toward the moonlit water. "About thirty yards offshore, there's a pod of dolphins. In a few minutes, they're going to surface. "

Dylan shook his head. "That doesn't prove anything. You're psychic. Everything you just said could come from you, not the ET."

"Ha. I'm good, George. But not that good."

Just then, Dylan heard a loud splash and someone on the deck shouted, "Dolphins, a pod of them!"

A dozen people hurried over to the railing.

Sofia touched Dylan's arm. "Hate to say I told you so."

Was she reading him through that touch? Was she seeing the rage in his heart toward these aliens? Dylan moved his arm and Sofia glanced over at Piper.

"You mentioned you've got your own plane, John. How many passengers does it accommodate?"

"Twenty-one and luggage."

"*Twenty-one?*" Dylan exclaimed. "Is it a private jet or what?"

This elicited a sly, quick smile from Piper. "It's a DC-3. My dad bought it in 1969. One of the best planes ever made. Some pilots argue that it's the best bar none. It's been flying since 1936, when my grandfather first flew it for American Airlines. I've flown it into Havana half a dozen times."

"Shit, John, you're full of surprises," Pierce said. "When you mentioned you had your own plane, I was thinking a Piper Cub. Or a Cessna."

"Had both over the years. But when my dad passed away, the DC-3 went to me and I kept it."

"Will a large group of Americas landing in a DC-3 attract

undue attention?" Aldridge asked.

"Nope. The government and the Cuban people are ecstatic that Americans are visiting the island and they don't care how we arrive—DC-3s, commercial flights, UFOs." He gestured at Cooper. "And it will be easier to get Cooper in on a private plane than on a commercial flight."

"He's certified as a rescue dog," Sofia said.

"Perfect. You'll just need his vaccination papers and rescue certificate."

"We'll still need visas," she said.

"And what kind of official stuff does your plane require?" Aldridge asked.

"One thing at a time," Piper said. "Tomorrow, I'll have to register online with the customs service and I'll need your full names and everyone's passport number. I'll request a landing permit for us—date and approximate time and I'll have to download at least ten declaration forms."

"So we're like, what, a charter flight?" Sofia asked.

"We're a private aircraft with a group of Americans and a rescue dog onboard. We can obtain our visas through American, fifty bucks apiece, and we'll have to leave from Key West. On the visas, we'll be asked why we're traveling to Cuba. There are twelve choices. We check number eight, *In support of the Cuban people*. And I think we should look for an airbnb. Then we can rent a driver and car to get to Viñales."

Dylan suddenly felt like he'd tumbled down the rabbit's hole and that Piper was the rabbit, hurrying past him, a stopwatch clutched in his palm as he murmured, *I'm late. I'm late for an important date.* Piper hadn't let on that he'd known the ropes.

What struck him most about the entire scenario was that three years ago, his frame of mind had been so fragile that insight and information like this would have blown his head apart. But now he understood that things finally were coming together for him. He would find these goddamn aliens and negotiate with them for his son's life. *My son lives and the last three years never happened.*

If they didn't consent to that or claimed that they couldn't, he would kill the whole stinking lot of them. He might be able to get a weapon into Cuba using his agency credentials, but if not, he had his hands, hands that could choke, pummel, hammer. Lethal hands.

"So we're good," Pierce said.

Piper shook his head. "Not entirely. We've got some prepping ahead of us. We need to change our American dollars into Canadian dollars so that when we exchange for the Cuban currency, we don't get socked with a ten percent surcharge. They only do that for American dollars."

"Payback," Dylan said. "For more than fifty years of an embargo that didn't work."

"Probably," Piper concurred. "And we'll need a couple days to plan."

"What's our weight limit on bags?" Dylan asked.

"About fifty pounds. If you all can keep your suitcases to that weight, we'll be in good shape."

"Fantastic," Sofia said. "We'll help pay for gas and we should give you money for our visas."

"We'll do that at the Key West airport," Piper said.

"When do we leave?" Dylan asked, aware of how eager he sounded.

"Between February twelfth and the fourteenth. Depends on how fast the process moves."

Dylan rubbed his hands together. "So, would you two like to see the craft?"

2.

Sofia had misgivings about seeing the craft under any conditions. But doing it after dark, when they'd been drinking, made her especially uneasy.

Yet, they were already in Piper's truck, headed toward the outskirts of Pirate's Cove where the storage unit was. It would be absurd to ask them to turn back just because she was terrified she would leave the place with webbed hands, a single nostril, gills, and double jointed knees.

She decided right then that she wouldn't read the craft, wouldn't touch it at all. Just a quick look. That was all she wanted.

Or needed. And she would take photos so that tomorrow, both Mike and McMullen could see it. Her phone dinged and a news headline appeared on the screen:

Cuba-bound ferry sinks, Facebook video shows alien creatures aboard

She stared at the headline, checked the source. *Huffington Post.* Heart pounding in her throat, Sofia clicked the link and watched a video that jumped around, blurred, faded, snapped into clarity. Two tall ETs fought each other on the deck of a ferry tossed about in high waves as frantic passengers scrambled for lifeboats. She hit the *pause* button, squeezed her eyes shut. *It's her. The one who's changing me.*

"What're you watching?" Pierce asked.

Unable to speak, she passed him her phone. He raised the volume and a man's voice filled the inside of Piper's truck. "We are now on an American naval ship from Gitmo. Forty-three of us survived. American and Cuban vessels are searching the waters for everyone else. They've demanded that we turn over our phones, that we shouldn't talk about what happened on board the ferry. But fuck that. I... I've uploaded my video to You Tube. This... this is... they were tall, seven or eight feet, with a single nostril, a weird spray of blue hair on top of their heads, strange knees that enabled them to leap high and far. Lydia Morales was caught in the restroom with these two... aliens. Lydia... can you tell us what happened?"

A child's voice, sobbing. Sofia leaned in toward Pierce, watching the video. The young girl looked ravaged, her eyes swollen, her face pallid. "My mommy... changed... she called me an ugly thing... I think I died and then something happened and I...I wasn't dead anymore and then it... it grabbed me and told me to find humans who would... would help me." She burst into tears and the video ended.

"Fuck," Dylan said. "She died and then she wasn't dead? Does CNN have anything on this? Any other networks? Websites? Twitter?"

Sofia took her phone from Pierce, clicked to CNN. It was the lead story: *High strangeness offshore Cuba.* NBC'S anchor looked to be on the verge of a breakdown. Twitter had exploded. The video was on Instagram and the likes had soared to more than a million. The Guardian, FOX News, MSNBC, The BBC, You Tube, the story had gone viral. Her head throbbed.

"The alien who's changing me is either dead by now or in Cuba," she said.

3.

Piper stopped at the gate, slid a card through the slot, and the metal bar lifted. The area was well lit, a relief, Sofia thought. Several other cars were parked in front of storage units, and people were loading and unloading stuff. His unit was at the back of the lot, where two bright street lights glowed like high noon. All the illumination alleviated her unease.

Even though the lighthouse's employee kitchen and the bathroom at the Fisher place had been lit, there had been sufficient shadows for the alien to blend into or pop out of. In Pierce's garage, though, the light had been plentiful and that hadn't stopped the stuff in the freezer from flying out of it, all those frozen foods battering her and McMullen and the van. And when she and McMullen had fled and the door had been wide open, flooding the garage with sunlight, the telekinetic activity had continued. So much for her little theory of light as protection.

Her anxiety ratcheted up another notch.

Piper stopped in front of his unit, Dylan got out and unlocked the door, raised it, and directed Piper into a tight space between furniture, cartons, airplane parts, boat parts. Dylan left the door half-raised to take advantage of the bright street lights and Piper didn't turn off the truck's headlights. Plenty of light, she thought, but held back like some little kid terrified of the dark. She was the last one out of the truck.

"It's upstairs," Dylan said. "In the loft."

Sofia looked up at the loft and estimated the climb was about forty feet. Not too bad even with weird, floppy feet wedged into uncomfortable shoes. As she started up the stairs, the memory of that child's face while she recounted what had happened to her on the Cuba-bound ferry lit up the inside of her head.

After her first few steps, the webbing felt like it was expanding, swelling, and that her feet were about to pop out of the shoes. She removed them. Her webbed feet looked larger, stranger, like the feet of a giant duck. They made ugly slapping sounds against the wood steps. But it was easier to climb the stairs.

When she reached the top, Cooper was already sniffing around the craft, and Dylan, Piper, and Aldridge stood on either side of it, holding powerful flashlights that illuminated its entire surface. Pierce moved slowly around it, videotaping, snapping photos, gawking. Sofia inched a little closer to the craft, but kept her arms at her sides, hands fisted. If the craft was shaped like a football or a cigar, as some witnesses and Piper himself had claimed, then judging by the size of this piece, the part that was missing would extend beyond the edge of the loft.

"I think it's total length is seventy to eighty feet," Sofia said. This kind of fact was easier to assimilate than the video she'd just seen.

Piper nodded. "Initially, I thought fifty feet. But since we got it up here in the loft, where you can see its size relative to something other than the floor of the gulf, I think eighty feet is pretty accurate. Right now, it's about half that."

Aldridge frowned. "That can't be accurate, John. Your boat is about thirty feet long, right? And when that piece we retrieved set down at the back of it, I don't remember any of it hanging over the sides."

Piper quickly consulted the photos on his phone, shook his head. "No, look at this picture."

He handed Aldridge his phone and the rest of them peered over his shoulder. Sofia thought the photo clearly showed about ten feet of the craft extending over the left side of the boat.

"I don't remember this," Dylan said.

"Me, neither," Aldridge concurred.

"It fucks with our memories," Pierce said.

"And with our sense of time," Sofia added. "And with our perceptions of what is true or not. It's why we have to pay close attention to time and document everything, when possible, with photos and video."

Dylan looked at the photo again, enlarging it. "Okay, if we're saying the total length of the craft is eighty feet, then this part of it that we found should be forty feet. But it looks larger than that to me."

Sofia took another look. "You're right. See Luke?"

He nodded his agreement.

"So it *grew*?" Piper asked. "Is that what you two are suggesting?"

"What we're saying is that we can't take anything for granted," Pierce told him. "Everything is possible. That's the most important thing to remember."

Dylan plucked a tape measure off a nearby chair, pulled it out, asked Aldridge to grab the other end. He did and hooked it over the edge of the craft and secured it there with the tip of his shoe.

"Okay," Pierce said. "What we have here is fifty-one feet in length. "Do we all agree?"

"Looks right to me," Dylan said. "Let's measure the width."

They did so. "Twenty-three feet," Piper announced.

"But we don't know which part of the entire craft you're measuring," Sofia said. "That could be the skinniest part."

"Good point," Piper said.

Pierce walked around the craft. "How do we get inside of it? I don't see a door or hatch or anything else."

Aldridge said, "We haven't found any entrance." He pointed at an inscription on the surface. "Minutes before any of us saw the dead, a fine mist drifted from right there and filled the loft. Any idea what that inscription means?"

Sofia moved even closer and studied it. As soon as she realized the words in the inscription ran together, she recognized them. *Gratias tibi ago.* The phrase she'd dreamed. "It's Latin and the closest translation I was able to find is *I give thanks to you.*"

"You've *seen* this before?" Dylan asked.

"I dreamed it."

"Shit," Piper muttered. "I think we need to video this entire surface and try to decipher what all these inscriptions and symbols are."

Aldridge ran his hands over the surface. "Some of them are worn away. To get really clear video, we need powerful lights."

"I've got some in the hangar where I keep my plane," Piper said.

Not tonight, she thought. *Not now. Please.* The closer she got to the craft, the more nauseated she felt. and the greater the sensation that the webbing in her feet was expanding, swelling. Her desperation to become fully human again felt like a lead weight in the pit of her stomach. All she wanted right this second was to get out of here, away from the craft and everything it represented. She started to suggest they return tomorrow, but Piper beat her to it.

"Let's tackle it tomorrow," he said.

"Good idea," Dylan agreed. "I don't know about the rest of you, but I need time to process all this."

Cooper suddenly started barking and backed away from the craft. The barks turned to snarls, he bared his teeth, the fur along his back rose. It shocked Sofia. The only time she'd seen him bare his teeth or heard him snarl was at the dog park months ago, when a Pit Bull tried to mount him. She moved toward him, took hold of his collar. "It's okay, Coop. We're leaving."

"Maybe he hears something we don't," Aldridge said.

A moment later, a shrill, piercing noise filled the loft. Sofia slapped her hands over her ears, but it didn't help, didn't block the terrible sound. It felt as if knives were being driven into her ears, through her brain. She stumbled back, barely able to breathe, her chest on fire.

She saw Piper lunge for something on a nearby shelf, Dylan and Aldridge crumpled to the floor, Pierce lurched toward her. He grabbed her hand, she tightened her hold on Cooper's collar, and they somehow made it down the first flight of stairs before they lost consciousness.

4.

When Dylan came to, Piper's face swam into view, Piper wearing headphones, terror etched into his face. He pulled Dylan to a sitting position, touched the headphones that covered Dylan's ears and blocked out that agonizing sound, and gestured his other hand wildly at Aldridge, also wearing headphones now, and at the craft.

It pulsed with pale blue light and the inscriptions and symbols that covered its surface were projected against the light as though it were a wall. Dylan scrambled to his feet, brought out his phone, started the video, and zoomed in, making sure he captured every letter, every symbol. At some point, he realized the shrill, piercing noise had stopped, but didn't dare remove the headphones for fear it was a trick and the noise would start again. But Piper had taken off his headphones and raced for the stairs, shouting something Dylan couldn't hear.

Had the sound triggered the light and the projection? Or was its purpose more insidious? But insidious in what way? If it intended for them to lose consciousness, then why bother with the projections ?

The only thing that made sense to him just then was that the projections weren't for them, but for the being that had piloted this craft and/or for its kindred. The projection was a message.

Then the blue light abruptly vanished, seemingly sucked back into the craft just as the mist had been. Dylan jerked off the headphones, emailed and texted the video to himself and the others, and approached the craft. He stared at it, hating it. "What the fuck do you want from us?" he shouted. *"Why did you kill my son?"* His knees buckled and he dropped to the floor, beating his fists against the craft, grief filling him until only choked sobs fell out of his mouth.

Piper pulled him back. "C'mon, man, we're outta here."

Dylan yanked his arms free, got clumsily to his feet. "Get the hell away from me. That sound, that light, the inscriptions mean something."

"It all means something, George. But we aren't going to find the answers this way. You need to calm down."

He sounded like the shrinks in the nuthouse. *Calm down, Mr. Dylan. Take the meds, Mr. Dylan. Time for your therapy group, Mr. Dylan.* Behave, comply, smile, go jogging, and you'll get out of here faster. Uh-huh, he got the message.

Dylan rubbed his hands over his face. Took long, deep breaths and struggled to contain his rage. His grief. "Sorry, John. I kinda lost it. Are the others okay?"

"Yeah. Yeah, we're all fine. They're outside with Luke. Let's go."

He followed Piper toward the stairs, his eyes raw and aching, his fists speckled with blood. Before he started down, Dylan glanced back once at the craft, dark and dormant now, its secrets held tightly within. Hatred welled up inside him again—hatred for the craft, for the ET that had piloted it, for what it or others like it had done to Justin. And he knew that if he allowed that hatred to consume him, to eat him alive as it was doing now, he wouldn't survive this. He would never know the full truth, he would never have the opportunity to bargain for his son's life.

5.

Pierce woke suddenly in the dark, aware of three things—the frantic beating of his heart, Sofia's soft, even breathing beside him, and that one of her webbed feet rested against his calf. He turned slowly onto his back and watched the play of light and shadows on the ceiling.

The light from the waning moon spilled through the blinds and passing clouds and the swaying of branches in the wind created the shadows. *Facts.* He clung to facts.

Fact: The futon wasn't as comfortable as his own bed, but his own bed had been so empty of human company these past months that he didn't care.

Fact: They all had been so freaked out by what had happened in the storage unit that Sofia had asked him to bunk in with her—*bunk,* which meant comfort each other, nothing more.

Fact: Piper, Dylan, and Aldridge were either on couches in the living room or in sleeping bags, McMullen was in his bedroom, and Mike was on a couch in the loft. He and McMullen had slept through their arrival.

Fact: He didn't know what the hell had happened back there at the storage unit. But he had the video on his phone and had emailed it to himself and everyone else.

He rolled onto his side and rested his arm in the curve of Sofia's waist. She moved closer to him, sighed in her sleep. Her skin smelled of lavender, the scent of her hair was as mysterious as the ocean. He brought his mouth to the back of her neck and she suddenly woke and turned toward him. "Don't stop," she whispered, and slid her hands through his hair, under his shirt, down the length of his spine, and into his gym shorts.

It had been so long since he'd been with anyone that he nearly panicked. But his body remembered Sofia's, his hands remembered how she liked to be touched, caressed, as though her body were an unknown country. Their clothes melted away, they were pressed together skin to skin, and her hands were as soft as silk and eager to know him again.

He peeled the sheet away from her exquisite body and explored her with his mouth, planting small kisses from her throat down the length of her to her belly, then lower. His tongue slipped over her, into her, and she clutched the sides of his head, whispering something he couldn't hear. He got lost in the taste of her, her nails dug into his spine, and when she arched her back and came, she shuddered, twitched, and guided him inside of her.

He felt the hammering of her heart against his chest, felt the moment their hearts pounded as one. They moved against each other with such ease and familiarity it was as if the last months had been a detour, a mistake in judgment, nothing more. Pierce, half-mad with his desire for her, drove on to his own completion, her groans muffled against his shoulder until they collapsed against each other.

They lay there afterward, hands clasped. "You love me," he said. "I knew it."

Her laugh was soft, husky. "I think the way it's sposed to go, Luke, is that afterward you say, *I love you, Sofi.* Or *Te amo.*"

He rolled onto his side and lifted up on an elbow, gazing down at her. "Just in case she's listening… " His finger inscribed coded words on her belly. *Te amo.*

She took his palm and tapped out, *Ditto.* Then she touched her mouth to his, brought his hand to her breast, and instantly fell asleep. Pierce lay there awake for a long time, her webbed foot pressed against one of his feet, his heart singing.

Part Two

HAVANA

"If I become President, I'll make every piece of information this country has about UFO sightings available to the public and scientists. I am convinced that UFOs exist because I have seen one."

- President Jimmy Carter during his Presidential campaign

In Hiding

*I*heard the chaos from the sinking ferry, the panic as passengers scrambled for lifeboats, the terrified shouts and sobs echoing through the darkness. Now I am swimming so deeply in the warm waters that there is only the hum of the sea and its creatures.

I don't know where Ravina is, how badly I injured her, if she even survived. How far am I from Cuba? It's so dark that I am swimming blind. I tentatively pluck at the web to open a private channel to Lotus, but instead am inundated with the calls and cries of Ravina's followers, a cacophony so loud and pervasive it overwhelms the web. I quickly detach and start swimming toward the surface, my exhaustion like a disease.

When my head pops through the surface, the gill at my throat closes without any problem and I breathe in the damp, humid air, a relief from breathing in the salt water. The sea is quiet and a highway of stars crosses the sky. I see a coastline in the distance, lit by bright lights. The Malecon, an esplanade and seawall that run for eight kilometers along the Havana harbor. Along the Malecon rises El Morro, the 500-year-old fort built by the Spanish, perched on a cliff like the Tango Key lighthouse. It's a place my tribe might have taken over if it were closer to fresh water, trees, wilderness. At this hour of the night, it's illuminated but undoubtedly empty of people. I believe I will be safe there for the night. But if I had Sofia's Sight, I would know for sure.

An abrupt change in the current signals that a large sea creature is nearby. I quickly sink beneath the water and come face to face with an immense hammerhead shark. It begins circling *me, its strange eyes perched at the very edges of its head pinned intently on me. I sense it is trying to figure out what I am, whether I'm edible.*

Then it lunges at me and I take off. But it's incredibly fast and agile and its spectacular vision enables it to turn as I turn, to see me as I come up behind it. It flips head over tail, jaws snapping down, barely missing my human feet. Enraged, I catch it on the next flip and sink my dagger teeth into the top of its skull. Its powerful tail propels it up through the water, it flips again, an acrobat, and as I'm thrown to the side, one of my teeth breaks off in its head.

Agonizing pain shoots through me, nearly beyond what I can endure. I emit shrill shrieks and wails that pierce the shark's senses and it dives to escape them. But my rage infuses me with strength and I fling a wave of pulsating energy that strikes the shark repeatedly, one savage blow after another from various directions, on different parts of its body. A second wave slams into its hammer head, one of its hideous eyes bursts, and it charges me again, fury radiating from it like a foul and powerful odor.

Suddenly, two figures shoot like bullets toward either side of the shark and in seconds, Jez shreds its head away from the rest of its body and Lotus flings its remains at a school of sharks racing toward us. Dozens of them converge on the corpse, tearing it apart, and Jez, Lotus and I move rapidly past them, the two of them supporting me.

I don't know how far they carry me. The pain in my mouth travels up through my head and into my eyes until my vision blurs, and I pass out.

Mira. Wake up. *Lotus's voice. I open my eyes, see her leaning over me in her natural form, her blue hair still wet from the sea.* Are you badly injured?

My tooth got ripped out. It's still in the shark's head. *I sit up. We're on a small beach hidden behind boulders and rocks, at the base of the high wall beneath El Morro castle.* Where's Jez?

She gestures toward the rocks and his head suddenly pops up, seaweed tangled in the sprig of his dark hair. Once you two head inland, I will follow you through the rivers, *he says.* For tonight, I will guard the waters here. *Jez, like other warriors with dark hair, can breathe outside of water, much as dolphins on this planet do, but is not able to walk on land.*

Thank you for helping me, Jez.

You fought that shark with such power and courage.

But we all know I wouldn't have survived had it not been for Lotus and Jez rescuing me.

We are going to leap to the top of this wall, Mira. *Lotus points upward.* We will be safe there for the night. You will have time to heal from your injuries.

Sixty feet? Seventy? Higher? I don't know if I can leap that high.

I can. I will leap for both of us.

With that, she gathers me in her arms, stands. She flexes her knees, focuses—and leaps. She lands on the wall's narrow ledge, but her balance is off and she nearly tumbles backward. She jumps down onto a wide stone pathway that seems to wind around the fort, sets me down. Can you move without pain? *she asks.*

It's my mouth that hurts. I can move.

I get up and we follow the scent of water along the walkway. I tell her about what happened back there with the hammerhead, before she and Jez showed up, how I couldn't move time back ten or fifteen seconds. Have you experienced anything like that, Lotus?

It is happening to all the Blues. Perhaps it is because of the gravity, the air or water or something else on this planet. But when your supporters and I were fleeing Acia and the caves, we discovered we could still rewind as a group, to save those who depend on us. One of Jez's warriors was wounded in our escape and we were able to rewind far enough to restore his health. What we can no longer do is rewind just to save ourselves.

Humans call that altruism. But if we can't save ourselves, what's the point of the skill?

She shakes her head and when she speaks again, her voice sounds like a lone note on a violin, sad, tragic. I don't know, Mira.

The scent leads us to old rainwater caught in in the overturned lid of a small wooden barrel used for trash. We crouch and drink and drink, splashing some of the water on our faces. Revived, we sit there by the lid and dip into the web together. Lotus knows her way around the web far better than I do, and adjusts it so that we can spy on Acia and her followers in the caves. Just brief glimpses, but it's all we need.

There, Acia standing on a stone ledge above the river, demanding that the changing humans, half-immersed in water, pledge allegiance to her. Of the dozens in the river, less than half pledge to her. Those that do not are slowly drowned.

In another part of the cave, half-changed humans are told to demonstrate their loyalty to Acia by killing one of their own. Those that do not comply, are tortured and killed.

I pull away, the senselessness of such brutality stirring such fury within me that I would leave tonight for the river country if I were stronger. I would leave and find Acia and eliminate her.

Lotus catches up to me. We should find a place here in the fort to sleep tonight so we will not be discovered in the morning. You see what I mean about Acia? She has become brutal, cruel.

A despot.

We walk in and out of small stone rooms that echo with the voices of the dead, climb up and down stairs, and as we round a corner, come face to face with a man in a uniform.

He takes one look at us and spins around, shrieking in terror. "Sirenas, ayudame!"

I fling a wave of energy at him and he lifts into the air, still shrieking, his legs still moving as though he's running, and he sails over the wall, to the rocks and water below. The waves will take his ruined body out to sea and he won't be found. Local fishermen and pleasure boats aren't permitted in the harbor. By morning, his body will be nothing but a carcass.

Does that make me a despot, Lotus?

No. Self-defense is never despotic. He would have brought police, the curious, the profane.

And then I hook my arm through Lotus's and we leap to the top of the old lighthouse tower. I break a window with my fist, and we climb inside. Once we're safe in the silent darkness of this place, the warm, wonderful air drifting around us, we curl up on the floor. I am finally here, where the fist of destiny has taken me.

I fall instantly asleep.

Chapter 12

Lia Graham stood in front of the tremendous fresh water tank, watching the bizarre aliens swimming through sunlight and shadow. The elongated bodies of these ETs, infinitely graceful, moved without resistance wherever the current took their elongated bodies.

Fleming once had referred to them as water dancers. But that name implied they were etheric beings, divine. What a fucking joke.

The current on which they drifted was finite, like the tank. Months ago, when they were learning the parameters of the tanks, they would bump up against the wall of the salt water tank, labeled #2, and a portal would open. They would swim into it with great exuberance, as though they believed they were free. It didn't take them long to learn that the salt water was just another tank. The only thing this told her was that they were equipped to survive in either environment, but that they were more comfortable in fresh water.

Most species of fish could survive only in one environment or another, based on how much salt their bodies could handle. The adaptable euryhaline species were able to endure a fairly wide range of salt levels and could migrate back and forth between ocean and rivers. There were two types of euryhaline fish: anadromous and catadromous. The former were born in fresh water, but spent most of their lives in the sea. They returned to fresh water only when they spawned. Salmon, smelt, shad, strip bass, and sturgeon fit into that category.

The disgusting creatures in front of her were none of those. Hell, they weren't even fish. Once upon a time, some of them had been human. But in all her months of observing and studying them, she couldn't say with any certainty which ones those were. *Hey, you with the dark weeds sprouting from the top of your head. Were you once human? If so, are you male or female? And where did you come from?*

In terms of other planets, that answer remained a gaping unknown. On this planet, the ETs had come from some coastal place, East coast, West Coast, either coast of Central America, northern, eastern and western coasts of South America, Europe, Australia, New Zealand, these fuckers were everywhere.

She'd seen the field studies, the statistics, and for the last year, she'd been seeing *them.* What she hadn't told Arleen Aldridge was that of the hundred her team had captured, many had died and now just fifty-three remained. They disgusted her, intrigued her, repulsed her, fascinated her, and when they fed, they made her want to puke. She hadn't told Arleen any of that, either, and yet, Lia knew she'd told Arleen too much.

Food was released into one or both of the tanks three times a day and sometimes more frequently depending on how agitated they were. The food that now poured into tank #1, their lunch feeding, included live frogs, frantic fish, seaweed, octopi, even sharks. Frogs appeared to be their favorite food, but they also coveted the human body parts that the agency collected from morgues and medical schools in the U.S. Like the barely recognizable arm that now floated through the water. A bunch of the creatures instantly went at it, going for the fatty part, shredding it with long, dagger teeth that appeared only when they fed or were riled up.

They were kept lightly drugged, which seemed to diminish their telekinetic ability, but maybe not. Maybe they had chosen not to use their telekinetic ability all these months. She didn't know, couldn't be sure. And that was The Agency's central challenge—they didn't know enough.

The glass of the tank that contained them was same thing used on the space shuttles—borosilicate, strong and heat resistant. It might withstand a telekinetic attack. She suspected they hadn't tried to break out of the tanks because if the water rushed out of the tanks too quickly, their gills wouldn't adjust rapidly enough and they would suffocate. Also, she figured they liked being well-fed three times a day.

Were any of these fifty plus ETs her husband, Neil, taken and transformed by these fuckers in 2011? She'd seen no evidence of that. She was fairly sure that the switched Neil she'd seen in San Francisco was it and that Neil in his alien form probably had perished.

Lia pulled a chair up closer to the tank and sank into it. She'd been up for nearly thirty-six hours and knew she couldn't last much longer. Her replacement hadn't shown up eight hours ago and Fleming had asked her to pull a double shift. Normally, she didn't mind because there wasn't much going on in the tanks. But today, the monstrosities seemed agitated and she couldn't grasp why.

Not enough food? Was the temp too cold or too warm? They preferred their water temp to be at least 80 degrees. The app on her phone read 81. The oxygen measurements were good. The food was more generous than usual. She texted Fleming.

Jerry, they're disturbed. Could you take a look?
On my way.

Lia leaned forward and pressed her palm against the glass. It felt warm but not hot. In five minutes, another supply of food would be pumped into tank #1. Nothing had gone into tank #2, where half a dozen of the creatures now swam. Would hunger drive them into the fresh water tank?

She had discovered that these little random experiments sometimes yielded surprises. At the feeding yesterday morning, food had been added to tank #2 but not to tank #1, yet not a single creature had left the fresh water tank to feed. Why not? These creatures were usually eager to feed. And what was that group of them doing on the far side of tank #1 right now? It looked as if they were commiserating, thirteen of them in a tight cluster, their webbed feet moving quickly, their long arms and webbed hands gliding up and down with precise, graceful movements. Another group formed a loose circle around the inner group, as if to protect them.

Were any of these creatures the son and daughter of Dr. Aldridge?

The door behind her whispered open and shut. "What's going on, Lia?"

"I'm not sure. They just seem really agitated."

Fleming stepped up to the glass, a tall, thin man so pale he looked as if he hadn't stepped outside in the thirteen months he'd been here. He probably hadn't. Once Obama had opened diplomatic relations with Cuba in July 2015, Fleming had gone to work making sure the agency could establish a marine research area on the island. Foremost among the Cuban government's requirements was an exorbitant amount of money the U.S. had to pay to lease the land. They also demanded that fifty percent of the facility's staff would be Cubans, paid at the same rate as their American counterparts, and that the research about the aliens would be shared with Cuban scientists and the government.

The arrangement had worked out surprisingly well. When the facility opened, twenty-six Cubans had gone to work for them—scientists, technicians, and fishermen who knew the rivers in and around the village of Viñales as only locals could. Within the first two weeks of operation, the fishermen had located more than two dozen of the alien creatures. Once they perfected a way to entrap them—essentially drugging the food that lured them into the open, then using nets to haul them in— it was relatively easy to capture them.

After that, though, the pods moved frequently and it took them weeks to locate the next batch. Fleming speculated that they needed to replenish their numbers, so she and her team followed stories about sightings, encounters, and abductions in the villages and towns in the province. This tactic had led to more captured aliens and when they had a total of a hundred and ten, they had stopped looking. Six of them initially had died, then others over the months and the forensic biologists went to work on the bodies, trying to figure out their physiology.

"What do you think?" she asked.

Fleming turned, hands clasped behind his back. "That cluster of them, Lia. They're protecting something. I want a closer look. Are the security cams online?"

"Yes. Of course."

"Bring them around."

Why hadn't she thought of that?

Because you're worn out, Graham.

She got up, went quickly to the computer. Her fingers raced across the keyboard until images popped up on the screen. The first one, taken from a cam mounted above the area of the tank where the ETs were clustered, showed figures without detail. She zoomed in, enlarging the image by two hundred percent.

Her breath rushed out of her. "My God."

"Holy fuck." Fleming snapped photos of the screen with his cell, then fiddled with keys, enlarging the image another fifty percent. "How the hell did *this* get past us?"

"Easy. We can't tell males from females and don't have a clue what to look for in terms of pregnancy."

Lia touched the screen, bringing the image into greater clarity. The ET the clusters protected was bald, less than a foot tall, with human features that looked underdeveloped. Lia couldn't see its feet, but it had just a single thumb on either hand and only one of its hands was partially webbed. It looked as if the group somehow was helping the webbing to develop more fully.

While she watched in fascination, Fleming paced and texted and yelled at someone over the phone. Minutes later, the door swung open and Sergio and Margarita Ruiz hurried in. Since higher education was free in Cuba, their Cuban staff—except for the fishermen—held the equivalent of doctorates in their fields. Sergio and Margarita were a sibling team of forensic biologists. Sergio, with his dark hair and eyes and excitable personality, reminded her of Ricky Ricardo.

"*Un bebe?*" he exclaimed. "These monsters procreate?"

Margarita, the calmer of the two, made a surreptitious sign of the cross on her forehead. "*Es un diablo.*"

"No, it's not a devil, Margarita." Lia pointed at the computer image.

"*Dios mio,*" Margarita murmured, peering over Lia's shoulder. "I understand something now that puzzled me before. One of the corpses that Sergio and I worked on had a kind of pouch, like a kangaroo, but on its back. We thought it might be a vestigial organ, but couldn't determine its purpose. Could that be the alien's womb?"

Sergio frowned and touched his fingertip to the screen, to the little alien's bald head, then to its partially webbed hand, its tiny gills. "This ET appears to have been born in an immature form, like an infant kangaroo, and perhaps stayed within the pouch as it nursed and grew."

"Nursed on *what?*" Margarita asked. "We didn't find any nipples in that being's pouch, nothing to indicate how it might feed an infant."

"What *do* you know about it?" Fleming snapped.

"Not enough," Sergio said.

"I want all the cams for the last six months to be reviewed," Lia said. "When was this alien born? Which alien gave birth to it?"

Sergio nodded. "I'll get the techs on it right away."

"That being on which you found the pouch. What number was it?"

"Thirty-two," he replied.

Lia made a note of it on her phone. "So the ETs with pouches are female?"

"I think so," Sergio replied. "But the pouches aren't visible."

"Were you able to determine its cause of death?"

Margarita laughed. *"Lia, escuchame.* You can't understand how something dies if you do not know how it lives. *Me entiendes?* "

"But you people have been studying these beings for months," Fleming burst out.

"We need *years,*" Sergio said. "Do they have blood that can be typed? It doesn't appear that they do. Only clear liquid comes out of them. Do they have organs? Lungs? Hearts? Livers? Kidneys? *We don't know.* They have some organs, but we don't have any idea what their function is. How do they procreate? Do they fuck? *We don't know.* The only things we know with any certainty is that their brains are larger than the human brain and are tricameral—right, left, middle brain. We suspect the middle brain, which is the largest of the three, is what enables them to communicate in much the same way that a hive of bees might. Or a flock of birds."

"Have you ever seen a flock of birds in an evening sky that suddenly turned in perfect unison?" Margarita asked. "They do a perfect one-eighty without skipping a beat. How do they do that?"

"Instinct," Fleming said.

"No." Margarita shook her head. "It's telepathic. That's how they communicate. That and the weird music that comes out of them."

"And now we know they can procreate," Sergio finished. "We just don't know how they do it."

The computer image changed. The group around the little alien loosened up and one of the other cams, positioned at a different angle, captured the webbing that now grew rapidly between its fingers on both hands. A second thumb started growing from its left hand.

Some of the protectors grasped the little ETs right hand and the rest of them gripped the being's right foot, which wasn't webbed. It shrieked, the sound like an orchestra badly out of tune, and the noise was clearly audible through the underwater amplifiers and microphones. Was it a shriek of pain? But from what? Were the adult ETs that gripped the little alien's foot hurting it in some way? Lia couldn't tell. Then the little ET shot toward the surface, its feet fully webbed now, beating frantically against the water.

"Something's wrong!" Fleming shouted. "Pump in more drugs, put all these fuckers to sleep! Fast!"

Lia slammed her fist against the red button on her computer and drugs shot out of portals in the sides of the tank, colorless, odorless, visible only because of the powerful, horizontal bursts that exploded through the tank. The little alien's misshapen head broke through the surface and it shrieked pathetically as one of the adult aliens raced after it, and nearly caught it by a webbed foot before it succumbed to the drug. It sank, body flaccid, arms and legs drifting this way and that with the current.

She hit another button that injected the drug into the tank #2, where the aliens were already racing toward the wall. A third button sealed off the portal in that tank. By then, Fleming and Sergio had clambered up the ladder to the platform at the top of the tank and donned diving gear. Margarita sounded the alarm, technicians poured into the room, and the two men tumbled backward into the tank.

Lia shouted, "They're rescuing an infant alien and it will have to be transferred to an isolation tank!"

Even though the security cam images had been transmitted to everyone on their team and they knew the protocol, bedlam ensued. Men and women scurried around like terrified insects, sealing off sections of the facility, preparing a transport. Snipers took their positions on platforms high above the two tanks, lights blazed.

The only other time something like this had happened, Lia remembered, was four months into the project, when several of the aliens had attacked one of their own. A domestic squabble, a heated difference of opinion, an attempted assassination, who knew? They had managed to extract the victim, which was heavily drugged, and got it into an isolation tank. Medics in scuba gear had gone to work on it, but because they knew so little about the physiology of these aliens, the being had died within hours.

Lia, now wearing earphones with a mike, kept tabs on the drug level and when it reached the max allowed, she shut off the valves and stood at the tank, watching Fleming and Sergio bringing the little alien toward the surface. Before they reached it, one of the ETs near the bottom of the tank suddenly came to and shot toward the two men. She screamed into the mike: "*Get out now! It's forty yards behind you!*"

The men swam frantically, snipers started firing, and the first three shots missed the creature. When it was just twenty yards from the men, it took a bullet to the head and fell slowly back through the water, long arms dangling above its head, long legs with those double jointed knees drifting at impossible angles in the current. It sank, touched down on the bottom of the tank and didn't move. Seconds later, Fleming and Sergio burst through the surface with the little alien and it was handed off.

Sergio started to dive again to retrieve the corpse of the ET that had been shot, but Margarita, now on the platform, grabbed her brother's arms and hauled him out of the tank. "No. You can't risk it, Sergio. Let them eat the goddamn monster."

Fleming was already out of the water, shedding his gear, breathing hard, his face drained of color.

Lia stood at the computer and continued to monitor the details. She stared at the dead alien on the floor of the tank, photographed it and the technicians who were preparing the baby ET for transport to one of the isolation tanks. *Proof, there's enough proof in this proof to create a worldwide panic.* And for the first time since she'd joined the agency in 1998, when she was a 26-year-old doctoral student, she seriously considered quitting.

2.

The buildings that surrounded Campo Viejo, the name of their facility, had been built in colonial times and hadn't been refurbished since the U.S. embargo had begun in the early sixties. From the outside, her building looked like the worn survivor of some terrible war, the concrete weathered and crumbling, windows missing, roof falling apart. But her one-bedroom place on the third floor had been restored completely and was a peaceful little haven. As soon as she entered the apartment, she kicked off her shoes and collapsed on the couch.

Four hours later, she came awake suddenly, so disoriented she didn't know if it was day or night. She showered, put on clean clothes, made coffee and fixed herself breakfast. She ate on the gorgeous rooftop porch with its hanging plants, colorful flowerbeds, and bougainvillea vines, their bright purple buds climbing trellises. The owner of the apartment had created this little paradise and each day, Lia spent time up here, embracing her solitude, her mind mercifully empty. Even at night, it soothed her.

A cool breeze drifted in from the surrounding hills, visible now only as distant silhouettes. But when the sun rose, light would spill across tobacco fields, rice paddies, papaya and mango groves, horse-pulled wagons, and *campesinos* on their way to work. Birds sang and now and then, she heard a car, diesel engine chugging noisily through the early morning.

She smoked the first of the five cigarettes she allowed herself per day, and wondered what else she might be doing with her life. She could write a memoir about the agency—but probably would be knocked off before she turned it in and even its posthumous publication would be killed. She could move to the farthest point on the globe—Tahiti, Bora Bora, New Zealand—and languish on the small fortune she'd saved. She could grow organic produce, raise sheep, have fifty dogs, and try to live happily beneath a sky strewn with stars. But eventually the agency would find her.

They could find anyone.

She felt miserable and lonely and what she really wanted was for Dylan to be here.

Pounding at the front door interrupted her fantasies.

Lia hurried downstairs, peeked out with the chain engaged. Fleming stood there in shorts and a t-shirt, glancing around nervously. "Can we talk?"

She removed the chain, opened the door, he came inside. "News?" she asked.

"Naw. I just can't sleep."

"Same here."

They went upstairs to the rooftop porch, Lia filled a shot glass with Cuban rum, and handed it to Fleming. "You think the big dudes in D.C. can eavesdrop on us here in Cuba?"

"Probably." He pointed at her phone. "Through that."

They turned off their phones and set them on the table with her breakfast dishes. She wasn't so sure that just turning off the phones would eliminate eavesdropping, so she scooped their phones off the table and carried them to the farthest corner of the porch, set them inside the empty washing machine, and shut the lid.

"Good idea," Fleming said.

"I should quit this job, Jerry."

"I've been thinking the same thing. In another month, I'm eligible for early retirement, so it would be easier for me than for you."

"I'm not eligible for another five and a half years, and that's for twenty-five years, not the thirty you've got."

His hands dropped to his thighs. "Today in the tank, as I brought that tiny alien to the surface, I thought about Larry Aldridge, the horror he went through, losing two kids to these fucks. He has been a friend of mine for years. He was one of my son's professors when he was in med school. I thought about Dylan, losing his son the way he did. My God, I wouldn't survive the loss of either one of my kids or grandkids, especially to an atrocity like these fuckers. And frankly, I'm terrified that if I keep working with The Agency, my kids somehow are going to become victims."

She didn't have children, couldn't. She and Neil had tried, then considered adoption, but in the end hadn't gone that route. Now she was grateful she didn't have any kids, just nieces and nephews. She was grateful she'd been able to help Dylan get out of a psychiatric facility and establish a life for himself in Key Largo, but regretted not contacting him when she was in Homestead several days ago.

"I'm not convinced that these ETs deliberately choose their victims, Jerry. It may just be random, a matter of convenience. Like with Neil. With Cat Aldridge and her husband. Like with Justin Dylan."

"What do you hear from Dylan?"

"These days? Nothing."

"You didn't contact him when you were in the States?"

"Nope."

He squeezed her hand. "I'm sorry, kiddo. You two were a stellar team."

"Yeah. We were."

His words opened a cavern in the pit of her stomach that begged to be filled with the sight of Dylan, the reality of Dylan, the passion of Dylan. If she quit the agency, she would seek the farthest point on earth from Washington D.C. and ask Dylan to join her.

"Text him, Lia."

"*What?* Why?"

Fleming sat back, elbows on the arm rests of the old plastic chair, fingers threaded together in an attitude of prayer. "If he's still as obsessed as he was when you last saw him, if he has used that brilliant mind of his to make a killing on the stock market or in the housing market or in some other way, then I'm betting he's on the trail of these ETs."

Lia stabbed out her third cigarette. A gust of wind played through the plants on the porch. Hanging vines swayed, leaves fluttered, orchids sang. She remembered that years before Dylan's son had washed up dead on that Sarasota beach, before they had become lovers, when they'd both been married to other people, they'd investigated a bizarre case in the Bermuda Triangle, where a private pilot in a single engine Cessna had an encounter with a lenticular cloud that was, in all probability, a UFO.

A book and countless articles had been written about it. The pilot had been on dozens of TV shows and because he was a pilot, his story was tough to dismiss. He claimed that shortly after he and his father had taken off from Andros Island in the Bahamas, they had encountered a lenticular cloud that had surrounded their Cessna. It formed into a tunnel of fog that kept pace with them, then trapped them. They'd experienced weightlessness, lost their electronic equipment, compass, communication with air traffic controllers. Everything had gone bonkers.

But when they'd broken free of the tunnel, the pilot's plane had covered nearly a hundred miles to the South Florida coast in less than thirty minutes—a trip that usually took more than an hour. In other words, their plane had been teleported.

In 2009, she and Dylan had traveled with that pilot and his co-author to Andros Island in the Bahamas where *Alien Hunters* filmed them and the pilot's story. She and Dylan tried to gain access to AUTEC, the secretive U.S. base on the island that was suspected to be the Area 51 of USOs—Unidentified Submerged Objects. But even with agency credentials, they weren't able to get in. When she had emailed Fleming about it later, he said he wasn't surprised. *Only the secretaries of state and of defense have that access.*

The reason that memory had surfaced now was because it was when she had realized she was in love with Dylan and that nothing would ever happen as long as she was married to Neil, whom she still had loved. "If I do this, Jerry, and he answers and he's doing what you say he is, what we both believe he is, then I want him reinstated."

Fleming tipped back in his chair, hands folded behind his head. "Hey, c'mon. The guy had a complete meltdown. I can't just... "

"Yeah, you can."

"Jesus, Lia. I... "

"Hire him back as an outsourced contractor. Or a consultant. I don't give a shit. Just make it happen. I'm not just going to text him and ask him to come here without offering something in return."

"Okay, okay." He poured himself another splash of rum. "Text him."

Lia thought about it, but not for long. She knew that Dylan would look at this as a sign. But that didn't guarantee a response. She went over to the washing machine, retrieved their cells, handed Fleming his, and turned hers on. She thought about it, then texted:

Hey, stranger, what's going on?

She had a response in less than three minutes.

Can I carry a gun into Cuba with agency creds?

"He's tracking, Jerry. He's coming here."

"Ask him why."

Fleming was wrong about that tactic, she thought, and texted:

Tango Key sighting?

Even you wouldn't believe this shit. We'll be in Havana in the next couple of days.

How many we?

8 and a dog. Aldridge is with us.

It didn't surprise her that he and Larry Aldridge had connected. People whose lives had been changed by encounters often found each other without trying. *This is what I'm doing,* she replied, and attached the photo of the dead alien at the bottom of the tank. *In Viñales. Let me know when u arrive.*

We're on the same track. Later.

She read the exchange out loud, except for the part about what she was doing in Viñales.

"*Eight people?* Fuck, why so many? We can't have eight people who… "

"Hire him back, Jerry. We need him."

"We don't really know that, Lia. We don't have any idea what he knows."

"I'll tell you this, Jerry. If he's headed to Cuba, then he knows more than we do."

As Fleming considered her argument, their phones dinged with simultaneous text messages from Sergio. *Get over here.*

3.

The infant alien sucked at the single thumb on its right hand. The fingers on that hand were no longer webbed, its head was no longer misshapen, its features looked nearly human. It basked in a wedge of moonlight on a rock, its gills closed, the webbing on its right foot slowly disappearing.

Lia went up to the glass that stood between them and the isolation tank and watched the infant closely. A pinkish stubble now covered its once bald head. Its almost human eyes kept glancing around the tank, but it wasn't clear to Lia whether it was curious, bewildered, terrified or just hoped to find an escape route. Or something else altogether.

"Did you insert a biometric chip when it was sedated?" Lia asked.

"Sure." Margarita, standing next to her, passed Lia her iPad. "These are the stats since we put it into isolation six hours ago. But other than the intake of oxygen and serotonin levels, nothing else registers, not even a pulse."

"The serotonin level has risen in the last two hours," Lia remarked.

"Makes sense," Fleming said. "After nearly being attacked by its own kind, it came to in unfamiliar surroundings. Serotonin helps mood—diminishes fear and anxiety."

"When did this transformation start happening?" Fleming asked.

"Three hours ago," Sergio replied. "It's been in and out of the water, then about an hour ago it climbed up onto that rock and has been there ever since. It's been snacking on seaweed we put in the tank. It looks vaguely female, don't you think?"

"Maybe," Lia replied.

"Should we feed it anything else?" Margarita asked.

"Sure," Fleming replied. "But since it isn't fully webbed now, let's start with something small tossed on the rocks rather than in the water."

"A frozen mackerel and a papaya," Lia said. "How's that sound?"

"Fish and fruit." Sergio nodded his approval and opened the door of a small fridge. He came over to Lia and Fleming with a Baggie that held the fish and a plump papaya in his palm. "Who wants to do the honors?"

"I'll do it," Lia said.

4.

This isolation tank, like the building and room that housed it, was a fraction of the size of the other two tanks. But it, like its siblings, was too high for even ETs with their dual-jointed knees to leap out of, Lia thought. It was covered with a transparent and porous material that allowed light and air to enter the tank. In the event that one of these aliens managed to leap seventy feet high and struck the covering, it would take repeated impacts to tear through it.

She hurried toward the metal stairs to her right, the Baggie in one hand, the papaya in the other, and watched the ET as she did so. It turned its head twice, eyes following Lia, then glanced back at its own hands, holding them up to the moonlight, turning them this way and that. At the top of the stairs, she walked out onto a small platform, opened an iron hatch in the floor, and dropped the mackerel and papaya through it.

The ET watched the food fall, then drew its long legs out of the water, double jointed knees fully visible, and leaped. It caught the fish and the piece of fruit in one hand, Lia slammed the hatch shut, and wrenched back, heart thundering. The being crashed into the hatch with such force that she felt the reverberations against her feet.

Before she fled back down the stairs, before she reached the others, the being landed feet first back on the rock, brought the mackerel to its human nose, sniffed loudly, and flicked it into the water. It tossed the papaya from hand to hand like a tennis ball, then hurled it above its head. As it came down, the ET opened its mouth, an immense cavern into which the papaya vanished. Then it bit down, slicing the large, football-shaped fruit in two.

Fleming's voice came through her earpiece. "Definitely not human. But not entirely alien, either."

"A hybrid," she said. "You think that's been their plan all along? That it might be why they're morphing humans? To create a race of hybrids?"

"Jesus," Fleming said. "It makes a kind of terrible sense."

The hybrid held half the papaya in one hand and chewed away at it, juice dripping from its mouth, and turned its eyes on them. As if daring them, Lia thought. Or challenging them. *Ha-ha, figure me out, you stupid humans. Ha-ha.*

It flung the other half of the papaya across the tank, toward them, and it splattered against the wall, seeds and innards dripping down the glass.

"Hostile," Lia said.

"And pissed off," Sergio added. "I think that might have been the two-year-old equivalent of a temper tantrum. Something that Margarita and I have been talking about is the effect the amphibious aliens still in the river and caves may be having on wildlife in this area."

Lia glanced at him. "Have you heard something?"

"There has been a massive die-off of frogs around Cuevo de los Indios."

"Since when?"

"In the last year, but it's been especially bad in just the last several months, which leads me to believe there are more of these ETs here now." Sergio said. "The government closed the cave to tourists. And since frogs eat mosquitos and other pests, like the hornworms that consume tobacco, their numbers have increased. A couple of the tobacco plantations in Viñales have been losing crops and have brought in parasitic wasps to control the hornworms."

"How do you know all this?" Lia asked.

"Our family owns a tobacco plantation in Viñales," Margarita replied. "There's concern among the locals that our facility is to blame because we're holding a bunch of ETs."

"Meaning what?" Lia asked.

"That more of their kind are arriving to liberate the ones we have here."

This kind of news and speculation worried her. In a country where the people had so little, the compound's relationship with the locals was vital to their continued existence. They bought food and supplies in town. They depended on the expertise of their Cuban employees. "Maybe we should offer to pay for the parasitic wasps, Jerry. And the loss of crops."

Fleming stood in front of a computer, hands flying across the keyboard. "Sounds reasonable to me. Sergio, can you send out an email to the tobacco farmers you know and get an estimate on cost?"

"*Claro que si. Gracias.* They will welcome this communication."

"The cams captured every second of the ETs temper tantrum," Fleming said. "I want the security cameras in here kept on this tank 24/7 with the continuous feed sent to each of us and backed up, like everything else, on the cloud. If this creature does anything unusual—*anything*—or starts changing in any way, I want a group text alerting us. And Sergio, two snipers should be in here at all times."

"Only two? I was thinking a dozen would be safer."

"Make it four. And I want six techs in here around the clock, checking and re-checking the... "

The rest of whatever he said got swallowed up by an explosion that nearly deafened Lia. Even as her hands flew to her ears and her head snapped up, she knew what she would see. And there it was, thousands of fissures running through the borosilicate glass and who the fuck knew how many hundreds of thousands of gallons of water would pour into this room as soon as those fissures gave way.

"Get out!" she screamed. "Get out now!"

She heard the snipers firing. She had no idea if they hit the ET or not, but either way, they knew the protocol and would exit through the top of the tank and escape down stairs on the far side.

She whipped out her phone to punch in the four-digit code that would seal off this room, but panic emptied her mind. She couldn't remember it. She tore toward the steel doors with Fleming, Sergio, Margarita, and three techs. Those doors would hold back the water for maybe thirty seconds. But then the sheer force of the tidal wave would crash through the doors and sweep into the hallways and other offices. It would eventually run through the patio and out onto the grounds, where it would empty into a stream that would carry it to one of the many rivers or out into a tobacco field, a rice paddy, a mango grove.

The last thing she saw before she made it to the other side of those doors was the hybrid flinging its arms above its head. Then it emitted a shriek so piercing, so shrill, the glass surrendered. In those final seconds, she and Fleming slammed the metal doors shut. He threw the bolt, the four-digit code popped into her head, she punched it into the control app on her phone, and kept racing toward the outer door.

Panels opened in the walls and an additional barrier of steel and iron sealed off the room that held the disaster, that shattered isolation tank and all that water. In a few minutes, drains would open in the floors inside and outside of the tank. She had no idea where that water would be carried or if the openings were large enough for the being to slip through.

Maybe it was dead already.

5.

They reached a field on a shallow hill. Lia's knees gave way, she sank into soft grass, pressed her hands to her thighs, struggled to catch her breath. She fell forward into that softness and lay there until she could breathe normally. Then she rolled onto her back, sat up, and looked at the isolation building in the distance. She couldn't tell from here whether the security wall had held.

It, like everything else here, had been built in haste.

She felt numb.

Fleming crawled up beside her, texting as he did so. "I just dispatched two dozen soldiers to search for that hideous thing and kill it on sight. My God."

"We may be fucked, Jerry. It may all be too late. We don't know how many governments around the world are dealing with these skin shifters. We don't know how many inroads these aliens have made."

"The most recent stats put the number at eleven that *admit* to dealing with these fuckers."

"Why didn't you tell me this before?"

"I only found out yesterday."

"There're probably another thirty governments who aren't admitting it." She glanced around, through the early morning flush of light. "Are we all accounted for? Hello?"

The seven of them called out their names.

"Here's my theory, people. We got taken. The whole helpless infant hybrid thing, where we thought it was being threatened by the adults, was a fucking ruse so we would isolate the little sucker. So it could do what it just did."

Sergio was the first to say anything. "We know that some of those ETs in the big tanks are humans who have been changed to aliens through a process we don't understand yet. They may have interbred with the ETs."

"C'mon, Sergio." His sister sounded pissed. "That *process* is what Catholics call *transfiguration* and what scientists call impossible. We don't have the knowledge to understand this."

They had been minutes away from dying, Lia thought, and were now doing what academics and scientists often did—intellectualizing it. Fuck that.

She moved away from the others, toward the rising sun, and stared at her phone. In the days before 2007, when the first iPhone had been produced, no one had any idea how it would change their lives. Change the world. Change everything.

On a professional level, it allowed her to work from nearly anywhere on the planet. On a personal level, it enabled her to communicate with anyone, nearly anywhere, and to do it instantaneously. She tapped in Dylan's number.

One ring and he picked up. "Graham?"

"Dylan?"

He started laughing. "We sound like first graders. What's up?"

Like no time had passed at all. Like they'd had coffee together yesterday. Like they'd just rolled out of bed and were continuing a conversation from the night before. Her heart swelled with love for this man, this stranger, this familiar. "These skin shifters—that's what we call them—are hostile. We have reason to believe our group of fifty-four now has a hybrid infant. "

"*Fifty-four?* You have fifty-four of these things? Where? And they procreate? Christ, Graham."

"Fifty-five now, counting the hybrid, and if it's not dead, it just escaped." She told him the rest of it, what had just happened. "Our facility in Viñales is known as Campo Viejo."

"Jesus. We're leaving in a few hours. Can you identify which of the ETs were once human?"

"Not yet."

"I'll text you when we arrive."

"Internet here is iffy. I'm texting you a link to our network. Use that. You flying commercial?"

"No. Private. A DC-3 owned by the pilot of Flight 516. See you soon."

She texted him a link to the agency's network and moments later, he replied. *Remember Sofia Lopez, psychic for Omega? She read an ET she and Pierce thought was dead. And began changing. She's in our group. Here's a photo of how she's morphing.*

Bile surged up Lia's throat, she nearly gagged. She squeezed her eyes shut, as if that would shut off the memory of what she just had seen, but the image loomed in her head in full 3-D color. She looked at it again and fought off her revulsion long enough to enlarge the photo, study it.

Where had this happened? When? Were her hands becoming webbed, too? Had she developed gills? Would her face morph? She started to text it to Fleming, then didn't. She convinced herself she needed more details first. True enough, but not the whole truth.

She desperately wanted to call Dylan back, pump him for the particulars, try to piece things together in her own mind before she sent this to Fleming. But she didn't do that, either. She simply sat there, staring at the hideous photo and struggling not to flee.

Chapter 13

Pierce thought the DC-3 looked like a time travel machine. It sat on the tarmac at the Key West airport, a relic of earlier times, its awkward body tilted steeply downward toward the rear wheels, its nose and propellers lifted into the noon light, haughty and proud.

He pulled his and Sofia's bags toward the rear of the plane, where Piper was loading bags into the cargo hold. Pierce kept glancing around, anxiously searching for cops, TSA officials, Mayor Willford, or any other authority that could detain them. But as passengers on a private plane, they had sailed through all the checkpoints. Even Cooper had passed the muster. The others now trailed out of the main building, Cooper in his rescue harness trotting along with Sofia, Mike, and Dylan. Behind them were Carmen, McMullen, and Aldridge.

"Did Sofia get a confirmation on the airbnb?" Piper asked.

"Yeah, someone from Casa Jose is going to meet us at the airport."

"Perfect."

"How long is the flight?"

"No more than forty minutes once we're airborne. Getting through customs and immigration in Havana may be a lengthy process if a bunch of commercial fights land around the same time we do."

"I'm going to hurry them up."

Once they were all seated in the plane, Piper announced they had clearance for takeoff in five minutes and were waiting for a 727 to land. His voice sounded smooth and calm on the intercom. "Send any last minute texts and emails now. Once we're rolling down the runway, phones go off."

Dylan, seated next to Sofia, suddenly stood, and announced they'd gotten a major lead. "First, I've texted all of you a link to a U.S. government network that will work in Cuba. Once we're out of the Havana airport, you can set up your own emails and passwords on the network."

"Is this for The Agency?" Aldridge asked.

"Yes. I received some photos earlier from my former partner there. The images are disturbing, but I want everyone to know what we may be up against. Group text. There're brief comments with each one, most of them mine."

Pierce's phone and everyone else's dinged and sang and hummed. The first photo and accompanying comment hurled Pierce into a shocked stupor. The picture was of a dead ET at the bottom of a gigantic tank of water. The comment read: *agency facility in Viñales, more than 50 skin shifters.* The second and third photos were of a considerably shorter ET basking on a moonlit rock. *Hybrid infant isolated from others after apparent attack.*

"Fuck," Pierce whispered.

The fourth and fifth photos showed the fissured glass of the tank that held this alien/human hybrid and a close-up of its face.

The sixth photo depicted two tremendous tanks, each one seventy feet or higher, where the ETs swam and where some of them clustered around the infant, which certainty didn't look like any human version of an infant. With this photo, Lia Graham had commented: *We were tricked into believing the infant was being attacked by the adults so we isolated it, exactly what they wanted us to do so it could reek the havoc in this next pic, all that's left of the isolation tank.*

Shattered glass, chunks of rock, twisted metal rods, downed trees.

Pierce knuckled his eyes, thinking of Sofia's webbed feet against his calves last night. Beside him, Carmen gasped and gripped his arm. "This really is... the mother lode, Luke."

Piper's voice came over the intercom again, no longer calm and smooth, and presumably disconnected from the Key West tower and controllers. "If any of you would like to get off the plane, I'll taxi back to the main building. Please speak up now."

Silence.

"Yeah, I kinda figured that. Okay, if at any point in this journey you wish to go back to the States, I'll fly you home."

Silence, then Aldridge shouted, "Let's get this tank moving, John!"

"Yeah!" Mike echoed, pumping his fist in the air. He cranked up the volume on his iPhone until Grace Slick's voice filled the DC-3. *Go ask Alice when she's ten feet tall... tell 'em a hookah-smokin' caterpillar has given you the call...*

A few minutes later, the DC-3 pulled into position, the engines loud and noisy and eager to rock 'n roll, and as it took off, Cooper howled. To Pierce, it sounded like a call to arms.

2.

After seeing the photos Dylan had texted everyone, the only thing Sofia could think of was that she would end up looking like the monsters in the tanks. Skin Shifters, Lia Graham had called them. Her webbed feet responded to those images with the webbing thickening, swelling. She was terrified that the nubs along the sides of her fingers would suddenly sprout with webbing or her hair would fall out and in its place would be a blue tumbleweed and she would be taken into custody in the Havana airport. The area on her left side that felt sensitive when she touched it now itched like crazy. So far, she had resisted looking at it for fear she would see a gill forming.

But all of this anxiety faded when she caught her first glimpse of Cuba at three thousand feet, impeccable white beaches, rocky beaches, landscape that was green, then dry, then mountainous, then flat, a dichotomy even at this altitude. She experienced a swell of emotion she hadn't expected.

Even though she hadn't been born in Cuba, her parents and grandparents had and throughout her childhood, she'd heard their stories. The brutality of Batista, the hope that Che and Castro and their revolutionary movement initially created, then the horrifying realization that Castro, like his predecessor, would rule with an authoritarian fist.

Her grandparents had gotten out in 1959 with the first wave of refugees, but her parents had stayed because they made a good living—her dad as an engineer for the government and her mother as a physician. But after the embargo began, it became obvious to them that they needed to leave as well.

They finally got out when her mother was assigned to a field hospital near Caracas, part of a medical exchange program that Venezuela and Cuba shared, and her father was assigned to an engineering project in the city. They lived with relatives, saved their money, and finally made it to South Florida in 1965, where she'd been born nine years later.

By then, her parents lived next door to her grandparents in a duplex in Little Havana, her dad was fluent in English and worked for an American construction company. Her mother also became fluent in English, but not enough to pass the medical boards in Florida. So she started tutoring kids in math, science, whatever they needed.

Sofia's memories of childhood were mostly good, but overshadowed by her parents' strict adherence to Catholicism. Only her grandmother Rosa had understood the visions that often besieged Sofia, the dreams that awakened her in the middle of the night, the impressions she picked up when she touched people or objects they had worn or handled. When Sofia was fourteen, Rosa had taken her to a *santero* in Little Havana who had thrown the *caracoles* for her—shells—and told her that when she was older, she would investigate *ovnis* and *extraterrestres*—UFOs and aliens—and would have a son who would share this passion.

The *santera*, she remembered, had conducted a *limpieza* on her, a cleansing that involved incantations, prayers, cigar smoke, a blessing with holy water, and the sacrifice of a dove as an offering to the *orishas*, the powerful saints in Santeria. At that point, Sofia had freaked out and bolted from the woman's house, sobbing, heartbroken that the *santera* had killed a dove.

But afterward, her life had changed dramatically. She was no longer bullied at school. She became a straight A student, graduated with honors from high school, and won a full scholarship to Cornell, where she majored in psychology, minored in science, and finished in three years. She and Steve had gotten married a week after she'd graduated and Mike was born thirteen months later. The marriage lasted only six years.

All of this rolled through her head as she stared out the window and wished she had called her parents before she'd left.

Thirty-nine minutes after takeoff, the DC-3 touched down at Jose de Marti International Airport and Piper's voice boomed through the headphones. *"Bienvenidos a Cuba!"*

They applauded and cheered. Mike reached across the narrow aisle and squeezed Sofia's hand. Cooper barked excitedly.

Carmen got up, lit a Cuban cigar, and pulled a small bottle of Florida water from her handbag, a type of cologne typically used in Santeria rituals. She moved slowly up the aisle, blowing a cloud of smoke at each of them, flicking Florida water over them and chanting, *"Con las orishas de Santeria caminamos."* With the saints of Santeria we walk. *"Con las bendiciones de Chango, orisha de fuego, estamos protejido. Elegguá abre las puertas, los oportunidades, y Ochun, orisha de amor, llena nuestros corazones."* With the blessings of Chango, the saint of fire, we are protected. Elegguá opens doors, opportunities, and Ochun, the saint of love, fills our hearts.

When she reached the back of the pilot's seat and blew a cloud of smoke at Piper, he waved his arm around. "Hey, c'mon, Carmen. No smoking."

"This is not smoke, my friend. This is the magic of Cuba."

Sofia suddenly understood that Carmen wasn't just the female half of a citrus fortune who had an altar in her Cuba room featuring little offerings of candles and sweets to the *orishas.* She was a full-fledged *santera,* Cuban born and bred, who had escaped in the Mariel boatlift at age nineteen, and used her magic to milk the American dream so that she could pursue her passions.

Piper, now taxiing toward the general aviation building, kept waving his arm through the clouds of smoke. "If you're going to smoke the damn thing, I should at least get a puff. Is it a *cohiba* cigar?"

"Of course, *mi amor.* Only the best."

She passed him the cigar, he puffed and coughed, and handed it back to her. She moved back down the aisle, flicking Florida water around the cabin and insisting that everyone take a puff on the cigar. When Carmen passed the cigar to Sofia, she leaned forward and whispered, "You aren't alone. You have the entire pantheon of *orishas* behind you. Even Ted and the Cuban government are defenseless against it."

Sofia wasn't so sure about the Cuban government being defenseless against Santeria. It had been rumored for years that when Fidel was alive, he'd consulted *mayomberos,* the practitioners of the black arts. And even though the country was now opening up, thanks to Obama, Cubans still weren't free to leave the island. From what she'd read and heard from Carmen, life here was still severely restricted. But Carmen's remark about her husband intrigued her. Sofia couldn't imagine Ted believing in anything other than his own power and wealth.

She puffed on the cigar, drawing the sweetness of the smoke into her mouth, and immediately felt lightheaded, as if she'd taken a hit of really strong weed. In the moments between that hit and when the plane stopped, she felt a strange sensation in her feet, as if the webbing reacted to the smoke, that inhalation of magic. The persistent itching at her side stopped.

Sofia experienced a fleeing vision of a red and white 1955 Ford station wagon that would take them to Viñales. It would have a flat tire in rural countryside that would detain them. She sensed the flat tire was the beginning of her *final chapter,* but didn't have any idea what that meant. The final chapter to finding the river ETs? The final chapter that was death, the ultimate transformation?

The next thing she knew, they were getting off the plane. The men were removing the luggage so they could pull their bags into the immigration building that commercial flights also used. Carmen fell into step beside her. "You okay, Sofia?"

I'm rocking. "You're a priestess initiated into the brotherhood of Chango."

Carmen shrugged. "When I was sixteen, three years before my family became Marielitos."

"And four years before you met Ted."

"Yes. Even though he isn't Cuban, he believes in the power of the *orishas*, of Santeria. But his ego is huge, Sofia. He thinks he's invincible and the fact that his entire team and his wife have defected is going to bring out the worst in him."

She said all of this calmly, in an intimate tone as they pulled their bags toward the faded blue building in front of them. "What's his worst?"

"Whatever money can buy."

3.

A number of commercial fights had landed around the same time as the DC-3 and the immigration area was packed, six lines, hundreds of people. Pierce hated lines, bureaucracy, and bullshit, and slipped into a row that was supposedly for employees only. No one told him he couldn't be there and he pulled way out ahead of the others in his group and sailed through immigration to baggage claim.

He spotted his bag and Sofia's on the carousel, retrieved them, and carried them over to a wall to wait for the others. Around him, he heard Spanish, German, French, a spattering of English. The airport smelled old, the floors were scuffed, the carousels creaked. But a deep excitement filled him that he was in Cuba. A thirty-nine-minute flight had deposited him in a country and culture he never expected to see or experience.

Yet, beneath that excitement ran an inexplicable current that warned him to be cautious, pay attention, look around, remain vigilant. He had experienced this sensation frequently when he was investigating sightings and alleged abductions. His creepy spider sense. He figured it was a genetic throwback to when man lived in caves and survival depended on knowing where the danger was, where your enemies were hidden. It had served him well in the past dozen years and he paid attention to it now.

His eyes moved slowly around the baggage area, studying the people closest to him. Two British women who looked like mother/daughter stood in front of him, checking their phones, waiting for their baggage. The Brits, like other Europeans and Canadians, had been traveling to Cuba for decades. He didn't sense anything particularly strange about them but wondered if they actually had cell service. Cuba's network, Cubatel, had appeared on his phone, but he couldn't access it. He hadn't yet activated the link Dylan had texted the group and hoped he would be able to connect once he did.

Pierce turned slightly, studying the couple slightly behind him and to his left. Nope. Nothing. The creepy spider sense remained quiet. But the guy directly across from him was staring at Pierce. Short, muscular, dark hair, late thirties, Hispanic. He wore black jeans and a black t-shirt with Miami Dolphins written across it in bright red letters. He looked away from Pierce, eyed the carousel, turned his attention to Pierce again and gestured at his bags. "You have your bags already," he said in Spanish. "That gives me hope."

"A lot of flights just landed. They're slow in unloading." His Spanish sounded like that of a first grader.

The man switched to nearly perfect English. "What flight were you on?"

"Private. You?"

"Cubana Airlines from Venezuela. You here on business?"

Ha. Here to find ETs. "Pleasure. Waiting for the rest of my group. You?"

"I work here, in a *casa de cambio*. I was visiting family in Caracas. Work in Venezuela is practically non-existent now. Really bad situation there." The man suddenly pointed at the carousel. "Finally! My bag. Enjoy Cuba. It's a beautiful and mysterious country."

Sofia and Mike joined him with Cooper. "We got lost and ended up in another part of the airport," she said.

"The signs here suck," Mike remarked. "The others are behind us somewhere."

She passed Cooper's leash to Pierce and she and Mike went over to the carousel. Pierce noticed that she moved strangely, awkwardly, and guessed her feet were bothering her. He also noticed that the traveler from Venezuela took an inordinate interest in her, said something to her that Pierce couldn't hear, then turned away with his bag. As he started past Pierce, he stopped. "Awesome dog."

"Cooper, meet..." He paused. "I didn't catch your name."

"Ari."

"Cooper, this is Ari."

Cooper's tail wagged enthusiastically and he barked once, sat down, and lifted his paw. Ari laughed and took it. *"Un placer,* Cooper."

Pierce noticed that the flight tag on Ari's suitcase was for Jet Blue's flight from Fort Lauderdale to Havana. Then Ari moved on and Pierce gazed after him, wondering why Ari had lied and bewildered by the dog's behavior. Usually when Cooper was in his rescue harness, he wasn't friendly with strangers. If Cooper hadn't greeted Ari like he had, Pierce might not have noticed the flight tag on the man's bag. Had Cooper somehow known that?

"Did you, uh, do that on purpose, Coop?"

The dog looked up at him and those amber eyes seemed to laugh at him. *Ha, dude. I don't give my secrets away.*

Sofia and Mike pulled their bags up to Pierce and Cooper. "What was *that* about?" she asked.

"No idea. Ask Coop."

Sofia poked him in the shoulder. "This sounds like the creepy spider thing at work."

"Hey, I remember that from when you investigated the Tango sightings," Mike said.

It surprised Pierce. "Why would you remember something like that?"

"Because it sounded like what mom does."

"No way. Your mom's in an entirely different league. But we haven't seen the last of that guy."

"Yeah?" Mike's eyes brightened. "Watch my bag. Be right back. I'll text the photos to everyone."

He followed Ari, snapping a couple of photos of him from behind, then pulled out in front of him, camera at his side, aimed at Ari, probably videotaping him. "Your son may be as weird as you are," Pierce remarked.

She laughed. "Look who's talking. Do you really think we're going to see that guy again? In a country of more than eleven million?"

"Yeah. When he spoke to you at the carousel. What'd he say?"

"That he needed a strong *cafecito.*"

"That's it?"

"Yup. Nothing strange, Luke."

"Wrong. Something is really wrong. Trust me."

She rocked forward and touched her mouth lightly to his. "Welcome back, creepy spider."

4.

It had been awhile since Sofia had witnessed Pierce's creepy spider sense.

She remembered how over drinks one night during the investigation of the Tango Key sightings in 2010, Pierce had described this creepiness as the sensation of a giant spider scrambling across the back of his neck. *A spider with long legs. When I don't pay attention to it, those legs get longer and curl more tightly around my neck.*

She had recognized it as a psychic skill, but one that was so specific it worked only when he was supposed to pay close attention to something or someone that might present a risk. She'd said as much that night, but he'd dismissed the remark with a wave of his hand.

Piper, Carmen, Dylan, McMullen, and Aldridge finally joined them. Dylan said he'd activated The Agency link and asked Mike about the man in the picture he had texted. His response made Sofia smile.

"Luke's creepy spider sense says we're going to see him again. We need a record, right?"

"What's a creepy spider sense?" Dylan asked.

"Like the fire in your belly," Piper replied.

By then, their bags were on the motionless carousel, they claimed them and Carmen and Piper led the way out toward the main lobby. Jammed with people, the air here was hot and sticky and stank of sweat and diesel.

Cooper stuck close to her and Pierce, his nose working the air. He tolerated the occasional squeals from children who subsequently rushed over to pet and fuss over him, but seemed more interested in the odors that drifted through the open doors.

When they were in the middle of crowd, Sofia handed Mike Cooper's leash and said, "You guys wait here. I'll go look for someone holding a sign for *Casa Jose.*"

She waded through the crowd of hundreds. Jostled and bumped into on every side, she stopped at one point, allowing the crowd to flow around her, and saw Ari. He rolled his eyes, a commiserating connection. "Still looking for that cafecito!" he called.

Sofia flashed him a thumbs up and strode off in the opposite direction, wondering if this sighting counted. She finally spotted a blonde woman holding a sign that read, *Casa Jose.* Sofia threaded her way through the crowd to the woman. *"Hola, soy Sofia Lopez."*

"Ay, mucho gusto. Soy Inez. Mi esposo esta aqui tambien, con el segundo carro."

Inez's husband was here with the second car. Of course. Most of the cars in Cuba were too small to accommodate more than four people- and five with luggage was a tight squeeze. Sofia waved at her group and they followed Inez toward the front door.

The first thing she saw as they left the terminal was a bright red Chevy, circa 1953. Then she realized the parking lot was filled with American cars from the 1950s, and felt like she was on the movie set of *American Graffiti.* Any second now, John Travolta would appear with Olivia Newton John and they would break into a song and dance routine and afterward, George Lucas would shout, "It's a wrap!"

They followed Inez across the road to the parking lot. Sofia, in a state of near shock, managed to keep pace with everyone in spite of her webbed feet. Her grandparents had left from this airport in 1959, on the last flight out to the U.S. before the air space was closed. She was walking where they had walked, seeing what they had seen, feeling the shock they had felt. Her parents had left from here to Venezuela, the first part of an escape plan that had lasted more than a year.

She blinked back tears and realized that for her, and perhaps for Mike, too, this trip wasn't just about the ETs. It was also about something ancestral, genetic. Had her grandparents and, later, her parents, not escaped, had she been born here, she might not have met Steve and Mike wouldn't have been born, at least not with Steve as his father.

Sofia suddenly questioned whether these skin shifters had ended up in Cuba and in Viñales by chance or by design. She sensed it was the latter. The island's isolation, its abundance of rivers and wilderness, its repressive government: an ideal recipe, she thought, for an invasion.

Dylan believed the ETs could manipulate time. Given some of their recent experiences, it seemed they could. But right now, surrounded by all these outrageously colored cars from more than half a century ago, she already felt like a time traveler, a displaced person chasing hallucinations, what ifs, maybes…

Inez stopped at the rear of a red and white 1955 Ford station wagon, popped the hatch. "Put your bags in here and let's get moving. Five and the dog should fit." She stroked Cooper. "That's you, big guy."

Sofia recognized the station wagon from her vision as the vehicle that would take them to Viñales and have a flat tire in a deserted rural area. She didn't know what it meant and had no desire at the moment to think about it too closely. She took solace from the fact that not all of her visions panned out and hoped this one didn't. She climbed into the rear seat, Cooper leaped into the station wagon, settled beside her, and Pierce squeezed in next to Cooper.

"Damn dog is a space hog," Pierce remarked, pushing against Cooper to make more room for himself.

"Just means he's got your back, Luke." Then she turned toward the open window, eager to lose herself in Havana, and suddenly spotted Ari hurrying through the lot. She twisted around to keep an eye on him through the rear window. "Hey,

Luke. Isn't that Ari?"

He craned his neck to see. "Yeah. Definitely."

"So now we've seen him again." Twice. "You were right."

Pierce ran his hand over the back of his neck and shook his head. "The spider's legs just got longer. Those sightings don't count."

Sofia watched Ari until he got lost in the crowd of people pouring into the lot, flagging down taxis. He worried her.

It all worried her.

5.

The station wagon lacked seat belts and AC. The windows were open and the warm, humid air of Havana rushed through the car, infusing Sofia's senses. She felt as if she were moving through her ancestral world. Now and then Inez's voice registered, a running commentary about where they were, why this corner and that building were so historic and famous.

"There's the Ciudad Deportiva de la Habana, where the Rolling Stones put on a free concert in March of last year." Inez gestured at a worn, faded sports arena on their right. "Half a million people saw them. People pitched tents for days before just to get seats."

"They started the concert with Jumpin' Jack Flash," Sofia blurted out.

"They did?" Mike asked.

Piper's head bobbed. "Yup. It was incredible."

How had she known that? In March 2016, she was in deep shit financially, and hadn't paid any attention to what was happening in Cuba or anywhere else. Now and then she had noted where sightings had occurred, then reminded herself she no longer worked for Omega. Even though she'd been oblivious to Cuba in the spring of last year, the ETs had not.

She saw one of them in her head, an awkward human—male? Female? She couldn't tell—who moved with a strange shuffle and wore a straw hat that shadowed his or her face. The person was taller than others in the crowd, shoulders slumped like that of an elderly person. She saw the individual push through the crowd of cheering fans and felt the awe the ET had felt when Jagger sauntered out onto the stage. *I am seeing history.*

Whose history?

Presumably there were shifters that still hadn't been captured by The Agency. When they had morphed successfully into human forms, did they venture out and do the tourist bit just to test themselves? To make sure they fit in? Was that what the alien had done that had attended the Rolling Stones concert last year?

I'm going to find you.

The next time she checked her surroundings, the station wagon approached a plaza dominated by a majestic statue. "That's Jose Marti, the golden hero of Cuba who fought to liberate the island from Spain," Inez announced. "It's the entrance to Habana Vieja. And down those mazelike streets, off Obispo Street, you'll find El Floridita, where Hemingway, Ezra Pound, Pablo Neruda, and Graham Green hung out. The most popular tourist bar in the old town and probably in all of Cuba."

Would ETs frequent the most famous bar on the island? It sounded absurd. But perhaps it was one of the places where they tested their appearances. Or chose their victims. She was here with webbed feet and vastly changed perceptions and couldn't afford to overlook any possibility that might enable her humanity to be restored.

El Floridita went onto her *must check out* list.

Chapter 14

Casa Jose stood on a narrow, cobbled street just inside Habana Vieja. The two-story building screamed for fresh paint, a new sidewalk and curb, new concrete steps that led to the second floor. Bars covering the first-floor windows were a testimony, Dylan thought, to a fear that the little you had would be taken from you.

Inez pulled up to the curb, her husband's cab parked right behind it. They hopped out, popped the rear hatches on their respective cars, and they all started unloading their bags. A short, lively man barreled through the porch door on the first floor and threw out his arms. *"Bienvenidos a Casa Jose!"* he bellowed. "Welcome to my home!"

Sofia introduced herself and Cooper, who was sniffing at the tiny Boston Terrier that had followed Jose out the door, and then went down the line, introducing everyone else. Dylan figured Jose wouldn't remember all their names, but the importance of names dimmed in the sheer exuberance he radiated as he shook hands with the men, hugged the women, and petted Cooper, who ate it up.

"Please, this way." Jose gestured grandly toward the crumbling stairs to the second floor and led the way to the front door.

He, Carmen and Piper jabbered so rapidly in Spanish that it sailed past Dylan. Before Justin's death, when he and Graham had been chasing sightings and encounters all over the world, his Spanish had been good. He blamed the nuthouse drugs for stealing that skill from him.

The apartment, longer than it was wide, had four bedrooms

and adjoining bathrooms along the hall that emptied into a spacious kitchen and eating area. Jose opened the fridge, gesturing at its contents. It was jammed with Cuba's Cristal beer, packs of bottled water because the water coming out of the faucets, he explained, wasn't good to drink. There were containers of sliced cheese, sliced mangos and papaya, a container of Cuban coffee, packets of dried fruit, boxes of crackers. Compliments of the house.

Dylan dropped his bag in one of the bedrooms and climbed the staircase of cracked concrete steps to a rooftop garden so beautiful that he immediately knew it would be his refuge from *people.* Yes, he liked this particular group, felt a kinship with them because of the ETs, because each of them had a score to settle or something to gain. But as a group, there were too many people for him. He'd had his fill of crowds in the nuthouse.

He moved among the hanging vines, the beds of colorful flowers, the orchids, the bougainvillea vines climbing trellises, and stood at the wall, looking out over Havana Vieja. The Old Town. The buildings, two and three stories, were wedged so close together you would hear your neighbor belch or fart. Odors filled the air—fresh bread, roasting chickens and pork, the stink of diesel. The street below was closed to traffic and pedestrians swelled across the cobblestones. Music infused the air—salsa, rumba, the lonely strains of guitars, the steady, rhythmic beating of drums that caused his feet to move.

Justin, he thought, would have loved this.

"Hey, George," said Piper.

He and Aldridge came toward him through the hanging garden and Aldridge handed him a cold beer. "Salud, amigo. Welcome to Cuba and we're only three hours from where we may find some answers."

Dylan clicked cans with both men, gulped down beer so cold it left him with a brain freeze. "What's the plan?"

"I paid Jorge for the cabs," Piper said. "And hired Inez to drive us to Viñales tomorrow. I also told Jose that we'd like to rent the place for a week, even if we stay elsewhere. I like having a base camp to return to. Right now, we should exchange money, then find a place to eat."

Piper, the organized guy who always had a plan. Dylan liked that about him, particularly right now when he felt completely discombobulated.

"Is it possible to fly to Viñales?" Aldridge asked.

"Sure," Piper said. "But it takes some planning."

"I don't think it's a good idea," Dylan said. "We want to make sure we have our own transportation."

"I hear some mistrust there," Piper said.

"Caution."

"Just as well. It would take me longer than the drive to get clearance, papers and so on. Let's round up the others and do our money exchange."

Let's not. How about if the three of us head out on our own.

"Guys?"

Sofia and Cooper joined them, her feet now free of shoes, those grotesque webbings so visible that Dylan felt a sudden urge to drop to his knees, touch them, whisper to them, beg them to return his son to him. Insanity. But who cared? He'd been to the dark edge already, had peered over the precipice, and returned without slicing his throat.

"Look at this view," Piper said, throwing his arms out in front of him.

"Stunning," she said. "But we need to go down into this view to a money exchange place before they all close, and repay John for the cab and whatever else he has paid for."

Piper shook his head. "Forget it. I'm grateful to just be a part of all this. I know this is going to sound stupid, but I'm finally beginning to understand what I'm doing on planet earth, at this strange juncture in time and space."

"Lucky you." Sofia held out her arms and tried to embrace the three of them at once. "Group hug, guys. Move in a little closer, George."

"Why?" Dylan snapped. "So you can read all of us?"

"Aw, c'mon," said Aldridge. "Don't be an asshole."

Sofia took Dylan's hand and held it tightly between her own. He could have wrenched free if he'd wanted to, but the curious thing was that he felt compelled to hear whatever she had to say. He wanted her to tell him his immediate future, to read him upside down and backward, inside and out, and to do it as far out in time as she could go.

"I'm enraged that these ET fucks have killed Justin and I hunger for the moment I can kill them..."

Sofia released his hand, her eyes snapped open. "I've thought the same thing, Dylan. But please don't do that until we know more, until we're sure that's the answer."

They're my only chance of getting my kids back," Aldridge added.

"You, Sofia, and your kids, Larry, will become fully human again once the ETs are annihilated," said Dylan.

Aldridge looked alarmed. "We don't have any idea which ETs were once human. You don't have any proof that killing ETs will fix anything."

"It may be the only thing I know," Dylan said, and hurried back down the crumbling steps to the first floor, found out from Carmen where the nearest money exchange place was, and set out on his own.

Relieved to be by himself, he turned on his phone, his connection to a larger world, and went to text messages. He looked again at the photos Mike had sent of Ari, the dude at the airport who had told Pierce he'd just arrived from Venezuela, but whose bag bore a Jet Blue tag for a flight from Miami. So many times over the years when he was with The Agency, mysterious people like this Ari had shown up repeatedly. These individuals had given rise to the urban legend of MIBs, the men in black made famous by Hollywood. Some of them were legitimate sources of information, most were not. He had no idea right now where Ari fell.

He texted Graham: *Settled in our place. Head out tomorrow for Viñales.*

A *delivered* message appeared. Moments later, Graham responded. *Be aware that nothing on this island happens quickly. Hybrid definitely escaped. Best way to get here is by car. I can send one. Or you can rent.*

We've rented already.

Paranoid, Dylan?

Bet your ass.

Of what?

Everything.

Give the network link to others in your group so you can stay in touch with texts, emails.

He sent a group text and reminded the others to create an account with a password and kept walking toward the money exchange place, up one block and down another. Traffic whizzed by in every direction, pedestrians were on the move. The heat was no worse than South Florida, but the stink of diesel lingered in the air. Now and then, a slight breeze would kick up, ushering in the distinctive scent of salt water.

Texts started coming through, everyone in the group thanking him, awed by the network's speed, asking where he was.

Getting in line at closest exchange place, he replied.

The small concrete building with *casa de cambio* inscribed over the door had a line outside several dozen people deep, and the guard at the door allowed only one person in at a time. No one complained. For Cubans, waiting seemed to be a fact of life. He began to understand what Graham had meant about nothing happening fast on the island.

When he finally neared the front of the line, the guard waved through the two people in front of him, poked his head back inside the door, spoke to someone, then glanced outside and motioned for Dylan to come in. He trotted up the steps, the guard opened the door for him, and he stepped into what felt like a steam room. No air conditioning, no open windows, just two tall floor fans stirring the hot, sticky air.

Two tellers, each with a customer. The guard motioned for Pierce to stay back from the teller windows. A third man appeared, short, muscular, dark hair. What the hell, Dylan thought. It was Ari from the airport, still wearing the black t-shirt with Miami Dolphins written across the front in bold red letters. No coincidence. That word didn't exist in the world of UFO research.

Ari came over to Dylan, smiling pleasantly, and introduced

himself. "Hello, I'm Ari Rey. If you could come with me, please?"

Dylan played along. "Where? I'm here to exchange money."

"I can do that for you. Otherwise you're going to be waiting awhile." He gestured toward the tellers. "They're incredibly slow in here."

He accompanied Rey out of the teller area, up a hall to an air conditioned office, where the window unit chugged and clanked noisily. "I saw you at the airport, Mr. Rey."

"Yes, yes. You were with a rather large group. Are the others waiting outside?"

"They aren't here yet."

"Please, have a seat. May I see your passport? Are you exchanging American dollars?"

"Canadian dollars."

Rey grinned. "Smart man. No ten percent surcharge." He brought out a keychain filled with keys, unlocked a drawer, and Dylan set his passport, visa tucked inside, on the desk. "How much are you exchanging?"

"Seven hundred Canadian." Dylan set his Canadian money next to his passport. The bills were so pretty they looked fake.

Rey ran Dylan's passport through a machine, counted out the equivalent of 700 Canadian dollars in Cuban CUCs, rang up a receipt, handed it, the passport, and the money to Dylan. "So, Mr. Dylan. Is your trip to Cuba for pleasure?"

Dylan decided this little game had gone on long enough. "I'm here looking for aliens, Mr. Rey. You know anything about that?"

"Aliens?" He blinked rapidly.

"Yeah, you know, the ones who look like grotesque mermaids."

"Ah, si, si." His head bobbed. "A visit can be arranged for you and your group."

"How?"

"For a price."

"How much?"

"That depends."

"Depends on what?"

"On what each of your value." Rey folded his hands on top

of the desk and leaned forward, dark eyes boring into Dylan's. "What price does Ms. Lopez place on being fully human again? How badly do you and Dr. Aldridge want your children..."

Dylan's pulse hammered in his ears, red poured across his vision, and he shot to his feet, towering over Rey, and grabbed him by the front of his goddamn Miami Dolphins t-shirt. Dylan jerked him forward so hard and fast that the fabric tightened around Ari's throat and he started to choke. "What value do you place on your life, asshole?"

Rey's fists shot toward Dylan's face and he wrenched sideways, releasing his hold on the man's shirt, and Rey sank back into his chair, rubbing at his throat, gulping at the air. "If I...call...the guards..."

Dylan leaned into him. Rey leaned back. "Let's get something straight, Mr. Rey or whoever the fuck you are. If you have information about my son or Dr. Aldridge's kids, then spit it out. Otherwise, you're wasting my time and I would just as soon kill you here and now. *Entiendes?*"

Blood drained from Rey's face. He straightened his t-shirt, struggled to compose himself. "I... I'm just a messenger."

"For who or what?"

"I... I don't even know. Four months ago, they... they took my wife. Changed her. They told me that if I delivered a message to you and your group, they would return her to me, whole, human again."

"What's the message?"

"Your son and Dr. Aldridge's children are at El Floridita."

"My son was killed by these fucks three years ago."

"No." He shook his head emphatically, almost violently. "El Floridita is not... of this world. It is *their* world. *They* control it. It has been that way for a long time. You'll see. When I go there, I see my wife, speak to her, embrace her. Illusion, all illusion. But it... it is all I have now." He started to cry, then sob, and pressed his fists against his eyes.

If it was an act, Dylan thought, then it was a damn good one. But he knew in his heart that Rey wasn't pretending. He recognized the rawness of the man's emotions and understood the profound shock he had experienced as a result of what had happened to his wife and, subsequently, to him. The late John Mack, the Harvard psychiatrist who had investigated alien abduction cases, had believed that the trauma for many abductees was so extreme that their worldview, everything they believed to be true, collapsed.

But this phenomenon was far worse than any alien abduction. A loved one was either killed by an amphibious ET or was turned into one. Or, like with Sofia, your own body was stolen bit by bit.

Dylan touched Rey's shoulder. "I appreciate your honesty, Ari."

His hands dropped to the desk and he looked at Dylan with his now swollen, rheumy eyes. "Please help me, señor."

"My hope is that all of us can find what he need. What can you tell me about the tanks of *sirenas* in Viñales?"

"What tanks?"

A messenger who was missing some vital information. "Where do the *sirenas* live in Viñales?"

"The river, the caves..."

"Which caves?"

"My wife... disappeared when we were touring Cuevo de Los Indios. Other people have, too. It has since been closed by the government. But I have heard these monsters live throughout the caves, in the river."

"Give me your cell number, Ari. Send me a photo of your wife. So I'll be able to identify her if I see her. "

"*Si, si, claro, Señor Dylan.*"

Rey quickly texted the photo, a lovely brunette with sad, haunted eyes. "I can take you to El Floridita."

"I can find it."

"But you must be close to Hemingway."

"Hemingway?"

"*Si,* his statue. His legacy is the reason El Floridita is the most famous bar in Cuba."

"Just show me the back door."

He shot to his feet and scurried through the office doorway and into a hall. "Through here."

"Why do they want Sofia Lopez?" Dylan asked.

Rey tapped his temple. "Because of what she can see. Even though they can do things we cannot, she has the *vision*, The Sight, that is what I was told. *Me entiendes?*"

Dylan nodded. Yeah, he understood.

Rey threw open a door at the end of the twilit hallway. The brightness of the late afternoon sun angled into the hallway, revealing the neglect and decay of the walls, the floor, the whole nine yards. Before Dylan stepped outside, he looked at Rey. "If I need help, if I need a bunch of people, a small army, how fast can you act?"

Rey grinned and snapped his fingers. *"Asi."* Like that. "I am just one of many who have lost loved ones to these *maricones*. We often meet in secret. There are more than a hundred of us now, from Havana, Cienfuegos, Santiago, Trinidad, from all over the island. But we're a small fraction. I believe there are hundreds more, but they are afraid to come forward. So far, we have not been able to do anything, so they use us to...to entrap others. People in the government know about these creatures, but are so paralyzed with fear they don't do anything."

"What's the best time to go to El Floridita?"

"Tomorrow. Midnight." No hesitation. "It truly is the bewitching hour there."

"Why not tonight?"

"It's closed." His voice dropped to barely a whisper. "I believe it's when they... make preparations, so they can choose their victims."

Dylan slung his arm around Rey's neck. *"Gracias, amigo."*

Then he hurried out into a shadowed alley, past overflowing garbage cans and skinny dogs and cats that scurried for shelter, and texted Sofia and Aldridge. *A lead. El Floridita. Midnight tomorrow.*

2.

Lia Graham and Jerry Fleming stood in the doorway of what had been one of the four isolation rooms on the property. The destruction seemed so massive and incomprehensible she felt their best option was to level the entire building and bury it under a shitload of dirt and rocks. They had tractors and land movers, shipped in from the U.S., that could do the job. Thanks to the money they'd paid the Cuban government for the use of this property, the authorities wouldn't question what they did. But they would expect the usual monthly report about the ETs.

These fucks can produce offspring. And one of them, an alien/ human hybrid, escaped.

That news might prompt a visit from the authorities, from some advisor to Raul Castro or his inner circle. And it might get her and Fleming fired.

At this point, she would welcome a forced resignation. So would Fleming. But in the back of her head, she clung to some small hope that when Dylan and his group got here, they would have information and insights she and Fleming lacked. And perhaps that information, whatever it was, would help them defeat these monsters and restore the transformed humans.

In the field of UFO/alien research, her hope would be considered a delusional long shot.

"Well?" she said.

Fleming ran his hand over his bald head and moved carefully across a floor covered with shards of glass, uprooted trees, broken doors, twisted spears of metal, and half a foot of mud. "Christ. We need to bury this. All of it. As soon as it's light."

"Any lead on the escaped hybrid?"

"Nothing. They're still looking."

She followed him into the ruined room, her heavy boots crunching across the glass, squishing through the mud. "And two of the snipers died. They both have families. What the hell do we tell their families?"

"They died in the line of duty in a special op and the insurance pays them three million apiece. The surviving snipers are reassigned stateside. We say nothing about the escaped hybrid and follow the usual protocol with the fishermen- they pursue whatever leads they hear. They get a raise."

"And Margarita and Sergio? They witnessed everything."

"We buy their freedom. They and their families can be

resettled in Miami. We need their skills, Lia, so they're welcome to remain on the team and they also get a raise."

"So essentially we're buying off everyone."

"Yeah." Fleming stopped at the large rock where the hybrid had been basking in the moonlight, climbed onto it, patted the space beside him. Lia joined him on the rock. "We have a huge budget, a black op bag of gold under the Department of Defense. But at some point, I'm going to have to submit my quarterly report for additional funding and I'd like you to start on that by delineating what we know about these aliens and what we don't know."

No small task, she thought. "We don't know much at all."

"The DOD is going to be interested in the fact that they can procreate and produced a hybrid. The hybrids have been suspected for some time—anecdotal stuff for the most part—but never proven in a tangible way like we saw. I'll need whatever video you've got on your cell. And we need a research team."

"We've got our team in Dylan and his group. I'd like them on payroll. All of them. I don't care how you do it, but it needs to be done."

Fleming nodded reluctantly. "He didn't answer your last texts?"

"They'll be here tomorrow. They rented a car and driver. He didn't say anything about working for us."

Fleming looked around at the ruin, at the mud and broken glass, the crushed doors and dead fish, dead octopi, dead trees, dead everything. He leaned back on his elbows and screamed, *"Fuck all of you! Fuck you and your morphing crafts and morphing bodies and whatever the fuck it is you're trying to do!"*

Lia looked over at him. Outbursts from Fleming were rare. "Feel better?"

In the waning starlight, tears glistened on his cheeks. "Not really. I'm still scared for my kids. If I had any sense, I'd put in for early retirement, like I was planning to do yesterday before all this shit happened. But now it feels like if I did that, I'd be betraying everyone who has been affected by these monsters. If we don't end this, Lia, they'll just keep coming here, taking people, turning them until they inhabit the entire planet."

"Maybe we should fill the tanks with drugs and kill the ones we've got."

"Believe me, I've considered that. The problem is that we don't know which ones were human."

They whispered now, both of them aware that the ETs might be able to hear them. "Maybe Dylan and his group can help us determine that. When Justin disappeared and Omega was investigating, I was impressed with Sofia Lopez's skills. She read that sail club site and later confided in Pierce and me that she felt Justin was dead. She picked up that he'd been dragged into the water by an alien and taken to a craft."

Fleming sat up. "An airborne craft?"

"She didn't say."

"She's with Dylan's group because of Omega?"

Lia hesitated. She still hadn't shown Fleming the photo Dylan had texted her of Sofia Lopez's webbed feet. Why? Did she really think he might try to hold Sofia prisoner? Or that he would put her in one of the tanks with the other ETs? Or that he would parade her before Congress so the politicians who controlled the money would understand the kind of threat they faced? No.

"That's not the only reason she's with his group." Lia brought up the picture and passed Fleming her phone.

"Sweet Christ," he spat. "She's *morphing?* " He raised his eyes. "How much of her has changed? When did this happen?"

"I don't know any of the details. But she could give us a distinct advantage."

"I want to know everything they know." Fleming held out her phone. "Until we know more, until we've spoken to her, it's not safe to bring her here. We'll meet them in town somewhere." He rubbed his eyes. "Shit, I need a drink."

She texted Dylan, asking for details. "Make that several drinks."

"We need drivers here at sunrise to start burying this shithole." Fleming stood, held out his hands, and pulled her to her feet. They stood there on the rock where the hybrid had basked, her hands buried in his, his eyes searching hers. "You're still in love with him."

She nodded. "And you still love your wife."

"Yeah."

But his wife and Dylan weren't here. Neither of them had been a part of what she and Fleming had experienced today or for the many days, weeks, months, and years since this project had begun. It made a difference. But she wasn't willing to go there.

Lia put her arms around him, hugging him. "About the only thing I'm good for right now, Jerry, is getting drunk."

He chuckled. "Agreed." As they climbed down from the rock, he took her hand. "My wife thanks you."

"I don't know if Dylan would thank you, but I do. I think we should consider each other siblings, like Sergio and Margarita. I always wanted an older brother."

"Done. Did Dylan reply yet?"

"No."

"Keep after him."

In River Country

*L*otus, Jez, and I reach river country near dawn of my second
day in Cuba. We follow the scent of water through groves of
fruit, into rice paddies. The paddies are wet, surrounded by pools
of fresh water, and Lotus and I immerse ourselves, stretching out
face down in the shallow pools. The gill at my throat opens, I
drink and drink until I can't drink any more. But I have trouble
breathing and my hand moves to my side, checking the injured
gill.

I don't feel anything.

I lift my head slowly from the water, giving my throat gill
a chance to close, and roll over, sit up, and look down at my left
side.

The gill is gone.

The skin there is beautifully smooth.

It means Sofia is in Cuba, that she now has a gill on her
side. She may not be close to where I am, not yet, but the closer
she gets, the more she will become like me and the more I will
become like her. That is my hope. But the transformation process
is different for each of us. When will I gain her Sight? Will I
have to wait until the final stage of her metamorphosis? Will that
happen when we are face to face?

Lotus and I grab handfuls of the green leaves of the rice plants,
jam them in our mouths, and move into the groves of mangos
and papayas, feasting until our hunger diminishes. What I really
crave now is meat—frogs, fresh water fish, turtles. Land animals
would satisfy that need, too. Chickens, pigs, calves.

Have you summoned your craft yet? *Lotus asks.*

I've tried. *Several times. But nothing happens.*

It should be healed by now.

Yes. It emitted one message, that it was now in a secure place and healing. But since then, nothing.

Perhaps the humans found it, hid it somewhere, and now it cannot communicate.

Worrisome.

Do you hear it? *Lotus asks, papaya juice oozing from her mouth.*

The music of our tribe. But the story it tells disturbs us. A hybrid was born in the tanks where some of my kin are being kept and it escaped. No one knows where it is.

Find it. *My demand races out through the web, but the song that answers it, a collective tribal song, smacks of cowardice.*

We are in hiding. Soldiers are hunting for the hybrid. If they see us, they will drug us and drag us off to the tanks.

You have powers! Use them!

They have weapons.

I warned you, Mira, *says Lotus.* I warned you that cowardice has infected your supporters.

Fools. They fear the very humans we are changing. Lotus and I leap up and race toward the river. My anger sweeps from me in waves and the web lights up as the tribe feels the rage that I feel.

Then I spot the river through the trees. It's wide, a beautiful blue that reminds me of distant memories that were passed onto me by my own ancestors when they died in The Tilt so many eons ago. Once, we had rivers like this, lush beauty and air like this, farms and groves like this. And now we will again.

As Lotus and I are about to leap into the river where Jez awaits us, two campesinos in a dugout see us and frantically paddle toward shore, jump out, and race into the trees, screaming, "Sirenas, sirenas!"

Watch this! *My demand rips across the web and Lotus and I hurl powerful waves of energy that knock the two men off their feet and sweep them up, up over the tops of the trees, their arms and legs flying out in every direction, both of them still shrieking. And when they are thirty or forty feet above the ground, a second wave throws them to the banks of the river.*

They are no longer shrieking. That's how you use your power. And you take them by surprise.

Now? We should do this now?

This stupid question appalls me. What have they been doing here for weeks, for months?

Abducting humans.

How many have you changed here?

Dozens. And dozens more are in the process of being transformed. But we have also been hiding from Acia and her supporters and waiting for your arrival, Mira.

It should be hundreds. Do nothing until I arrive.

With the two campesinos now dead, Lotus and I leap into the river and start swimming toward Viñales. The absence of my webbed feet slows me down, but my hands and arms are strong and my determination is a force that drives me.

As I swim, I gobble fish, a couple of delectable frogs, and in the quiet of the river, I connect with her, with Sofia. She feels it, tries to block it. She can't. So she frantically builds a wall around herself that proves impenetrable for me. But I saw enough. She knows about the tanks in Viñales and her plans for getting there were delayed. Right now, she and her group are waiting for a tourist bus in Havana that will take them around the city.

Her group: I glimpsed them only briefly, but all are familiar to me. Pierce, whom we chose long ago; her son; the old man who found me; the pilot who saw my craft crash; the santera, Carmen; Aldridge, the physician whose children are now part of my tribe; and Dylan, who has hunted us for years. Of them all, I believe Dylan is the most formidable.

Three years ago, a rogue in my tribe took his son, tortured him, inserted an implant behind his ear, and the young man's terror killed him. Dylan's hatred toward us is profound and dangerous. He will stop at nothing.

There is something else I glimpsed, but I'm not sure how it fits and must dip into the web to find the answer. Ari Rey. El Floridita. Hemingway. I understand the connections immediately and know that members of my tribe control the place. Does Acia also have her supporters there?

I suddenly wonder if, all along, this web that connects the tribe is our collective Sight, *the very thing I'm seeking from Sofia. But as I skim its surface, dive into it, and swim around inside it, I understand there is nothing here about our future.*

This web is a pool of our collective knowledge and experiences. Even the humans we have transformed have access to it, but most of them are too traumatized to realize what it is. Yet, those of the tribe who now walk in human bodies and retain their identities as part of us, use it sometimes. It's our equivalence of the human Internet. And it's here I discover a private message from Neil King, a man who worked for The Agency, the same government organization that employed Dylan.

He addresses me by name in our language, a series of high and low notes that roughly translate as Mira, a giant red star in the constellation of Cetus. But the message itself is in human languages—English and Spanish:

Mira,

I was transformed six years ago and now live in San Francisco, where an enclave of our kind work in the tech industry. Three years ago, I began recovering memories of my human life and learned how to dip into the web that connected us when I was part of your tribe.

The people who run the compound, where members of our tribe are imprisoned, are my former boss, Jerry Fleming, and the woman I was married to when I was changed—Lia Graham. My recommendation, to use a phrase humans love, is that you *do not fuck* with them. You won't win.

There are other factions of humanity you can conquer easily. I suggest you pursue anything but this. Allow the fist of destiny to play its hand with those who are captive. Humans call them collateral damage. As for Acia and Ravina, they have sent out calls to those of us who are now human and demand that we join them, that we unite against you.

I have refused that call. If you need my help at any point, please let me know.

I withdraw from the web and swim faster.

Chapter 15

Shortly after midnight at the beginning of their third day in Havana, Sofia spotted El Floridita. It stood where it had stood for decades, several blocks off Obispo Street, the main pedestrian route through Havana Vieja. Even in the moonlight, Sofia could see the building's pinkness, with three large white, rectangular tiles—signs—hanging above the entrance that read: MI DAIQUERI... EN LA FLORIDITA... and then, in a fancy script, ERNEST HEMINGWAY.

This was the place the ETs supposedly controlled.

The gill in her side opened as if in response to that control. She felt it as it happened, like a mouth opening to suckle greedily, lips puckered. *Feed me, feed me.* She experienced a slight difficulty in breathing and pressed her hand to her side. Panic poured through her, she nearly spun around and ran. But if she did that, then the alien won and she might as well just lay down here in the street and let a car run over her.

She'd discovered the gill in the shower yesterday, the horrid thing fluttering open as soon as the water hit it. It had scales with sharp edges and inside of it, visible as it opened, were layers of more scales the color of rust. It had been preceded by the awful itching, as if she'd been bitten by something. As soon as she'd seen it, she had known the ET no longer had its side gill, that its skin there was as smooth and flawless as hers had been.

What next? A throat gill? A single nostril? A tuft of blue hair that replaced her own?

In the moments when the gill opened like this, she sensed it was another conduit between herself and the ET. She hastily slapped together a mental wall around herself and her knowledge, but information still leaked through. The ET knew where she was, who she was with, what was happening with her metamorphosis.

In turn, Sofia sensed the ET—*Mira, her name's Mira*—traveled with two allies, Lotus and Jez. Her tribe was fractured, a power struggle of some kind with Acia, and she and her allies were being pursued by another alien, Ravina, with whom Mira had battled once before for dominion over the tribe. There was something here about a battle with a hammerhead shark and with Ravina on the Cuba-bound ferry that had sunk.

This works two ways, bitch.

Mira heard her. *In terms of information, yes. That's only fair, right? You humans are so big on fairness. So know this: when you enter El Floridita, you step into my world, governed by my rules. Your suppositions about how reality works will no longer apply.*

I'll take my chances.

Laughter. Or, at any rate, what Sofia interpreted as laugher, a series of off-tune notes, like badly played chopsticks, that made her want to grind her teeth. *And what chances are those, Sofia? That you will overpower me? Kill me?*

Sofia felt something else about this web, that she could open a private channel to others in the tribe, to Mira's foes. But she didn't yet understand how this web worked, the machinations were beyond her. Yet, she understood enough to detach from it by placing her attention elsewhere, on her dog, moving along between her and Dylan. She dropped her hand to Cooper's head, stroking it, combing her nails back through his fur.

The last thing she heard, a faint echo, was Mira reprimanding her followers for not using their power against the humans who held some of them captive in tanks. As long as she kept her attention on Cooper and her goal—walking into El Floridita- the communication between her and the ET shut down. And so did the gill at her side. She was left with nothing more than her clumsy webbed feet and the nubs on her fingers that promised the webbing would grow back when the ET commanded it to do so. A sour residue coated her tongue. The scent of lavender clung to the air.

It controlled her still, but she was learning the control wasn't absolute.

"Sofia?"

"Yeah?" She glanced at Dylan as they crossed the street to El Floridita, moving between parked taxis and throngs of pedestrians enjoying the old town's night life.

"You okay? "he asked.

The question made her laugh. *Okay*? What was *okay*? Communicating with an alien? Webbed feet? A gill? Hearing so acute she could listen to a woman a mile behind her arguing on the phone with her husband? Was it *okay* that she could smell the women in this crowd who were having their periods? Was it *okay* that she was no longer entirely human?

"I don't even know what that means anymore, Dylan."

Pierce, Mike, and Cooper were behind them, and Aldridge, Carmen, Piper and McMullen brought up the rear. They were entering El Floridita as three separate groups, and each group would be reporting to the others through the agency network link Dylan had provided.

If she could figure out how to access private channels in the alien web so that she could communicate with Mira's adversaries, she would have an edge, however slight.

They had spent most of the day on the tourist bus, orienting themselves to the labyrinthine city. The bus cost the equivalent of ten bucks, was good all day, and they could get off and on as they pleased. They had gotten off and walked around the old town, had stepped inside El Floridita to orient themselves, then boarded the bus again. In another part of town, they'd gotten off at the University of Havana campus, where the 1959 revolution had started. Sofia had found the science department and when she and Carmen were inside, she'd asked a clerk a reference question. *How's the frog population doing in Viñales?*

She'd expected she would have to go through several supervisors to find her answer. But to her surprise, the young woman had told Sofia she'd been getting official inquiries recently about that very thing. "Our government is conscientious about our wildlife areas and is concerned that the frog population in Viñales has suffered greatly in the past months."

"And what effect does that have generally on the area?" Carmen asked.

"More mosquitos, more hornworms, greater destruction to the tobacco crops. Since tobacco is one of our major money producers, it means less money for the farmers."

"Why are the frogs dying off?" Sofia asked.

"No one knows."

But Sofia knew why. The ETs were arriving, a rendezvous in Viñales to save their captive brothers and sisters, to take over the island, and they had an appetite for frogs.

"And what did that tell you?" Carmen had asked when they were outside the building.

"When frogs vanish from an area, things get screwed up ecologically. I think hundreds of ETs are headed to Viñales, Carmen, there could be thousands already here, and they're consuming the frogs."

She worried that they should have left for Viñales today. But Inez had car trouble and since it was the height of the tourist season, they hadn't been able to find another driver with a car large enough for all of them on such short notice. She was discovering that nothing on this island happened quickly. And besides, Dylan was adamant about going to El Floridita around midnight, to find out if what Ari Rey had told him was true. The gill at her rib, now closed, told her it was true, that the ETs controlled El Floridita, a confirmation of what Mira had said.

... when you enter El Floridita, you step into my world, governed by my rules. Your suppositions about how reality works will no longer apply.

She didn't have any idea what the specifics might entail.

Just outside the front door of the place, Dylan grasped her hand. "No intimacy intended, Sofia. I just need to make sure that if there's weirdness here, you and I don't get separated."

"I get it. But I think you should know, Dylan, that I keep seeing you married to or living with a really pretty blond. She reminds me of your former partner, Lia Graham."

"You're a spooky person, Sofia."

"I've been called worse."

As they walked into the building, Cooper's tail wagged

and he endured endless pats and smiles and exclamations of how beautiful he was. No one said he couldn't be here, which Sofia took as a positive sign. Her watch read two minutes after midnight. El Floridita, jammed with people, rocked with live music.

They made their way through the crowd, a feat made easier by Cooper's presence, who caused the crowd to part like the Red Sea. They moved past the band, to a crowded space against the wall. There, to her left, stood a large bronze statue of Hemingway, his left elbow resting on the edge of the bar, his head turned toward it, as if he were watching someone on the other side of the room. His profile, rendered in such exquisite detail, right down to the wrinkles at the corner of his right eye, couldn't be mistaken for anyone else. People were crowded around it, taking selfies with Papa.

The wall behind and above the statue were covered with photos of Hemingway with Fidel Castro and other political figures from the Fifties and of various Hemingway family members. Sofia recognized Hemingway's niece, Hilary, daughter of his brother Les. She was a friend of Sofia's and had provided her with invaluable information for a paper she'd written her senior year in college on Hemingway's bipolar disorder during his final days in Cuba. She snapped a photo of the wall and texted Hilary, but it didn't go through.

Was that part of the aliens' control over this place?

They squeezed their way to the bar. The bartenders wore white shirts and trousers with aprons the same shade of red as the cabinet that held glasses and bottles of booze. Across the front of the cabinet were the words, *Cradle of the Daiquiri*. "Is that true?" Dylan asked, gesturing at the cabinet.

"Beats me. I figured this place was the cradle of the *mojito*."

"What would you like to drink?"

"A cold beer would be great."

She saw Pierce and Mike on the far side of the bar and Carmen and the others edging their way through the crowd at the front. The mood inside the place was festive and loud and it lifted her spirits to see so many people enjoying themselves. Aldridge, she noticed, was no longer using his cane and she didn't remember him using it yesterday, either. Was this significant? Probably not, but now she questioned everything.

Dylan ordered two beers from the bartender who came over. His name tag read, *Constantino Ribalaigua.* He handed Sofia a dog treat and a metal bowl filled with water for Cooper. *"Muchas gracias,"* she said, setting the bowl on the floor in front of Cooper. He sat back, eyeing the treat, and she handed it to him.

"De nada. Come se llama el perro?"

"Cooper."

A shadow flitted across his face. *"Eres Sofia?"* He glanced at Dylan. *"Y tu eres Dylan?"*

"Si," Dylan replied. *"Por que?"*

"No deben estar aqui. Hay mucho peligro."

"Is he saying what I think he's saying, Sofia? We shouldn't be here, there's danger?"

"Yes. *Que tipo de peligro?"* What kind of danger?

Ribalaigua glanced around uneasily. *"Ya sabes."* You already know. He quickly turned away, popped open two cold beers, set them on the counter. *"Seis CUCs, por favor."*

Dylan paid, then added another three CUCs for a tip. *"Gracias. Salud,* Sofia."

As he clicked his glass against hers, the doors of El Floridita opened and more people poured into the place. The music and laughter got louder, men and women crowded into the space along the wall and took more selfies with Hemingway. The press of bodies behind them, the warm air and noise, brought on a wave of claustrophobia. Sofia started to tell Dylan she needed to get out of here, but noticed that the door to the building was still open and wisps of fog now eddied through it. The wisps quickly elongated, lengthened, thickened, then curled and uncurled and whipped along the floor like snakes.

Cooper tensed and tugged on his leash. Sofia held him back and reached down, stroking him. "Dylan, do you see... "

"Yes." His voice sounded tight, alarmed. His fingers curled around Cooper's leash and her hand.

The fog kept moving across the floor, thicker now, weaving

its way between people's legs, separating her, Dylan and Cooper from the people behind and around them. Alarmed, Sofia checked out the crowd to see if anyone else noticed the fog. No one seemed to. In the midst of laughter, drinking and dancing to the rhythmic salsa beat from the band, the fog moved along in no particular hurry.

Now it crept around the statue of Hemingway, along the sides of the bar, then across it. The bartenders kept mixing drinks, filling shot glasses, whipping up daiquiris. The band kept playing, laughter continued to ring out. Fog formed a wall between them and the bartenders and customers that crowded around the bar. She still had Mike and Pierce in sight, but it was like seeing them through a billowing, translucent curtain.

Dylan's hand tightened around hers. "Everything feels surreal," he whispered.

The skin at the back of her neck tightened, goose bumps erupted on her arms. And then the statue of Hemingway suddenly moved and she understood what the ET had meant... *when you enter La Floridita, you step into my world, governed by my rules. Your suppositions about how reality works will no longer apply.*

Hemingway's elbow dropped away from the bar, he stretched both arms overhead, and stood. "My God, sitting in that position makes my back ache."

Sofia, too shocked to say anything, just stared, her mind racing, stumbling around for answers. *It's him, it's really him.*

Dylan drew back. "Holy fuck."

Hemingway looked at them, saw Cooper. "I'm a cat person myself, but your dog is beautiful."

"Cooper," she managed to say. "His name is Cooper."

"Mucho gusto, Cooper."

Sofia felt as if she'd awakened inside a myth, a legend. What could she possibly say to Hemingway? *Hey, you're still famous fifty-five years after you died. Everyone in this place is here because of you.* Did he understand what was happening? She finally blurted, "Your home in Key West is now a museum with several dozen cats living on the grounds. Some of them are descendants of the six-toed cats you owned."

Something sad happened to his eyes, he looked down at the floor, and pointed at the fog that slithered around. "Oh. Shit. This again."

"So you, uh, understand what's happening?" she asked.

"When the fog is here, I come alive for awhile." He met her gaze. "We didn't have cats in Key West. We had peacocks. Mary and I have cats at Finca Vigia here in Havana, where we live now... where we lived then... Christ, this time thing gets so confusing. Anyway, Mary and I got the cats to keep down the rat population that comes in from the mango groves."

The bit about the cats was news to her. Sofia had taken the tour of his home in Key West several times and the guide invariably had commented on the cats as descendants of the felines Hemingway had owned. PR bullshit. Ironic that she'd had to come to Cuba in search of ETs to find out the truth on that piece of trivia.

Dylan leaned across Sofia, thrust out his hand. "I'm Dylan. I'm a huge fan of your work."

"Thanks." Hemingway shook Dylan's hand. "You've got excellent taste."

Dylan laughed and raised his phone to take a photo of the full-blown, flesh and blood Hemingway.

"Interesting gizmo you've got there. Everyone in here has them. What's it do?"

"It's a, uh, phone. With a camera. And some other features."

"You're going to take pictures of me?"

"I'd like to. If it's okay with you."

"It probably won't work, Dylan, but try anyway. Sometimes they overlook stuff."

"They?" Sofia asked. "Who are *they*?"

Hemingway made a dismissive gesture. "The ones who make it possible for me to be alive for awhile. Spirits...malign energies...aliens. I've heard all kinds of theories. All I know is that they're powerful, come with the fog. Or the fog comes with them. I'm never quite sure how it works."

"Yeah, okay. But what's that mean?" she asked.

"I don't know." Hemingway shook his head. "It just

happens." He waved down the same bartender who had warned them they were in danger.

"Buenas noches, Señor Hemingway. Lo mismo?"

"Si, Constantino, un mojito grande."

Ribalaigua's eyes met Sofia's briefly. She thought he looked apologetic. He seemed to be the only bartender who could see Hemingway, talk to him, serve him. As he fixed the mojito, Hemingway said, "Back in the day, Constantino used to fix Mary and me the best mojitos in Havana. I'm not sure how he manages to bridge the real world and this one, but he does. He's always here when I come alive."

"You realize this isn't normal, right, Mr. Hemingway?" Dylan asked.

Hemingway rolled his eyes. "I may be technically dead, Dylan. But I'm not stupid. Yeah, I realize it isn't normal. Then again, when I wrote *The Old Man and the Sea*, I knew it wasn't *normal*. For me, *normal* is boring. That may be one of the reasons this… " He moved his hands, as if grappling for the right word. "… this strangeness happens."

Ribalaigua set the mojito on the bar and waved at someone. "Pablo just got here."

Sofia and Dylan glanced toward the door. A short, balding man hurried in and came over to them, his arms thrown open. *"Amigo."* His voice boomed as he threw his arms around Hemingway. "How good to see you. You're looking well."

"You too, Pablo. Since you're here, I guess it means the usual?"

"So I'm told."

"What's it like outside?" Hemingway asked him.

"Cooler. Foggy. Strange. Like it always is when we meet here."

Dylan's eyes looked like they were about to pop out of their sockets. "My God," he murmured. "Pablo Neruda, the best poet of the twentieth century."

Huh? Dylan was a fan of South American poetry? "Where'd that come from, Dylan?"

"Graham gave me some of Neruda's books."

Sofia and Dylan snapped photos of both men. Even when

Neruda turned toward them, they kept taking pictures. "Who are your friends, Ernesto?" asked Neruda.

"Dylan and Sofia." Hemingway gestured at the dog. "And Cooper."

"*Mucho gusto,*" Neruda said, shaking hands with both of them. Then he stooped over and rubbed his hands along the side of Cooper's face. "*Dios mio, que perro mas hermoso!*" Cooper licked Neruda's face and he laughed. "The dog is coming with us, too?"

"Since he's here, I guess so," Hemingway replied.

"We're going somewhere?" Sofia asked.

Hemingway nodded. "Wherever you need to go."

She and Dylan exchanged a glance, then Sofia pointed at Mike and Pierce, now on their feet, moving toward this end of the bar. "Those two men need to come with us."

As Mike and Pierce worked their way through the burgeoning crowd, Sofia caught glimpses of their faces. Their expressions told her they couldn't see her and Dylan any longer. She searched the crowd for Carmen, Aldridge, Piper, and McMullen, but didn't see them anywhere. Had they left? Or were they just invisible to her?

"They're friends of yours?" Hemingway asked.

"My son and partner," Sofia said.

Neruda looked bewildered. "I wasn't told anything about two other passengers and a dog, Ernesto. Were you?"

Hemingway sucked down the last of his mojito and shook his head. "But what the hell. That's not unusual. Most of the time, I'm told only what they think I need to know."

"How do they contact you?" Sofia asked.

"They come through the door, just like everyone else. If there's fog, then I know I will come alive. Otherwise, they come in looking like clumsy drunks, find seats next to my statue, and talk away."

"Are you supposed to write about this or something, Ernesto?" Neruda asked.

"I don't write science fiction." He sounded indignant.

"Maybe you should."

"No writer of science fiction has ever won the Nobel," Hemingway countered.

"But writers of speculative fiction have," Sofia said. "Doris Lessing. 2007. She was the oldest Nobel winner and the eleventh woman."

"Pearl Buck, 1938," Hemingway said. "But she didn't write speculative or science fiction."

"Gabriela Mistral, 1945," Neruda said. "Her poetry was exquisite. But how do you know who wins in 2007, Sofia?"

"What year is it?" Sofia asked.

"The year?" Neruda frowned. "1958. I think." He gestured at Sofia's phone. "But that's not from 1958. What year are you from?"

"2017," Dylan replied quickly. "How far back can they rewind time?"

Neruda and Hemingway looked stunned. It was Neruda who spoke first. "Uh, no one has asked us such a question before. When most of *their* victims see Ernesto get up from the bar and stretch his arms over his head, they pass out. Or flee. That makes it easy for *them*. I can't remember anyone who has conversed with us as you two have done."

"So you always arrive after Ernest has gotten up?" Dylan asked.

"No. Sometimes I am already here. You two are now nearly sixty years in the past, my friend, so who knows how far back they can go?" Neruda leaned toward them, his voice soft. "But notice that they have created a point in time where Ernesto and I are still alive."

"I always wondered about that, " Hemingway remarked. "I've never come alive after July 2, 1961."

"Can they create a new timeline?" Dylan asked.

"Unknown," Neruda replied.

While this existential conversation unfolded, Sofia was thinking about 1958, what she knew about that year. In 1958, Hemingway was suffering from diabetic highs and lows and was probably bipolar. He and his fourth wife, Mary, were living in Finca Viglia in Havana that was, in 2017, a museum.

Politically, Batista received a million bucks in military aid from the U.S. All of his weapons, planes, tanks, ships and military supplies came from the U.S. The three branches of the military in the States trained his army. But the rebel forces of Fidel Castro and Che Guevara were gaining ground and in July of 1958, in the Battle of Jigue, the rebels won a decisive victory that proved to be a turning point for them. In late December, Che Guevara took the city of Santa Clara and captured a thousand prisoners. She remembered her grandmother's story about that. And on January 1, 1959, the rebels ousted Batista and the exodus to the U.S. began. She remembered that family story, too.

"What month in 1958?" she asked.

Hemingway looked annoyed. "What the hell difference does *that* make?"

"We're not sure," Dylan said. "In 1958, Pablo was already internationally famous because one of his major works had been published four years earlier—*Odas Elementales*. It was a happy time for him and his poetic output between then and 1973 was phenomenal- twenty books, with eight others that were published after he died."

"*That* many?" Neruda exclaimed. "My memories of all this are foggy."

"And your point?" Hemingway asked.

"He's as recognizable here as you are, Mr. Hemingway," Sofia replied. "You won the Nobel four years ago—in 1954- and are already considered Castro's favorite *yanqui*. That could create problems for Dylan and me."

"Or it could play to your advantage," Neruda said. "The Guardia of this time know Ernesto and me. They won't stop us. Some of them are minions of whatever this is. But most of them just don't want to lose their jobs. We can get you to wherever you need to be. Viñales, right?"

"How do you know that?" Dylan asked.

Neruda ran his hand over his bald head, shrugged. "I just do."

"So they control you, too?" Sofia asked.

Neruda's face shifted and the pixels blew apart like a faulty You Tube connection, then the image came together again. It looked solid and dependable, even though she knew it wasn't. "I'm controlled only to the extent that I allow it, within the parameters *they* have established." Neruda paused. "When do I win the Nobel? Do you know? Like I said, some of my memories have become confused over the years."

"1971," Dylan said. "You were pretty sick then. With cancer. You died in Chile not long after you got the prize and Allende died a few days later, during a right-wing coup."

"Allende. A wonderful man, a visionary. That pig Pinochet took over, right?"

"Yeah," Dylan replied. "And hurled Chile into chaos for years."

Hemingway looked sad. "You outlived me by ten years, Pablo."

"Ah, my friend. I remember that day. My heart wept for you."

Ever since Sofia had written about Hemingway's bipolar disorder, she'd wondered about the rumored friendship between Hemingway and Neruda. Were these interludes evidence that such a friendship had existed or was this just more of the ETs spinning illusions?

"If they can manipulate time in this way," Dylan said, "then they may be able to manipulate time in other ways. Suppose they created a timeline, Mr. Hemingway, in which you don't die on July 2, 1961?"

His expression changed, parallel lines jutted down between his eyes. Sofia thought it was strange to watch a man contemplate his own suicide three years from now and how things might unfold if he lived. "If Mary and I hadn't moved to Ketchum in 1959, things probably would have been much different. After all the years we spent in Cuba, I felt... I don't know... lost, I guess. Displaced. Havana and Ketchum were two very different worlds. I also had extreme highs and lows because of diabetes."

"Would they create a different timeline for you?" she asked.

"I've never really thought about it."

Neruda slung his arm around Hemingway's shoulders. "Some things, amigo, should not be considered."

"Maybe they should, Pablo. We don't know what these... these beings are... "

"Yeah, we do," Sofia said. "They're aliens."

"Aliens? We're all aliens," Hemingway said. "We're all from elsewhere."

"Not like these beings."

"The U.S. government calls them Skin Shifters," Dylan said.

Sofia swiveled her chair around and worked the shoes off her feet, revealing the grotesque webbing. "These aliens are amphibious creatures from elsewhere who are morphing... " She didn't know if that word existed in 1958. "... changing, transforming... humans into creatures like themselves so they can take on our human attributes."

Hemingway stared at her feet, raked his fingers back through his hair. "Fuck. So an invasion is underway?" He raised his eyes. "Is that what you're saying? These clumsy humans who lumber in here when there's no fog are actually from another planet? Another star system?"

Sofia shrugged. "We don't know. Maybe they're us from the future. Or from another dimension. And we don't know if it's an invasion yet. But if you're going to invade another planet, it's a brilliant way to do it."

Neruda stooped over, studying the webbing. "May I... touch it?"

"Touch away."

He brought his fingers to the webbing and touched, explored, examined. "It is... repulsive." He straightened up. "Your hands?"

"That webbing disappeared." She held up her hands, fingers spread. "There are still nubs on the inside of the fingers on my left hand where the webbing withdrew."

He ran his index finger up and down the fingers on her left hand. "This is why ...you're here? In Cuba?"

"I want my humanity restored."

"And you, Mr. Dylan?" Neruda asked.

"They killed my son."

"Ah." Hemingway nodded. "So that's why you spoke of a new timeline."

"Exactly."

Sofia pulled her shoes back onto her webbed feet and kept reminding herself that even though these two literary giants looked real, felt real, and their conversations seemed real, ET magic made it all possible. But if she was right that the webbing turned her into an ET spy, then the E.T., Mira, and perhaps her allies and enemies as well, had eavesdropped on all of this.

She saw Mike and Pierce headed for the door and quickly texted them. She didn't know if it would go through, she hadn't gotten any texts from either of them. But maybe the rules in this game were flexible.

Following u 2 outside w/neruda & hemingway

No response.

"Is your car nearby?" she asked Neruda.

He nodded. "Ernesto, you are going with us, yes?"

"That's what I was told."

Sofia figured the bartender must have refilled Hemingway's mojito at some point in the last few minutes. He tipped the glass to his mouth and chugged the whole thing. "They let you drink and stuff?" she asked.

Hemingway drew the back of his hand across his mouth. "They let me do pretty much what I want, except come truly alive. But that's good enough for me. Maybe better. I haven't stuck a gun in my mouth yet. And after listening to you two, maybe that doesn't need to happen."

"Do you have any bargaining power?" Sofia asked.

Hemingway got a kick out of that. "Hey, I'm dead."

"You're not dead right now."

"You remind me of Mary. She was a war correspondent for *Time* and *Life* magazines, you know, a pushy woman who could talk her way into anything. At one time in our marriage, I was jealous of her talent. I wasn't always nice to her, one of my deepest regrets."

Sofia barely resisted a comment about Hemingway's macho shit. "Technically, right now, she's as alive as you are. She's probably the best wife you had, Mr. Hemingway. She outlives you by twenty-five years, and as executor of your estate, makes sure your novels are published after your death. She contributes to your legacy in a major way."

He shrugged. "I loved all my wives. But no question that Mary was special. Like Pablo said, though, our memories have dimmed and become confused."

He rubbed his palms against his thighs, his body

and expression similar to how he had looked as a statue, contemplative. Sofia took several photos. She had no idea whether any of these pictures would show up on her phone, but if they did, they would be reminders of how she and Dylan had entered the impossible when they'd walked into El Floridita.

"You asked me about bargaining power. I think I do have some." Hemingway rapped his knuckles against the bar. "This place. Because of me, thousands of tourists flock here and that enables *them* to mingle, to choose their victims."

Her cell vibrated. A text message from Pierce: *WTF?*

Then from Mike: *Fog everywhere, mom.*

Step into it, she replied.

They started toward the door, following Dylan and Neruda, Cooper straining at his leash again, eager to lead the pack. "The tourist draw may be enough, Mr. Hemingway."

"To do what, exactly? Get rid of your webbed feet? Stop what's being done to you? Prevent my suicide? Keep Pablo alive past 1971? Make it so Mr. Dylan's son doesn't die? Change the course of history in Chile? In Cuba? It's all so fucking complicated."

"Let me put it this way," Sofia aid. "A week ago, I didn't think it was possible for me to be in 1958 Cuba, talking to a couple of Nobel authors. In my senior year in college, I wrote a paper on you." She didn't mention that it was about his bipolar disorder; she didn't know if that word had existed, either, in 1958. "Les's daughter, your niece, Hilary, is my friend. She and a famous actor in my time produced a movie about your and Mary's lives here. It was nominated for an Oscar. How does any of that fit anywhere in what we think we know about the way the world works?"

"It doesn't." He linked his arm through hers. "But right now, I'm okay with it. I think that as long as I feel like that, as long as Pablo is okay with this strangeness, we can help you and ourselves."

As they left El Floridita, she glimpsed her son and Pierce just ahead of them. "Mike!" she shouted.

He didn't hear her. The fog moved in around them, eddying across the ground, twisting up their legs, hugging cars, blocking her view of Mike and Pierce. Cooper suddenly broke away from her, raced through the fog—and vanished.

"Cooper," Hemingway said. "He just disappeared."

And then reappeared with Mike and Pierce as they entered the fog. She shouted their names and they spun simultaneously and raced toward her.

It was as if Cooper had alerted them, reminded Mike about the fog. They barreled into her, nearly knocking her and Hemingway over. Neruda and Dylan joined them and hasty introductions were made. They piled into a 1956 red Ford station wagon. The car in her vision had been a 1955 red and white Ford station wagon, a year older and a color off. She hoped that meant they wouldn't have the flat tire she'd seen.

The driver turned. "Thank God you're here."

Aldridge. "Larry!" Sofia exclaimed. "How... "

He looked completely freaked out. "I... I was standing with John, Josh, and Carmen and someone tapped me on the shoulder. When I looked around, I swear, I nearly fell over. This young woman could've been my daughter's twin. Except she was taller than Cat and her dark hair was... was longer than I remember. She said my friends were outside and needed a driver to get to Viñales She... headed for the door and I ran after her, I wanted to... to get a better look at her. I saw her pause next to this car and then she vanished into the fog."

"*Cat?*" Hemingway exclaimed. "That's your daughter's name?"

"Yes. Why?"

"*Caramba,*" Neruda murmured. "She's our most recent contact among *them.*"

"But... that's not possible. Two years ago she was...was changed by these bastards, she..." Aldridge looked helplessly at Dylan. "I don't understand any of this."

Dylan patted the older man's shoulder, trying to comfort him. "The only thing we need to understand right now, Larry, is the possibility that the woman who led you out here to the car is the ET who morphed your daughter."

"Let's call it what it is," Sofia said crossly. "That woman is the ET who *stole* Cat's body."

"But if that's true," Aldridge said, "why would she be helping us?"

"Maybe she doesn't like being human," Mike speculated.

"Or maybe they aren't all hostile," Pierce said. "Or both."

"Or maybe none of the above," Dylan said.

Hemingway slapped his hand against the edge of the seat. "I think we'd better get moving before *they* change their minds." He thrust out his hand toward Aldridge. "By the way, I'm Ernesto. This is my friend Pablo."

Neruda nodded. *"Es un placer. Tienes que seguir adelante."*

Aldridge now seemed completely confused. "I recognize you." He pointed at Hemingway. "You're... "

"Yeah, Ernest Hemingway," Sofia said. "Pablo said you should go straight."

"Into the fog?"

"Uh-huh."

"Ernest Hemingway." Aldridge shook his head. "Fuck me." Then he slammed the old car into gear and it plunged forward into the fog, rattling inside and out, the diesel engine spewing smoke.

Chapter 16

Hours passed. Or at least that was how it felt to Dylan. His watch had stopped, there was no clock on the Ford's dashboard, and when he briefly turned on his phone to check the time, the numbers were frozen at two minutes past midnight, about the time they'd walked into El Floridita. He turned the phone off to conserve the battery.

The old Ford accelerated at an impossible rate, its shocks so worn he felt every bump in the road, every pothole, every imperfection. Now and then, the radio suddenly came on, blaring with salsa music or propaganda. Fog whipped past the windows, the stuff so thick he couldn't see anything outside— not a tree or car or even a landscape. It disoriented him.

When he finally turned his phone on again, the time still showed 12:02 AM. Two bars appeared in the upper left-hand corner, indicating that he was connected to Cubatel. He clicked the agency's icon. It didn't work.

Dylan clicked the photo icon. Some of the Hemingway and Neruda photos were there, pictures of them as living human beings. Strangely enough, the dates the pics were taken showed up as June 16, 1958. How? The phone didn't display a date, its calendar was blank, yet the date for the photos had appeared. This kind of inconsistency had to mean the ETs allowed him to see only what they wanted him to see.

You really were in 1958 when you took these photos, Dylan. We're going to keep you off balance now, ha-ha.

His phone hadn't made a sound for hours, but started dinging now, one text message after another.

From Graham.

Fleming is offering everyone in your group a job. As a research team.

Dylan? You there?

Fleming said to keep texting you till you give him a yes or no.

Just saw the aftermath of our tank disaster. The entire site's going to be plowed under. You still coming?

He saw that the first group of texts had been sent yesterday morning and the next bunch had been sent today.

Now the mess will be plowed under tomorrow. None of the earth movers worked. Got some techs to fix them. ETs are messing with shit, am sure of it.

I'm hoping the reason you haven't responded is because you're on the road.

There were more texts, a string of them, a running dialogue of observations, thoughts, and speculations about the aliens and what their ultimate purpose was. Graham had texted some photos, too, of what the isolation tank looked like before and after, and a video of agitated ETs in the main two tanks. Dylan watched the two-minute video several times, alternately repulsed, intrigued, enraged, his emotions all over the place.

"Does everyone have cell service now?" Dylan asked the group.

The consensus was yes. "I'm not sure how or why, though," Pierce said. "I couldn't get anything inside El Floridita or out here, either, for the longest time."

Mike agreed. "I wasn't getting anything until we walked outside into the fog."

"I think the how and why are obvious," Aldridge said, and lifted his hands off the steering wheel. "I'm not driving this sucker."

"The fog," Hemingway said. "This has happened before. It takes over."

"So you and Pablo have accompanied others elsewhere?" Dylan asked.

Hemingway nodded. "To Cienfuegos, Verdadero Beach, Santiago, Trinidad. Then at some point it all ends and I'm a statue at El Floridita and Pablo is a photo on a wall."

"At some point, Ernesto and I are robbed of life," Neruda added.

"Fucked up," Aldridge muttered.

"But tonight we're supposed to stop at the Ferris wheel," Hemingway said.

"A Ferris wheel?" Dylan exclaimed. "Here in the middle of nowhere?"

Neruda's head bobbed up and down. "Sometimes, the Ferris wheel is part of what Ernesto and I do. I do not like that place."

Dylan didn't like any of it.

"Would you sign these?" Mike passed a pen and paper napkin to Hemingway and the same to Neruda.

"What should we write?" Hemingway asked.

"Your names and the date," Mike said.

"I'd like a little more than that," Sofia said. "Mr. Hemingway, could you write, *To my beloved niece Hilary. Keep writing!* And sign your name, the date, and Cuba."

"Hilary, whom I haven't even met yet," Hemingway remarked.

"Who won't be born until three weeks before you pass on," Sofia said. "You never saw her because you and Les hadn't seen each other for a decade. He didn't, uh, like Mary."

"That's true," Hemingway said. "But if I can negotiate for a different timeline with these aliens, that's something I'll change." He signed the napkin and gave it to Sofia, who asked Mike to hold onto it.

"And what should I write?" Neruda asked.

Dylan spoke up. *"Thank you, Lia, for buying Dylan my books.* Then sign your name, date, location."

When he'd finished, he passed the napkin to Dylan. He snapped a picture of it, then folded it carefully, slipped it inside his wallet.

"So now there're two written records that you went back in time," Neruda remarked.

"Now there's a record that we experienced the impossible. " Dylan sent a group a text of the video Graham had texted him. "Just so we all know what we'll be dealing with." He passed his phone to Hemingway. "Here's what the ETs look like, Mr. Hemingway."

"A *movie*?" Hemingway exclaimed. "These phones make movies?" He paused. "Shit, these images are... terrifying." He handed the phone to Neruda.

"*Que feos.*" How ugly.

"Can they be killed?" Hemingway asked.

The right question, Dylan thought. "That's part of what we intend to find out."

Just then, Dylan heard a popping sound, the station wagon shuddered, Aldridge grabbed the wheel and tapped the brake, slowing down. The fog continued to hug the Ford, blocking their view of everything outside the car, and Aldridge wisely stopped where they were rather than pulling to the side of the road.

"I think we've got a flat," Aldridge announced.

"They heard you, Dylan," said Sofia. "This is straight out of my vision."

"What vision?" Pierce asked.

"When we walked out of the airport. I saw us having a flat in Inez's car. Which is almost identical to this one."

Neruda glanced back. "You have visions?"

"She's psychic," Pierce explained. "Her feet became webbed when she psychically read what we thought was a dead alien."

"You people talk of strange things, show us movies on telephones, images of aliens," Neruda said. "But the only knowledge Ernesto and I have is what has happened on previous trips in the fog. And never have the people involved been so... *talkative*, so willing to share. We have learned a great deal from you. It's extraordinary."

What was extraordinary, Dylan thought, was how easily they all accepted the impossibility of what was occurring. If he had related any of this to the shrinks who had treated him in the nuthouse, he would find himself in a padded cell, drooling from all the drugs they'd given him. His ex would get a restraining order against him.

"How do you read something psychically?" Hemingway asked, rubbing his palms over the foggy glass in the windows.

"Usually by touching it," Sofia replied.

"If I give you my wedding ring, can you read that?"

"I can, but, uh, probably not right this second, Mr. Hemingway. We've just had a flat in thick fog in the middle of fucking nowhere."

They all peered through the windows, but no one, Dylan thought, rushed to get out. The headlights lit up the fog but it merely reflected the light and didn't enable Dylan to see anything beyond it. Cooper whined and pawed at the door.

"We can't just sit here," Dylan said. "Is there a spare in this car, Larry?"

"How the hell should I know? I was led to it by an ET. Maybe it's booby-trapped."

Dylan moved next to Hemingway so he could slide open the side door, but just then, lights appeared in the fog and John Lennon's *Imagine* drifted through the air. A Ferris wheel appeared just ahead of them and they all leaned forward, staring at it. "What the fuck," Dylan muttered.

"It's an illusion," Sofia said. "Another trick. We should ignore it."

The Ferris wheel, fully lit, was inside of an enclosed patio surrounded by tables. Dylan could see customers at those tables, eating and drinking, their laughter ringing out, the eerie light from the Ferris wheel spilling over them. "We can't ignore it," Dylan said, "It's blocking the road."

"We're supposed to go inside Betty Danger's Country Club," Hemingway said.

Mike laughed. "You're kidding. That's what the place is called?"

"Its full name is Betty Danger's Country Club for the ninety-nine percent," Neruda remarked. "In that place, your feet can become normal again, Sofia. Your grandmother is there. Your ex-husband. Dr. Aldridge's children. And your son, Dylan, he's there, too. And even if you do not want to go inside, you can't go around it. You'll see. Ernesto and I have been here."

"This music," Hemingway said. "It's extraordinary. What is it? I have never heard this."

In 1958, Dylan thought, the Beatles were six years away from their appearance on the Ed Sullivan show on February 9, 1964. Seventy-three million people watched and a legend was launched. "The Beatles, John Lennon singing. A visionary group. You were alive then, Mr. Neruda. Do you remember hearing about the Beatles?"

"A vague memory, yes. One of them was, hmm, Harrison. George Harrison. George, like you, Mr. Dylan."

"Wait," Hemingway said, excited. "I remember something. This man, John Lennon. Others we've taken through the fog have mentioned him. He was assassinated in… I don't recall the year, but it was after I died."

Dylan found it fascinating that Hemingway and Neruda seemed to have two tracks of memories—that of their normal lives as they'd lived them, as history had recorded, and this other track. "December 8, 1980. That was the day Lennon was killed."

Hemingway seemed to absorb this information, gave a slight nod, and slid open the side door. Fog rolled in, Dylan really didn't want to step outside. "Pablo is right that we can't move past it," Hemingway said. "But if we avoid the seduction and emerge on the other side, all of us can be free."

"What the hell does that mean?" Dylan demanded.

Hemingway turned, looked at him. "This is where the world of the dead and the world of the living intersect and co-exist."

"What does it mean, the club for the ninety-nine percent?" Neruda asked.

Ironic, Dylan thought. "It means all the rest of us."

Cooper leaped out first, his leash slapping the edge of the door, and Dylan followed him, the fire in his belly burning so bright and hot that he couldn't do otherwise even if he wanted to.

2.

Cooper led the six of them toward Betty Danger's, the darkness on either side of them lit up by the Ferris wheel. *Imagine* had ended and now the Rolling Stones sang, *You Can't Always Get What You Want*. Sofia thought the critical line of this song, the message to the six of them, was that even if you didn't always get what you wanted, you might find what you needed *if you tried.*

What she needed right then was to see her *abuelita* Rosa, who would advise her. What Dylan needed most was to see his dead son. Aldridge needed to see his children. Mike needed to talk to his dead father. Pierce needed to see the bigger picture so he could figure out what the hell they were supposed to do.

She didn't have a clue what Hemingway or Neruda needed. She felt they had all stumbled down through the rabbit's hole into Alice's nightmare.

When they stepped through the gate, her feet lost their webbing and she saw a small crowd of the dead moving toward them—her ex, her grandmother, Dylan's son, Aldridge's son and daughter. She rushed into her grandmother's arms. Rosa felt real, smelled real, was as solid and alive as she had been in life. Rosa whispered, "Get out of here fast, *mi amor.*"

"How?"

"Close your eyes to the lies around you, and run. *Fast.*"

Close her eyes? What kind of advice was that? She saw Mike with his dead father, Dylan with his dead son, Aldridge with his changed kids, and Pierce with Hemingway and Neruda, paralyzed with shock as the nearby Ferris wheel turned slowly against the unnaturally lit dusky sky.

"You're now on the warrior's journey," Rosa hissed.

Sofia suddenly found herself in a gondola on the Ferris wheel, sitting across from a woman who looked like her twin. The surreal light touched her skin in such a way so that beneath it, Sofia saw her alien features. "Let's make this simple, Sofia. Let's walk out of this place together."

Panic lurched inside of her, the gondola swung in a breeze. "Let's not."

"Everything will be much easier if you just come with me now. Otherwise Mike dies, your... "

She lunged at the ET, shrieking, *"You're lying, you sack of shit! Die!"* She slammed into the alien with such force that the gondola swung violently in the air and Sofia tumbled out of it, falling slowly through the strange light, everything below her changing swiftly, the patio and customers melting into darkness, sunlight, a pulsing twilight, then darkness again.

She landed in the road where the car's tire had gone flat,

landed as lightly as a leaf, her hands now as fully webbed as her feet. The others were hugging the sides of the station wagon, creeping toward the rear of the car, fog closing in on them. The Ferris wheel and Betty Danger's were gone, she couldn't see anything beyond the fog, and Pierce clutched her hand tightly.

"I... I don't understand," she whispered. "Did you see the Ferris wheel?"

Pierce glanced back at her. "What're you talking about?"

"Did anyone see the Ferris wheel?" she asked, loudly enough for the others to hear her.

Only Hemingway responded. "Yes, yes, I remember now. Betty Danger's. Pablo, do you..."

"*Ay, dios mio, si, si.* I remember. But... "

"I saw my son," Dylan said.

"I saw my kids," Aldridge said.

"I saw my dad," Mike said.

"Christ," Pierce said. "Let's just get that spare tire on the car and get the hell outta here."

3.

Pierce's spider sense had slammed into overdrive from the second the tire had gone flat, but now it went wild, radiating out from him like spokes in a wheel. He vaguely recalled the Ferris wheel but it didn't fit into any context he understood and right now his primary concern was the thickening fog, moving closer.

"Eerie," Aldridge remarked.

"I do not like it," Neruda said.

"I can think of better adjectives," Hemingway said.

"Is *fucked up* an adjective?" Pierce asked.

Hemingway snorted. "It can be. Let's link arms."

"Good idea," Pierce agreed.

Pierce heard his own frantic heartbeat, the sour taste of fear coated his tongue, the spider on the back of his neck tightened its legs around his throat. He heard Sofia breathing hard and she suddenly tugged on his hand, urging him closer to her. Her finger tapped out a message in their secret code.

ETs close. Feet swelling, gill opening. Webbing on hands aching.

"Okay, hatch open," Dylan said. "We still connected, people?"

"We're good," Hemingway called out.

Should we run? Pierce tapped out against her palm.

Never.

The fog kept thickening, shoots of it twisting along the ground, climbing up into the wheel wells, around their ankles. What would happen if it started winding around his legs and slithered up under his khaki shorts and t-shirt, across and up his chest, around his throat and across his face? Would it swallow him? Jesus, he hated the feel of the stuff against his bare skin, cool and slippery, like raw, slimy fish. "Is there a spare?" Pierce asked.

"Yeah," Dylan replied. "Yeah, I think so. Gotta move some shit around and lift this panel in the floor."

Hurry, Christ, hurry. He crept forward until he stood at the right tail light, close enough to Dylan to see what he was doing. "Lemme hold the flashlight, man," Pierce said.

"Thanks."

Pierce was so uneasy and nervous that the flashlight's beam danced around, revealing the beads of sweat rolling down the side of Dylan's face, the tightness of his mouth, the determination in his set jaw that screamed, *I'm scared shitless. We're gonna get outta here.*

"I, uh, think I just saw something moving through the fog," Hemingway whispered. "Did you see it, Pablo?"

"Nada," Neruda whispered back.

Pierce glanced around, dropped his head back and peered upward. The fog blocked the sky, blocked everything. It encased them completely. "I don't see anything. Mike? Do you?" Just the act of saying the kid's name out loud made him feel more grounded, more secure. Mike, behind Sofia, always said it like he saw it.

"Nothing, Luke."

"Me, either," Sofia said. "But my swelling feet say otherwise."

Pierce realized that light now penetrated the fog. The rising sun? Even these goddamn ETs couldn't control the movements of the sun, could they? He looked at his watch, but it had stopped at two minutes after midnight, probably around the time they had walked into La Floridita and Rod Serling's twilight zone.

"Mom, the webbing on your hands...it's thickening."

"I know." Sofia's words sounded choked.

Pierce thought he saw dark figures, silhouettes, moving through the fog to the Ford's right, where they now waited for the verdict about the spare tire. Hoping he was wrong, he blinked to clear his vision. It didn't change anything. The figures remained, four of them darting quickly through the fog. The stuff swirled and eddied to accommodate them. Tendrils shot out from the base of the fog, short, thick things like nails or bolts that abruptly flipped upward and drilled into the ground. Pierce's terror ratcheted upward, his heart hammered wildly. They had no defense against something like this.

Cooper barked ferociously.

"Dylan, to your right!" Pierce shouted.

Dylan's dead son stepped out of the fog, whole and alive, looking just like he had at Betty Danger's, the vivid details of that place suddenly bursting into Pierce's awareness, confusing him. Had he been in two places simultaneously?

Dylan dropped the spare tire, rushed forward, and embraced his son, ribbons of fog swirling around their ankles and legs. A young man and a young woman ran toward Aldridge, shouting, "Dad, Dad!"

Frightened that the fourth figure was intended for Sofia, Pierce jerked her past the rear of the station wagon, to the other side, trying to put distance between her and the advancing fog. If he could get her inside the car...

Cooper went nuts, barking and snarling and leaping until he broke away from Mike. The dog ran back and forth alongside them, a protector, a line of defense, and Mike yelled, "Inside the car, Luke. Get her inside!"

Then the fourth figure emerged from the fog. It didn't look like Sofia's dead ex-husband. It looked just like her, a tall, svelte woman with dark hair falling to her shoulders. She wore the clothes that Sofia wore, denim shorts and a black t-shirt with *blah, blah* written across the pocket. Her Sketcher running shoes were identical to Sofia's. She stood several inches taller, but otherwise could have passed for Sofia's twin.

"*No!*" Pierce shouted, and jerked her around to the other side of the Ford, Sofia's webbed feet stumbling clumsily, Mike guarding her back, Cooper barking at her side. Pierce struggled to slide the side door open, but the goddamn thing was stuck.

The woman came steadily toward them, in no particular hurry. They reached the driver's door and Pierce yanked it open and Cooper lunged at her. The ET stumbled back, human arms pin wheeling for balance, and the door slammed shut. Pierce grabbed the handle to open it again, but it was locked, the ET had locked it.

"*Stay the fuck away from her!*" Mike shouted, and he and Pierce threw their arms around Sofia.

Cooper ran circles around the ET, keeping her off balance, and then he leaped at her. He was flung away, yelping and howling with pain, and Hemingway tackled the ET and they slammed into the ground. Neruda charged like an enraged bull, screaming something in Spanish, and threw himself on top of Hemingway and they rolled away, the ET trapped beneath them. Aldridge raced toward them, hurling rocks. Dylan tore forward, clutching a tire iron above his head, yelling like a fucking madman. Pierce somehow got the side door to slide open and he and Mike pushed Sofia inside.

She sprawled on her back on the station wagon's middle seat, her webbed hands raised into the air, her ripped shoes in the road, her webbed feet moving frantically. She now had a gill at her throat that opened and closed like a fist. She wheezed for air.

Mike scrambled inside, Pierce right behind him. He jerked the door shut and crawled over the front seat with some half-baked idea that he would start the Ford and get the fuck out of here. The key wasn't in the ignition. He patted his pockets frantically, remembered Aldridge had been driving. Pierce climbed into the back again, where Mike held his mother tightly.

The side door slammed open, fog rolled in over them. Pierce was dimly aware that everyone was shouting, nothing was what it was supposed to be, all order had collapsed. He wrapped his arms around Sofia and Mike, so she was sandwiched between them.

"Mike, Luke," she wheezed. "Let me go. For now, just let me go."

"We're going with you. Mike and I are going with you."

"You can't." She struggled to breathe.

And then, just like that, he found himself sprawled on the dirt road with the others. The air smelled scorched, old, used up. Sunlight beat down. Birds sang from the trees on either side of the road. The fog was gone. Hemingway was gone, Neruda was gone, 1958 was gone. Sofia was gone.

Part Three

VINALES

"The truth is out there."

- Fox Mulder

Chapter 17

Pierce struggled to his feet, his despair so profound he could barely breathe. Behind it rushed dizziness, disorientation, a terrible nausea. He leaned against the car until the sensations passed, then lurched toward Cooper's whimpers, his choked sobs like punctuation points. *Done, done, done.*

He found the dog three hundred yards from the car, conscious but unable to rise. Pierce slid his arms under Cooper, lifting him, all one hundred and ten pounds of him, and staggered back to the Ford. He set Cooper gently on the middle seat where he and Mike had set Sofia, where they had seen her last, and ran his hands over the dog's body. "You'll be okay, boy, you'll be fine."

If Cooper wasn't fine, if his injuries killed him, if these aliens fucks turned Sofia completely or killed her, then Pierce would—what? Join Dylan and kill the fucks? Things had reached that point already, *them versus us.* Regardless of the language any of them used to describe what was happening, these events all screamed that an invasion was underway.

Forget *Childhood's End, E.T., Independence Day.* This was more *like Invasion of the Fucking Body Snatchers.* But instead of human bodies being grown in pods in some field in the 1950s, they transformed human bodies, exchanging body parts with their victims until they were fully human and their victims were fully alien. A Kafka metamorphosis.

He scooped a bottle of water off the floor, poured some into his hand, coaxed Cooper to lap at it. He sipped at it, too, and moved his hands over the dog's body again, checking for broken bones, blood, obvious injuries. He couldn't detect anything. He gave Cooper more water and this time, the dog raised his head, lapped eagerly at the water, and licked the back of Pierce's hand.

"You stay here, Cooper. Rest. I think you're just bruised. We need to get outta here."

He raised the bottle of water to his mouth again, but it was empty. Pierce ran over to Mike, who was sitting up, blinking, looking around in confusion. Pierce crouched beside him. "You okay?"

"Where's…"

"Gone." He could barely utter the word. "She's gone, it's all gone."

"Where the fuck are we?" Dylan. "Do we have any idea?"

Pierce glanced over at him and Aldridge, both of them sitting up.

"Not in Havana," Aldridge replied. "That's for sure."

"What do you two remember?" Pierce asked.

"I got a good whack at the fucker," Dylan said. "With the tire iron." He reached out and plucked it off the ground.

"I remember being in that place with the Ferris wheel, seeing Cat and Duncan," Aldridge said. "Do you…remember that place, Luke?"

"Vaguely." He didn't want to think about it right now. "Larry, do you have the car key?"

"In the ignition. That's where I left it."

No, Pierce thought. It hadn't been in the ignition, and he tore back to the station wagon.

The key *was* in the ignition. The ET bitch fucked with his perceptions. He turned the key, making sure the engine fired up. It did. He turned it off. "We need to change this flat and get to Viñales. To those tanks. And Mike, Cooper got injured. I think he's okay, but you'd better keep an eye on him."

"Right before…Mom vanished, she said we may need an army."

"An army," Dylan said. "She's right. I can contact Ari Rey. He said that group he meets with in secret, who've lost loved ones to these fucks, are willing to fight."

"John Piper could fly them to Viñales," Mike said. "With Carmen and McMullen."

Pierce had been there right before Sofia and the fog and Hemingway and Neruda and everything else had disappeared and hadn't heard anything like that. It didn't mean Sofia hadn't said it, only that he hadn't heard it. The ETs were manipulating everything, even who heard and saw the minutia, the tiniest details, the connect-the-dots stuff that might make a significant difference in their next move.

"Let's take things a step at a time," Pierce cautioned. "First up is the spare tire."

"I'll take care of it," Dylan said.

"Wait," Pierce said. "Time check. I've got...shit, nothing."

"No internet now," Mike said. "We really need to get away from here."

Changing the tire on a car that weighed nearly 3,500 pounds—Pierce looked it up in the manual in the glove compartment -was no easy task. It took a long time, with the four of them involved. Cooper waited in the shade of a tree and appeared to be all right, except that he was panting hard from the heat. They all needed water and food, Pierce thought, and longed for a Google map that would indicate where the nearest market was.

Hunger and thirst distracted him from his dark thoughts about Sofia. He felt she was still alive, but beyond that, he ran into a wall of anxiety and fear.

2.

Sofia came to suddenly and realized the ET—*Mira? Is it Mira?*—carried her in her arms, and the cool dampness against her skin told her they were in the fog. She knew if she opened her eyes, she would freak the fuck out and her final chapter would be death out here in nowhere land. The alien moved rapidly, leaping from one spot to the next, and when Sofia heard footfalls to her right, understood Mira wasn't alone. At least one other ET accompanied her.

She tried to keep her breathing soft, even, as though she

were still unconscious. But it was hard. Panic burrowed through her, quickening her pulse, turning the inside of her mouth desert dry. She focused on her breath, slow, easy breaths, like when she entered the zone. She no longer felt the gills at her throat or side and wondered if the gills would come and go as the webbing in her hands did. Or had the ET messed with her perceptions so that she merely believed she had gills? So that she and Pierce and Mike believed she was suffocating? This possibility suddenly seemed plausible to her, but that didn't necessarily make it true.

As the ET moved, her grip on Sofia tightened and now and then, she was able to read the alien psychically, but only in bits and pieces. Otherwise, it was too horrifying, too chaotic. This being's strange consciousness didn't follow any linear track; it was all over the place. One track began with her craft crashing into the gulf offshore of Tango Key, another track picked up on her planet in the midst of a worldwide disaster, a third track weaved among countless others.

But Sofia learned that the alien was accompanied by her advisor, Lotus, and that her other ally, Jez, was in a nearby river. Millions of these ETs existed all over the world, with the majority in warm, tropical climates. Here in Cuba, the aliens numbered between five and ten thousand; even Mira and Lotus weren't sure of the exact number. Both of them had blue hair, which signified the highest authority in the tribe.

Once again she sensed that she could access the web that connected these aliens, but she didn't want to be identified. Had the ETs who had been transformed into humans retained their memories of their lives before? Maybe some of them did.

She felt that the ultimate goal of the aliens, aside from taking over this planet, was to produce a race of alien/human hybrids that would be perfectly suited to Earth's environment. So far, there had been only one—born in a tank on The Agency compound. And it had escaped.

Sofia felt the fog was thinning; the excessive moisture no longer clung to her skin. And what would happen once they were out of the fog? Would they toss her in the river to swim with the others? To be guarded by Jez? Would they take her to the caves? Would the final steps of her metamorphosis take place there? *You go in no longer fully human and emerge as totally alien.*

Her panic broke through, collapsed into terror, and her aching bladder abruptly let loose, soaking her shorts, urine running over Mira's arms. The alien made a strange noise, a series of musical notes, low and drawn out, that were immediately answered with other high, shrieking notes from Lotus.

Mira abruptly dropped Sofia and she struck the ground hard, and her eyes snapped open. The aliens hopped around, making a lot of noise, a medley of musical notes that sounded badly off key. The two of them, tall, grotesque figures in the fog, frantically wiped themselves and each other with fallen leaves and palm fronds. She nearly screamed, nearly leaped to her webbed feet and took off. But she would never outrun them, didn't have a weapon...

You do have a weapon. Rosa materialized at her feet, between her and the ETs. *You're a warrior. Read their future. Let your eyes roll back and tell them that in moments, the escaped hybrid will be killed by the armed soldiers pursuing it. Now, do it now.*

Sofia bolted upright, her eyes rolled back in their sockets, and she shouted, "In just moments, the hybrid that escaped from the tank is going to be killed by armed soldiers who're pursuing it!"

The air around her exploded with a wild cacophony that sounded like a bunch of coked up teens in a high school music room. Hands slammed piano keys, violins screeched, trombones and horns and clarinets hooted and tooted. She kept shouting it over and over again and then, beyond the thinning fog, rapid gunfire.

Mira and Lotus crashed out of the fog, forgetting about her completely.

Sofia struggled to her feet and took off in the opposite direction, shocked at how fast her webbed feet moved. She had no idea where she should run, where or who the soldiers were, or even if those shots had been fired by soldiers. And where was she relative to where their car had had a flat? How many miles had the ETs traveled since she'd been taken?

She tore ass until the fog abruptly ended, bright, hot sunlight spilled over her, and she found herself at the edge of a half-paved road riddled with potholes, lined with palms and ceiba trees. A wooden cart pulled by a donkey trundled slowly toward her, hauling mangos and papaya. An elderly man, a campesino in faded shorts and a t-shirt, held the donkey's reins in one hand, and a cigarette in the other. Two boys sat in the back with the fruit.

Sofia waited until they were closer, then stepped out into the road, waving her arms. Her webbed feet were fully visible but the driver stopped anyway. *"Necesitas ayuda, señorita?"*

"Donde queda Viñales?"

"Quince kilometros." He signaled straight ahead. *"Por alla."*

Viñales lay fifteen kilometers away, straight ahead. A little more than nine miles.

"Puedo ir con ustedes?" May I go with you?

"Si, si, claro."

He motioned at the back of the wagon and told the boys to make room for her. They moved around and Sofia climbed into the wagon and leaned back against a pile of ripe papayas. The boys giggled and snickered and pointed at her feet. She asked if they'd heard gunfire and the taller of the two boys nodded. Soldiers from Campo Viejo, he told her in Spanish. About five kilometers from the town where the Americans kept the mermaids. The old man glanced back, pointing his cigarette at her feet. "Feet like yours."

"You know about them?" she asked in Spanish.

Everyone in Viñales knew about them, he said. The Americans were capturing them, studying them. The gunfire meant they were after one of them.

"No tienes miedo?" Aren't you afraid?

"Siempre." Always. *"Pero tenemos que comer."* But we have to eat.

She explained she'd been abducted by two of the *sirenas* when the car she and her friends were in had a flat tire and they ended up in a place with a Ferris wheel and suddenly she was in a gondola with the alien who now looked exactly like her and... Sofia rambled and sounded like a nut and abruptly shut up. *"Me puedes llevar a Campo Viejo donde queda mis amigos?"* Could he take her to Campo Viejo so she could meet up with her friends?

He shook his head. *"No, no, tengo miedo de ese lugar."* He was afraid of that place and offered to take her to the police station in town. He assured her the police would help her. Then he handed her a bottle of water and instructed one of the boys to cut open a papaya and give her a big slice. Sofia guzzled down half the bottle of warm water, then the older kid handed her a fat, dripping slice of warm papaya. Nothing had ever tasted so good.

Now and then, a car clattered past, a relic of the Fifties, but none of them were the red Ford Aldridge had been driving. She no longer had her cell phone and the old man didn't have one, so she didn't have any way of getting in touch with Pierce or anyone else. But she had about a hundred CUCs zipped into her back pocket and gave the old man two tens and asked him to drop her outside of town. She wasn't about to walk into any police station with webbed feet.

She sat back against the papayas, the hot morning sun beating down, and knew that if it hadn't been for Rosa, she wouldn't have escaped. Tears rolled down her cheeks. The younger boy noticed and took her hand, holding it gently in her own.

3.

When the tire was finally mounted, Pierce volunteered to drive and with a quick turn of the key, the engine kicked to life. This stick shift, protruding from the steering column, was huge, a monster compared to the stick shift on the first car he'd owned, a 1965 VW bug. He slammed it into gear and sped up the road, the engine roaring.

Beside him in the passenger seat, Aldridge's hands were pressed over his face, his shoulders shaking as he wept. "It was her, it was Cat. She was real. And Duncan... my God, they were both so real. We... had a drink together, a bite to eat, and were talking about going on the Ferris wheel when... I don't know what happened, but suddenly I was back on the road by the car."

Pierce's heart ached for Aldridge. "We're going to find them, Larry, and one way or another, we'll figure out how to restore their humanity."

His hands fell away from his face. "I honestly don't know if such a thing is even possible, Luke. It's not just their appearance that has changed. It's their entire physiology, their organs, nervous systems, *brains*. I'm a neurologist, okay? You know how many miles of nerves there are in the human body? You know how fucking complex the human brain is?"

"You're depressing me," Pierce said.

"Shit, I'm depressing myself."

"My dad and I were in one of the gondolas," Mike said. "We...saw Mom throw herself at this woman who was in the gondola with her and then she...she fell over the side and kind of fell in slow motion and I...leaped up, shouting, and...and found myself back by the car."

Pierce didn't know what alarmed him more—Mike and Aldridge's experiences or the fact that he didn't recall much of anything now about Betty Danger's. "What about you, Dylan?"

"Same sort of trick," Dylan replied. "But Justin told me they need human bodies because in their natural form they're allergic to a number of things in our environment. Something in tobacco, he said, is lethal to them."

"The nicotine?" Mike asked.

"He was about to explain when everything went haywire."

Pierce felt a surge of hope and waved his arm at the fields they passed. "Plenty of tobacco out there. If it's true, then they picked the wrong area of Cuba."

Mike, excited, suggested, "We should find a field of tobacco and start harvesting."

His excitement, Pierce thought, smacked of desperation. "Not a good idea, Mike."

"No kidding," Dylan said. "These plantations are either government or privately owned. I don't think we can just walk into any field and start harvesting. I texted Graham about this."

"Has she responded?" Pierce asked.

"Not yet."

The station wagon sped along the dirt road lined by dense trees on either side. Eventually, the woods thinned and the dirt road gave way to pitted asphalt where wagons pulled by horses or donkeys were the most common method of transportation. They passed rice paddies, groves of mango trees, tobacco farms.

The distraction of driving, of what they passed, helped Pierce move beyond what had happened back there, the Ferris wheel he barely remembered, the silhouettes in the fog, the ET who looked like Sofia's twin. He believed the ET had manipulated their perceptions so they would see her as Sofia. But if he ever saw her again, he expected her to look like the alien McMullen had found, the being they'd hidden in a floor freezer, with the blue tuft of hair, the single nostril, the webbed feet and hand, the dual thumbs, and double jointed knees. He expected her to be an amphibious alien.

"Did your kids tell you anything about the ETs, Larry?" Mike asked.

Aldridge turned in his seat, looked at Dylan. "What they told me was intended for you, George. They're begging you not to kill the creatures unless you can distinguish them from those that used to be human."

Pierce glanced in the rear view mirror and noticed that Dylan looked ashamed. "I give you my word on that, Larry."

In all of Pierce's years of investigating alien encounters, he'd never experienced anything like this. There was no protocol, no process, not even a suggestion in the Omega handbook for dealing with a complete metamorphosis from alien to human or vice versa. No mention, even though Ted and Carmen Fisher had been investigating this very thing here in Cuba. He had entered new, unchartered terrain, untouched by Google, a place you traveled with nothing more than raw instinct. He was now no different than a guy who lived in a cave with his spider sense on high alert.

"How's Cooper doing?" he called out.

"Better," Mike said. "He's sitting up. But he needs water and food."

"So do we," Aldridge said.

"Any idea how far out we are?" Pierce asked.

"The GPS on my phone isn't working," Dylan said. "But the agency's GPS puts us about sixty miles out from the facility."

In the bigger scheme of things, Pierce thought, sixty miles was nothing. Unless you were hungry and thirsty.

A couple of miles later, Pierce spotted a gas station and a small store. A slick new tourist bus and numerous cars were parked at the pumps or in front of the store. A crowd. Good. Crowds were a welcome change. Since he didn't have any idea where the next gas station might be, he decided to top off the tank, too. But when he checked the needle on the gas gauge, it pointed at full. One more impossibility. Or a trick.

"Larry, when you initially got into this car, did you notice what the gas gauge read?"

"Sure. It was full."

"It's still full."

Aldridge leaned over to take a look. "They're tricky bastards. Maybe it's on empty and we're just seeing it as full."

"Try topping it off just to be safe," Mike suggested.

Pierce got in line at the pumps and the others hopped out and headed into the store. Cooper hung his head out the window and whined to go with Mike. "Hey, it's okay, big guy. He'll be back with food and water."

The car in front of him pulled away and Pierce drove up to the pump, got out, reached for his wallet, and realized he couldn't pay with an American credit or debit card in Cuba. Rather than going inside and battling a crowd in order to pay, he decided to take his chances that the tank was still full. He drove over to a field where four men with small coolers were selling sandwiches and sodas to passengers from the tourist bus. He snapped on Cooper's leash and they walked over to the vendors.

"*Que tipo de...*" Pierce stopped. He suddenly couldn't recall the word for sandwich. Screw it. Spanglish would have to do. "*...sandwiches tienes?*"

"*Pollo, puerco, jamon...* "Chicken, pork, ham.

Pierce asked for four chicken sandwiches and the man

opened the cooler, withdrew four sandwiches. *"Diez CUCs."*

As Pierce handed him a ten CUC bill, two small police cars arrived, lights spinning, their sirens making a sharp, staccato noise, like loud hiccups. All four vendors took off, racing away through the field.

Pierce suspected that unless vendors were licensed by the government, who probably got a cut of everything sold, they weren't allowed to sell their goods. Just in case he was wrong, he and Cooper walked off into the field, where the dog was content to sniff and do his business. The last thing he needed was to be questioned by Cuban police or hauled in.

Back in the car, he and Cooper shared a chicken sandwich. He remembered doing this when Cooper was just a pup and he and Sofia had taken off for a long weekend together. They'd been living in Miami then and had driven to Key West, where he'd rented a conch house that allowed dogs. His ex-wife and daughter had moved back in with her parents because he'd told her he wanted a divorce, none of which he'd mentioned to Sofia.

His life back then had been one lie after another—to Sofia, his ex-wife, his daughter. As he sat here now with Cooper, feeding him small bites of the sandwich, Pierce hated himself for those lies of omission, for the mess of things he'd made back then, for the year he and Sofia had wasted after she had resigned. Now she was becoming an amphibious alien because he'd asked for her help. He was bad news for her regardless of how he looked at it.

He slung his arm around Cooper's neck, rubbed his cheek against the dog's fur. "Let's go inside, Coop. I need to take a whiz. You're still wearing your rescue harness, I don't think anyone will tell us to leave."

Cooper drew his tongue across Pierce's cheek. The dog forgave him, he thought, and that lick felt like a small redemption.

4.

The market lacked many of the basics that Dylan expected when he walked into a grocery store at home. Like choices. Whatever the product, it was carried in just one brand, the Made in Cuba brand—cereal, soap, milk, bread, razor, eggs. But the refrigerated area was filled with bottled water and he loaded his cart with it. Mike then added a small bag of dried dog food, two cans of dog food that might or might not be edible, and called Dylan's attention to the fresh deli. "Of sorts," he added.

"Sandwiches?"

Mike rocked his hand from side to side. "See you over there. Larry's checking out the choices. I grabbed t-shirts for all us and some razors, soap, basic shit."

"Thanks, Mike." Dylan's phone dinged, he glanced down at it. A text from Ari Rey. *Got your message. Have informed others. We're ready.*

Since they were communicating through the agency's network, Dylan felt certain their communication couldn't be seen by the Cuban government. But he wasn't sure about the ETs. They had proven to be almost omnipotent in terms of surprise, in locating their group, in fucking up their plans. Their knowledge could have come through Sofia, as she'd speculated. Since she was turning into one of them it made her an inadvertent conduit of information. If that was true, and Dylan suspected it was, then what info would they be able to obtain now that they'd taken her?

They weren't gods, he reminded himself, and sent Rey a text that CCed their entire group:

Contact John Piper at jpiper@ss.gov *He'll send you instructions on where to meet and how many of your team to bring. John will text you privately on where we are & what has happened.*

The response from Piper came in less than thirty seconds.

Have been frantically worried. What happened to you all, where you are, what happened @El Floridita, WTF is going on? What's the plan?

Dylan had thought about this, about how Pierce had cautioned one step at a time and how Fleming would freak when a bunch of pissed off locals descended on the agency's hideaway in Viñales. But what Fleming didn't understand—and what Pierce and Mike had only come to understand in the last few hours— was the emotional devastation that happened when your loved ones were abducted, transformed, or killed by these amphibious freaks.

Tell Rey to meet you @airport with as many of his group as you think will fit in the DC-3. Bring them all to Viñales airport. Let me know your arrival time. One of us will pick you up. Sofia was taken. These fucks drew 1958 around us @El Floridita and we traveled part way with Neruda & Hemingway. They fuck with time, perceptions, but aren't ubiquitous. Justin says something in tobacco is lethal to them.

While Dylan waited for a response from Piper, he hurried over to the so-called deli counter where Mike and Aldridge were waiting for their orders, which looked to be mostly meat and cheeses. "Let's get moving, guys."

"Nearly done here," Mike said.

Just then, Dylan received a response from Piper:

Carmen says Ted has paid off a Viñales police chief to find Sofia and Luke. If you're stopped, offer them $. Average pay for gov't worker is $20 a month. She thinks Ted paid $200. Then get your asses fast to agency facility.

The front door of the market opened and a cop strolled in, spotted them, and came toward them. "Shit," Dylan murmured. "Take what's ready and let's get outta here."

The odd convergence of the text message and the cop walking in seconds later convinced Dylan the ETs had arranged this. Nuthouse thoughts. Except now he knew better. The man behind the counter laid out four packages wrapped in newspaper, Dylan scooped them off the counter, and they turned toward the register. But the cop stopped them. *"Pasaportes y visas, por favor."*

They handed over what he asked for. He flipped through everything, returned it all, spoke rapidly to Mike, who announced, "He says our passports and visas are in order. He wants to know where Luke Pierce and Sofia Lopez are."

"They left our group back in Havana Vieja," Dylan said, and Mike translated.

"Y ustedes, adonde van?" And you people, where are you going?

Mike looked at Dylan. His mind scrambled back through text exchanges and that call with Graham. He knew she'd provided the official name of the facility, the name by which authorities would know it, but all he could recall was the word *vieja*. As in Havana Vieja. "Vieja," he said.

The cop's eyes came alive. *"Ah,* Campo Viejo?"

Gender agreement between nouns and adjectives. The nuthouse had robbed him of that detail. "Si," Dylan said.

"Cuesta doscientos CUCs para ir alla." It costs two hundred CUCs to go there.

"No problema," Dylan said, and handed the cop two hundred CUCs.

The cop looked like he'd just won the lottery and quickly pocketed the cash. *"Pueden ir. Bien viaje."* You can leave. Have a good trip.

They thanked him, got in line at the register and a few minutes later, nearly bolted out of the store. When they reached the station wagon, Dylan found Pierce slumped down in the front seat, Cooper pressed flat on the floor in front of the middle seat. "I heard some guys talking about a *yanqui* with a red dog and we hid. What the hell is going on?"

"Stay down," Dylan said. "I'll drive. Get into the rear seat and lay low. Ted Fisher paid off some police chief in this region to find you and Sofia."

"Not surprising."

Mike set their purchases on the floor in front of the middle seat, spoke to Cooper as he got into the station wagon, Dylan scooted behind the steering wheel, Aldridge slipped into the passenger seat. Pierce slithered like an eel to the rear of the station wagon and didn't pop up until they were on the highway. He asked for water and Mike, the official caretaker of water and food, dispensed them. "And I've got a bowl for you, Cooper. And hey, can we go any faster, Dylan?" Mike asked.

"Guys, just to set the record straight. My name is *George* Dylan, okay?"

"Sorry." Pierce snickered. "You're not a George. You're a Dylan."

Dylan started laughing because it was the same thing Sofia and Graham had said to him. Maybe when this was all over, if it ever was, he would officially change his name. "Okay, whatever. My GPS says it's fifty-two miles to Campo Viejo and I really don't want to go any faster, Mike, because this road is riddled with potholes and we don't need another flat."

"No more delays," Aldridge said. "I don't have my Parkinson's meds with me."

It suddenly struck Dylan that Aldridge was no longer using his cane, that he hadn't even seen that cane since—when? Yesterday? "Where's your cane, Larry?"

"I guess I lost it at some point." Aldridge frowned, held up his hands. "My hands don't shake anymore. And I've been walking fine."

A memory rushed back. "When John Piper and I experienced that weird thing with the craft, when it dragged us through the air and then we dropped onto the deck of his boat, he hit his head and sustained a bad gash at his temple. It was healed before we headed back to shore."

"I remember that," Aldridge said. "So... these encounters we've had... healed my Parkinson's? Is that what you're saying?"

Dylan shrugged. "Maybe the combination of that and our experience the other night with the craft."

"It's a medical impossibility. You know that, right, Dylan?"

"It's not impossible if it happened," Mike said. "You were walking fine in that store, Larry."

"Hey, the way I see it now," Pierce said, "anything is possible."

The old Ford slammed over one pothole after another and because the shocks on the car were shot, it was like being inside some nauseating ride at Disney World. "You're barely doing forty, Dylan," Mike griped.

"If we lose this tire, our only other option will be to hitch a ride on one of those." Dylan pointed at a donkey-pulled wooden wagon moving slowly along the side of the road, a middle aged man and a teenaged boy inside. The back of the wagon was piled high with tobacco leaves.

"Pull alongside him," Mike said, and opened the side door. "I'm buying that tobacco."

"Brilliant," Pierce burst out. "It gives us a head start. That tobacco is headed to market somewhere."

Dylan drove alongside the cart and Mike shouted, *"Señor, cuanto quieres para todo ese tobacco?"*

The cart's driver glanced at them, reined in the donkey, the wagon stopped. Dylan braked. Mike and Cooper hopped out of the Ford, Dylan pulled to the shoulder of the road and he, Pierce, and Aldridge got out. Dylan tried to keep up with the conversation between Mike and the wagon driver, but they were talking too quickly.

"How much does he want?" Dylan asked.

"We haven't gotten to that yet. He says the tobacco is from a local plantation that doesn't use pesticides. None of it has been frozen. He's supposed to deliver it to a factory in Viñales that processes cigars. They're paying him two hundred and fifty CUCs for the load."

"Tell him we'll double it for just half of what he's got in the wagon," Dylan said. "That way he doesn't have to explain what happened to the shipment."

"Let's really make it worth his while," Pierce suggested. "Tell him seven-fifty."

"Nos pagamos setecientos cincuenta para un medio del tobacco que tienes aqui," Mike told the man.

His eyes lit up. *"Esta bien. Muchas gracias. Hay espacio en su camion?"*

"Is there room in the station wagon for half his load?" Mike asked.

"Bet your ass," Pierce said.

"Si, claro," Mike told the driver.

Dylan peeled off another two hundred and fifty CUCs from his nearly depleted supply of money, passed it to Mike. Pierce and Mike added their two-fifty apiece and Mike handed the man the money. He and his son climbed down from the wagon to help them load the tobacco into the back. Dylan wasn't convinced any of this was worth seven hundred and fifty bucks and the delay. But he wasn't about to overlook anything that might give them an upper hand in defeating the ETs who had killed Justin, transformed Aldridge's kids, nabbed Sofia, and planned to take over the fucking world.

He hurried over to the Ford and opened the rear hatch.

5.

Lia Graham stood in the warm, bright light, watching three earth movers destroy the remains of the isolation building. With every pass, something solid was reduced to rubble, then turned over in the earth until it became part of the earth. But not a single machine touched the rock on which the young hybrid had basked in the moonlight. Why not?

She finally walked over to the lead machine, waving her arms until the driver stopped. "Something wrong, ma'am?" he asked.

An American. "I'm just curious about something. Why aren't your men tearing apart that large slab of rock over there?" She pointed at the basking rock.

The driver looked in the direction she pointed, then tilted his shades back onto the top of his head. "No offense, ma'am. But I, uh, don't see anything over there."

Not good, she thought. Not good at all. Had the hybrid rendered the slab invisible to everyone except her and maybe Fleming and the others who had been in the building when it had escaped? If so, then it might mean the slab retained a certain power. Or maybe the slab simply couldn't be seen from where he sat.

"May I come up?"

"Sure."

He gestured at some steps on the right side, she climbed them, he pulled her up into the driver area. Lia sank into the second seat. She could still see the slab. "I'm going to direct you to it," she said.

"Excuse me?"

"I can see it. You can't. So I'm going to direct you to where that slab is so you can plow it under."

He dropped his sunglasses back onto the bridge of his nose. "I don't understand why I can't see it. But you're the boss. Direct me."

From her raised perch, Lia told him to go slightly left, then straight, a little to the right, then straight again. When they were within twenty yards of the slab, she asked him to lower the plow, increase his speed, and just keep going straight. He did. And when the plow struck the slab, it made a high-pitched shrieking sound and a translucent bubble was released into the air. It expanded so quickly that within seconds it encompassed her and the driver and the entire earth mover.

She was snapped back against the seat by a force as powerful as gravity, nausea gripped her, she thought she might puke. The driver gasped, his hands flew off the steering wheel, and the earth mover lifted the entire slab and did a crazy one-eighty. The plow flung the slab into a gully of raging water that hadn't been there seconds ago, she was sure of that much, and it bobbed away, headed for the river, the sea, who the hell knew?

The earth mover suddenly died and a great screeching sound sundered the air as the metal plow tore away from the rest of the machine and hurtled across the field, dangerously close to the main buildings, where the other two shifter tanks were. She and the driver snapped forward, her head struck something. She thought she blacked out briefly because the next thing she knew, the driver was scrambling to the ground, shouting that he was done, he'd had it with the weirdness, the place was possessed.

Lia stared after him until he vanished in a thicket of trees near the parking lot. She didn't move. Hot sunlight poured over her. Cuban sunlight. Tropical sunlight. Beads of sweat oozed down the sides of her face. Sweat covered her upper lip, a perforated line that she licked, then wiped away with the back of her hand.

"Lia?"

She turned her head toward Fleming's voice and saw him racing toward her, waving his skinny arms. She was so shaken when she pushed up from the seat that her knees turned to water and she collapsed, falling back and rolling down the earth mover's steps to the ground, a tumbleweed. Lia lay there on her back, staring into the sun struck sky, and thought, *We're fucked.*

She started laughing hysterically. Fleming reached her, crouched down, touched her arm. She saw her reflection in his sunglasses and her laughter shriveled up. She looked like a maniac, her blonde hair wild, dirt smeared across her cheeks, her eyes haunted by unspeakable things.

"Are you all right?" he asked.

"Will any of us ever be all right after what we've seen and experienced?"

She pushed up, looked around slowly, and explained what had happened. Fleming stood, pulled her to her feet, and they walked over to the ruined earth mover. "I won't even bother asking what force ripped off that plow and hurled it."

"The same fucking power that destroyed the isolation tank. It was...in the slab of rock where the hybrid was basking."

"I was afraid you were going to say something like that. What was that weird bubble or whatever it was that I saw when the plow hit the slab?"

"I don't know. But it created some kind of force, a power that I think wrenched the plow from the earth mover."

"Well, here's another piece of information. Forty-three minutes ago, the head of the hybrid search party radioed that they'd sighted the hybrid and were firing at it when two of these alien fuckers leaped out a thicket and let loose. Fourteen soldiers were killed. I've requested backup from Gitmo and Homestead. Several hundred are on their way here. We're now on lockdown."

"And the hybrid?"

"Unknown."

Trickery

Sofia tricked me. She peed on me while I held her in my arms, perhaps knowing her urine would burn me, that it would throw me into a panic. But how would she know that? Is it the kind of thing her Sight reveals to her? And then she screamed what she saw coming in the immediate future, screamed with her head thrown back, only the whites of her eyes showing. What she screamed was genuine. Does she know the hybrid is the only thing more important to me than she is in terms of my tribe's survival? Did her Sight show her that as well?

How powerful is this vision of hers? Has it shown her who will win this war? Or how many of us there are—thousands scattered throughout the islands in Caribbean and thousands more in South America, on the coasts and inland in the wilderness? Has it shown her those of us who have even adapted to life in the mountains, where mountain rivers run cold and clear? Or has she learned to access our web? Does she know the hybrid is the first of its kind, the offspring of a blue and a transformed human male?

Lotus and I are standing in the wooded area where we were when Sofia started screaming. I can hear Jez calling to us, a soft, mournful cry. He understands what has happened. Lotus, do you think the two of us, working together, can move us back to the point where we entered the fog with her? We must understand what has happened here.

We know what happened. Sofia tricked us.

Intentionally?

I don't know, Mira.

It's something we must know.

It may work since we are not trying to save ourselves, it's not about defense. It's about understanding what happened. Let's try it.

She takes my hand and we struggle to do something that until recently has been so effortless. Nothing happens. Nothing changes.

My frustration builds. If we can't do this single thing, then we might as well surrender now.

Surrender? NO! *Lotus tightens her grip on my hand and suddenly we are in that moment when Sofia peed on me and I dropped her to the ground. Lotus and I are* there, *but we are also* here, *able to watch what happened, where we made wrong choices.* I should not have dropped Sofia. My first mistake.

I should have kept watch on her while you were cleaning yourself, *Lotus says.*

And I should have done the same. As the humans say, We fucked up. *In our language, that phrase sounds like a howling wind and Lotus winces and slaps her hands over her ears.*

And then I notice something that escaped me when it was actually happening. Something or someone takes shape at Sofia's feet. Lotus, do you see it?

Yes. But... how is that possible?

A short, plump woman with a braid threaded with gray is clearly visible now. A dead woman whom Sofia can see, hear, talk to without my creating a climate conducive to contact between the living and the dead.

We didn't know humans could do that, *Lotus whispers.*

My deepest fear is that there are many things we don't know about these humans. Do you think we can change it, Lotus?

As long as it's not for defense but for understanding, for broadening our knowledge. Yes, yes.

We won't fall for her trick this time.

Chapter 18

Sofia could see Viñales just a quarter mile ahead now, a little town with little buildings, little Russian cars, a lot of bikes, a lot of people. She started to tell the driver he could let her off at the first stoplight but something happened to the air. It crinkled like aluminum foil or cellophane, like a special effect in a movie, and for a moment she seemed to be in two places at once.

She was here on the wagon with the two boys and the old man, where the cart bumped along, the donkey snorted, the air smelled scorched. But she was also back in that wooded area with the ET carrying her through the fog. It disoriented her, nauseated her, made her feel like she was being ripped in half. She clutched the edge of the wagon to keep from falling off, then the sensation stopped.

What the fuck just happened?

Suddenly, she was back in the wooded area, in the fog, in the ETs arms, and her bladder let go. *I lived this before.* It felt like a massive déjà. She knew the alien would drop her, strange sounds would erupt from the ET and her companion, Rosa would appear, Sofia would scream her vision of the future and would escape. It was as if she'd dreamed it, wished it, hoped that escape into being.

Then she suddenly understood the ET had rewound time and intended to change the events so that Sofia couldn't escape.

She abruptly shrieked and jackknifed her legs up toward her chest and slammed her webbed feet into Mira's face, into her disgusting single nostril. The ET pitched backward, weird, discordant notes erupted from her, her grotesque hands flew to her face, a thick, clear liquid like corn syrup poured through her fingers. Lotus emitted a string of high-pitched, piercing sounds that felt like hot needles drilling into Sofia's eardrums.

Sofia leaped to the ground, swept up a fallen branch, swung hard, and it cracked against Mira's back. She stumbled around, shrieking, and Sofia swung again and slammed the branch across her throat. She gasped and fell back and slammed into the ground.

Lotus emitted a weird cry and hurled her arms into the air, causing dirt and rocks and fallen branches to spin into a tornadic wind, and stuff pelted Sofia from every angle. "Fucker!" Sofia yelled, and swung the branch once more, aiming low, and it lashed across the ET's double jointed knees and she sank to the ground, her hands slapping her knees as if to revive them. Or heal them.

The branch had snapped in two and Sofia tore away from them and suddenly was back inside the donkey-pulled wooden wagon with the two young boys. And a mountain of mangos and papayas. They seemed completely unaware that she'd been gone. Her breath burst from her, her heart slammed against her ribs, she was covered in sweat, dirt sheathed her face and bit into her eyes. Alarms shrieked through her. She shoved bills into the boy's hand and leaped off the back of the wagon.

Sofia ran toward the direction of Campo Viejo the old man had indicated the first time she'd lived this scenario. The alien, she thought, had just shown her what she and her kind could do with time, but they seemed to have some trouble doing it. Why? None of this would serve Dylan, who wanted the last three *years* erased and a new timeline created, but it certainly helped her.

She ran until she was drenched in sweat and could hardly breathe. Then she crawled to a spot in a wooded area, where she was protected by trees and large boulders. She curled up in a nest of fallen leaves, her exhaustion so profound she fell asleep.

2.

Pierce drove the last twenty miles to Campo Viejo. It stood at the edge of a lake and was bordered on one side by a river. Another

Gitmo, walled and fenced like a prison, posted with signs that claimed it as American soil. The only difference from Gitmo was that it involved a lake, not the ocean, and aliens, not terrorists. He doubted that any Cuban seeking asylum in the U.S. would come here in the hopes of finding passage to America, but maybe that was why the ETs had chosen this spot.

He pulled up to the imposing six-foot tall steel gate guarded by a small army of soldiers armed with assault weapons. A soldier stepped up to the driver's window. "Your business, sir?"

"We're here to see Lia Graham."

"The compound is in lockdown. No one is permitted in or out."

Dylan leaned forward from the back seat. "She's expecting us."

"Your name, sir?"

"George Dylan."

"I'll check. Please remain in the car." He whipped out his phone, spoke to the person on the other end, his voice too low for them to hear, then nodded. "I'll need your passports, visas, and the papers on the dog. What's in the back of your vehicle?"

"Tobacco," Pierce replied, and collected passports and visas from everyone. Mike handed over Cooper's papers.

"Why tobacco?" the soldier asked, shuffling through their passports.

"Ms. Graham asked us to bring it," Pierce replied.

The inside of the Ford smelled so thickly of tobacco that even the warm humid air drifting through the car didn't mitigate it. Was the stuff really lethal to these fucks? Who knew? Last night, they'd followed a lead from Ari Rey to El Floridita, the ETs had pulled 1958 around them so that Hemingway and Neruda were still alive, Aldridge and Dylan had seen their transformed or dead children, Sofia had been taken, now here they were. Pierce didn't know what to expect, but felt that he was now prepared for almost anything.

A Jeep raced down to the gate, Lia Graham hopped out in khaki shorts, a t-shirt, Adidas. A tall, pretty blonde, she looked just as she had three years ago when she and Dylan were investigating his son's disappearance. She belonged in a boardroom, Pierce thought, in an expensive suit and high heels, not here working for a government agency in a remote area of Cuba, in charge of more than fifty ET monsters.

When the gate creaked open, she took their passports and visas from the soldier and motioned for them to follow her. The unpaved road wound through a wild growth of trees—ceibas, palms, papayas, mangos. Now and then, he glimpsed a large tobacco plantation of on the east side of the lake and scattered wooden structures beyond it—barns, stables, several small houses.

The compound's main buildings, barely visible through the trees, looked like so many concrete buildings in Havana—old, neglected, a relic of colonial times that hadn't been refurbished during the nearly sixty-year embargo. As they neared, he spotted several other similar buildings to either side of it, none of them large, none with signs. The dozen or more vehicles parked to the right of the building included a fleet of huge flatbed trucks that held large aluminum tanks. Pierce parked next to an old VW van and they got out. "Are those what I think they are?" Aldridge stabbed his thumb toward the aluminum tanks.

"For moving the monsters," Dylan replied. "That's my guess."

Lia hurried over to them. "I was worried you guys had gotten lost." She hugged Pierce hello. "It's wonderful to see you again, Luke. I regret that it's under these conditions."

"We're going to find her," Pierce said. "We know how to do this kind of thing, Lia. All of us do."

"Damn straight," Mike said, and introduced himself. "Plus, we've got Cooper."

"It's a pleasure, Mike. You look a lot like your mom." She petted Cooper. "You're going to be an asset, Cooper."

"And you already know these two guys," Pierce finished.

She hugged Aldridge first, an embrace that held a lot of history. "Larry. Thank God you're here." She stood back from him. "I don't have any idea how you connected with this group, but Jerry and I are glad you did."

Aldridge didn't waste any time with amenities. "Have you determined how to tell the ETs apart from the ones who used to be human?"

"Not yet. We're hoping that once we put our heads together, we'll come up with answers. Maybe that's where Cooper comes in."

She hugged Dylan last, an embrace that spoke tomes about their previous relationship, Pierce thought. "It's good to see you, Dylan."

"You too, Graham."

Pierce noticed that Dylan's embrace lingered. Then Lia glanced around uneasily. "We've got food for everyone," she announced. "Even for you, Cooper. If you'd like to shower, use the restroom, change clothes or whatever, there're three bathrooms and your bedrooms are set up. Let's go inside."

3.

Dylan was beat and knew everyone else was, too. But none of them took the time to shower. They changed into the t-shirts Mike had bought—clean t-shirts—and met up with Graham in the large kitchen.

It had been modernized, with large sliding glass doors that looked out into trees through which Dylan could see yet another building. A buffet had been set out on a long metal table with a tiled surface and his stomach cramped with hunger just at the sight of all the food. Omelets, arepas, bacon, muffins, cereals, coffee, juices, a cornucopia compared to that shitty market where they'd stopped.

Dylan and everyone else took paper plates and utensils and helped themselves. Cooper went over to a large bowl of water on the floor and lapped until it was nearly empty. He sniffed at the equally large bowl beside it that held dried dog food and a generous portion of chicken and went to town.

When Jerry Fleming joined them, his appearance startled Dylan. He looked older, thinner, balder than he had since Dylan had seen him last a year ago. He never had been a man who wasted time and they got down to the business of exchanging information. It became emotional for Aldridge, Mike, Pierce. The only emotions Dylan felt during this exchange was rage toward the ETs for turning his life inside out like a dirty sock, and a deep longing for Graham, for the intimacy they had shared during his recovery from the nuthouse. Extremes.

"This tobacco," Fleming said. "It's in your car?"

"Yes, we bought it from a campesino," Mike replied.

"There's a tobacco plantation across the lake," Graham said. "But nothing has been harvested yet. Do you know what about the tobacco is lethal to them?"

"Not yet," Dylan replied.

"I'll ask some of our guys to unload it. We'll run tests."

"We'd like to see them," Dylan finally said.

Graham glanced at Fleming. "Are they out? Is it safe to go in there?"

Fleming nodded. "Sergio just texted me. We're good to go."

"What do you mean by *are they out?*" Mike asked.

"We keep them drugged, but increased the dosage before you guys arrived," Graham explained. "We don't want to take any unnecessary risks about how they might react to seeing other people. We already got duped by the hybrid and she's still out there somewhere."

"Let's do it," Pierce said.

They left through the kitchen's sliding glass doors, crossed the patio, and entered a concrete passageway, an above ground tunnel that looked newly constructed compared to the other buildings. Graham fell into step beside Dylan, her hand brushed his. "I'm glad you're here. I just wish the circumstances were different, Dylan."

"Me, too. I wish the last three years never happened." He quickly added, "Except for the recuperation time with you. That was one of the happiest periods of my life since Justin died."

Graham caught his fingers and he squeezed her hand. "Mine, too." Then: "Did you really meet Neruda? Hemingway?"

"Yeah." He slipped out his phone, navigated to photos. Out of the dozens of pictures he'd taken of Neruda and Hemingway, only a handful had come through, with the actual 1958 dates the photos had been taken.

"Wow. My God. So these ETs really can move around in time."

"Either that or it was a clever illusion they perpetrated. But if, at the end of all this, Hemingway dies later than July 2, 1961, then we'll know it actually happened and that he successfully bargained with them to create a new timeline for himself." Dylan paused, slipped out his wallet, and removed the folded napkin. He handed it to her. "A note to you from Neruda."

"What?" She gave a short, clipped laugh, as though she thought he'd slipped into nuthouse mode. Then she unfolded the napkin. "My God," she whispered. "This is incredible, Dylan. Thank you." She tucked it into a zippered compartment in the bag that hung from her shoulder.

He slipped his hands along the sides of her face and kissed her. Graham's body melted against his, her mouth opened to his, he inhaled the citrus scent of her hair, the spicy aroma of her skin, loved the familiar taste of her mouth, loved her as fully and completely as he ever had.

"Jesus, Dylan," she whispered, her body pressed against his, her mouth close to his ear. "I've missed you."

He stepped back, his hands still at the sides of her lovely face, his thumbs stroking the contours of her jaw. "Look, I want you to know something, Graham. I'm willing to negotiate with these monsters if they do something for me—create a new timeline where the last three years never happened, where Justin doesn't die, and Larry's kids are never changed. But that won't change my feelings for you, which existed long before his death, when I was still married and miserable."

Tears glistened in her eyes. "I understand. But bargaining with them right now won't be possible because they're unconscious. If you get a chance, keep in mind they're tricksters. They'll fuck you over somehow. That's what the hybrid did. Besides, what do you have to offer them?"

"I'll tell them where we hid the craft that crashed off Tango Key."

"They probably don't give a shit about their craft."

"I think they do." He told her about the message the craft had transmitted when they'd hidden the part of it they'd found. He didn't tell her where for fear the ETs might hear. "It's partly biological and, in some sense, it's alive."

Graham looked surprised. "How do you know this?"

"Some experiments that John Piper, Larry and I did. Is the compound well-armed?"

She laughed, but it sounded harsh and cold. "Sure. To the teeth." They hurried to catch up with the others, her hand still in his. "But even assault rifles and grenades aren't much of a defense against what these ETs can do."

"You could kill the lot of them while they're drugged."

"We've considered that. But we still don't know which ones were originally human and we're actually learning stuff about them."

"Like what?"

"Their language consists of sounds, they're definitely telepathic, and now we know that when one of them has sex with a transformed human, that union may produce a hybrid. The females have pouches on their spines where the infant is nurtured and fed until it's mature enough to get along on its own. But there's a whole lot more that we don't know. How do they feed their young? They don't have nipples. What's the gestation period? How do they have sex? I'll email you the report I'm preparing for the Senate Intelligence Committee."

They stopped behind Fleming, Pierce, Mike, Aldridge, and the dog, and Dylan let go of her hand. He immediately felt that same crippling loss he had the day he'd told her that his only goal in life was to find the alien fucks who had killed Justin. He loved her, but he loved his dead son more. No one should have to make the choice these aliens had forced on him, on any of them.

Fleming slid a card through the security slot, a vacuum sealed door whispered open, and they entered a windowless, twilit control room. A dozen or more employees sat at computers or stood around with iPads, monitoring the grotesque beings that floated in a pair of tremendous tanks. Dylan's initial impression was that they looked like ETs in a badly made horror movie. But the longer he looked at them, the more details he noticed.

The dual thumbs on their hands were longer than their fingers and had two joints. Their double jointed knees made their legs seem floppy, like a doll's, as they floated. The single nostril and the throat gill struck him as especially hideous. But their weird hair that came in four different colors puzzled him. Dark brown, blue, red, yellow.

"The hybrid in that video you sent, Graham. It had pink stubble on its head, right?"

"Yes." Her eyes widened. She immediately understood his implication. "Shit, Dylan. You may have hit on something. I was thinking it was pink because it was still an infant."

"Maybe it's pink because it's a hybrid."

"And that would mean the hair color indicates a hierarchy."

"Exactly."

While Graham texted the theory to everyone on her and Fleming's team, Dylan moved closer to the glass. The control room was separated from the tanks by sheets of glass that Dylan suspected was borosilicate, the same stuff used on space shuttles. Given what he'd seen of the capabilities of these ETs, he didn't think borosilicate would do much of anything except irritate them if they went ballistic telekinetically. The video Graham had sent him of the destruction the infant hybrid had perpetrated was proof of that. The snipers positioned on platforms above and around the tanks, a small army of them, were their best defense.

Dylan pressed his hand against the glass. *Which one of you killed Justin?* Was it the one with the tuft of red hair lying there on the bottom of tank #2, sprawled on its hideous back like it was sunbathing? Or was it the one with the spray of yellow hair, floating facedown, arms perpendicular to its body? If pink hair indicated a hybrid, what did the others colors mean? How did this hierarchy work?

Cooper crept over to Dylan and lifted his paws to the railing. For the longest time, the dog stared the way dogs did when stalking squirrels in trees. Then he growled, the fur on his back stood up, and he leaped at the glass, his claws dancing against it, his ferocious snarls echoing in the control room.

Dylan grabbed his leash and yanked him back and Mike rushed forward and took the leash and hurried to the rear of the control room, trying to calm him down.

He knows you took his main human.

Sergio shouted, "Get more drugs pumped into the tanks!

The dog's reaction registered for them."

Graham looked at Sergio's iPad and yelled, "Margarita, a double dose fast! Sergio's specs show they're coming to!"

Margarita's hands flew across a computer keyboard, Fleming spoke quickly into a mike on his shirt and alerted the snipers, and a milky liquid shot out of the walls of both tanks. But before the stuff filled the tanks, an ET with a sprig of blue hair in tank #1 sprang forward. It pressed its hideous face against the glass, its hands with those twin thumbs at either side of its head, its eyes boring into Dylan's.

I took your son, and an image of Justin filled his head, Justin being dragged out into the ocean that evening on a Sarasota beach as he kicked and fought and shrieked. Dylan wrenched back from the glass, his horror so profound that he tripped over something and went down, landing hard on his ass, air rushing out of his lungs. It severed the communication between him and the ET.

The drug reached the ET and it fell away from the side of the tank, unconscious. Dylan watched as it drifted to the bottom of the tank and lay there, motionless.

4.

The afternoon heat radiated from the ground where Lia walked. Not a breath of air blew in from the water. The trees on the compound stood straight and still. She felt like she was inhaling steam, sweat trickled down the sides of her face, her damp hair clung to the back of her neck. But she kept walking, unable to sleep like Dylan and the rest of his group, who had collapsed finally from exhaustion.

Movement kept her mind active.

Movement kept her from despairing.

Movement kept her from doing something foolish, like returning to the main building, slipping into Dylan's bedroom, shedding her clothes, and climbing into bed with him.

Movement was her salvation.

Here and there, she found ripened papayas on the ground, collected them, dropped them in a fabric bag she carried over her shoulder. She added a couple of coconuts and wished that the mangos were ready to be harvested. She wished, oh Christ, she wished she'd never joined The Agency, that she'd been a professor at Yale or Berkeley, and had been able to have children. She wished for an ordinary life.

Maybe some summer night in that ordinary life, she would see a weird light in the sky and wonder about life on other planets. But in that probable life, she wouldn't pursue a path that led here and now to Cuba, to Campo Viejo, to desires unfulfilled, to strangeness she could barely comprehend.

Behind her, barking. She glanced around. Cooper loped toward her, Aldridge trotting along behind the dog. Aldridge, who used to walk with a cane because of Parkinson's and now moved along at a respectable clip with no aid whatsoever. In fact since he'd arrived, she hadn't seen him use the cane at all. Why not?

"Hey, Lia. Hope you don't mind company."

"I'd love some company, Larry. You're walking great, by the way."

"This is going to sound nuts, but I think these encounters have cured my Parkinson's. Medically impossible, but here I am."

Graham stopped, her thoughts swirling with the myriad possibilities. "My God. When...did you first start noticing your symptoms were improving?"

"The night Piper, Dylan and I moved the craft, it emitted a fine mist that supposedly made the atmosphere more conducive to contact with his dead son and my morphed son. That's when I started noticing the improvement. But it wasn't until a couple of days later, on the flight, that I realized my hands weren't shaking anymore. Then, the night we set out for El Floridita, I accidentally left my cane in the apartment. After our encounter on the road, when this mist or fog surrounded us and we ended up at Betty Danger's and I talked to my kids again and Dylan talked to Justin...and they...took Sofia, I realized I could walk fine under my own steam."

So, it was something in the mist and the fog that had cured him? That was what it sounded like. "As a neurologist, Larry, tell me what would have to happen physically for a complete cure of Parkinson's."

"Wow." He paused. "Okay, a simple explanation. The dead nerve cells in my midbrain would have to come back to life and start producing dopamine again. The midbrain controls motor skills, vision, hearing and other things. Dopamine is a neurotransmitter that allows messages to be sent to the parts of the brain that coordinate movement."

"Could the mist or the fog contain dopamine that somehow, I don't know, seeped into your brain?"

"No. Parkinson's patients can't just take dopamine as a drug because it can't cross into the brain. So the treatment gets around that with drugs that are converted to dopamine in the brain or with dopamine agonist drugs that act like dopamine and stimulate the nerve cells. That's what I think happened. The mist and the fog stimulated an incredibly rapid growth of the nerve cells in my midbrain."

"Jesus, this is huge, Larry."

Aldridge touched her arm. "It's more than huge, Lia. It means that these beings, as grotesque and strange as they are, may not be all bad. They facilitated contact with my kids...."

"Whom they initially changed, Larry."

"But maybe they chose Cat and Duncan because they knew I had Parkinson's and that they could cure it and offer the world a cure."

It's all about me. Lia had heard this kind of rationale for years—from abductees, the loved ones of abductees, even from researchers like herself. *The abduction woke me up to a more evolved idea about the world I live in,* an abductee might say. Never mind that you had probes shoved up your ass, ovum and sperm removed from your body. *I learned to appreciate everything I have,* the loved one of an abductee might say. But never mind that you ended up in a psychiatric hospital like Dylan had. Then there were the researchers, some of whom believed the aliens were here to save humanity and the planet, that they were the good guys, like Spielberg's cute E.T.

She didn't say any of this to Aldridge. The miraculous thing was that he appeared to have been cured of an incurable neurological disease and that warranted closer scrutiny. "Why did they kill Dylan's son?" she asked. "What did he get out of that except for a stint in a psychiatric facility and his life unraveling like a fucking spool of thread?"

Aldridge looked less certain now. "Why do *you* think they're here?"

"What they're doing is a clever way to invade a planet, Larry. That's what I think."

He nodded and they started walking again. "Sofia said the same thing."

But the bottom line, she thought, was they really didn't know.

Before she could reply, half a dozen transport planes flew in low over the compound, and suddenly, the afternoon air filled with hundreds of parachutes. Their backups had arrived.

Lia texted Fleming and she and Aldridge and the dog hurried back to the main building.

In the Caves

*T*he call that went out to my supporters is answered. They emerge from their hiding places, our numbers swell. This network of caves—separate from Cuevo de los Indios, which Acia and her supporters have claimed- looms large and high enough to accommodate all of us and our changelings. Nearly fifty in my tribe are now fully human, true changelings, and we converse as humans do, something made possible only because I am partially transformed. They are Cubans as well as Canadians and Europeans, Asians and South Americans who came to the island as tourists and were brought here through El Floridita months ago. They stand ready to join our battle against the American compound so we can free our trapped kin. And conquer Cuba.

The changelings wait in small groups to be transported in tourist launches at the pier. Two groups will be escorted out of the cave by Jez and several of his warriors, who will follow them to a place by the riverbank where cars await them. In their human form, they no longer have the ability to affect matter with waves of energy and the warriors will protect them from humans. From Acia and her followers. From Ravina, if she's still alive. But they can still access the web. They have that advantage because their transformation happened here in the caves, so they remember who they were.

Do you understand what you're to do? *I ask those in the launches.* Do you have any questions?

Yes, I do. *A young man, Charles, once from Canada.* So we're the first line of defense. Is that correct?

Yes, *Lotus says.* You're the ones who will enter the compound first.

By posing as humans who have escaped the alien clutches. *He snickers.* I love it.

You won't need weapons, *I tell him.* Jez and his warriors will protect you. But we have weapons if you would like to take them.

Show us how the warriors can protect us, *says ex-Canadian Charles.*

Jez raises up from the water, to his full height of eight and a half feet, and throws his arms into the air. The pulsating energy he releases blows away tons of rock and stone at the back of the cave, then a bright light leaps from his webbed fingers and burns the hole into a beautiful, perfect arch, our new exit.

Like that, *he says.*

The man shouts and pumps his fist into the air. Are we ready for this battle, people?

A chorus rises in the caves and it's echoed by what sounds like music so divine that we all pump our fists, cheering them on. A human thing, but it drives home the point. Then Jez and his fellow warriors lead the launches out of the cave and for the first time since my craft crashed, I feel hopeful.

Chapter 19

Sofia came to with her clothes stuck to her like Velcro from the heat, her knees aching and throbbing, and a young girl standing beside her, staring at her, sucking hungrily on her thumb. She raised up on her elbows. "Who're you?"

The girl—Cuban?—sucked harder on her thumb and didn't speak or move. A fuzz covered her skull, her ribs showed through the tight shirt she wore, her shorts were too large for her, her legs pencil thin, the tattered sandals on her feet threatened to come apart. She looked like photos Sofia had seen of children who survived Buchenwald.

"What's your name?" Sofia asked.

Silence.

Maybe she didn't speak English. Sofia asked her the same question in Spanish. The girl's thumb fell out of her mouth and she quickly rubbed her hands over her head, knocking away dried mud that revealed that the fuzz covering her skull was pink. Alarmed, Sofia sat straight up and the little girl grinned, her dagger-like teeth lining up in her mouth, and lunged for Sofia.

The hybrid.

She rolled to the side and the girl struck the ground, her head slammed against a rock, and the blow knocked her out. Sofia leaped up and ran to her, turned her over. The gash on her temple bled, but the blood was pale pink, as though she were badly anemic.

Sofia lifted her shirt and saw the small, closed gill at her side. She checked the inside of the girl's fingers and felt the familiar nubs where the webbing would emerge. She saw the mounds where her second thumbs would come in. She had nipples, genitalia. She removed the girl's sandals and found the same nubs on the inside of her toes. She touched the discolored mark at her throat and guessed it was where a larger gill eventually would form.

This was the hybrid the soldiers had been chasing, the ETs best hope, the one they'd run off to save when she'd screamed what Rosa had told her to scream. Human face, alien teeth, a pink fuzz that would grow into a little tuft of pink. An aberration.

Terrified, Sofia backed away, then loped clumsily into the trees, moving rapidly, her webbed feet slapping the ground. Miles later when the trees ended abruptly, she stopped. Winded, hot, her heart throbbing, she doubled over from exhaustion, palms pressed to her thighs. She finally raised up and wiped the back of her hand across her sweaty face.

Directly in front of her lay sprawling fields of some sort of crop, surrounded by a low wooden fence. She saw a ramshackle wooden barn that looked on the verge of collapsing. Cows, goats, and horses grazed in a pasture to the left of the crops. Several long water or feed troughs lined the sides of the field. Water and a place to hide.

She would be fully exposed when she left the trees, but she couldn't risk staying where she was until it got dark. If that hybrid kid's knees morphed into the dual jointed wonders, she could close in on Sofia suddenly, without much warning. She took off toward the field, arms tucked in close to her ribs, and hoped the *campesinos* who worked here were at home for their afternoon siestas. She didn't want to endanger anyone else.

As she neared the field, pigs squealed and oinked and several little piglets waddled quickly into the field and vanished in all the greenery. She followed them until the crops reached her knees, then veered right to a water trough. Sofia crouched in front of it, between two of the piglets.

The water looked clear and came from a hand pump. Even if dead ants had been floating in it and the trough had been coated with algae, it wouldn't matter. She scooped handful after handful into her mouth and splashed it on her face and arms and neck, then drank some more. It felt so refreshingly wonderful that she worked the pump with one hand, stuck her head under the stream of water, opened her mouth and the cool water ran down her throat.

She plopped back into the leafy crop, the piglets moved up next to her, one of them curling up against her leg. She stroked it, the peace and quiet of this field surrounding her long enough for her to remember the evenings in Key West when she and Cooper had sat out on the dock together, welcoming the dusk. In spite of her financial difficulties then, she missed those peaceful times. Another life.

A terrible, high-pitched squealing shattered the quiet.

The sound came from the woods.

The piglets took off, screeching as though they were being slaughtered. The hybrid girl leaped out of the trees, taller now, her legs with those dual jointed knees enabling her to move with incredible speed. Sofia leaped up and took off, adrenaline pumping through her. She raced toward the pasture where cows now scattered, mooing frantically, goats bleated and fled, horses galloped wildly, rearing up, neighing with fear. As they started leaping the fence, seeking refuge elsewhere, Sofia glanced back.

The girl plunged into the field, her stubbled pink hair clearly visible in the late afternoon sunlight, standing straight up on her head like a flag, a sign that screamed, *Here I am, ha-ha, and I found you!* Like it was a goddamn game of hide and seek.

Sofia neared the fence. Any idea she'd entertained of jumping on the back of one of these horses and galloping off to safety evaporated. The horses were long gone, halfway across the meadow beyond the fence and headed for the distant hills. Sofia climbed awkwardly onto the fence, her webbed feet so clumsy that one of them slipped, her hands lost their grip on the railing, and she fell back into the field of crops.

She bolted upright, looked back once more. The hybrid girl had stopped in the middle of the crops, webbed hands darting around, grabbing leaves, stuffing them in her mouth. She turned slowly in a circle, slapping the crops this way and that, and stuffed another handful of leaves into her mouth. Sofia used the girl's distraction to run toward the nearest structure, a barn. Small houses stood several miles beyond it.

Sofia plunged into the barn. Chickens and roosters wandered about freely, pecking at the dirt, the trough, clucking away. A huge male pig occupied one stall, a donkey neighed in another stall. The third stall held a monster pale green 1950 Chevy. Perfectly preserved. Shiny. The large fenders gleamed and reflected her face like a mirror. She looked half-mad, a possessed witch who belonged in some nineteenth century institution where electroshock was the only treatment.

She jerked open the driver's door, hoped to find a key in the ignition, but didn't. *C'mon, I know there's a key in here somewhere.* She searched frantically—under the visor, in the glove compartment, under the seat. She finally found the key under the passenger seat floor mat.

She jammed the key in the ignition, realized she needed to open the gate to get out of here without taking the entire barn down with her. She leaped out, unlatched the gate, saw the hybrid girl in the distance, still moving through the field, gobbling down leaves. *Keep chowing down, kid.*

Back to the car, fast. She turned the key, the engine clicked. "Please, start, c'mon." She turned the key again, pumped the accelerator. The engine clicked once, twice, then died. "Shit, just turn over."

And it did. Relief poured through her. She slammed the massive gear into first and the Chevy roared out of the stall, taking part of the gate with it. As it tore up the dirt road, the hybrid girl glanced up, her body stiffening with recognition, and leaped.

She landed several yards in front of the Chevy, bared her horrifying teeth, and Sofia didn't slow down, didn't swerve to avoid her. *I'll mow you down, bitch.* Seconds later, the car struck her, throwing her back with such force that it hurled her body over the fence, into the field. Her body slammed to the ground. The Chevy stuttered, the engine threatened to stall, she pressed the accelerator to the floor, unwilling to stop, to check. She'd been fooled before. These ETs were tricksters, and it could all be a ruse, an act like that of the helpless little girl with the fuzzy hair, sucking her thumb. She kept moving, fast.

In the side mirror, she saw the girl lurch to her feet and

stumble around, confused. How the hell could she still be alive? She jammed the accelerator to the floor and the Chevy zoomed up the road. Several miles later, the road to one of the houses climbed and she shifted gears.

It would be dark soon. That scared her. She didn't want to be stuck out here after the sun went down. Another mile and she reached the top of the hill and pulled up in front of the house. Four vehicles were parked to the right side of the porch. A barn stood a quarter of a mile away. Sofia turned off the engine, pocketed the key, swung her legs out. Her webbed feet touched the ground.

She looked out over the field, didn't see the girl.

Sofia hurried up the porch steps to the front door, pounded frantically. *"Por favor,"* she shouted. *"Necesito ayuda."*

The blinds that covered the window to her right moved, eyes peered out, the lock clicked, the door opened. The woman who stood there was *old*, pushing a hundred, and wore a cotton housedress, her gray hair pulled back in a ponytail. Around her neck, hung a necklace with a charm Sofia recognized as Chango, the *orisha* of Santeria that symbolized fire, cleansing, new beginnings. Her tired gaze dropped to Sofia's webbed feet, flicked to her face. *"Ay, dios mio,"* she murmured, and made a hasty sign of the cross on her forehead and opened the door wide. *"Entra."*

"Gracias. Muchas gracias."

Sofia stepped inside, the door shut, and the first thing she saw was a long, wide altar along the wall to her right, lit up with candles that illuminated a statue of Chango and the numerous offerings of sweets, candies, honey, flowers, loaves of bread, bags of sugar, flour, coffee. Tucked in between these offerings were slips of papers, requests people had made of Chango.

" Hay...un monstruo afuera." There's a monster outside.

"I believe it is dead," the woman said in heavily accented English.

"My car hit it."

"Not the car, the tobacco. Please, sit. I will get you food, something cold to drink." She vanished into the kitchen and reappeared moments later with two bottles of cold water, a plate of yellow rice, black beans, chicken, a small loaf of warm, buttered Cuban bread, and set everything on the table. Sofia, famished, dived into the food. "You are Sofia Lopez?"

Sofia raised her eyes to the old woman's face. "How... do you know my name?"

"Certain news travels quickly in Cuba. I must drive over to the barn. I will be back in a jiffy." She smiled. "I have just learned that word. *Jiffy*. Like American peanut butter. It means quickly, yes?"

"Very quickly. Do you have a cell phone I can use?"

"*Si, claro.*" She slipped a cell out of a pocket in her housedress, handed it to Sofia, slipped out the front door.

As Sofia continued shoveling food into her mouth and downed half the bottle of water, her grandmother materialized across the table from her. Rosa, with her braid, her wise eyes. "*Abuelita*, you saved my life out there."

"The first time, I just helped you out. The second time, when the ET rewound time, you knew exactly what to do and saved your own life. That's the way of the warrior, Sofia. You're going to be walking this path for many years. And shortly, you will become one of a kind, *mi amor*." Rosa gestured at the phone. "Call Luke."

Then she faded away and Sofia stared at the cellphone, trying to remember Pierce's number. Her fingers started tapping out a number. They remembered.

2.

The tank area was filled with security monitors that not only watched the ETs, Pierce thought, but also showed the perimeter of the compound. The several hundred soldiers who had parachuted from the transport planes now surrounded the compound. Pierce felt they needed more soldiers, tanks, B52 bombers, a massive army. But several hundred was a vast improvement over a few dozen.

He glanced back at the tanks, where ten men in full scuba gear separated the drugged ETs according to hair color. Another team of divers started sliding petitions into place so that each tank would consist of two areas, essentially creating four tanks, one for each color.

When they were done, tank #1 held ETs with dark brown and yellow sprigs of hair. Tank #2 held the ETs with blue and red hair. There were six browns, 15 blues, 11 yellows, and 28 reds. No pinks, not since the human/alien hybrid had escaped. Pierce moved closer to the viewing area and wished he could see their eyes. It wasn't likely that Sofia was among them since these ETs had been here awhile. But if she was, he would recognize her eyes.

Aldridge also moved closer. "Luke, do you feel that any of them are Sofia?"

"Unlikely. But honestly, Larry, I don't feel much of anything except horror. What about you?"

He shook his head. "When we were at Betty Danger's, Cat and Duncan told me a lot of stuff. I'm just starting to remember some of it. Cat said they were in tanks. She was terrified she would never be... be human again and even more terrified that if she did become human, she would be so changed she wouldn't be able to live with herself."

"I've been standing here wondering why that whole Betty Danger's thing happened, why they allowed you to speak to your kids, why they let Dylan speak to his dead son. And I think it was all a big fucking distraction so they could nab Sofia. Maybe it didn't even happen, maybe it was all some clever illusion... "

"It's no illusion that Sofia was taken."

The hole in Pierce's heart opened wider. "True."

"If we were just tourists on that road, would we even see Betty Dangers?" Aldridge asked.

"I doubt it. I think Hemingway was right. Betty Dangers is where the world of the living and the world of the dead intersect."

"What the fuck." Aldridge shook his head. "In the medical world where I come from, the consensus is generally that when you're dead, you're dead. End of story."

Pierce slipped his arm around Aldridge's shoulders and

leaned in close to him. "Here's something weird to consider, Larry. A lot of abductees have reported that during their abductions, they see and communicate with loved ones who are dead. That's led some researchers and experiencers to speculate that ETs and the dead inhabit the same dimension."

Aldridge looked at Pierce. "*You* inhabit a strange and incomprehensible world, Luke. And thank Christ you're here."

Mike came over to them with Cooper. "I'd like to take Cooper into the main tank area and let him look at these beings up close."

"If he goes nuts like he did before, it might rouse them," Pierce said.

"I think he understands what he did wrong before, Luke. I'm going to try."

"It's up to Lia and Jerry."

"I already talked to them. They're willing."

"Let's go do it, then. I'm going in with you."

"Count me in, too." Dylan came up behind them with Lia.

"Uh-uh,"Lia said. "Forget it, Dylan. That Blue had a violent reaction to you. At this point, with them divided up, we can't risk one of them becoming conscious."

"It had a reaction to me because it was the fuck who dragged Justin off into the water on Sarasota Beach," Dylan snapped.

"I understand. But please." She touched her hand to his chest. "Stay here with the others." She motioned at Pierce, Mike, and Aldridge, gave Cooper a reassuring pat, and they followed her to the steel door that separated the viewing area from the tank area. "Remove your shoes. Their hearing is acute. Sergio and Margarita will shoot in more drugs if the monitors indicate they're coming to."

They slipped off their shoes and Lia opened the steel door. Pierce felt excited but scared, intrigued but uncertain. Once they passed through the door, he noticed how attentive the snipers were, several dozen of them positioned on the platforms above the tanks. It was strangely quiet in here and the air smelled humid, felt thick, viscous, uncomfortable, and it creeped him out.

Mike and Cooper walked ahead of him, Aldridge, and Lia,

the dog sniffing the air. Mike held his leash loosely, so that if Cooper wanted to stop, the leash wouldn't keep him from doing so. The dog paused in front of tank #2, stared at the floating beings, the Blues and Reds. He brought his snout up to the glass, Mike patted him, whispered, "Good boy."

Cooper moved his snout to the left, sniffing at a Blue close to the glass, then at a Red nearby. He moved on to tank #1, did the same with the Browns and the Yellows, and looped back to the second tank. He went up to the Red, pawed at the floor, and stretched out on his belly, staring with that peculiar focus usually reserved for squirrel watching.

Holy shit, Pierce thought. *Are the Reds the transformed humans?* Suddenly, the Red's eyes opened, a quick, desperate look that screamed, *Help me, dear God, help me!* Then its eyes snapped shut again.

Cooper whimpered and Mike wrenched back, nearly stumbling into Pierce and Aldridge, and Lia gestured for them to leave, quickly. The instant the steel door shut behind them, Mike burst out, "Did you *see* that? The Reds were once humans! Good boy, Coop, great work!"

Lia was already issuing instructions to the divers to separate Reds from Blues, to isolate them, and to activate the second partition in tank #2. She told Sergio to give the tanks another blast of drugs. Pierce stood at the viewing area window, his thoughts racing.

What that look in the Red's eyes meant, he thought, was that even when a human was fully changed, even when it had become one of these repugnant ETs, a remnant of its humanity remained. Or it remained in some of them. It gave him hope that even if Sofia had been among them, she would recognize him, her son, her dog.

"Where're the rest of the Reds?" Pierce asked Aldridge. "There have to be more than twenty-eight. Somewhere."

"Probably still in the river or in the caves."

His phone vibrated. He didn't recognize the number, a Cuban exchange, but he hurried out of the viewing area to take the call. In the long tunnel, he answered it. "Luke Pierce."

"It's me." Sofia's voice, breathless. Choked up.

"Jesus." He experienced a euphoria unlike anything he'd ever felt before. "Sofia..." The signal crackled and he loped up the tunnel, hoping the signal would be clearer outside. "My God, where are you?"

"In a house near a tobacco field. Where're you?"

"The Agency compound. Campo Viejo."

"On the lake, right? Near the river?"

"Yes."

"I think I'm only a handful of miles from you. I...I was chased by a hybrid into a tobacco field. It stuffed tobacco leaves into its mouth. The woman...a *santera*...thinks it's dead. Her friends are coming up from the barn and then...I want to check and see if it's really dead."

Tobacco. "We have a shitload of tobacco."

"Dump it in the river."

"We just discovered that the ones with red hair are the changed humans. Will the tobacco kill them, too?"

"I...don't know."

"There are twenty-eight Reds in the tanks."

"*That's all?*"

"That's all they've captured. The locals think some of these aliens live in the caves. The river that borders the compound runs into those caves."

"I think the ones with the blue hair are in charge. Like the one who's changing me."

"What about the others?"

"I don't know. Shit, Luke, there's so much we don't know yet. Before you dump the tobacco in the river, we have to know if it will harm the Reds."

She sounded frantic and distraught. It scared him. "How... changed are you?"

She took a deep breath. "Just webbed feet now. I don't know if the gills were real or an illusion. The woman's coming back. We can text on this number."

The phone went dead. Pierce stood there, breathing hard, his head pounding, then ran back through the tunnel.

3.

Dylan was outside of the main building with Fleming, walking the property, talking with some of the soldiers, trying to get a sense of the lay of the land before the sun went down. One road in and out. Any vehicle coming up the road would be visible as soon as it emerged from the tree-lined curve twenty feet below him and would be spotted long before then from the upper back deck.

"If we're on the upper back deck as the final line of defense against an advancing army of these alien fucks, Jerry, what kind of protection do we have?"

Fleming gestured toward the upper deck. "See the glint of metal just above the deck?"

"Yeah."

"They're like hurricane shutters, except they cover the entire building, turning it into a titanium dome. On the deck, there are portholes for weapons. I don't know if a titanium dome can withstand a telekinetic assault, but it at least will protect everyone inside against airborne debris. And there are exits that lead to other protected areas in the event the tanks are breached."

Anxiety churned through Dylan's stomach. "These soldiers from Gitmo."

"Special forces, not just soldiers," Fleming said. "And they aren't just from Gitmo. I tapped our units at AUTEC, in the Bahamas, and at Homestead Air Force."

"Are they aware of what they may be up against?"

Fleming kicked at a stone in front of him, gave a reluctant nod. "Yeah, they were informed. I had to be up front about this before I could get anyone to sign off."

"Yeah? You mentioned aliens?"

Fleming looked pissed now. "Yes, George. I mentioned fucking aliens. They've got video, photos, reports, all of it. What the hell. Who do you think is funding all this?" He threw his arms out to his sides. "Not Ted Fisher."

"Okay, okay." Dylan patted the air. "I just need to know in case… "

"In case what?"

In case there's a time anomaly. In case another impossible thing happens. "In case those two vehicles down there are filled with aliens." He gestured toward a pair of 1950s cars coming out of the turn on the road below them.

"They'll be stopped at the gate."

"And then what?"

"Lia and I will be contacted about whether they should be admitted."

The fire in Dylan's belly suddenly burned so hot that his hand tightened on the assault rifle over his shoulder. "Let's meet them at the gate, Jerry."

Fleming looked uneasily at Dylan. "Why?"

"Major gut feeling."

"We'll take one of the Jeeps."

They trotted over to it and Dylan slid behind the wheel, the fire in his belly scorching his insides. The key was in the ignition, he turned it, and the Jeep tore down the hill toward the gate where the two old cars had stopped. One soldier spoke to the driver of the first vehicle, another spoke to the driver of the second vehicle. Fleming's earpiece was connected to the Jeep's Bluetooth, so Dylan could hear the soldiers' conversations with the drivers, Charles and Amy.

"Please, dear God, let us in," Charles babbled. "We escaped from the caves, they're after us, we don't have anywhere else to go." Sobbing and pleas from the people inside the car.

"How many are you?" the soldier asked.

"Seven sandwiched inside this car," Charles said, his voice crackling with fear. "Eight in the other. Please, please let us in. We... "

Dylan looked at Fleming, mouthed, *No.* When Graham had run into a man in San Francisco who was the spitting image of her husband, Neil King, dragged off a Costa Rican beach three years before Dylan's son had vanished, he hadn't recognized her. He'd lost whatever memories he'd had as the human Neil King.

"Ask him who the president of the United States is, soldier," Dylan instructed.

"Will do," the soldier replied. "Sir, who is the current

president of the United States?"

The Jeep shrieked to a stop in front of the gate and Dylan and Fleming leaped out and ran over to it as it slid open. The driver of the first vehicle, Charles, eyed them uneasily through the windshield, then opened his door and stepped out, a young man, handsome, well-spoken.

"Excuse me, but… "

"Answer the goddamn question," Dylan snapped at Charles. "Who's the president of the U.S.?"

"Obama… is president."

Just then, a pulsating wave shot out of the trees that bordered the river. Dylan saw it, the air wavering, quivering, like heat above a scorching hot pavement, and shouted, "Hit the ground!" Then he threw himself at Fleming, knocking him to the grass, and Dylan dived on top of him. Seconds later, the pulsating wave tore away the front fence, the gate, the nearest trees, and a tornadic whirlwind of dust and debris tore over and around the cars and swept past them.

Dylan rolled away from Fleming and started shooting at the people scrambling out of the two cars. Charles fell back, his human eyes wide and shocked, and began changing into his alien form before he hit the ground. Fleming leaped up and he and Dylan ran toward the cars and kept firing at the human-looking aliens. The soldiers who were still alive riddled both cars with bullets, the stink of death filled the air.

And when it was over, fifteen aliens lay scattered around two ruined cars. Dylan and Fleming moved rapidly out among them, firing at the alien bodies, making sure they were dead. "Did we just liberate the humans these fucks changed, Dylan?"

"I sure hope so."

Fleming turned to the several dozen soldiers still alive and shouted, "This is what you're up against! Load the bodies, bring them onto the compound, dig a hole, and burn the fucks. And all of you move back toward the compound."

Then the sun slipped beneath the horizon. Somewhere nearby, perhaps from the river, Dylan heard the jarring calls that traveled through the darkness, alerting the other ETs of what had happened, that their preliminary convoy was dead.

Chapter 20

When the door opened, the old woman came into the room accompanied by Carmen, Piper, and McMullen. Sofia was so shocked and relieved to see them she burst into tears. Carmen hugged her, smoothed her hands over Sofia's hair.

"It's okay, Sofia. We're here, *mi amor.* "

"But *how* are all of you here? "

"This beautiful woman... " Carmen gestured at the old woman. "... is Teresa, my teacher and mentor, who first inducted me into Santeria when I was just sixteen."

That part didn't surprise her. But everything else did. "But... c'mon, the odds that I would be here right now are past the stratosphere. Is this more ET manipulation?"

Teresa gestured at her altar, suggesting that Chango had a hand in all this. But Sofia didn't believe in the power of the *orishas.* She'd been an interested bystander of Santeria, nothing more. Yet, here she was, confronted with so many impossible things it was impossible for her to *not believe*—in something. The orishas, synchronicity, an order that unfolded from some deeper place, a universal intelligence.

Piper said, "Dylan arranged this with Ari Rey. He and his army of men and women are in the barn out back. I flew two dozen of us here, the rest drove. All of these people have lost loved ones to these aliens, Sofia. They want them back."

But the odds, Sofia thought, that they would be on the same property where she sought refuge bewildered her. She felt as if she were in the presence of some sort of quantum force or power that she couldn't understand or decipher. She motioned at Teresa's altar, the little statues, the offerings to the *orishas*. "What do the *orishas* have to say about that monster outside, Teresa?"

Teresa fingered the Chango metal that hung around her neck. "That it cannot be purified or cleansed, but can be destroyed by fire. But that is not how it or its kind will die. May I have my phone? I know people in town who have warehouses of tobacco and many of them have lost loved ones to these creatures. They'll help us."

Sofia passed her the phone and Teresa walked quickly out onto the porch, jabbering away in Spanish.

"We're going to check on the hybrid," McMullen said. "Make sure it's dead."

"Because she ate tobacco and is allergic to nicotine or what?" Sofia asked.

"Not quite that simple, but close," Piper replied.

"The aliens enjoy eating tobacco," Carmen said. "And the caterpillars that destroy the crops are probably an added bonus. But we don't think that's what kills them. Those caterpillars—hornworms—are where a parasitic wasp lays its eggs. Farmers have brought in a bunch of wasps recently to control the caterpillar population. The wasp larvae feed internally on the caterpillar and once an ET has consumed the caterpillar, we think the wasp larvae go to work on it. In other words the alien is eaten from the inside out. Now we'll finally be able to prove that theory."

"Have you known this since you and Ted returned from Cuba?" Sofia asked.

"We suspected a lot of things, Sofia. But Teresa got in touch with me after you all left El Floridita. She told me her sons found several alien bodies in their fields. They burned the bodies, though, so she was never able to verify anything. Now we can. If that hybrid isn't dead already, my hope is that it will be shortly."

"Do Pierce and the others know you're here?" Sofia asked.

"Not yet," McMullen replied.

"They're at The Agency compound," she explained. "I called Luke on Teresa's cell. They have a load of tobacco and I told him to dump it in the river, the tanks. Except there may be Reds in the river."

"Reds?" Piper looked confused.

"Humans who have been changed. They're the ones with the red hair. Luke found that out. I don't know if the tobacco will harm them."

Teresa stepped back into the house. "The owners of two tobacco warehouses are bringing truckloads here. The army is about to grow by at least several hundred."

"Let's go check on that hybrid," Sofia said, and dug into her pocket for the key to the Chevy.

"I'll drive," Piper said.

"Wait," Teresa said, and disappeared into a back room and emerged with half a dozen unlit torches and lighters. She handed them out. "Chango's suggestion. His element is fire."

The Chevy was large enough to accommodate twice their number. Its huge windows were open to the humid evening air and even though Sofia was no longer alone, the open window made her feel vulnerable. Suppose the hybrid girl wasn't dead? At any second, she might leap out of the dusk and hurl the Chevy into oblivion. Sofia's unlit torch was upright between her knees, a long metal stick with a mass of cloth wrapped around it that smelled of kerosene. She clutched the lighter.

"Sofia, do you remember where she fell?" Dylan asked.

"Near a cross carved into the fence. In the field."

"I know where that cross is," Teresa said. "About three kilometers ahead."

"Do we have any weapons besides torches?" Sofia asked.

"The tobacco, knives, pitchforks,"

In other words, Sofia thought, not much.

If the hybrid body wasn't there, then their theory was wrong and they needed to get to the compound with their little army. Sofia didn't harbor any hope for an army of several hundred men and women armed with torches, pitchforks, and knives against these ETs. They could kill the aliens The Agency kept in tanks, but what about the rest of them out there in the caves, the rivers?

Piper stopped just short of the cross on the fence. The road was empty. "Are you sure it was here, Sofia?"

"Positive."

"I'm going to have a look."

He got out of the car, lit his torch, and the rest of them stayed where they were, no one speaking. Then McMullen threw open the back door. "Fuck it. I want to see."

"Me, too," Teresa said, and she and Carmen got out, lit their torches.

Being alone in the car was worse than finding out the truth and made Sofia feel like a coward. If she was what Rosa considered to be a goddamn warrior, then she needed to start acting like one. She got out, lit her torch, and hurried up the road through the dusk toward the others. Stars began popping out against the sky, the air hummed with night sounds.

In the distance, the cows, goats, and horses seemed calmer now, grazing in that starlit meadow where they'd fled. When she glanced back to make sure the hybrid horror wasn't sneaking up behind them, she saw dozens of torches flickering in the dusk, moving slowly forward. The army that Ari Rey from the airport had amassed. She guessed their numbers to be at least fifty, maybe more.

She broke into a run, her webbed feet noisily slapping the road. The Piper group was just inside the fence, flashlights and torches illuminating something on the ground. Sofia climbed over the fence and joined them.

At first, she didn't know what she was looking at. It resembled the carcass of an animal that had been attacked by a larger predator. Its insides spilled through its ribcage and leaked onto the ground. Then she saw its severed arms about a yard from the carcass, and one of its severed legs with a webbed foot, dual knee joints. She scooped a stick off the ground and poked at the thing.

Green caterpillars with seven white lines on their bodies slithered out of the stinking mess, but they were dying. Some of them had holes in their bodies where the wasp larvae had eaten through them, but continued to crawl, perhaps in the hopes they could escape death. The hybrid's head lay a foot from the carcass, severed at the neck, covered with what looked like foam. When Sofia poked at it with the end of the stick, the foam separated enough for her to see the larvae, hungry little suckers that continued to gnaw at the skin, to work their way up the hybrid's face, into her mouth, nose, eyes.

And there, at the top of her skull, the weird sprout of pink hair.

"My God," Sofia whispered. "The larvae *consumed* her."

While they inspected the hybrid carcass, three Cuban tree frogs hopped out of the tobacco leaves, crossed Sofia's webbed feet, and hopped on toward a pond where other frogs splashed around. Sofia stared at them, awed by this peculiar timing, and suddenly knew how to prove whether the Reds could be killed by the parasitic wasps. This was what Rosa had meant when she said that Sofia was about to become one of a kind. Who else here right now could even attempt to prove such a thing?

She stuck her lit torch in the ground and hurried away from the disgusting carcass. Rosa faded into view again, keeping pace with her. "This is how a warrior fights, *mi amor*. You know what to do."

"Be sure and tell that to Luke and Mike and Cooper if it turns out that I'm wrong, *abuelita*."

"That *ovni* we saw so many years ago when you were little," Rosa said. "It was the same object Luke saw. It targeted the two of you, uniting you even before you had met. This is how they work, Sofia."

"How do we defeat them?" She grabbed a handful of leaves with the strange hornworms stuck to them, and stepped into the pond, past the croaking frogs, her webbed feet sinking into the mud, and hoped the pond was deep enough to do what she intended. "Tell me that, Rosa. I want to be human again. I want Dylan's son alive, I want Larry's children to be human again, I want to spend my life with Luke as a human being, not a freak."

"You win by doing what you're doing now."

Her grandmother faded into the darkness and Sofia felt completely alone. And scared. *Suppose I'm wrong and die in this fucking mud hole?* She reminded herself that she was partially alien right now and hoped that partial would be enough. She kept walking and midway across the pond, the bottom abruptly dropped deeper and she sank beneath the water.

She nearly panicked. Then she vividly imagined a gill at her throat and willed it to open. When it didn't happen, she had to surface for air. If she couldn't do this, then the ET still controlled her, it would continue to use her, it would morph her completely and steal her humanity. *You can do this.*

Sofia inhaled deeply, sank underwater again. This time, determination surged through her like a force of nature. She felt a terrible itching at the skin on her throat, then a weird discomfort as the gill started forming. Once the formation began, the rest of the gill came in quickly. It opened, she was able to breathe. She willed the webbing between her fingers to move into place. She felt the smaller gill at her side opening. Something happened to the roof of her mouth that felt like a small snake burrowing into it. She nearly shrieked, nearly shot toward the surface of the pond, into the air.

But her resolve kept her submerged.

Now cartilage and bone on the roof of her mouth shifted, her teeth grew longer, sharper. Bones and cartilage in her knees rearranged themselves, the dual joints snapped into place. The pain was considerable. Then, the part that she dreaded most: her skull, face, and hair started morphing. The bones in her face rearranged themselves, a transformation so agonizing that she almost passed out. But with her single nostril, her sense of smell exploded.

She could smell the tobacco she clutched in her webbed hand, the hornworms that clung to the leaves, the wasp larvae inside their bodies. She smelled the diesel of the cars and trucks that chugged uphill, toward the tobacco field. She smelled sweat and fear and rage.

The ends of her clump of red hair brought tastes—of the water, the mud, the tobacco that grew here, of dead flies and mosquitos, of the cute little piglets that had played and shit here. Her hearing enabled her to hear footsteps in a house miles away. Her nictitating eyelids showed her what lay above the water, a 360-degree view of the pastures, fields, hills, sky, even Teresa's house.

If she flicked her webbed hand, if she kicked her webbed

foot, if she was pissed off or afraid or defending herself, she could create a telekinetic carnival. But what she lacked was *vision*, what the alien called Sight—what *might* happen when she stuffed the tobacco leaves in her mouth and tore them apart with her dagger teeth. What danger *might* show up moments from now. Who she could trust. This was what the ETs were after. That was what Mira wanted from her.

Fuck you. It's mine, you can't have it.

These ETs lacked the most basic psychic sense—the hunch, the tightening in your gut, the rising of the hair on the back of your neck, Pierce's creepy spider sense, Mike's emotional clarity, the fire in Dylan's belly and his and Aldridge's profound love for their children. And that trumped all of it. Love. That was where it all started. That was the power.

And these alien fuckers couldn't feel it.

Sofia stuffed the tobacco leaves in her mouth, tore them apart with her hideously sharp teeth, tasted the caterpillars—their cool, silk soft, slivery skin, the crunchy nut taste of the seven white lines on their body. She knew she should be throwing up by now, but those white lines reminded her of the yogurt-covered pretzels she bought at Whole Foods and often crumbled into her most tasty salads.

The wasp larvae tasted sour, but that taste lasted only until they began gnawing at her intestines, trying to eat her alive. She shrieked in pain, the sound muffled by the water. Her immune system quickly kicked in, pouring something acidic into her stomach, and she felt the larvae scrambling around, trying to avoid whatever this was.

It took her a few moments to realize she had survived, that the Reds wouldn't die if they ate the tobacco leaves, the hornworms, the parasitic wasps. Her head popped above the water and the bones in her face instantly started shifting and rearranging themselves. It wasn't as painful as the first time, but for long, terrible moments, she imagined herself stuck in between physical forms like this, not quite alien, not quite human. The gill at her throat closed up, enabling her to breathe air again, the single nostril gave way to two, the nictitating eyelids slid away.

She became aware of dozens of people crowded around the pond, watching her. Some of them drew back in horror, others leaned forward in fascination, some stayed where they were, pitchforks and torches held high just in case. Her knees rearranged themselves even before she pushed to her feet. She felt her hair sprouting like a weed. The webbing between her fingers withdrew. And then, for the first time since she'd read that ET in the lighthouse kitchen, the webbing between her toes vanished.

It was like a virus, she thought. Once it had infected you, it could lay dormant in your system for years. Unless and until an ET summoned it. Or unless and until you learned to control it yourself.

When she could finally speak again, she screamed, "John, call Luke! Tell them the Reds won't die if they eat the tobacco. Dump the shit in the river. All of it!"

Dozens of trucks and cars clogged the dirt road paralleling the field. Hundreds of torches now flickered in the darkness. This army, four or five hundred strong, were armed with fire, machetes, pitchforks, and some of them even had guns. But their most powerful weapon was rage.

"*Los vamos a matar!*" one man shouted, pumping his torch in the air. We're going to kill them.

"*Estan en el Campo Viejo!*" a woman with a pitchfork yelled.

Others in the crowd started shouting and Sofia turned, threw her arms up in the air. "Please!" she shouted in Spanish. "Listen. These monsters who have taken your loved ones want just one thing: to turn us into grotesque clones of themselves so they can seize our planet."

"Kill them!" shouted a man, and the chant was taken up, fists pumped the air, pitchforks and shovels and knives appeared.

Among people who had been oppressed for so many decades by a brutal dictatorship, the idea that another oppressor had appeared in their midst was unacceptable. She understood that. But Sofia also knew this oppressor had powers that even the Castro brothers had lacked.

"Your loved ones are those with red hair. Save them."

"Will they remember us?" a woman shouted.

"I don't know. But in my heart I believe that even those humans who have been fully changed retain a memory of their humanity, their families and loved ones. Those that aren't in Campo Viejo may be held captive in the caves... "

"In Cuevo de los Indios!" a man yelled. "They have been seen there and the cave has been closed for weeks."

"The rest of them—blue hair, yellow hair, dark brown hair, pink hair- must be annihilated. There are millions of these aliens all over the world. We know the parasitic wasps in the hornworms kill them."

Shouts echoed through the torch-lit darkness.

"This battle begins and ends here, tonight," she yelled. "We're the resistance!"

By the Numbers

We have not heard from our convoy of changelings, the web reveals nothing. But we can't wait any longer. We're prepared. Now that the sun has gone down, our scouts move out of the caves, some in the river, others on foot, and scatter like ghosts through the darkness. They report that Acia and her fighters are hidden everywhere—in the river, the lake, the trees, the brush— waiting for us to leave the caves.

Since I can no longer rewind time as a means of defense, Jez and several dozen of his warriors unleash the first attack against our enemies, buying us time to leave the caves by the back exit Jez burned through the rock. Other members of our tribe have arrived from nearby islands so we now number more than 5,000 and, as far as we can tell, the numbers on the compound are less than a thousand. We move rapidly through the labyrinth of caves for several miles, the ground rising, dipping, the river filled with warriors. The exit brings us out behind our enemies, into a swirling maelstrom of uprooted trees, flying branches and stones, and raging fires that the warriors have set.

Acia and her fighters are so consumed by their hatred for me, so hungry for my destruction, they don't realize they're battling just several dozen warriors and scouts. We wait, hidden in darkness, for them to exhaust themselves as they fling wave after wave of energy that whips the swirling debris into a frenzy that blocks the light of the moon, turns the river into a frothing storm, and flattens most of the nearby woods. When I'm sure they have nearly exhausted themselves, we move forward en *masse, an advancing wall of warriors hurling pulsating waves that catch them by surprise. We leap and attack over and over again. Horrific sounds echo through the darkness, shrieks and cries, the tearing of flesh and bone.*

Some of Acia's fighters take off, leaping away into the darkness, fleeing like the cowards they are. Lotus chases a small group of them, I chase two of the others and tear the head off one and tackle the other.

Acia.

I pin her to the ground, my teeth inches from her face. Such a careless coward, Acia. How foolish of you to run.

How foolish of you *not* to run. *Her eyes flick away from my face, giving away that one or more of her allies is behind me. I jam my fingers into her eyes, blinding her, and as she writhes and screams, I simultaneously lift my legs and slam my feet back, into her ally behind me. I pull my fingers out of Acia's eyes and flip around, leap, and land hard on Ravina's chest.*

You again?

She struggles to throw me off, but her breath is a pathetic wheeze and she has exhausted her ability to fight with energetic waves. I grab her by the throat, yank her forward, and poke my fingers into her eyes, blinding her, too. She shrieks and leaps up, but because she is crippled from the confrontation back on our world, she stumbles, pitches forward and slams into the ground.

She doesn't move.

Lotus races over to me. Mira , the changelings have been killed and didn't make it past the front gate of the compound. The humans whose appearances they took have been freed.

A terrible fear crashes through me. Nothing is working out as planned. I summon my craft, as I have done countless times since Lotus and I hid in El Morro, but it doesn't respond.

Unless it's completely destroyed or is in a place that it can't escape, it should respond. It frightens me.

Discordant music echoes through the darkness. Those of my tribe who are still alive and uninjured are prepared to attack the compound at my command. But even as I hear this, my human feet begin to give way to webbing, sprouting like weeds between my toes. The gill at my throat flies open and I nearly suffocate as I stand there, struggling to speak.

The only thing this can mean is that Sofia has freed herself from my control. Such a thing has never happened before and I have no idea how it happened now. But I'm forced to dive into the river in order to breathe and the survivors in my tribe follow me.

We are now thousands, swimming rapidly upriver, toward the compound.

Chapter 21

From inside the electric cart where he and Mike were, Dylan saw waves of flickering firelight moving across the landscape. The advancing army of resisters—which had started with Ari Rey's army of enraged locals—had grown to include hundreds, maybe thousands, of people from the closest towns. And in the distance, perhaps ten or fifteen miles from here, in the vicinity of the caves, the dark sky lit up with what could only be raging fires. Dylan didn't have any idea what that meant, but it couldn't be anything good.

He, Mike, and dozens of soldiers in electric carts loaded with containers of weapons, moved out among the resisters, distributing assault rifles, dynamite, grenades, dart guns, Tasers, hand guns, rifles, ammo for everything. Weapons were abundant and, if nothing else, the compound could defend itself because this was something Americans did well. They loved war.

The resistance welcomed the weapons, but Dylan worried. The compound had an army of less than a thousand. They didn't have the might and power of the U.S. military at their disposal. No fighter jets, tanks, nukes. Forget Will Smith in *Independence Day* and Tom Cruise in *War of the Worlds*. While Graham and Fleming and their team were in the tank area attempting to move the red-haired ETs to safety and keep the other ETs drugged, all he wanted was a chance to bargain for Justin's life. *Give me a different timeline. I'll tell you where your craft is.*

His earpiece carried Graham's voice. "Where's the resistance now, Dylan?"

"All around us. Everywhere." He spoke into the radio clipped to his shirt pocket. "Has the tobacco been loaded into the tanks?"

"Yeah. And what's left has been scattered between us and the river. We're still moving the reds. The rest of them are drugged. Twenty minutes ago, Jerry requested help from naval pilots at Gitmo. And we're going to need them. The infrared cameras are indicating an army of ETs moving toward us from the far side of the lake."

He glanced in that direction, but it was too dark to see anything that far now. "There's also activity in the river. We're hurrying up here. But Graham, if we get through this, will you marry me?" He couldn't believe he'd blurted the words, that Mike had heard him, but realized that his desire to be with her for the rest of his life was as great as his need to see his son alive. "I mean, if that's what you want."

She sounded choked up when she replied. "Can we find some peaceful place by a lake where we can have dogs and go swimming every day and never think about any of this shit?"

"In the mountains?" He handed out a container of grenades to several men. "I've kinda had it with Florida and the tropics."

"In the mountains."

"It's a deal, Graham."

"Uh, Dylan." Mike elbowed him and pointed off to his left, the direction of the river. "Something's definitely happening over there."

"Graham, security lights need to burn up this place."

"On it." She disconnected.

Seconds later, untold numbers of brilliant security lights blinked on, burning through the darkness like a thousand suns, casting light for miles. And Dylan saw them, an army of the alien fuckers leaping forward on the far side of the river and another battalion of them moving toward them from the other side of the lake. Others were in the river itself, so many of them the water spilled over its banks.

He called Sofia, turned on the speaker, and she answered on the first ring. "We have them in sight, Dylan. We're going for them. I think we're five or six hundred now. People keep arriving with weapons. From the cops. The Guardia. We're on foot, in trucks. Some of us will go for them, the rest of us are headed toward you."

"We're ready. We armed the resistance that's here already."

"Have the Reds been moved?"

"Still in progress."

"Is Mike with you?"

"Right here, Mom. Cooper identified the Reds. He knew."

"Best dog in the universe. Is he with Luke?"

"In the viewing area."

"The titanium dome now covers this building," Dylan said. "Okay, I hear the first of the navy jets."

And then the first F-16 from Gitmo or AUTEC or somewhere roared through the airspace above the river, across Campo Viejo, flying low enough so Dylan could feel the reverberations of its passage in his toes. And behind it were three more. Dylan drove the electric cart as fast as it would go—a damn snail's pace— toward the main building. He pulled alongside it, he and Mike leaped out, and scrambled up the stairs to a door that slid open. They hit the floor, slid open a couple of panels in the titanium shutters, and started shooting, creating a shield of constant gunfire.

As the first F-16 circled in low over the beings crossing the lake, dropping missiles on the ETs, it suddenly blew up, the fireball spewing smoke and flames everywhere across the sky, the land. The second and third jets circled at a higher altitude, and their missiles decimated the front lines of the aliens, the fucks falling like dominoes.

But more of them kept advancing. Hundreds or thousands of them, Dylan couldn't tell. It looked like something out of *Star Wars*.

"Kill the lights, Graham," he snapped into his radio.

Dylan grabbed another assault rifle, a bag of grenades, more clips, and ran through the door, down the stairs, and outside. The security lights went out and he loped forward, weaving between the trees, the shadows, his body remembering what it had been like when he'd seen Justin's body on that autopsy table three years ago. Burns on his arms and legs, surgical cuts on his face and eyes, his scrotum sliced open, and then that scurrying implant during the autopsy.

Fuckers, fuckers, fuckers.

He made it to a mound of rocks and trees near the river and saw the ETs up close, grotesque giants with blue and yellow sprouts of hair, their dark brown haired minions shrieking from the water, egging them on, and red-haired beings at the front.

Reds: humans who had been changed.

He couldn't fire at them. So he ran toward them, gesturing wildly for them to move toward the dome, to duck and run. And as they scattered in his direction, he hurled grenades at the ETs around and behind them. They crumpled like puppets whose strings had been cut. Dylan turned toward the ones on the other side of the river and opened fire, mowing them down. Some had dived back into the water with the browns and he hurled grenades into the river that burst like exploding suns and blew their despicable bodies into oblivion.

Wave after wave of telekinetic energy ripped apart the landscape, uprooted trees, a tornadic maelstrom. On the other side of the river, the alien army advanced, leaping across the lake like giant grasshoppers. Dylan threw himself to the ground as another Navy jet shrieked up behind them, leveling a bunch of them, but it didn't make any difference. Behind those fallen aliens came more. And more. Their numbers numbed him.

Then the noise and the horror faded and a tall being that looked entirely human strode toward him, arms open, no visible weapons. Of course, none of their weapons were ever visible. It—she? He?—spoke to him in English. "Mr. Dylan, can we talk?"

Dylan rocked back on his heels, shot to his feet, his assault rifle aimed at whatever this was. "Sure, talk away."

He thought it was female, but she didn't have a bust, her blue hair didn't reveal her gender. Something about her eyes. At this point, Dylan was sure he was in the midst of a full-blown psychotic episode. In the past, medics would have rushed in, pumped him full of drugs, and when he emerged on the other side of the experience, he would have been in isolation, in a straitjacket. But not now. The ET sat on the ground by the river, Dylan continued to stand. "This path is useless, for both of us," it said.

Authority. In charge. "I agree. So where do we go from here?"

"I regret what happened to your son. It was not my doing.

The rogue who was responsible is dead. I killed her. But I can undo your don's death and create a new timeline. If that happens, your son will never be fully your son again and we will still overtake your planet because we can flourish here and can't return to our planet, which is dying. In return, I want to know what you did with my craft."

Dylan pinched himself, felt the discomfort. Real. What was happening was real, not a dream, not some psychotic hallucination. And the part about his son was a lie, intended to undermine his determination. The dying planet stuff sounded like it had been borrowed from a bad science fiction movie. "I'm sorry your planet is dying. But that doesn't give you the right to invade our planet, steal human bodies and devastate lives."

"Our intent was never to devastate. But we, like you, have rebels in our midst, those who believe you're a barbaric race that deserves annihilation. You're destroying your planet, you can't come to a consensus on the most basic issues—climate change, poverty, health care… "

Dylan started laughing, he couldn't help it. Listening to an alien shithead talking about American politics had to be a joke. "C'mon, you people could install one of your own and we wouldn't know the difference."

"We already have."

"Then you don't need me."

"Oh, but I do need you, Mr. Dylan. I need you for my one and only altruistic act."

And just like that, the alien, Campo Viejo, the gunfire, all of it disappeared.

2.

Dylan was on Sarasota Beach with Justin and his girlfriend, Barbara, helping them refurbish a sailboat for the college sail club. Late afternoon. Hot. Much too hot to be out here.

"Hey, guys," Dylan said. "Let's knock off and get a bite to eat. We can finish this tomorrow morning when it's cooler."

"Sounds good to me," Justin said.

"Yeah, me too," Barbara agreed. "I'm starving."

"When do you go back, Dad?" Justin asked.

"Not till Monday."

"Fantastic, that gives us two more days. Barb and I want to take you to our favorite music place. We can get a bite to eat there."

They pulled the sailboat into the main area, beneath a tin roof that looked like it would collapse in a gust of wind. Dylan trotted back to the beach to gather up their tools and abruptly felt displaced, as if he wasn't supposed to be here. It startled him and for moments, he heard gunfire, chaotic shouting. He glanced around uneasily, half-expecting to see some crazed, armed student mowing down the group of young men and women in bathing suits headed this way.

"Hey, man," one of them called.

"What's up, Carl?" Justin asked.

"Is the club still open? We were hoping to take out a sailboat."

Dylan decided the noise he heard was coming from the kid's iPhone. Music pumped from it, raucous heavy metal.

"Sure. Just sign the sheet, dude, and have it back before dark."

Dylan deposited the tools in a large plastic container and set it on the sand next to the sailboat they were working on. Then he, Justin and Barb started up the path toward the campus and dorms.

Awhile later, they were seated at a table on the open patio of a restaurant in downtown Sarasota, waiting for their drinks. A local band was setting up, more people were arriving, dusk settled around them. "Hey, they forgot to give us a basket of chips," Justin said. "Be right back."

He left to search for a basket of chips, their drinks arrived. "Cheers, Mr. Dylan," said Barb, holding up her draft beer.

"Cheers, Barb."

They clicked glasses and she leaned forward. "Justin told me you investigate UFO sightings for the government. I thought he was joking but he swore he wasn't. Is it true?"

"All true."

"So you're like, what, Fox Mulder?"

He laughed. "Not quite." But he did have a Dana Scully, knockout Lia Graham.

Barb's blue eyes widened. "Wow, totally awesome. But isn't it frightening at times?"

"Yeah, it can be. I'm betting he told you about our camping trip when he was just a kid."

She looked sheepish. "It's that obvious, huh? It's not, like, classified intel or anything, I hope."

"Classified only in the sense that I don't think he's ever told the story to a woman he was dating. He always felt women would think he was strange."

"He knows I'm into this stuff. That's how we met. Whitley Strieber gave a talk on campus seven months ago and Justin and I ended up sitting next to each other. We were both blown away by his talk. Do you know Strieber?"

"Nope. Love his books, though."

"You think the stuff he writes about really happened?"

The question troubled him and he wasn't sure why. Before he could reply, Justin returned with a basket of chips and dip and the band started tuning up. "Did Barb tell you where we met, Dad?"

"That's what we were just talking about." He suddenly saw Justin on an autopsy table, a coroner drilling through his skull, chasing an object that, on the computer monitor, looked like an implant. The image horrified him and he leaned toward his son. "Have there been any more incidents, Justin?"

He looked surprised that Dylan even asked. "Nope. Nothing."

Their meals arrived, the band started playing, and Dylan focused on his food, the music, the company of his son and Barb. But in the back of his mind, he saw that implant exit through Justin's ear and drop to the surface of the autopsy table, as vivid as a memory.

During the band's break, Barb looked up from her phone, horror etched into her face. "Shit, we need to get back to campus, Justin. That guy who asked us about taking out a sailboat? Carl? He... he got dragged away by... something. The people who were with him witnessed it."

"What the fuck?" Justin spat. "What did they see?"

"I don't know."

"I'll get the bill," Dylan said, and tossed Justin the car keys. "Bring the car around."

As soon as they hurried out, Dylan's legs felt weak, strange, and he realized he already knew what had happened to Carl. He'd had an encounter. The other people in his group had seen whatever he'd seen and had run off, but Carl had stood there, spellbound, fog gathering around him, thickening, and had been dragged off into the ocean by an ET. In three days, his body would wash ashore and by then, UFO investigators would be swarming Sarasota. Among them would be Lia Graham, his partner at The Agency, and Omega's people, Sofia Lopez and Luke Pierce. He wasn't sure how he knew this, but felt certain it was true.

His job would be to interview the witnesses and get Graham here as quickly as possible. Just as he started punching out her number, his cell rang and her number came up in the ID window.

"You're psychic, Graham. I was just about to call you. There's been… "

"I know. An incident on Sarasota Beach. But this time, it isn't Justin."

Her words felt like a fist chopping into his esophagus and nearly choked him. He stopped where he was on the sidewalk. "What… "

"I'm in Sarasota with Larry Aldridge and his two kids, both of them biologists at the University of Miami."

Aldridge. The name seemed vaguely familiar to him, but he didn't know why. "Who's he? And what're you doing here? I thought you were in Maryland."

"He's a neurologist at UM. I called Sofia Lopez and Luke Pierce. Turns out they're already on their way here. We'll meet you at the campus sail club."

She disconnected, his son pulled up to the curb, and Dylan hopped in the car. He wanted to tell himself he didn't know what the hell was going on, that he didn't have any idea what Graham had meant when she said it wasn't Justin this time. But the truth was that some of this felt familiar to him. He just didn't know why.

3.

When Dylan, his son, and Barb arrived at the sail club, Graham was already there with a tall, gray-haired man leaning heavily on a cane. He looked familiar to Dylan, as if they'd met at some time in the past. The two of them were talking to several freaked out students and four campus cops were roping off the club and part of the beach. One of the young women saw Justin and Barb and ran over to them.

"I saw the whole thing," she said breathlessly, her eyes red and swollen from crying. "It came out...of the ocean. A fog, it was a big, thick mother fog and inside it was a light and a shape and..." She began sobbing, Barb put her arms around the woman's shoulders.

"Hey, it's okay, Rita," Barb said, gently.

"Everyone started running, except me and Carl. I kept shouting, 'C'mon, Carl, it's a fucking UFO, an alien, we need to get outta here!' But he was, like, in trance. Or something. I ran."

I know this story, Dylan thought. "And did you come back to the sail club later?"

"Yes. With a professor and a bunch of people. But...Carl was gone."

As Rita spoke, Dylan noticed how Justin's face grew progressively paler. He looked like he was about to puke. Barb led Rita back to Graham and Aldridge and Justin hurried over to Dylan. "Dad... I think... this is going to sound totally nuts... but I think what happened to Carl was supposed to... happen to me. And that Barb was supposed to see what... Rita saw. Carl's body is going to wash up in two or three days and it'll... be covered with burn marks, his eyes... Jesus, his eyes will be all cut up, his scrotum cut...open. The... " Tears poured from his eyes and he turned suddenly and tore up the path past Graham, Aldridge, and nearly collided with Sofia and Pierce and another young man and woman.

Dylan ran after his son, shouting, "Justin, hold on!"

Justin paused, Dylan caught up to him. "Listen, you're talking crazy... "

Except that he wasn't. *You were pulled into the ocean and your body washed up three days later covered in torture marks and during the autopsy, the coroner found an implant behind your right ear and chased it with a drill through your brain and I saw it exit your left ear...Sweet Christ, it all happened. I ended up in a nuthouse and...and...*

Dylan threw his arms around his son, holding him close, whispering, "I remember, Justin, I remember..."

"I'm 'sposed to be dead, Dad... " He sobbed against Dylan's shoulder. "I remember being dead, I remember how... the ETs made it possible for us to communicate when I was dead. I remember... We met at some weird spot, Betty something, with a Ferris wheel."

"Sofia had webbed feet," Dylan added. "They were turning her into an amphibious being, that... "

"... an invasion was underway." Sofia came up behind them. "Do you remember that, Dylan? Do you remember that next year, in 2015, Dr. Aldridge's daughter and her husband go to the Dominican Republic to find her brother, Duncan, who had been abducted by these alien fucks and turned into one of them? Do you recall that his daughter, Cat, was turned as well, that you and Graham investigated the case?"

Her words exploded like bombs inside of him, tearing him apart, melting his organs. He wanted her to shut up, but she didn't.

"Three years from now, you and I and Dr. Aldridge end up on Tango Key because Josh McMullen finds an ET on the side of the cliff and he and Luke put it in a freezer in the lighthouse and Luke hires me to read it. Does any of this sound familiar, Dylan? Do you remember our Cuba trip? The agency's compound in Viñales? El Floridita and..."

"Hemingway, Neruda."

"Yes!" she said, excited. "You're remembering. Keep going."

"And you're going to have a Golden Retriever, Cooper, who comes to Cuba with us and helps identify the ones who were once human."

Pierce, Graham, Aldridge, and his two kids were now crowded around them. Dylan leaped to his feet, slung one arm around his son's shoulders and another around Graham's. "I asked you to marry me, Graham, and you said yes." Then he yelled, *"It's up to us to defeat these fucks!"*

The beach, the people, all of it evaporated like water from a kettle.

Chapter 22

Dylan stood over the human-looking alien by the river. It said, "So I kept my end of the bargain, Mr. Dylan. My single act of altruism. Are you going to tell me where my craft is?"

"You traded one kid for another. And hey, you're the one who manipulates and rewinds time. You can find it easily enough."

"No, I can't. Not anymore."

"I don't see my son here."

The ET gestured toward the porch where Mike and the soldiers were firing, and he saw that Justin was with them. "It might be an illusion."

"It's not."

"So we're back to trust again? I'm sposed to take you at your word?"

"And Dr. Aldridge's two children are with him in the viewing area."

"I'll ask him." Dylan texted Aldridge. *Are Cat and Duncan with you?*

The reply came quickly. *Yes. Of course. Why?*

Dylan realized that Aldridge's response, as though it were perfectly natural that his son and daughter were with him, indicated that he didn't remember things as they used to be.

"You humans are so distrustful," the alien said.

"With good reason. We're being invaded."

"Well, yes, there's that." Then the human-looking alien grinned, its dagger teeth flashing.

"Okay, your craft. I've decided I'm not a man of my word, you miserable fuck," and Dylan fired the assault weapon repeatedly, kept firing as the alien's head exploded and its wretched body shook and twitched and fell back in pieces on the ground. The head rolled toward the river, its human face gone, its single nostril and the sprig of blue hair a mockery of the illusion it had created for Dylan's benefit.

One of the dark-haired fucks shrieked and struggled to climb out of the water and Dylan shot it, too. He kept firing at the advancing aliens on the other side of the river and backpedaled toward the main building.

An F-16 swept past, engines shrieking, and the burgeoning army of locals came at them from the south, hurling torches, shooting. Waves of energy rippled through the darkness, ripping out trees, whipping through Ari Rey's army. A second fighter jet exploded, but another half dozen roared in behind it, dropping missiles as they passed over the aliens advancing from the lake side of the compound.

Dylan raced back to the building and Justin threw open the door in the dome and pulled him onto the deck. *My God, he's real, he's here.*

"Jesus, Dad. What were you doing down there? "

Fuck, you're here, please don't suddenly vanish... "Do you remember?"

Justin's face crumpled like a piece of aluminum foil. "All of it," he whispered, and threw his arms around Dylan.

Mike ran over to them. "One battalion of aliens has paused! They found the tobacco. My mother is on her way here with more tobacco, stuff from warehouses brought in from town. Other trucks of tobacco are headed to the caves."

The local army now swarmed over a hill and more soldiers raced onto the deck, some of the snipers Dylan had seen on the platforms above the tank. Pierce was with them. "We'll take over here," he shouted above the shriek of another jet. "I want to make sure Sofia gets through and we'll help her unload the tobacco and spread it!"

"Are the Reds all separated?" Dylan asked.

"Just about." Pierce clasped Dylan's arm. "Good work, man. I don't know what the hell you promised in return, but you've got Justin and Larry has his two kids."

"You remember, but Larry doesn't."

"Not yet. He will," Pierce said.

"I didn't keep my end of the bargain," Dylan said. "I shot the fucker. Even if we win this battle, Luke, it may not matter. They're here already and they may number in the hundreds of thousands."

"I'm staying here with Luke," Mike said.

Dylan and Justin raced for the door.

2.

Sofia drove like a maniac, the truck's headlights off, Piper, McMullen and Carmen squeezed into the front seat with her. She had a vague memory of being on that Sarasota beach three years ago when she and Pierce had investigated Justin Dylan's disappearance and then his death. But in this memory, she was leaning into Dylan's face, firing questions at him. Did he remember that an invasion had been underway? Did he recall the trip to Cuba?

She clearly remembered him leaping to his feet, flinging one arm around Justin, the other around Graham, and screaming, *It's up to us to defeat these fucks!*

Justin. *Alive* in that memory. Alive now? On a different timeline?

If so, it meant Dylan had made his bargain with the devil— but in exchange for what?

Nothing. He wouldn't do that. Had he killed the alien who had tried to change her? If the aliens who changed the Reds were killed, did they immediately become human again? Or would they, like her, have to discover how to control it themselves?

If this was a new timeline for them all, what had changed in their lives beyond this place? Would the changes extend to the larger world? Would there be a different president? Would her place in Key West still belong to her or would she return and find someone else living there? What were the larger repercussions of what the ET had done?

She flinched as another jet swept in low overhead, dropping missiles over the lake. Piper, her navigator, shouted, "The driveway for the compound is coming up, Sofia. Turn!"

She swerved and the truck squealed onto a winding driveway. She flashed the headlights once, twice. On the third flash, she saw Pierce, Mike, and a half a dozen soldiers tearing toward them. She slowed, stopped long enough for Pierce and Mike to pass weapons through the windows, then they scrambled into the bed of the truck with the soldiers and the tobacco.

"Loop around," Pierce yelled. "Then head straight for the river and then across to the shores of the lake!"

Piper took up a position at the passenger window. McMullen and Carmen climbed into the back seat and positioned themselves at the rear windows. Sofia made a tight loop, floored the accelerator, headlights on now, and aimed the truck at the river.

ETs lined the banks, chowing down on the tobacco, stuffing it in their mouths just as the hybrid had done. But behind them, on the other side of the river, thousands more advanced, leaping forward. Piper, McMullen, Carmen, and the men in the back started firing at the feeding ETs. They were so stupefied from the tobacco and the caterpillars that many of them didn't even try to defend themselves. They simply fell.

Sofia swerved into a sharp right and sped parallel to the river. The barrage of gunfire continued and Pierce and Mike started shoving the tobacco leaves out of the truck. Hundreds of the ETs now crossed the river, another jet shrieked over them, dropping missiles that wiped out dozens of them. Even as those ETs fell, the others kept moving ever forward, waves of telekinetic energy sweeping from them. When they reached the newly dropped tobacco, they scooped it up and shoved it in their mouths, gluttonous fucks.

But they were larger and more mature than the hybrid and Sofia's fear was that it would take much longer for the wasp larvae to do them in. She spun into a turn and sped toward the lake. Alien bodies littered the shore, floated in the water, but thousands of them kept coming, leaping across the lake, a surreal army. She swerved so she would be parallel to the shoreline and the truck slammed over alien bodies, tires crushing their miserable bones. "Toss the rest of the tobacco into the lake!" she yelled.

As Pierce and Mike threw great bundles of tobacco leaves into the water, the soldiers, Carmen, Piper, and McMullen maintained a steady assault of gunfire that mowed down the ETs closest to shore. Those telekinetic waves kept rolling toward them, whipping up sand and water, branches and stones and debris, all of it swept into the whirlwind above and around them.

Stuff rained down over the truck, visibility shrank, and she worried that one of the men in the rear would be struck and injured or killed and felt an immediate urgency to get away from the lake. She turned sharply. In the side mirror she saw the trunk of an uprooted tree slam to the beach where she'd been driving moments ago. Random or directed? *Does it matter?*

The truck tore away from the lake, bouncing and slamming across the field toward the dome that now covered the main building.

She pulled up in front, they all leaped out and raced for the door, the soldiers at their backs.

3.

When Dylan and his son ran into the viewing area, the shock of seeing Justin alive shook Graham so profoundly that she suddenly had two tracks of memories—the one she'd been living and this new one, where Justin hadn't died. She remembered being on that Sarasota beach three years ago because some kid had been taken. The wrong kid, Carl someone instead of Justin, and that Aldridge and his two kids had been there, too, just as they were here now. The alien had kept its promise to create a new timeline.

She remembered Sofia leaning into Dylan's face, demanding to know if he remembered, and Dylan had looked at Graham and said, *I asked you to marry me.*

"My God," she whispered, and rushed toward Dylan and Justin and threw her arms around both of them. Then she turned toward Aldridge, who looked as shocked as she was, and sputtered, "Larry, do you..."

"Yes. Holy crap, yes... Just now..."

"Something's happening to the Reds!" Fleming shouted.

They all rushed to the glass. In tank #1, the Blues, Browns, and Yellows grabbed at tobacco leaves, munching away with a kind of wild abandon. But in tank #1, the Reds were coming out of their drugged stupor. Some of them swam around frantically, panicked by the circumstances. Two of them swam toward a large rock, scrambled onto it, and shrieked with agony as their knees and faces began shifting, rearranging themselves into some semblance of a human.

Cooper started howling, almost as if he felt their pain, Lia thought, and his howls and the shrieks of the Reds on the rocks roused the aliens in the first tank from their tobacco feast. "Tranquilize the Reds on the rocks!" Lia yelled into her radio.

Two of the snipers shot darts at them and they slumped against the rock. But they continued to transform, their dual thumbs melting into their hands, their faces turning human once more, the single nostril giving way to two, the red sprout of hair on their otherwise bald heads turning to their natural colors, lengthening quickly, the gills at their throats and sides closing up, vanishing. A third Red sped toward the rock and when its head broke the surface of the surface, it shrieked, *"Ayudame, ayudame!"*

Its screams pulled a Blue away from the tobacco and it moved so fast toward the Red it didn't realize that glass separated them. It slammed into the partition with such force that the glass cracked and then it turned its strange, misshapen head toward the viewing room, dropped its head back, and emitted a shriek so shrill and piercing that it shattered the effects of the tobacco-induced stupor on the other Blues and they snapped into full awareness.

The air filled with their collective, high pitched shrieks. Fissures appeared in the tank glass and Graham, who had been through this before with the hybrid, shouted, "Get out now!"

They raced for the doors, the snipers started firing, but it was all too late. Another collective shriek shattered the partitions between the tanks and a third shriek brought down the glass on both tanks. They fell like towers brought down by controlled demolition.

By then, she, Dylan, Justin, and Cooper were on the stairs that led to the platforms and they scrambled down the back stairs to the rear exits, slightly elevated above the tank area. They stumbled outside and ran. Graham didn't know where Fleming, Sergio and Margarita were. She wasn't even sure where she was. Exploding missiles lit up the landscape, the eerie light illuminated thousands of ETs on the riverbanks, in the fields, by the lake, feasting on tobacco leaves, falling where they stood. The river frothed with dying aliens.

As Graham ran for the hill where she'd run when the hybrid had escaped, she tripped over rocks, roots, bodies, and ran until she couldn't run anymore and fell to the ground. She lay there, inhaling the sweet, oppressive odor of tobacco and fertile earth, then twisted onto her back and bolted upright.

She and Dylan were in the backyard of their mountain retreat in Colorado, laughing at the antics of their grandchildren, Justin and Barb's identical twin girls. Then his cell rang and he put it on speaker and Luke Pierce's voice rang out.

"They're back, Dylan. We need your and Lia's help."

She rolled again, sat up, and saw the devastation below, the dome on fire, Blues falling on the tobacco, consuming it as the fully human Reds scattered into the crowd of locals with their torches, their cries of triumph. Some distance away, Aldridge was sprawled in the grass with his son and daughter, and Sergio and Margarita were near them. Dylan was leaning over Justin, who was on his knees, puking.

Beside her, Cooper whimpered and struggled to his feet. She slung an arm over his back. He licked her hand and sat back and howled, the most mournful yet triumphant sound she'd ever heard.

A lone F-16 swooped in low over the river, missiles dropping, blowing apart the remaining ETs with their voracious appetites. The army of locals converged around the Reds who had escaped, then there was only a disquieting silence, thick, pervasive. Cooper licked her hand again, and raced down the hill in search of his main humans.

4.

"We did it," Sofia whispered.

She, Pierce, Mike, and Cooper sat in the back of the empty truck near the compound, huddled together, watching the soldiers move among the dead ETs. The dawn light revealed devastation beyond her ability to comprehend. Bodies everywhere—alien, human.

Carmen, McMullen, and Piper walked through the killing field with the soldiers, finishing off any aliens that weren't fully dead. Every shot made her flinch. Now and then something went airborne, a tree, branches, a clump of flowers, the last, feeble wave of telekinetic power from a dying alien. One of those waves flattened the tires on the truck, all four of them, and she felt the vehicle sinking to the ground.

"I guess we'll be walking back to Teresa's place," she said.

"It's not over," Pierce said.

"For now, it is."

She grasped his hand and Mike's, whistled for Cooper, and they left the back of the truck and started walking.

5.

Two days later, Sofia and Pierce, Dylan, Lia, and dozens of locals entered Cuevo de los Indios and loaded hundreds of dead alien bodies into trucks and freed Reds who were fully human but starving and confused. The trucks hauled the alien bodies to a remote area of the island, holes were dug, the bodies deposited inside. Then Sofia poured gasoline over the mass grave and Dylan touched a torch to the gasoline and the bodies burned fast and furiously. Afterward, they covered the scorched remains with dirt.

It wasn't her best day.

They remained in Cuba for another week, aiding authorities in identifying the restored humans and helping them to acclimate to their experience.

During the flight back to the U.S. in Piper's DC3, Sofia

Googled Ernest Hemingway and discovered he had died of natural causes on the same day that JFK had been assassinated in Dallas. He had lived more than two years beyond what he was supposed to and suicide hadn't happened on this timeline. Neruda had been at his memorial service and recounted a story that most of those present had believed was the beginning of a new series of poems for him In the foreword, Neruda had written:

"In June 1958, my friend Ernesto and I experienced something extraordinary... "

Sofia stared at those words and the rest of his speech for a long time—and then a chunk of information dropped into her, a massive, collective download that answered her questions about the ramifications of the new timeline the ET had created.

By the time they landed in Key West, each of them understood the personal implications of this new timeline. It was both a blessing and a curse, Sofia thought. A blessing for what they had gained and a curse because they remembered how things had been before.

Sofia's parents were dead, but Rosa was still alive and in a nursing home. Her ex-husband, Steve, was still alive. Her own genetic makeup was completely altered now. She could change at will into an amphibious ET.

Carmen was now a widow; Ted Fisher had passed away from a heart attack. Aldridge's beloved wife had passed away. American Airlines had never recovered from its bankruptcy after 9-11 and Piper now flew for Omega. Pierce's ex-wife had remarried, he was estranged from his daughter, and he and Carmen headed Omega.

Dylan's ex had died, he still worked for The Agency and had been appointed acting director after Fleming's retirement. Graham had a daughter from her marriage to Neil King, and she and Dylan were married, Justin was engaged to Barb, and now worked for The Agency. McMullen worked for Omega.

In this massive download, the details revealed to one were revealed to all of them. So when they followed Cooper off the plane, they staggered like drunks, all of them talking at once, and Sofia pressed his hands over his ears, struggling to ground herself. They still didn't know the broader implications of this new timeline. That would come as they re-entered their daily lives.

She hurried to catch up with Pierce, caught his hand, and he slung his arm around her shoulders, pulling her against him. "What happens now, Sofi? Can we get married and live happily ever after?"

"I don't know about the last part, but the first part sure sounds good."

But that lay in the future. Right now, only one thing mattered: although the ETs had been decimated in Cuba, there were thousands more worldwide and the war against them, Sofia knew, was just beginning.

Epilogue

*L*otus and I walk through Betty Danger's place, and I'm eyeing that Ferris wheel, wondering where my craft is. Ever been on one of those, Lotus?

No.

Let's try it.

I'm dead, Mira.

Not here. Remember?

Her expression brightens, she laughs. That's right! I forgot!

We hurry toward the Ferris wheel, that revolving strangeness of lights and swinging gondolas, where I once sat across from Sofia, my nemesis. I was so arrogant that I believed I owned her, that I could conquer her, control her, bend her to my image, take her Sight.

Lotus stood in for me with Dylan. I've tried repeatedly to rewind the moments of her death but it hasn't worked. She insisted on negotiating with Dylan and we agreed that a single altruistic act would change things in our favor. But it didn't benefit us at all. Is that the meaning of altruism? You surrender and hope for the best and have no expectations? Instead, it killed my advisor and closest friend, the one I trust above all others.

Something profound has shifted for us. On this new timeline, our ability to rewind has been lost. But Lotus and I found our way back here, where the world of the living and the dead intersect. For now, we are safe.

We step into gondola 9, sit close together, and the attendant, a Yellow in our tribe, shuts the door. No standing, *the Yellow calls.*

No leaping from the gondola. *And she laughs as she says it.*

As the Ferris wheel starts moving, Lotus throws her head back, squealing with delight. We're moving, Mira, up, up, into the moonlit sky. *She looks at me, then down and sweeps her hand across the patio, the restaurant and bar, where hundreds in our tribe have taken refuge or have died and ended up here for healing.* Is there hope for us?

Always.

Except for the warriors, Mira, we're all female. We can't procreate with Jez and his kind. But we can procreate with transformed human males. The hybrid was proof of that. To survive, we need those hybrids.

I don't want to talk about any of that right now. When I think about what my life will be like when I leave Betty Danger's and move back into the world of the living without Lotus, grief nearly crushes me. I have never felt anything like this. All these years, decades melting into centuries, she has been there for me.

Sofia believes we do not feel love, that love is a stranger to us. Perhaps that has been true. But no longer. I lean into Lotus, touch her chin, turn her face toward mine, touch my mouth to hers. The contact is ecstatic, like what Sofia felt that night she and Pierce made love, when her webbed feet enabled me to feel what she felt.

I whisper, I love you, Lotus.

And her body presses against mine and the gondola swings gently in the moonlight.

About the Author

T. J. MacGregor is the author of 42 novels and in 2003 won the Edgar Allan Poe award for Out of Sight. She was born at Ballantine Books in 1987, when her editor told her that her maiden name, Trish Janeshutz, was too difficult to pronounce and that mysteries by men were outselling mysteries by women. Could she please come up with a name that had initials? By then, she was married to novelist Rob MacGregor, so she became T.J. MacGregor. A few years later, she wrote Tango Key and by then, mysteries by women were outselling mysteries by men and her editor asked her to create a new female name for that book. So, she became Alison Drake.

She lives in South Florida with her husband, novelist Rob MacGregor, their daughter, Megan, a cat and two noble Golden Retrievers.

Curious about other Crossroad Press books?
Stop by our site:
http://store.crossroadpress.com
We offer quality writing
in digital, audio, and print formats.

Enter the code FIRSTBOOK
to get 20% off your first order from our store!
Stop by today!